Rider of the Wind

Book Three of The Bardic Isles Series

Marla Himeda

Print ISBN: 978-1-959900-07-8
.mobi ISBN: 978-1-959900-08-5
.epub ISBN: 978-1-959900-09-2
audiobook ISBN: 978-1-959900-10-8
Library of Congress Control Number: 2025911205

Published in Kaneohe, HI, US

*For Charis, the catalyst for the birth of this story,
and the one who never lets me settle for less
than the best I can do*

Author's Note

As a reader, I don't usually like it when a series takes me forward or back in time from one book to the next, thus breaking my contact with characters I've come to love. Yet here I am as an author, finding it necessary to do the same thing to my readers. I assure you, Kaelin's story will continue in book four, *Harp of Stone,* but before that tale can be told, we must go back in time ... back to when the Gift was prevalent, the possession of Bards and Masters who knew and understood its power. Back to the months leading up to the exodus, over two centuries before the birth of Kaelin. I hope you enjoy your trip to Eire and the musical adventure that awaits you there.

I blissfully invented most of the names in the Bardic Isles, but used more authentic Irish names in Eire. I quickly discovered that Irish can be a complicated language to pronounce from the written word for those of us not born to it. A pronunciation guide for the names, places, and terms used in the book is included for your convenience.

The Bardic Isles Series

Master of Music
Cry of the Kestrel
Rider of the Wind
Harp of Stone (to be released)

Contents

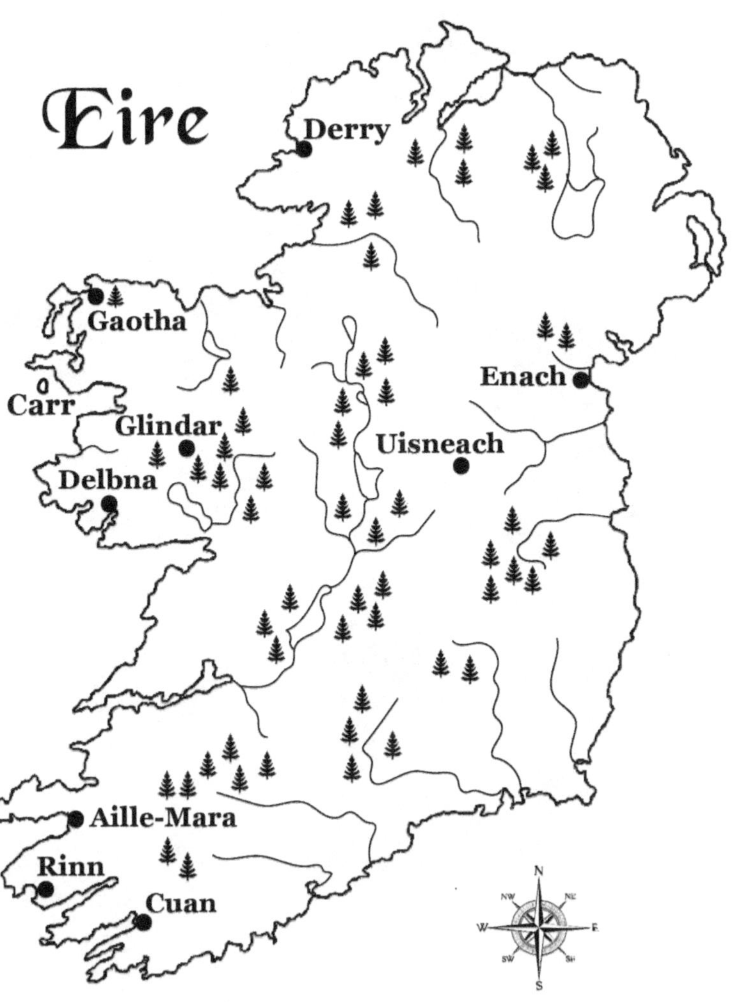
Éire
Derry
Gaotha
Carr
Glindar
Delbna
Enach
Uisneach
Aille-Mara
Rinn
Cuan
N
NW
NE
W
E
SW
SE
S

The Bardic Isles
221 Cycles After the Exodus
Kestrel
Skirling Mts
Vale
Tennyk
Bronig
Loch Daevon
Maran
Eyrie
Skirl
cabin
Alana
Lynd
Kyet
Zephyr
Braelach
Riona Springs
Shoal
Loch Lyon
Mt Tiern
Aille
Rilla
Kyria
Oriel
Skye
Elba
Loryn
Bardic Mountain
Mt Carag
Glyn
Shay
Bard's Landing
Clary
Council Grounds
Caer Wynd
Chyrn
Rhys
Nessa
Loch Senan
Loch Glynda
Tryl
Lyssa
Fiadh
Loch Culyn
Raelyn
Daithi Springs
Wyndle
Caerlach
Ferghus
Faeron
Ciara
Tuirling
Sharna
Elegy
Lyra
N
NW
NE
W
E
SW
SE
S

Irish Pronunciation Guide

Names

Aisling (*ash*-ling) – 'vision'
Balor (*bah*-lur)
Barrach (*bar*-ukh) – 'pointed'
Cailleach (*kahl*-yakh) – the hag of winter storms
Cairbre (*kahr*-bree) – 'charioteer'
Cathair (*kah*-hir) – 'man of battle'
Cillian (*kil*-yun) – 'little church'
Cormac (*kor*-mack) – 'raven'
Daevon (*day*-vun) – 'beloved'
Dáire (*dye*-ra) – 'fertile'
Daithi (*dah*-hee) – 'swiftness'
Diarmuid (*deer*-mid) – 'without enemies'
Donn (dunn) – "the dark one"
Dorcha (*dur*-uh-kha) – 'dark'
Dughan (*doo*-gun) – 'dark or swarthy'
Eoin (*oh*-in) – 'God is gracious'
Faolán (*fway*-lun) – 'little wolf'
Fionn (fin) – 'fair-haired'
Fionn mac Cumhaill (fin mac cool)
Kieren (*keer*-en) – 'little dark one'
Liam (*lee*-um) – 'strong protector'
Marcach Gaoithe (*mar*-kukh *gwee*-heh) – 'Rider of the Wind'
Odhran (*oh*-run) – 'little pale green one'
Réiltín (*rayl*-cheen) – 'little star'
Ruairí (*ror*-ee) – 'red-haired king'
Sásta (*sah*-stah) – 'happy, satisfied'
Seamus (*shay*-muss) – 'supplanter'
Tadhg (tye-g) – 'poet'
Tiernan (*teer*-nan) – 'little lord'

Places

Aille-Mara (*all*-yuh or *eye*-la *mar*-uh) – 'cliffs of the sea'
Armorica – NW corner of France, corresponding to Brittany
Blasca (*blas*-kuh) – old term for the Blasket Islands
Carr (kahr) – 'rock'
Connemara (*kon*-uh-mar-ah)
Cualann (*koo*-uh-lahn)
Cuan (*koo*-ahn) – 'harbor'
Delbna (*delv*-nuh)
Easach (*ess*-ukh) – 'cascade'
Eire (*ay*-ruh or *air*-uh or *eye*-ruh) – Ireland
Gaotha (*gway*-huh) – 'wind'
Ganach (*gan*-ukh) – var. of 'garden'
Scaelaga (*skal*-uh-guh) – old term for the Skellig Islands
Uisneach (*ish*-nukh) – 'place of the hearth'

Miscellaneous Terms

Aes Sidhe (ace shee) – faery folk of Eire
Ard Rí (ard ree) – the High King of Eire
Arrach (*arr*-ukh) – 'monster'
Bealtaine (*byal*-tin-uh) – festival marking the start of summer
currach (*kur*-ukh) – light raiding boat, oars or sails
cycle – one year
fianna (*fee*-uh-nuh) – a local warrior clan (fian is singular)
fortnight – two weeks
furlong – 8 furlongs in a mile; 4.97 furlongs in a kilometer
Imbolc (*im*-olk) – festival halfway between winter and spring
Rí (ree) – 'King'
Rí Túath (ree *too*-ah) – the local King of a single territory
sean sionnach (shahn *shin*-ukh) – 'wise old fox'
sionnach glic (*shin*-ukh glick) – 'crafty fox'
túath (*too*-ah) – a territory or tribe of Eire
túatha (*too*-a-ha) – plural of 'túath'

Movement One

The Seaport of Aille-Mara

221 cycles before the birth of Kaelin

Chapter 1

On a cold, wind-swept winter morning, a small stone washed up on the southwest coast of Eire near the seaport of Aille-Mara, named for the sea cliffs that lined much of the rocky coast. The rising sun lit the stone as it settled into the sand, the receding tide allowing it a few hour's rest before it would return to claim it once again. The stone did not seem remarkable as it lay there, merely one rock among many on the bleak shore. It was black in color and smoother than most of the others scattered about the narrow beach. Otherwise, there was nothing about it that particularly drew the eye, nothing that suggested the stone was anything other than what it appeared to be. Yet the elderly Master Bard that picked his way across the beach toward it seemed to think otherwise. He lifted the stone cautiously, as if he couldn't quite trust what it might do. Turning it over in his weathered hand, he inspected its dark surface with a keen eye. Frowning, the Master took the stone with him to where the sand was dry, then carefully placed it down. He unslung his travel bag and removed a Bardic harp from the protective leather case inside, then seated himself in silent contemplation of the stone, the harp held motionless on his lap.

Abruptly the Master turned his attention to a different rock nearby, a piece of granite not usually found so far from the inland mountains. About the same size as the dark stone, its light gray surface was streaked with translucent white patches and sparkled with silvery flecks that caught the sunlight. Keeping his gaze on the granite, he began to softly play his harp. A listener would have been astonished to find his own senses pulled by the music toward the piece of granite, would have marveled at the sensation that he was being pulled into the rock itself. Had he managed to keep his wits about him, he might have realized that the music did not come solely from the instrument. For there was music coming from the granite itself, skillfully duplicated across the strings of the Master's harp. A fleeting realization at best, for the observer would have been utterly taken with a vivid experience of the inner rock, as a chorus of three distinct melodies twined together across the background of his mind. One was a steady, rhythmic pulse echoing the heartbeat of the earth itself. Above this, notes shimmered like streaks of moonlight on water. Yet another overlaid both with a sprinkling of light, delicate staccatos ... the glistening of frost, perhaps, on a wintry morning. Had the music lasted longer, the listener might even have experienced the birth of the rock untold millennia before in the cooling of silicate magma deep within the earth beneath him. The Master's hands, however, stilled the strings, and the blended music of harp and rock stopped. The piece of granite lay undisturbed upon the sand ... one rock among many. One song among a symphony of songs coming from the rock-strewn beach, though only the Gifted could hear them, or those who heard the echoing music from their harps.

Once more the Master turned his regard to the dark, smooth stone. His amber eyes narrowed in concentration, his fingers positioned themselves on the strings of his harp in readiness to play. He bent his mind toward the stone with a force that would have made the observer gasp.

Despite the Master's best efforts to hear it, the dark stone was silent.

～ ⸙ ～

The following afternoon, on the porch of a spacious home that overlooked the coast twelve furlongs north of Aille-Mara, a tall, lean young Bard knocked firmly on Master Ferghus' door. A rain-spattered pack and an instrument bag showing the outline of a lap harp were slung over his shoulder. He shivered slightly in the breeze coming from the bluffs and smiled as the door was opened.

"Cyral, my boy," the Master said, motioning him in out of the rain. "I appreciate you coming so quickly."

"When my Master summons me, I don't dally along the scenic route ... not that there's much to see in this weather." His smile faded at the Master's serious expression. "Is something wrong?"

"Not at all." The Master seated himself at the large dining table, motioning Cyral to join him. "Just something I've found that I think you'll find ... intriguing."

Cyral hung his pack, lap harp, and wet cloak on a peg near the door. It was hard to believe it had been seventeen cycles since he first hung a much smaller cloak on that same peg as a lad of eight. Being apprenticed so young to a Master was unusual, for Masters only apprenticed the few who were Gifted, and the Bardic Gift usually emerged between fifteen and twenty cycles of age. Cyral's early apprenticeship had undoubtedly accounted for his rapid rise through the Bardic ranks, becoming a Harpist at fifteen and a Bard at twenty. He had then served a two-cycle term in Master Liam's territory in the north before being rotated to Master Barrach's on the southern coast. Near the end of that term, Ferghus had called him back to Aille-Mara, where he had served for the past cycle. As Prime of the Bardic Order, Ferghus had every right to recall him, but he had given Cyral no reason for the unusual transfer, nor for the extensive testing the Bard had undergone upon his return. And Cyral hadn't asked, for if it had anything to do with Bryan's death ... well, that was a subject the Bard would not discuss, swiftly shutting down every attempt Ferghus made to do so.

Cyral looked with curiosity at the two rocks sitting on the surface of the table. One was granite, its veins of translucent white and scattering of sparkling flecks attracting the eye. The other was smooth and dark, with no gleaming traces on its surface. Either would fit easily in the palm of his hand.

"Look at the granite," the Master instructed him, "and tell me what you hear."

The Bard glanced up in surprise, for the request might well have been a training exercise for an apprentice. Ferghus looked pointedly at the granite, and Cyral turned his attention back to it, his eyes resting on its surface for a moment as he listened. He broke the contact and glanced at the Master.

"I hear its song," he said. "Do you wish me to play it?"

"That won't be necessary," Ferghus said with a fleeting smile. He raised a brow and nodded toward the rock's companion.

Cyral turned his attention to the dark stone. Hearing nothing, he frowned and shook his head, then listened once again as minutely as he could, his brow creasing in concentration. After a time, he looked up in bewilderment. "What's wrong with this stone?"

"What did you hear?"

"Nothing," the disconcerted Bard said. "The stone is silent!"

"As it is for me," Ferghus said gravely. "Can you explain that?"

Cyral shook his head. "If stones were living things, I'd say that this one had died. I didn't think any object could exist without music ... and yet, here one sits."

The Master frowned. "Surely, I taught you better than that. You know perfectly well there are no such things—"

"—as impossibilities. But everything is created with music!"

The Master did not dispute this. "I summoned you because your Gift is the most acute among us. I thought, if even a trace of music existed in that stone, you might be able to hear it."

Cyral shook his head, gazing curiously at the silent stone. "How can it exist without the music it was created with, the music that infuses it with energy?"

"Let's see if you can answer that for yourself."

The Bard regarded the stone thoughtfully. "Its music might have been drained from it, I suppose," he said dubiously.

"And what is the problem with that theory?"

"Well ... if it had music to begin with, that music should have imprinted itself within the rock the way our memories are imprinted into our instruments. Yet there's no hint of an imprint."

Ferghus lifted his brow. "Have you another theory, then?"

"Only that it wasn't created with music in the first place."

"Which means?"

"Perhaps the stone came from some other part of the world."

The Master's mouth quirked. "Do you really suppose that Eire is the only place in the world where everything was created with music, be it stones, trees, animals, people, or the very elements themselves? I've traveled, my boy, and I can tell you that the laws governing this world apply everywhere, to everything in it."

"Are you saying that the Maker overlooked this stone?"

Ferghus snorted. "No need to blame the Maker. I'm saying that perhaps this stone didn't *come* from this world."

The Bard darted a nervous glance upward as though half-expecting a rain of ominously silent stones.

His Master apparently suffered no such trepidation. "Just imagine, my boy! A Stone of stones, made without music and hurled from the heavens to the ocean to wash up here, practically on my very doorstep." Ferghus gave the Stone an approving nod as he slid it into a small drawstring bag and cinched it firmly shut. "I want you to curtail your usual activities," he told his Bard, "and devote yourself to the study of this Stone. Discover what you can about it. If anyone can figure out a way to enter the Stone and uncover its secrets, I believe that person is you."

Matching amber eyes held each other, the Master's in challenge, the Bard's in anticipation. Many of those born with amber eyes, a rare color to begin with, were often Gifted with the ability to hear the songs of whatever they focused on. Trained to play that music, they could send their conscious awareness into the object and see it from within. To attempt to enter an object that had no music of its own was a unique, irresistible notion.

Ferghus pushed the bag toward Cyral. "Report to me within the week, whether you've made any progress or not."

"Through our bond, or do you wish me to come here?"

"I'd prefer you to come here." The Master's expression lit with anticipation matching his Bard's. "We might need to run a few experiments."

Cyral suppressed a smile and nodded. He stowed the Stone in his pack and headed toward the door.

"One more thing."

The Bard paused on the threshold.

"This conversation—*and* the existence of this Stone—is highly confidential. You're not to speak of it to anyone, in or out of the Bardic Order. The Druidic Council is becoming troublesome, and I do not wish any word of this to reach them. If the Ard Rí gets wind of the growing friction between our two Orders, he's likely to solve the problem by restricting the free movement between the túatha we both enjoy now."

Cyral stared at his Master in dismay. There were many túatha, or territories, scattered across Eire, each with its own Rí, or lesser King. The Ruaidrí were greater Kings with several Rí under their control. Above them all was the Ard Rí, King of all Eire. The thought of the Bardic and Druidic Orders being as restricted as the common people of Eire were, unable to move freely between territories without permission from their Rí, was a sobering thought.

Looking at the grim expression on his Master's face, the question Cyral was about to ask died on his lips. As he took his leave, the Bard wondered what Odhran, First of the Druidic Council, was up to now. And what on earth did a silent Stone that had apparently dropped from the heavens have to do with it?

Scattered through the woods and along the shores of southwest Eire were a number of small cabins used by the Bards assigned to Master Ferghus' territory, or by any traveling Bard in need of shelter. One such cabin, a half hour's brisk walk north of the Master's home, was situated next to a tributary of the Easach River where it spilled over the cliffs into the northern side of the bay. Cyral had gladly taken occupancy of the cabin when his Master recalled him, for the sound of the falls was soothing after traveling his rounds all day. Now that his work with the Stone was done here, however, the river was dismally failing in this role.

The Bard glared balefully at the dark Stone on his table. His second report was due in the morning, and he did not want to arrive empty-handed yet again. Master Ferghus had not seemed disturbed by his Bard's failure to enter the Stone and wrest any secrets from it, but Cyral was beginning to think the endeavor was a waste of time. The Master's quiet confidence in his Bard's eventual success was all that kept him from giving up in despair.

Of course, Master Ferghus knew everything Cyral did with the Stone because of the bond between them. Since the Master had apprenticed him and touched Cyral's song with his own, anything Cyral did with his Gift was instantly known to Ferghus. This enhancement to their bond would not be removed until Cyral became a full Master himself, a custom that ensured that Gifted members of the Bardic Order could not break their vow to do no harm with their Gift. Ferghus, therefore, was well aware that Cyral had spent hours trying to probe the inner depths of the Stone, receiving nothing but a splitting headache for his trouble. Whatever else might be true of the Stone's properties, one thing was certain. There was no music in its dark depths. Not a single whisper of sound, not a stray note broke the stillness within. *Perhaps the Maker tossed it from the heavens specifically to drive one Bard stark raving mad,* Cyral grumbled. That, at least, was one theory with ample evidence to support it.

The Bard pushed the Stone away, thinking to relax for awhile with his lap harp, but as he rose to fetch it, he caught sight of a full-sized Bardic harp lying in its case in the corner. *Bryan's harp.* His chest tightened and tears filled his eyes. Angrily, he shoved his emotions aside and, ignoring both harps, went to get himself something to eat. The mental focus he'd been exerting on the Stone was exhausting, he told himself sternly, accounting for this absurd emotional reaction to a perfectly good harp. *A harp you've never had the nerve to play,* his mind traitorously pointed out.

Too upset to bother with making a meal, he settled for taking some dried fish, a crock of honey, and a loaf of bread over to the table. He cut a thick slice of bread with his belt knife, then laid the knife next to the Stone. He was about to drizzle some honey over the bread when he paused, struck by a slight movement of his knife. To his utter amazement, it vibrated slightly, then moved the width of his smallest fingernail to rest against the side of the Stone.

Cyral blinked. Surely he couldn't have seen what his eyes were insisting he had. Yet there was his knife, nestled up against the Stone, which was not where he had placed it. He took hold of the knife's handle, pulled the blade away from the Stone, and felt the resistance at once. Clearly, the two objects did not wish to be separated. *So, I've finally discovered a second property. The Stone is magnetic! It reacts to the iron in my belt knife.*

Gratified to have something tangible to report to his Master the next day, Cyral finished his meal and decided to reward himself by working for the rest of the evening on his new harp. He could hardly wait to finish it ... indeed, he'd somewhat resented the Stone for taking him away from the harp's construction. It had taken two cycles for him to save enough coin for the expensive rosewood, bought from a merchant who specialized in importing rare woods. Then it had taken months to season it, along with the spruce and beech he would use as inlays, to be certain the wood wouldn't split or crack under his tools. After constructing all three parts of the frame—soundboard, column, and neck—he had carefully stained them ten times. The beautiful, glistening parts were now ready to assemble, and Cyral smiled in eager anticipation.

Any other member of the Bardic Order would think him crazy to make a harp of such unprecedented size and weight. Though a full-sized Bardic harp was twice the size of a lap harp, either of them would fit on a harpist's lap. The harp Cyral was constructing would stand upright before a seated harpist, and its pillar would reach above his head. Crazy or not, he had dreamed of this harp since he was a young boy avidly watching every Harpist he had the chance to listen to. His parents had died when he was four, leaving him to be passed from relative to relative, then given away to Harpist Ultan when he was seven. The man had scoffed, however, at Cyral's stuttering request for lessons.

I'll not waste my time teaching a boy who can barely speak. Let's see how well you handle your chores before I allow you to handle a lap harp.

For over a cycle, Cyral did an endless round of chores, enviously watching others take lessons he longed for and surreptitiously learning all he could. Then one day Master Ferghus had appeared at the door and, after a few heated words with the Harpist, had taken Cyral away with him, promising to instruct him in the making and playing of his own lap harp. Of all the times he had been given away, it was the first time he had gone eagerly, for the Master's promise was the first step toward his dream harp, a dream which had remained bright and true over all the cycles since.

He smiled as he laid out his tools and set to work. "I promise you," he told his vision of the completed instrument in his mind, "you will be a harp like no other in Bardic history."

Chapter 2

The following morning, Ferghus watched as Cyral demonstrated the Stone's magnetic powers. Fascinated, the Master took hold of the knife's handle and applied enough force to separate the two objects. "It's a powerful attraction."

"Yes, though I'm not sure what good that is." Cyral said with a shrug. "We've no particular need to attract belt knives."

Ferghus snorted. "No, belt knives won't be much use against men armed with swords."

Cyral looked up, startled. "Who are you worried about? The Druids bear no arms. And what have the Rí to complain of? We provide music and songs lauding their exploits, our excellent healers are available to all, and we arbitrate disagreements the Rí would otherwise have to bother themselves with. And at no cost!"

"Which is part of the problem. The Druidic Order would prefer to provide such services themselves—and be paid for it—making themselves even more useful and indispensable to the rulers who fund their Order. Both of us want peace, but the Druids would prefer it to be maintained by *their* efforts, not ours."

Cyral stared at him. "And you think their Order is becoming so upset by this that they would move against us?"

The Master shook his head. "That alone would not be enough, no. However, Odhran has apparently cast his greedy eyes on Glindar, our mine in the Connemara Mountains."

Cyral was astonished. "But why would he be interested in a mine that produces so little? Our own Council has been talking about closing it down for cycles."

Ferghus cleared his throat. "That is what the Council has let it be known ... and what Diarmuid has scribed into our records."

"You mean—"

"I mean that you are now one of a very small number of Bards who know differently. There are a number of small abandoned mines scattered throughout the mountains, furthering the belief that we have yet to find a decent one, but..." He shrugged. "Suffice it to say that there's a reason our Order is self-sufficient, able to care for those who can't afford the services of the Druidic Order. A reason we do not compete with them for positions within the households of the many Rí of Eire as teachers. A reason that Odhran has apparently discovered." The Master snorted. "I can just imagine the look on his face when he found out. How could mere *musicians* have discovered such rich veins of crystals and gems?"

"How, indeed?" Cyral murmured dryly.

"If you can't figure that out for yourself," Ferghus chided, "you'll be even more confused when I tell you that only three Bards are needed there ... one of mine, Brenach, who has a permanent position as supervisor, and two Gifted Bards who rotate monthly from the other Masters, lending further credence to the impression that Glindar is a poor mine, unworthy of anyone's attention."

"Three Bards?" Cyral echoed in astonishment. "To *mine* them?" When Ferghus merely looked at him, Cyral chuckled. "I see. Apparently the mastery of earthsong comes in handy."

Amusement crossed the Master's face. "Indeed it does. What need to dig from above when the earthsong can push up from below? The mining is done by each of the Masters on a rotating basis at the beginning of each month, using the excuse of checking on the mine's progress or lack thereof. The gems and crystals are then hidden in caches, and two Bards are more than enough to alternate in bringing them to their Master, small amounts at a time. The Ard Rí is aware that we have a single mine he believes we barely manage to support ourselves with," he added. "Having a vested interest in both Orders peacefully coexisting, he turns a blind eye to it. You will keep this information strictly to yourself," he added.

"Of course, Master." The Bard fell silent, wrestling with the discovery that matters in Eire were not what he had thought they were. "How could Odhran have found out about Glindar's productivity," he wondered, "if the Ard Rí himself thinks it's barely worth having and most of *us* don't even know about it?"

"That's a matter of conjecture," Ferghus replied, "but the signs all point to one man ... Cathair, the young Overdruid of Connemara. He has a few spies of his own, one of whom might have ferreted out the truth about our mine. And, in fact, one of the Bards was waylaid last month, a day after leaving Glindar. He survived the encounter, but the small bag he was transporting was taken. Cathair is ambitious and quite willing to fight for what he wants."

"With what?" Cyral scoffed. "His stave? Druids are no more fighters than we are!" When his Master made no reply, Cyral went cold. "You can't think ... surely Odhran wouldn't send *fianna* to take the mine," he said, his eyes begging to be assured that Odhran wouldn't dream of using one of the local warrior clans against them. "His Council would never stand for—" But his Master was shaking his head.

"If *I* wished to make a move against *them,* without anyone in my Order—including my Council—knowing anything about it—"

"You would *never—*"

"No, I never would. But I *could.* And so could Odhran."

"Surely the Druids have no more desire to attract unfavorable notice from the Ard Rí than we do!"

Ferghus snorted. "Whatever else he may be, Odhran isn't stupid. He wouldn't arrange things himself. He'd do it through an overly ambitious, expendable upstart. If the venture fails, Cathair's life would be forfeit, his body sent to the Ard Rí with apologies for the reprehensible actions of a rogue Druid. But if it succeeds, Cathair will get what he wants ... a position on their Council."

"What? But he's no older than I am!"

The Master nodded. "And quite unwilling to wait. Discovering we have a lucrative mine would have sent him scurrying straight to Odhran. Which explains, perhaps, the lengthy, closed session he had with him just last week."

Cyral's face paled. "How could you possibly know that?"

Ferghus chuckled grimly. "Odhran is not the only one with an extensive network of spies. He uses his to see what fires he can light. I use mine to put them out, or prevent them from kindling in the first place. One of my sources is privy to the doings of the Druidic Council and lets me know when something occurs that might threaten the balance between our Orders, a balance *most* of us are anxious to maintain." He tapped his fingers against the armrest of his chair. "What concerns me is that Odhran might have just been given reason to upset that balance. And *that* fire, once kindled, will be very difficult to put out." He gave the Stone an appraising look.

Cyral fell silent, wondering at his Master's look. *What has this Stone to do with any of this? And why is it so important for me to spend all my time studying it?*

Before he could ask, Ferghus arched a brow in his direction. "What do we know about this Stone?" the Master asked, as if he were lecturing to a hall full of ignorant apprentices.

"It has a force that attracts iron," his single listener answered.

"And what stops the attracted object?"

Cyral frowned in thought. "Its own material boundary."

"And what could be pulled toward the Stone that doesn't *have* a material boundary to stop it?"

The Bard's eyes widened. "Music? You think the Stone might be able to pull music into itself?" The fascinating idea held Cyral entranced for a moment. "But why, then," he muttered, "wouldn't the Stone have pulled the songs from every rock on the beach? Not to mention every sea creature in the ocean it washed up from?"

The Master sat back in his chair and smiled slightly when Cyral rose distractedly to his feet and began to pace. After several trips back and forth across the length of the living room, he stopped in front of the fireplace.

"If it could pull music into itself," Cyral lectured the mantelpiece, "it would be packed so full of songs that we'd go mad if we tried to untangle them all! And clearly it's not." Restlessly, he moved on to the living room window.

"So, no," he concluded as he came to a stop and stared out at the bluff beyond. "The Stone cannot pull music into itself."

"And does that preclude music being *placed* there?" the Master quietly asked.

"Well, no," Cyral said thoughtfully. "Music, taken from something else, could perhaps be placed into the Stone, unable to leave until it was taken back out again." He frowned. "But why would anyone want to do that? What would be the point?"

"Just indulge me, my boy, in a purely theoretical exercise."

Cyral snorted. "Well, it's certainly theoretical, since no Bard or Master is allowed to remove the inherent song of anything."

"No Bard or Master is allowed to break Bardic Law," the Master corrected. "Or their vow never to cause harm with their music. Not removing songs is merely a stricture, which applies to all Gifted members of our Order except for Masters. Nevertheless, no Master would remove the song of something if it caused harm, for *that* would break his vow. So, while we can use living things for food or fuel, we would not use our Gift to alter their nature and desecrate them from within."

The Bard's gaze slid uncomfortably away from the Master's.

"So, what music might be put into the Stone?" Ferghus asked.

Cyral glanced at the vase of wildflowers on the kitchen window sill. "Removing the song of a living thing wouldn't be an option," he assured the flowers, "since that would certainly harm it." He glanced out the window. "A small portion of elemental music like water or wind would seem to be the best choice, since its removal is unlikely to do its vast host any harm. And the music of an element is a single song, in contrast to an object, which contains an ensemble of songs that would require untangling first. On the other hand, elemental music has incredible force, which might be difficult for the Stone to handle and might cause unexpected, possibly catastrophic results."

He turned around and fixed his attention on the granite sitting on the table. "So, all things considered, it might be best to try to untangle and remove one of the songs of that piece of granite." His gaze shifted to the Stone. "One could then attempt to place the freed song into the Stone ... although that might be problematic. Since the Stone has no song of its own, we can't take it there ourselves. An external force would be needed to push the song into the Stone directly from the granite," he said consideringly. "It would need to be a force generated from within the granite and capable of propelling the freed song through the boundary of its host." He glanced at the Master. "You, perhaps, could do it. Holding the freed song, you might be able to move within the granite with enough momentum to propel the song into the Stone."

Ferghus nodded thoughtfully, his eyes bright.

Cyral turned his attention back to the window, frowning in thought. "I can see no reason why a song couldn't be placed inside the Stone in this manner if it was untangled and freed from the structure it was held in first," he announced, his brows raised as though somewhat surprised at his own conclusion.

"And who," Ferghus quietly asked, "has made a successful attempt to do just that?"

Cyral froze, staring sightlessly out the window. "I have no idea what you mean," he said tightly.

"Then let me make myself clear. Bry—"

"Has nothing to do with this! He was just a friend who died. People have friends who die all the time." His voice rose in panic.

"Not like—"

"Stop trying to make me remember! You don't understand."

"I understand what you're doing to yourself, and you remember it quite well on your own," Ferghus told him. "Over and over you see it happen, guilt tightening its hold with every repetition. What you don't want me to do is make you face it."

"You can't make me," the Bard whispered hoarsely.

"I can, my boy," the Master said quietly. "And, if you keep refusing to face it on your own, I will."

Cyral turned at this. "You think I don't *know* I broke my vow?" he demanded. "Isn't having to face that fact every single day enough without having you bring it up as well? Why don't you just take my robe, bind my Gift, and send me away? I expected you to when you ordered me to return to Aille-Mara. "Do it now," he said bitterly, "and stop this torture!"

"Your torture is of your own making, not mine," Ferghus said sternly. "And you did *not* break your vow, for if ever you were about to, do you think I wouldn't stop you? Until you're a Master yourself, it's my responsibility to do so." His voice softened. "What you did with your Gift was a mercy, requested by a friend who knew exactly what he was asking of you. Had I stood in his place, I would have asked the same. Had I stood in yours, I would have done the same."

Cyral turned abruptly back to the window, his mind filled with the deep pain of a memory he wished only to forget. He had never stayed in one place long enough as a child to have any close friends, and Bryan was the first friend he had made as a Bard, the only person besides his Master whose song had touched his own to create a bond of entwined music. And then ... *No! I won't remember it again!* His Master's hands gripped his shoulders.

"Let go of your guilt, my boy," Ferghus urged. "It will strangle your song if you keep playing that memory with undeserved guilt attached to it. When you became my apprentice, you vowed to do no harm with your Gift. You have never broken that vow."

The Bard barely heard him as the memory he had resisted with all his strength streamed effortlessly into his mind like the water streaking the rain-washed window in front of him.

Cyral had been late that day, held back by a mediation that had taken longer to settle than it should have. After the two quarrelsome merchants left, satisfied at last, the Bard snatched up his lap harp and pack, then hurried as fast as he could to meet Bryan for a hike up to the top of Solas Falls. He smiled as he strode through the trees to the clearing where the upward trail began, looking forward to the rare pleasure of a free afternoon. He reached the clearing in time to see the answering grin on his friend's face ... and to see the tall ash tree on the embankment behind Bryan begin to fall as the earth abruptly slid out from under it. Cyral froze in horror as everything seemed to happen too fast for thought, yet every moment of it was captured in his mind to be replayed again and again with agonizing slowness. His shout of warning that came too late ... his friend turning in alarm ... the scream that split the clearing as the cursed tree slammed into Bryan. Then a moment of utter silence, broken by the sound of Cyral's boots racing across the clearing—for surely the rest of him was still standing frozen in place. Unfamiliar hands frantically shoved aside leafy branches to finally reach the broken body beneath. Amber eyes opened into his, filled with anguish.

Release my song ... please...

The words rang hollowly in Cyral's mind as he tried to make sense of them. He gasped as realization forcibly struck him. Bryan's lower body was crushed under the trunk of the tree. Trying to move it, if it didn't kill him outright, would only cost his friend more agony. But that wasn't the release his friend was asking for.

I can't! ... I can't! The part of Cyral that was trained not to tamper with or move the unique songs inherent in all things kept up the mute, two-word monologue. The rest of him put aside his own anguish and focused, not on the song of his friend's conscious awareness or that of his broken body, but on his soul ... the song that was the essence of who he was, unique among all other people. The song that was Bryan. It leapt into Cyral's mind with perfect clarity, as though anxious for him to hear it. He removed his lap harp, set a strong block, and began to play, his fingers firm and sure, though his own soul trembled with the import of what he was doing. Then he moved his song forward to touch Bryan's.

Memories assailed him at its touch, memories of the person who meant more to him than anyone but his Master. Holding Bryan's song firmly to himself, he withdrew from the mangled body and released the song to float on the wind. The strings stilled under fingers too numb to feel them. His friend's eyes were closed forever, the slight smile on his face a parting gift he would never give again. And Cyral clung to his lap harp and wept, tears trickling down his cheeks and harp to fall into the earth below.

The Bard came back to himself as his Master released his shoulders. "I will leave the matter be ... for now," Ferghus said gently. He gestured toward the living room window. "The rain has finally given way to a bit of sunshine. Go out to the bluff and enjoy it while you may. I've a few things to attend to here. When you come back, we'll continue our discussion of the Stone."

Cyral nodded and left the house, grateful for the time he needed to calm his turbulent emotions and think about what his Master had said. He walked to the bluff and felt the welcome warmth of sunlight on his face. He heard the windsong as it rippled his robe and blew capriciously through the tall grasses, letting it dry the unshed tears in his eyes. He had known, of course, that his Master had to be aware of what he had done with his Gift. Indeed, Cyral had returned to Aille-Mara soon after Bryan's death on his

Master's orders, fully expecting to be censured, if not cast out of the Bardic Order altogether. When Ferghus made no move to do so, Cyral thought he was simply giving him time while keeping him under close watch. Time to grieve for his friend, time to come to grips with what he had done before pronouncing judgement on it.

He honestly doesn't believe I broke my vow. He took a deep breath and closed his eyes in relief at having unexpectedly received his Master's absolution. He stood on the bluff with the wind buffeting him, wondering how he would ever receive his own.

The moment he opened his Master's door, Ferghus motioned imperatively to the Stone as though the Bard had never left.

"I believe an experiment is in order, my boy!"

Cyral's eyes lit with interest. "Are you going to try placing a song into the Stone?"

Ferghus shook his head. "No, my boy. *You* are."

"Me! You're giving me permission to move a song?"

"Have I not just done so?" The Master indicated the chunk of rock on the table. "This piece of granite, I believe, could spare a bit of its music for you to test your theory, especially if you're successful in returning it afterwards."

Cyral scrutinized it. "It's a complex specimen," he mused. "A trio of songs, one of which must be untangled from the others."

"Best leave the quartz and feldspar alone," Ferghus advised. "We have no real idea what might happen, but we know the music of an object infuses it with energy, and I've often wondered if at least some of that energy is what holds it together. If so, you must be careful how much energy you remove. I'd just as soon *not* have an explosion on my dinner table." He lifted a finger. "As I recall, there's very little mica in this sample. I doubt the loss of its energy would disturb the rock overmuch."

Cyral nodded, then took a chair and set it in the farthest corner of the room. "If you please, Master," he said, indicating the chair with a flourish. "If things don't go well, someone needs to be here to give me a glowing eulogy."

Ferghus got to his feet, grumbling about young, sarcastic Bards who thought they knew better than old, experienced Masters regarding things neither one of them knew anything about in the first place. He took his new seat and looked at Cyral expectantly.

The Bard gave the two rocks on the table a calculating look, then positioned the granite up against the Stone.

"Very good, my boy," Ferghus said. "When you enter the granite, its translucent wall will be darker where the Stone touches it, showing you its precise location."

The Bard nodded. "With the Stone up against the granite, I'm hoping to propel the freed song directly into it, for I can see no reason why the material boundary of either object would stop it. Once inside the Stone, the song should be caught by the Stone's internal structure and held there."

"And what of your *own* song?"

"I ought to remain in the granite. If so, I'll return to myself and try to enter the Stone by playing the music I sent into it."

Cyral removed his lap harp and sat near the table. Then he took a deep breath and settled his emotions. This rock, he firmly told himself, was *not* a living person begging for release from mortal injuries. It was an inanimate object with no feelings and no life to lose. Nevertheless, the Bard swallowed hard as he focused on the rock's surface and began to softly play its music.

As his conscious awareness moved into the granite, Cyral saw the trio within. The pure, crystalline song of quartz threaded through the granite like liquid moonlight. A steady rhythmic pulse, firmly played on the lowest strings of his harp, wrapped itself around the beautiful melody, evoking the stability and strength of the smooth grey feldspar. Sprinkled over both was a constellation of silvery staccatos that twinkled like tiny stars of mica. Cyral never failed to be enthralled at the realization that each substance had its own song, its own part to play in the ensemble of the whole.

The harpist focused solely on the song of mica, his fingers playing the sparkling staccato notes on the highest strings as he carefully untangled them from the trio. At last they stood free as a separate composition of their own. He moved toward the scintillating song until his own song touched it, then held it firmly. He was thrillingly aware that what he was about to do now would place him in uncharted territory. When the Bard had removed his friend's song, he had released it into the wind as he returned to himself. To his knowledge, no one had ever untangled a song from something and attempted to push it directly *into something else*. Much less, the Maker willing, put it back where it had been.

Cyral searched the translucent walls until he found the darkened area that pinpointed the location of the Stone. Holding the freed song tightly to his own, he raced toward the shadow and released the mica's song like a musical arrow from a bowstring. Too late came the realization that he was still playing the full trio, including the music of those sparkling notes. For one breathless moment he remained in the granite; the next moment he was swept through its boundaries and sucked into the dark recesses of the Stone. Barely managing to keep his fingers on the strings, he quickly segued to playing only the mica's song. The shimmering staccatos were scattered, swirling toward the dark cavern's perimeter as though intent on investigating their new domicile, oblivious to the Bard they had just yanked into the Stone with them.

Feeling somewhat scattered himself, Cyral brought the wayward notes into some semblance of order, then decided to follow their bright path and do some exploring of his own. But the moment he moved forward, he froze, caught in the powerful gaze of what he could only call an awareness ... one that was utterly unlike his own. Indeed, it was unlike anything he had ever encountered. And this awareness was not fixed on the song drifting around the perimeter. It was fixed on his *own* song. A strange drowsiness overcame him. The music of the harp slowed.

Block your mind! Now!

The command ripped through his mind, shaking Cyral's awareness free of the Stone's scrutiny. Swiftly, he constructed a block and slammed it into place. The intense feeling of being inspected disappeared. The song of mica finished its slow circuit of the Stone and began another, moving more slowly as the impetus that had brought it here lessened. Cyral tore his wondering gaze away from the mesmerizing display and looked suspiciously into every dark crevice he could find. Nothing met his searching gaze, no lurking awareness looked back. Gradually his emotions calmed and he carefully drew his conscious awareness out of the Stone and back to himself. As his hands stilled the vibrations of the strings, he was startled by a voice spoken in whispered excitement mere inches from his ear.

"Look!" Ferghus hissed, pointing at the Stone. "It's shining!"

Sure enough, the dull black Stone was now gleaming with flecks of light. Both heads swiveled toward the granite, whose surface was no longer as shiny as before. The smooth grey feldspar was unchanged and the translucent veins of quartz still gleamed, but the flecks of mica no longer reflected the light.

"Fascinating!" Ferghus settled himself into the seat next to Cyral. "Now, tell me what you should have done that you didn't do," he said mildly. "For, although neither of us expected you to be pulled into the Stone, that was a serious mistake you must *not* make again."

"I should have set a block beforehand," Cyral said ruefully. "I should have expected the unexpected and been prepared for it. I won't make that mistake again. And I ought to have realized that if I continued to play the song I was sending out of the granite, it would exert a pull on my own song once I released it."

"See to it that you keep your fingers firmly on the strings, as well," Ferghus told him. "You came far too close to releasing them. Understandable, but potentially disastrous if you have not yet brought your awareness back." The Master turned his attention back to the Stone. "What an unusual object! I'm quite certain now that this world is not its home. Instead of being created with music, it seems to have been created with some kind of awareness. Despite my curiosity, I do *not* want to know what would have happened to you if you had remained under its scrutiny." He glanced pointedly at the granite. "Now, are you recovered enough to collect the results of your experiment, or must a decrepit old Master do it for you?"

Cyral chuckled and focused on listening to the granite. A few moments later he reported back. "The song of the granite is different now because the song of the mica is almost totally absent from it! I can only hear its echo within the rock, like an imprint that has no ability to reflect light. The granite's song is now a duet ... a duet with an imprinted memory of having once been a trio." He turned his focus on the Stone. "The Stone is no longer silent," he said in awe. "It's filled with the song of mica, and that song is far clearer than I've ever heard it before."

The Master nodded thoughtfully. "The Stone is definitely a receptacle capable of holding music. You could use this to study individual songs, for the Stone takes on the properties of the music within it. Fascinating!"

"Takes on the properties," Cyral echoed, feeling slightly ill. "Would it have taken on *my—*"

"Whatever it would have done," Ferghus firmly interjected, "it didn't do. Just be very careful not to find out. Can you put the song back into the granite?"

Cyral took a deep breath. "I'll try." He took up his lap harp and set the strongest block in his mind he had ever created. Then he focused on the Stone's surface and began to play the song that emanated from it. He moved effortlessly into the Stone and the scintillating world it had become, enormously relieved when no uncanny awareness seemed to be in residence. Searching the Stone's perimeter, he found the place where the Stone and granite touched. He took hold of the glittering song, but when he began to move toward the darkened area with it, he found himself encountering great resistance, as if he were suddenly traveling through a quagmire. The Stone, it seemed, did not wish to relinquish its sparkling prize.

Cyral broke off with a gasp as he returned to himself. "I can't move it out of the Stone." He thought for a moment. "When the song of mica was in the granite, it was the lesser song, with far fewer notes and complexity of rhythm than the others. Inside the Stone, however, it's a dominant song of its own, with nothing to compete against or overshadow it. One would think, with no other songs to be entangled with, it would be easier to move. Perhaps it's entangled with the structure of the Stone itself. Whatever the reason, its resistance is too great for me to overcome."

The Master pursed his lips. "Too great for a lap harp, perhaps." He picked up his Bardic harp and held it out. "Try this."

Cyral obligingly took the larger harp and tried again. This time, with great effort, he was able to overcome the Stone's resistance and return the song to the granite. He sat back, exhausted from the mental and physical strain, but noting that the granite gleamed with shining flecks once again. The Stone was silent and dull, and Cyral thought it had taken on a brooding aspect, as if sullen from having the captured music taken from it.

"Continue your study of the Stone," his Master said, "with my authorization to move the songs of inanimate objects into and out of it. I assume you have a full-sized Bardic harp by now?"

Cyral hesitated. "I've kept Bryan's harp in good working order. His family gave it to me after he passed on."

Ferghus observed the emotions flickering across his Bard's face. "I see. Will you be able to use it to work with the Stone?"

The Bard nodded wordlessly.

The Master accepted this without comment. "And how is the construction of your own harp coming along?"

Cyral raised his brows in mock surprise. "I thought you didn't care for ... how did you put it? ... ah, yes, that foolish testament to my massive ego."

The Master chuckled. "On the contrary, I have the greatest respect for your monstrosity of a harp," he said. "I simply reserve the right to tease you about it unmercifully." The Bard laughed, and Ferghus turned a thoughtful gaze to the Stone. "And I've decided the bigger the instrument, the better ... provided I'm not the one who has to carry it."

A few weeks later, Cyral sat working on his harp as a heavy rain lashed his cabin. He had finished constructing the harp's frame, its column, base, and body fitting together with tight precision. Now he was using the leftover pieces of rosewood to make the tuning pegs, which would then be stained with the same painstaking care he had used with the frame. Cyral refused to hurry, for replacing parts was costly and time consuming, and he would accept nothing but the best in materials and workmanship.

As much as he looked forward to actually playing his dream harp, he would be sad to see its construction come to an end. He talked to it frequently as he worked, telling it what a wondrous harp it would be, what incredible music would flow from its strings. He shared his hopes for the future with it and told it all the things he could never bring himself to share with anyone else, not even his Master. For, although Cyral enjoyed his work as a Bard—playing at every village and hamlet he came to on his rounds, helping anyone who needed aid, and fixing any instrument that came to his hand— he loved his solitude even more. His harp, he was certain, was the only companion he needed.

Although memories besieged him whenever he took hold of Bryan's harp, Cyral had persevered with his study of the Stone. He had become adept at separating single songs from inanimate objects and transporting them into the Stone, careful never to enter it without setting a strong block first. This, however, had become progressively more difficult to do, for after only a few days, he had noticed a weakening of his block. Thinking the lapse was his own—for setting and maintaining a block took energy he was also expending in his work—he swiftly reinforced the block. When it happened again a short while later, he became worried. His Gift was strong, none of his blocks having ever been breached in the testing of his Gift every Bard must undergo each cycle. Cyral stopped his work with the song and continued to softly play, focused only on the block he had set. It was not as dark as it had been, and as he watched, the edges rippled and lightened to a dark grey. A shiver ran through Cyral's song. Was the Stone rhythmically probing his block for weaknesses, patiently chipping away until it ... what? Cracked open his mind like an acorn?

You're not getting in! he snarled at the Stone and slammed a second layer of darkness over his block. The rippling stopped. Since then, he had kept vigilant while working in the Stone, stopping often to inspect and reinforce his block. It was exhausting, but his strength was increasing, as though his Gift, like a muscle, was increasing in strength as it was flexed and used.

Cyral's knowledge of songs was growing with it. He had successfully taken two songs together into the Stone and studied their interactions with each other, how they combined in a slightly different way than they had in their original host, like two members of a large ensemble who suddenly found themselves playing together as a duet. Further experimentation revealed that repeatedly playing the lesser song could make *it* the dominant song, supplanting the former one in the hierarchy of the ensemble. Every alteration he made was instantly reflected in the outer traits of the Stone. Ferghus, aware of everything Cyral did with his Gift, found this so fascinating that he immediately wanted to enter the Stone and try it himself. Cyral's vehement objection left his Master in a rare state of speechlessness, which the Bard took instant advantage of.

"I can't forbid you, but I beg you to forgo your curiosity and listen to me!" Cyral said. "This is *not* the time for the Prime of our Order to put himself at risk." To his surprised relief, Ferghus merely nodded and did not bring it up again.

When Cyral realized that he could separate individual phrases of a song and successfully put them back, he asked Ferghus for permission to do this in the song's original host, for separating a single phrase from a song and transporting it into the Stone took far less energy than it took to untangle and take the entire song. The Master agreed to let him try, and when it was successful, gave him permission to continue doing so. All this painstaking study had revealed a wealth of information Cyral was certain no one had ever known before. How this information could ultimately be used to benefit the Bardic Order, he didn't know. And, though he suspected his Master did, questioning him proved useless.

Nor did Ferghus bring up the growing tension between the two Orders of Eire again. Cyral was admittedly isolated in his cabin, restricted from his normal responsibilities as a Bard while he continued his studies of the Stone, but even he was aware that the Druidic and Bardic Orders were becoming more estranged. What had long been a friendly rivalry of sorts, with villages taking sides for one or the other, had become a growing undercurrent of overt disharmony. He had been shocked and dismayed when he last visited the marketplace of Aille-Mara and heard whispered comments as he passed, accompanied by suspicious frowns directed at his Bardic robe. A few discreet questions to one of his colleagues revealed that rumors were circulating throughout Eire that the Bards were practitioners of the dark arts, even insinuating that the instruments themselves were tainted with sorcerous music. There was little doubt, Cyral thought, where such rumors had originated.

Ironic, Cyral reflected as he stoically continued working on his harp pegs, considering that the two Orders came from the same ancient tree of the Celtic religious belief system, which originally had three branches. The Druids of old had been philosophers, judges, and teachers. The Ovates had been healers and seers. And the Bards had been musicians who kept alive the stories of their history and lore. Over time, the three branches had become two, as the healers were absorbed into the Bardic Order, and the seers into the Druidic Order. And now, it seemed, the two remaining Orders were on a subtle, but potentially deadly collision course. If his Master was correct in thinking that Odhran's greed and Cathair's ambition were going to result in a move against their mine, and quite possibly against their very existence, then little wonder his Master seemed to be aging, lines of worry etching increasingly deeper paths across his face. The Bardic Order was armed with musical instruments, not weapons of warfare. They would stand no chance against a band of warriors armed with swords.

Cyral put aside his grim musings and tuning pegs and went to get himself a meal. Though the bowl of cooked oats and dried fruit looked good when he took it to the table, he ate without tasting, lost again in contemplation of his experiments with the Stone. Would he get the same results if he ran the same experiments in an object with music of its own, he wondered. If he sent the sparkling song of the granite into a piece of slate, would the slate suddenly have gleaming flecks on its surface? Or would its structure remain unchanged or be damaged beyond repair?

Most things were created with a complexity of songs, a veritable symphony of music that blended harmoniously into a unified work, like the individual parts of an ensemble that created a single piece of music. It staggered Cyral's mind to think of the endless combinations that could exist within the same substance. In all the many samples of granite he had explored over the cycles, not once had he heard the exact same song, though their similarities had been striking, as if individual phrases had been dissected from a single piece.

Using the Stone as a receptacle, Cyral had discovered that, just as the trio of songs in the granite corresponded to the three types of rocks that formed it, each of those individual songs was itself a choir of its own, with music that apparently described the physical substances that formed it. He had even managed to separate the song of one of these mystifying substances, astonished to find that it, too, was an ensemble of songs. How far down, he wondered, did the layers of songs go? Could they be untangled and separated until only a single song remained? The primary song—or perhaps the primary note—of creation itself?

The incessant hammering of the rain finally abated as the sun set outside the cabin, casting shadows that gradually darkened into night, but the Bard inside made no move to light a lantern or stir the fire to life. For it seemed to Cyral that nothing else existed but his own mind, filled with questions and thoughts of the song of creation, and the Stone sitting before him, filled with nothing but dark, impenetrable silence. His mind reeled with possibilities. The Stone could easily contain the song of an object, but what about the song of a living thing? What if he were to fill the Stone with the song of a tree or a flower? Could it be returned to its host, or would it immediately die? He would never know, he told himself wryly, for he had no right to do such a thing.

The only living thing he had the right to experiment on was himself. But how could Cyral transplant his song—the song of his soul, not just of his conscious awareness—without killing himself on the first try? And how, he wondered as he sat in the growing darkness, would he ever bring himself back?

Suddenly aware of the coldness penetrating the cabin, he shook himself from his reverie and went to build up the fire. Such idle speculations, he told himself, were best put aside. Especially if they took him away from his harp.

Chapter 3

On a blustery day in early spring, the marketplace of Aille-Mara was unusually quiet, most of the seaport's inhabitants unwilling to venture out on this unseasonably frigid day. Those who did finished their haggling quickly and hurried home, the wind whipping the hems of their cloaks around their boot tops and threatening to take their purchases from tightly clutched grasps. The dock stood empty this day, but at the jetty a currach of disgruntled fishermen tied their small vessel securely in place and headed for the comforting embrace of the nearest pub.

The youngest among them veered off from the others, ignoring the good-natured jibes accusing him of preferring the company of his newly handfasted bride to the company of his friends. He pulled his cloak tighter around him as he left the thatched buildings behind and headed uphill, where a tall stone building stood in regal indifference to the weather. His desire to go inside and warm himself before continuing on home was quickly squelched as he neared the imposing structure. The Council Hall of the Bardic Order was not something to be lightly entered by a mere fisherman. And, as if to underscore this, the sound of raised voices cut through the wind, hurrying him on his way.

Had the young fisherman been so bold as to walk up the wide

stone steps and open one of the tall double doors, he would have found himself in a narrow, unoccupied anteroom that spanned the length of the outside wall. A long row of pegs on either side of the entrance, ten of them with packs and instrument bags hanging from them, would have informed him that ten Masters were in residence within the hall, the imposing doors to which were firmly shut. Had the fisherman dared to push one of them open, he would have stood there immobile, his mouth open in wonder. For such a room as this was indeed worthy of far more than a cursory glance.

The hall was large, as one would expect who knew there were as many as fifteen Masters who must be seated there, and when a general conclave was called, upwards of a hundred and fifty Bards looking on as well. The ceiling was high, and the white granite walls were adorned with murals of music scores and symbols. Centered on each wall was a single tall window, letting in an abundance of light. Above each window was the symbol for one of the four elemental songs, each done in a mosaic of stones and crystals. It is doubtful that any fisherman would have heard of the wonder of these mosaics, displayed where only Bards and Masters came, but seeing them in person would have taken his breath away.

Windsong adorned the northern window, a vortex of clear quartz crystals spiraling upward against a sky of crushed aquamarine. Watersong was featured above the western window, a rocky beach of corkite and cinnebar sprayed with sparkling waves of blue azurite. The eastern window's mosaic was of earthsong, striking cliffs of connemara marble with serpentine grass bending in the wind on the bluffs above. The southern window's mosaic looked to be in flames, shimmering yellow heliodor, orange gmelinite, and red jasper twining together in a hypnotic pattern that drew the eye to their white, chabozite centers, each one delicately laced with crushed blue fluorite.

In the corner closest to the door stood a table where a small man sat poised to write, his quill quivering as though impatient to be dipped into the gleaming ink pot nearby. He emitted a soft sigh and regretfully set the quill down. His tunic of seafoam green with a silver quill embroidered on the front left shoulder proclaimed his status as a Scribe, one with only a few remaining wisps of white hair left to him. Except for those matters deemed too dangerous to be recorded, such as the one being discussed now, Diarmuid, Scribe of the Council, had kept a detailed record of every Council session for untold cycles. Dozens of scrolls in cubicles on the wall above his table bore silent testimony to his efforts. Next to these, several shelves of books, including the original book of Bardic Law, were arranged in neat rows. As if knowing the fastidious Scribe would swiftly put an end to them, not a speck of dust was to be seen on any shelf, nor were any so bold as to show themselves elsewhere.

The Council table itself was enormous, spanning half the length of the hall itself, and could seat as many as twenty-two people. Eight marble pedestals supported the polished marble surface, empty this day except for a mallet and three graduated chimes that stood at the head of the table in front of Ferghus, the Master strongest in the Gift and Prime of the Bardic Order. Nine other white-robed Masters were seated in order of their strength in the Gift, beginning with Barrach, Second of the Council, to the Prime's right and Liam, Third of the Council, to his left. At the moment, both were frowning at Ferghus.

"This insistence of yours that Odhran is going to attack our mine ... with all due respect, what are you basing it on?" Barrach shook his head. "I haven't heard anything yet that would justify calling this session, close on the heels of the last one."

"I must agree," said Liam. "You've given us much to think on—and it's legitimate cause for concern—but in order to act, we need proof ... or at least *some* clear evidence."

A murmur of agreement came from around the table, and the Prime slapped the arms of his chair in frustration. "What will it take to get you to see reason?" he demanded. "All the signs—"

"Signs, Ferghus? Really?" snorted Fionn, seated to the right of Barrach as Fourth of the Council. "Coming from the Master who insists we back up every opinion we have with *reasons?* And yet here you are, expecting us to commit ourselves to a drastic course of action without any real evidence to justify it!"

Barrach nodded agreement. "You say that Odhran had a meeting with Cathair, one of his Overdruids. Well, and why shouldn't he? If *you* had a meeting with a *Bard,* do you think Odhran would panic and call for a Council session at Uisneach, insisting you were clearly about to commit an act of violence against them?"

Ferghus snorted. "When have you ever known me to panic or act without good reason?" His eyes swept the table. "When have any of you? And that's hardly the only thing that's happened! Two weeks before that meeting, Dunn was waylaid only fifteen furlongs from Glindar, his sack of stones and gems stolen. We must *not* take lightly the very real possibility that Odhran now knows where our mine is, and has proof that it's productive!"

"No one's taking it lightly," Liam said in a conciliatory tone. "We're simply not willing to *act* on what you admit yourself is only a *possibility.* You say that Cathair has spies. Well, what Overdruid does not?" He opened his hands and shrugged. "What Master seated at this table does not? You say that one of his spies may have discovered Glindar's location. You don't actually *know* that he has, nor do you know that he's the one who attacked Dunn. You say that Cathair immediately ran off to tell Odhran to use it as leverage for a seat on the Council, but all you really *know* is that they had a meeting." He shook his head. "You know you have my greatest respect, Ferghus, but I think I speak for most of us when I say we need more than speculation."

"We need *proof,*" Barrach said bluntly. "And without it, what action do you expect us to take? March to Uisneach and demand an accounting of Odhran for his 'obvious intentions'?" He snorted. "You know perfectly well he would laugh in our faces and advise us to have your head examined by one of our healers."

"We should at least close down some of the more productive tunnels," Ferghus insisted, "leaving only what we need open for a few seasons. If Glindar is taken, they will eventually discover the tunnels, but it will at least give us more time to prepare."

"Prepare for what?" Aidan asked from farther down the table. "With Glindar taken, wouldn't we simply open Lóis, our alternate mine, with none the wiser?"

"And, having been successful the first time," Ferghus countered, "what makes you think Odhran wouldn't do the same thing again?"

Barrach sighed. "We're moving in circles, getting nowhere. There's been enough talk. As Second of the Council, I call for a vote. How many think we should do as Ferghus suggests and close down most of Glindar's tunnels?"

The Prime's hand went up alone.

"How many think we should wait until we have clear proof before acting on it?"

Every hand but Ferghus' went up.

For a long moment, Ferghus sat staring at the Council table, his expression unreadable. Then he picked up the mallet and struck each of the three chimes once. The sweet sounds filled the air and died away. "This Council session is ended."

One by one, the Masters rose and left, until only Ferghus and Barrach were left at the table.

"I'm sorry, my friend," Barrach said quietly. "I know you truly believe we're in danger. But perhaps the one who does not believe in impossibilities ought to consider the possibility that he might be wrong."

Ferghus looked up then, his amber eyes gazing steadily into Barrach's. "I sincerely hope that I am."

Barrach nodded and left.

Ferghus sat staring at the smooth marble surface of the table.

If I gave them the proof they want, they would not believe it. He looked up and saw the Scribe looking at him uncertainly.

"Forgive me, Diarmuid. I didn't mean to keep you."

"It's no trouble, Master Ferghus, to stay as long as you have need of me." The Scribe rose, bowed to the Prime, and left. A few moments later, Ferghus sighed and rose as well.

"I will do what I must," he murmured regretfully as he turned to leave. "And let the pieces fall where they may."

$\mathcal{B}$arely two hours later, Ferghus opened his front door and smiled at Cyral, who was stamping the dirt from his boots and blowing warmth into his cupped hands.

"Come in out of the cold, my boy!" the Master exclaimed, then stood stock still, blocking any possibility of Cyral doing so. For on the Bard's back was the most enormous Bardic travel bag Ferghus had ever seen. "By the Maker himself! Is that what I think it is?"

"That depends," Cyral said, shivering and burying his hands deep in the pockets of his cloak. "At the moment, you're looking at a Bard with a giant harp on his back. But he's about to become a frozen porch ornament if you don't let him in soon. Apparently, the weather didn't get your notification that spring began last week ... or did you forget to send it?"

The Master laughed and stepped aside. Cyral lost no time shedding his cloak and taking himself and his harp to a seat near the fire. Ferghus eyed the giant tasseled bag with delight. "You've finished it! Where did you find a case and travel bag to fit it?"

"I ordered them custom-made. Bren refused to accept the dimensions I gave him until he saw my harp for himself."

Ferghus chuckled. "It must have cost you a small fortune. Bren is meticulous in waterproofing his leather and isn't shy about charging extra for it. I'm surprised you went to the trouble of lugging it this far."

Cyral shrugged. The harp was indeed heavy, but not unmanageable for his own size and strength. "I would lug it a great deal farther to show it to you."

"How does it sound?"

"I don't know. I haven't played it yet."

Ferghus gave his Bard a startled look. "I'd have thought you'd be playing it night and day, my boy!"

"I want its first performance to have a very specific audience." The Bard's deep amber eyes rested on the Master's. "The one who made its existence possible."

Ferghus gazed at him for a long moment in silence. "I'd be honored to be your first audience," he said at last. "After your hands have stopped shaking, that is."

Waving off Cyral's objections to being served, the Master brought two steaming mugs of mulled ale to the table, then went back for a jug of honey and a plate of scones. "Eat up," he said, happily slathering his own scone. "If that harp takes half the energy to play as it does to haul it around, you'll need all the fuel you can get."

They ate for awhile without speaking, enjoying the crackling of the fire and each other's quiet company.

"Do you miss your usual activities?" Ferghus asked.

"Well, not as much as I thought I would," Cyral admitted. "I've always enjoyed being—" he stopped abruptly.

"—alone," Ferghus finished.

"Well ... yes. Is that so wrong?"

"No, as long as you don't become like the hermit crabs on the beach, dragging their shells around with them." The Master arched a brow. "The Stone and your harp are hardly good candidates for your only friends," he said pointedly.

"I have friends," Cyral said stiffly.

"Name one." The Master held up his hand as Cyral indignantly began to answer. "Friends, not acquaintances. Friends you know well and have created a bond with ... and I, as much as I treasure our bond, do not count."

Cyral's mouth abruptly closed.

"Exactly, my boy." The Master brushed a few crumbs off his robe and finished his ale. "Well, there will be time enough later to redress your charmingly reclusive nature. Right now, let's hear this wondrous harp of yours!"

Cyral chuckled, then rose and eagerly removed his harp from its bag. He set it on the floor in front of his chair and took his seat. Ferghus' eyes widened at his first sight of the magnificent instrument, the pillar of which rose well above the Bard's head. The polished rosewood gleamed in the firelight and the strings glistened invitingly as the harpist adjusted their pitch.

The tuning complete, Cyral closed his eyes and plucked a soft arpeggio from the lowest strings, then inverted it upward, each note played with fluent skill. The sound that filled the air was so sweet, so mellow and full, that the Master drew a sharp breath, and the harpist's eyes flew open in pleasure as he drew the notes up to the highest strings. The maiden voyage of the instrument's range complete, the harpist reversed his direction. The arpeggio tumbled head over heels down the dominant seventh as Cyral began playing the music of a memory, a memory his listener would experience exactly as he himself had so many cycles ago.

The listener's senses were swept into the music, surprised when the dominant seventh did not resolve. Instead, with the alteration of but a single note, the suspense increased with a firmly plucked diminished seventh. As it rose ever higher up the strings, the listener's senses were taken thirty furlongs to the east. He found himself in the home of Harpist Ultan, who pushed a pack into his hands and gave him a stern look. The listener bit his lip and listened with apprehension.

You'll do fine, boy, as long as you do as you're told. Mind the Master, now, and give him no cause for complaint!

Y-yes, H-harp … Harpist Ultan, the listener stammered in the treble voice of a young boy. He turned and gazed wonderingly at the Master Bard standing at the open doorway, robed in white with a golden cord around his waist. He had never seen a Master before. In contrast to the heavy-set Harpist, the Master was short and wiry, his eyes lively, his demeanor fairly bristling with energy.

The Master spoke to him kindly. *Come along, lad, we've a long way to travel. Have you any instruments to bring?*

The listener stared at the ground and shook his head. He cried out as a sharp clout caught him across his ear.

Look up and answer the Master, boy!

Fearfully, he looked at their visitor. *I d-don't have any, S-sir.*

The Master was glaring at the Harpist. *Hit this boy, or any other youngling again, and your robe will be forfeit.*

Ultan blanched. *I apologize, Master Ferghus!*

Amber eyes smiled suddenly into the listener's own. *Your first lessons, then, will be about constructing your own lap harp.*

The listener felt a burst of pure joy. He didn't care how hard a Master he must serve, if only he could have a harp of his own. It wouldn't be the great harp he dreamed of making one day, but it would be a start. The first step toward his dream.

The music of the harp swept the listener up and away. He found himself sitting in a corner of a living room, surrounded by the unfinished parts of his lap harp. He held the maple base firmly against his lap, a strip of spruce already inset to create the sound-board, and a strip of beech running along the center of the spruce, where the strings would be affixed. He was sanding the base in preparation for staining. He worked industriously, pausing only when Ferghus entered. The Master's uncharacteristically grim expression quickly erased the listener's own smile.

Come here, Cyral.

Alarmed, the listener set aside his harp and quickly obeyed the stern voice. The Master only ever called him "lad."

Didn't I tell you to go to the tanner's home and rub salve into his joints and muscles for me, since I couldn't go this morning?"

Y-yes, Mas-ster. The listener hung his head.

Then why did you not do so? I stopped by his house on my way home and found him in terrible pain. You know that he is old and bedridden, unable to move, and that the salve is the only thing making his last days bearable.

I w-was going to go as s-soon as I finished the s-sanding— The listener broke off at the expression on the Master's face.

You put your harp above the welfare of someone who needed you ... and let him suffer for it?

The listener was filled with shame. *I'm s-sorry.*

I've been tolerant of you occasionally putting your harp above your assignments, but this ... this is not something I can let pass. The Master's face was filled with sadness, and worse, disappointment. *Go to the kitchen and fetch the paddle used for scraping the butter churn.*

The listener bit his lip and rose to obey, more devastated by the Master's disappointment than the imminent punishment.

The Master accepted the paddle and spoke to him gravely. *The maximum number of strokes given to a youngling for wrongdoing is ten ... for something very serious, like lying or stealing. Five might be given for insolence or disobedience, two or three for more minor infractions. Think about what you have done this day, and what it caused. Then tell me how many you deserve to have, and that is how many you shall receive.*

The listener was astonished. He could choose how many strokes he'd receive? He wanted to say that he hadn't meant to hurt anyone, that he only deserved two strokes, but the Master was still regarding him, and the listener couldn't pull away or bring himself to lie to those golden eyes.

I d-deserve ten s-strokes.

Why ten? Why not five for disobedience?

I caused s-someone to s-suffer.

Yes, for even stealing something from him wouldn't have caused him such suffering as this did. Receiving your ten strokes, however, will not pay your debt to the tanner. Can you think of something you could do that would.

This required some thought. *I could help him every d-day.*

The Master nodded. *Well thought of. The tanner's daughter can't come until afternoon to help him, so you will go there after breakfast every morning and stay there until she arrives. You'll use the salve to ease his pain. You'll help him relieve himself and clean him afterwards. You'll help him eat and drink what he's able to ... talk to him to keep him company through the long hours he's usually alone.* He paused for a moment, holding the listener's eyes with his own. *You may take your harp to work on only when he's sleeping, for I know I can trust a youngling who has just been as honest as you've been to obey me fully this time.*

Once again, the music swept the listener away. He found himself lying on his stomach near the fire, his backside still sore from the paddling of the day before, listening to the Master play his harp. The skillfully played music created fascinating pictures in his mind. He could see the rocky coast of Eire, could hear the cries of the gulls, the surf pounding against the cliffs. The music came to an end, and the listener cocked his head at the Master, who smiled.

Do you have a question for me?

The listener nodded and chewed on his bottom lip. Questions were hard.

I like questions, the Master said quietly. *But I must hear them to answer.*

H-how ... d-d-d—

Hold on, lad. Close your eyes and use your Gift the way I taught you, to enter your own mind.

The listener closed his eyes and nodded.

Do you see the cord that links us together?

The listener nodded, smiling at the shining cord that sparkled in his mind with music. Since the Master had shown it to him, he had loved listening to it every night when he went to sleep. The bad dreams he'd had before coming here had all but gone away.

I can travel that cord into your mind so you can see my song there, the Master said. *Would you like to see it?*

The listener nodded eagerly, and immediately a shimmering shape appeared in his mind. He stared in awe at the beautiful, sparkling notes as the voice of the Master spoke to him from the notes themselves.

What you're seeing is the song of my conscious awareness, and now we can speak to each other here in your mind. I see the cord you created with me is a beautiful one. You took good care of the tanner today, and now you'll be able to reach me from there—or from anywhere—if you need me. Just focus on that cord and call to me and I will come. Now, then, ask me your question.

How do you do that? The listener marveled at the novelty of asking a question without a single stutter.

Do what, lad?

Make pictures in my mind with your music.

An excellent question. You know that everything in this world is created with music that gives objects their energy, plants and trees their life force, animals and people their soul that will continue on. And you know that your Gift allows you to hear such music, and when you've learned how to play it, it will allow your listeners to experience it as well. What you just heard me play was a memory of my walk on the beach this morning.

Memories have songs? the listener asked in surprise.

Your memories are the captured impressions of what you have experienced. You create those memories yourself. Look deeper into your mind and you'll see your own memories: orbs filled with music, some bright and some dark.

The listener looked and was filled with excitement at all the songs he saw, dozens of glowing orbs filled with scintillating notes of color. *I see them!*

Those are the memories you've created, and the swirling colors are emotions. The memories you see the clearest are those you think of often, reinforcing their emotions. The more obscure orbs are memories of things you refuse to think of, so streaks of grey anxiety or black fear darkened them, causing you to push them even farther back. Those ghostly-looking songs are memories you pay no attention to. They recede and are eventually forgotten, though they never disappear completely. Right now, you're paying attention because you're interested in learning the answer to your excellent question. You're creating a memory in your mind that won't fade, that will still be there for you to think about tomorrow or a fortnight from now. And whatever emotion you experience in this moment will be there for you to experience again as well.

The listener gazed spellbound at the many colorful memories before him, wondering which emotion was reflected in each of their myriad colors. Before he could ask, the Master continued.

Each of your memories is a song of its own, complete with a time and key signature. The time signature, the pulsation of the memory, can be slow or fast. The one we created together yesterday was in a minor mode, filled with smoky blue sadness for us both. The key signature of this moment is in a major mode, and thus a pleasant one, likely the small orb glowing with amber light right there in front. If you listen to the memory of it later, you will hear its song in your mind. If you play it, your listener will be drawn into it and experience the memory with you, just as you experienced my memory of walking along the beach.

The listener thought for a moment, absorbing the Master's words. *How come Harpist Ultan's music never did that? Isn't he Gifted like you are?*

Regardless of whether a musician is Gifted or not, his music will create an experience for the listener only if the performer himself is having one. When I played for you, had I been thinking of nothing in particular, you would have experienced nothing from my music except the outer shell of it ... the notes, the timing and articulation. The same is true of a performer who is not Gifted, like Harpist Ultan. He also must immerse himself in the experience, and if he does, the listener's experience will be drawn from his own memories and feelings. Never doubt the power of music, lad. Whether a performer is Gifted or not, his music has the power to reach inside both himself and his listener and draw out innermost thoughts and feelings. Music shapes experiences that will remain and affect who we are and how we act toward others. It can create balance and incite conflict. It has the power to heal and to destroy. If I apprentice you, you will begin a journey to discover that power for yourself ... and how and when to use it.

The listener could hardly believe his own ears. *Don't apprentices have to be of age?*

Normally, yes. They're apprenticed by Harpists and Pipers until they progress far enough to complete their training with an ungifted Bard. An apprentice whose Gift manifests in their eyes as an inner ring of amber is transferred to a Gifted Bard. An apprentice with completely amber eyes like yours is given immediately to a Master, all of whom are Gifted."

And ... you would apprentice me? After what I did yesterday?

There is no shame in making a mistake, only in refusing to acknowledge and rectify it. I will apprentice you if you want me to. If you do, the cord connecting us will become a bond of our combined songs, and I will enhance it in a way that gives me complete access to your Gift. This means that anything you do with your Gift, I will be instantly aware of. Think well before agreeing to this, lad, for the enhancement will remain until you yourself become a Master, and that, if ever it happens, will be many cycles from now.

What will you do if I don't want to?

I will block our cord so it can't be traveled and bind your Gift so it can't be used, for the Gift is too dangerous to be left in inexperienced hands.

And then ... you'll give me away. His voice rang hollowly.

Certainly not to Harpist Ultan. I'll find a new home for you, with parents who love you and treat you well. This I promise you. I'll be sorry to see you go, but the choice to leave me and refuse the development of your Gift is your own to make.

The listener thought of his nearly completed lap harp in the corner, and of the Master who was making it possible. The Master who answered his questions and took away his bad dreams. The Master who wanted to keep him. *I want to stay with you! I want to finish my harp and be your apprentice.*

The Master's song brightened in his mind. *Then so it will be. We'll speak our vows here, where you can speak freely, then I will touch my song to yours and enhance our bond. I will give you your apprentice robe and cord afterwards, twist the ends of our cords together, and pronounce us Master and apprentice.*

What are vows?

They're promises that must be kept. The Master vows to teach his apprentice to the best of his ability, and to always act in his best interests. The apprentice vows obedience to his Master, and promises to never use his Gift or position in the Bardic Order to harm anyone. Do you have any questions about these vows?

The listener thought for a moment. *No.*

Then I will speak mine first. I take you, Cyral, the Master said, his voice ringing with conviction, *as my apprentice in the Bardic Order. I promise to teach you to the best of my ability and to do my utmost to develop your Gift. I will treat you fairly and always act in your best interests.*

The listener's vow was spoken with all the earnestness of his heart. *I take you, Master Ferghus, as my Master. I promise to obey you and learn everything you teach me. I promise to never use my music or my position in the Bardic Order to harm anyone.*

The listener watched in awe as the Master's song approached his own and touched it. And in that moment, it seemed to him that their two songs combined as one, a duet that sang through his mind with the clarity of a bright summer morning. Then the Master's song withdrew and disappeared from his mind. Before the listener's wondering gaze, the bond connecting him to the Master shone with increased brilliance, sparkling with notes from their combined songs. The listener called out in the new radiance of his own mind.

Are you still with me, Master?

I will always be with you, my boy.

The listener opened his eyes to find deep amber eyes resting on him. He scrambled to his feet and threw himself into his Master's arms with a glad cry.

I won't ever disappoint you! The declaration filled the room without a single stutter to mar it.

I know you won't, my boy. I know.

The music of the harp swept the listener up and took him home.

Ferghus opened his eyes, slightly disoriented at finding he was once again himself. Cyral was gazing at his harp with a look of such transparent wonder on his face—*truly, it's a look of adoration*—that the Master couldn't bring himself to speak and break the spell.

Oblivious to the Master's existence, Cyral closed his eyes and pressed his forehead to the harp's frame, his arms wrapped possessively around it. "Didn't I tell you?" he murmured to it. "You're everything I knew you would be."

At last, he released his harp and looked up at the Master with the same shy smile he had worn so often as an apprentice. "Well, Master? What do you think?"

"I think," Ferghus said emphatically, "you have in your hands a harp that Bards will one day compose ballads of, my boy! Never have I heard a more beautiful sound from any harp, nor have I ever had such an exquisitely clear experience from one. To see myself as you..." He shook his head. "There are simply no words to describe what you just did."

Cyral smiled in pleasure, then packed his harp back into its case and travel bag. "I'd best be on my way. The weather seems to be getting worse."

"Why don't you stay here for a few days?" Ferghus offered. "There are a few things I'd like to discuss with you now that your harp is finished, and the weather is too bitter for traipsing back and forth with it. Your room is always ready and waiting for you, and you're more than welcome to anything you need."

Cyral sat back down with a smile. "I'd be happy to stay!"

The corners of Ferghus' mouth quirked. "Because you enjoy my company, or because my home is warmer than your cabin?"

"Because I can hardly wait to hear how you plan to redress my charmingly reclusive nature."

Ferghus chuckled. For a time, they spoke of Cyral's harp. The Bard eagerly recounted his various trials with its construction and how he had triumphed over them all. The Master listened with interest to the lengthy list of improvements Cyral had made and how each contributed to the harp's incredible tone quality. Ferghus said little but noticed much. He saw the young face, lit with animation, and realized that this dream harp meant more to Cyral than anything else in the world. The Master's heart twisted. *How can I bring myself to do what I must, now that his harp is finished?*

No one meant more to Ferghus than this young Bard, his face flushed with the pride and love of his harp. In all the world, there was only one thing that mattered more, one thing that could make him erase the joy from the young Bard's face. Ferghus wished he could wait and let his boy—for Cyral would always be his boy—bask in his happiness for longer than this one short evening. But the harp had taken far longer to complete than he'd anticipated, and after the morning's fruitless Council session, time was no longer something he could afford to lose. He turned abruptly to the fire, staring at the flames for so long that Cyral fell silent as well.

"I applaud your dedicated work with the Stone," the Master said at last. "You have learned things no one else in the history of our Order has ever known, and have become a true Master of Songs as a result. And the strength of your Gift has grown with it."

"I've thought so as well," Cyral admitted. "It's almost as if—"

"As if what?"

"I don't know, really, but it seems to me the Stone has grown with every song I place inside it, as if it's ... hungry for them, and grows with the eating." He shrugged helplessly.

Ferghus frowned. "You're saying that the Stone feeds on songs and grows stronger? And that, in turn, has made *you* grow stronger in order to block it and keep it from ... feeding on *you?*"

"Well ... yes. I know how crazy—"

"Crazy doesn't necessarily mean wrong," Ferghus said wryly. "But regardless, your Gift has grown to unprecedented heights because of it. It's far stronger than that of any Master I've ever known, quite possibly stronger than any in Bardic history."

Cyral shifted uncomfortably and Ferghus turned his attention to the fire for a long moment, fingers drumming lightly against the arm of his chair as he studied the flickering flames. *It must be done now.* His fingers stilled as he turned and locked eyes with Cyral.

"The Stone could not have arrived at a better time," the Master told him, "for we will need such strength in the coming days, and I intend to make good use of yours. To that end, I want you to stop working with the Stone. I'm about to ask you to flout tradition in a far more serious way than untangling and moving songs. It's time to *use* the considerable strength you've gained from it."

The Bard frowned. "I won't break my vow again," he said in a low voice.

"Flouting tradition is hardly breaking your vow, but why say 'again'? I told you that releasing Bryan when he asked you to and was facing a horrible death did *not* break your vow. Now ... why don't you believe that?"

Cyral flinched and said nothing.

"Answer me," the Master said quietly.

"Because," the Bard said slowly, the words coming with effort, "there's a trace of doubt in my mind that tells me if I hadn't interfered, he might—just might—have survived. And if that's true..." He stared out the window into the darkness.

"You did *not* murder your friend," the Master said with flat certainty. "The moment you accessed your Gift, I was there and saw for myself that his injuries were mortal. Had a dozen healers been there the moment it happened, they could have done nothing except dull his pain, remove the memory of his terror, and calm his spirit before the end. What you did was far better. Bards are forbidden from doing certain things, not because they're wrong, but because they could lead them in the wrong direction, ultimately causing them to break their vow. For instance, if you enjoyed the power of moving songs about so much that you couldn't resist the idea of moving the song of a *tree* into the Stone—"

"I would *never*—"

"I know you wouldn't, which is why I can trust you to do what I would normally forbid. I, more than anyone, know you will not break your vow, and that's a good and admirable thing. Your adherence to the strictures of tradition is also admirable, and well and good during peaceful times. These times, however, are not." The Master's face hardened. "I expect we'll soon be called upon to put aside our strictures, perhaps even our vows, and do what we must to ensure our survival."

Cyral shook his head. He had a strong dislike of conflict, and consequently rarely stood up for himself, but this ... this he would challenge. "Do what we must ... even break our vow to do no harm with our Gift? Would you choose to become that which we most despise?" Cyral forced himself to look his Master in the eye. "Have you considered that the price of survival on such terms might not be worth paying?"

The Master's eyes flashed dangerously, but the Bard continued, undeterred. "Would you do anything, no matter how heinous, if it saved us? That is *not* the Master I know!"

It was long before the silence was broken by Ferghus.

"No ... not anything."

"Then how far are you willing to go?" Cyral demanded. "I must know that before I follow you down such a path, if that is what you're truly asking me to do. Would you kill with your Gift, in order to save us all?"

"Yes ... and I would accept the consequences."

Cyral took a deep breath. "Would you ask *me* to kill with my Gift, if it saved us all?"

"Yes. I would ask, but never force you to do so. The decision to break your vow is your own to make, just as it is mine."

The two regarded each other in silence. At last, Cyral broke it.

"What is it you want me to do?"

Ferghus spoke with measured emphasis. "I want you to play and master all four of the elemental songs."

The Bard might have laughed if the Master's' words hadn't rung with deadly seriousness. Instead, he stared aghast.

"Come now, my boy," Ferghus said testily. "I've hardly asked you to hunt down the nearest Druid and murder him."

"*No* Bard is allowed to play the song of an element!"

"Thank you for reminding me," Ferghus said dryly, "since I, as the Prime of our Order, have trouble recalling such details."

"Master! You're asking me to break—"

"—a *stricture,* not a vow! *None* of those strictures prohibit acts that are inherently wrong, and breaking one at the request of your

Master does not break your vow. Indeed, most Bards would quite enjoy the rare opportunity to break a stricture with impunity!"

Cyral's eyes flashed. "It annoys you that I haven't broken one?"

"No. It worries me that you've never even *considered* breaking one!" The Master got up and paced restlessly in front of the fire. "Don't get me wrong, my boy. You've been a model apprentice, Harpist, and Bard, always doing what you're told. In all of Eire, I could have asked for no one better. But in times like these, models are of no use to us!" He stopped his pacing directly in front of Cyral and held the Bard's eyes firmly.

"You are on your way to becoming a Master, but you're young, and there are several others on the same path with far more seniority than you. I can't afford to wait ten cycles or more before you rise to that position in the normal order of things. So, I intend to train you *as if you were already a Master*. I intend to teach you everything I know, whether it's forbidden to Bards or not. I intend for you to gain command of all four elemental songs. I will do this because it is *necessary,* and I believe our very lives depend on it. Your Gift and your harp are without equal in all Eire, and I intend to make of you a powerful force that will give Odhran himself pause!" The Master's eyes flashed with a resolute will that would have given the collective members of both Councils pause.

"Such power will give you the ability to do great harm, yes," the Master acknowledged in a quieter voice, "but it will also give you the ability to do great *good* for our people, and the choice of how to use that power will always be your own to make. I ask this, not command it of you. You are free to refuse me, for no one can master such forces who is made to meet them against his will."

The color leached from Cyral's face, and the Master's tone softened. "I realize you can't fully understand the need as well as I, for there are some things I will not yet share with anyone. I am relying heavily on our bond and your trust in me. If that is not enough, say so now and I will never trouble you about it again. You may return to your duties as a Bard of my territory ... until Cathair's warriors take our mine. For make no mistake," the Master warned. "It will not stop there. Once they discover how productive Glindar is, the precarious balance between our Orders will vanish, for Odhran will then view us as a threat. He will assume, having our independent means of support cut off, that we will infringe on their teaching positions with the Rí in order to survive, for that is something he knows we can do at least as well as they. He will not stand for that, knowing the mine will eventually play out, and there are not enough of such positions to support both our Orders. So, while he has the means to do so, he will send warriors against *us*, and that," he concluded grimly, "is a strike we will *not* survive."

The Bard's face was ashen. "You ... truly believe—"

"Yes," the Master said with flat finality. "I truly believe."

The silence that fell between them this time was by far the longest. Cyral abruptly stood and walked toward the door. For one awful moment Ferghus thought he had lost him, had pushed too hard and too soon for the young, idealistic Bard to accept such unpalatable truths that the Council of Masters themselves could not. Instead of reaching for his cloak, however, Cyral picked up his harp, slung it across his back, and returned to the Master. Then he knelt on his right knee, in the Bardic manner of taking a vow, and looked up into his Master's eyes.

"I pledge myself and my harp to you, Master, and will learn whatever you feel is needful to ensure the survival of the Bardic Order. I do so because I trust you as my Master and my Prime, and because I believe what you have told me."

"Will you obey me without question, even if I ask you to do something terribly difficult, something you do not understand and for which I will give you no explanation?"

"I will."

Ferghus closed his eyes, loath to do what he must do now.

"Even if I ask you to place your harp in my room and not touch it again until I give you leave?" Ferghus would have given the remaining cycles of his life not to have to open his eyes and see the devastation on Cyral's face. When at last he opened them, however, the Bard was no longer there. A softly murmured voice came from the Master's bedroom, then the Bard returned without his harp.

"Even if, Master." Cyral's voice was not quite steady.

"I'm truly sorry, my boy. I know you love that harp more than anything."

"But not more than any*one*. I put my harp above the welfare of someone else once before and let him suffer for it. I will not do so again and let the entire Bardic Order suffer for it. My Master taught me far better than that."

The Master's eyes were suspiciously moist as he tried his best to look stern. "You'd best get off to bed then," he said gruffly, as though Cyral were no older than eight. "For your lessons begin at dawn, and not a moment later!"

The Bard nodded, then turned and retired to his room.

Ferghus remained by the fire for most of the night. Of all the many difficult decisions he had made as Prime of the Council, this had been the hardest. He had just hurt the person who meant more to him than anyone. *It had to be done*, he told himself sternly. With a deep sigh, he finally rose to get what little sleep he could.

In his own room, Cyral stared sightlessly at the ceiling, trying vainly to understand the reason for the restriction his Master had just placed him under. If he was expected to command elemental forces, didn't he need the best instrument possible to do it with? At last, giving up the attempt to make sense of what had just happened, he closed his eyes and tried to sleep, wondering how long he would be denied the use of the harp he did indeed love more than anything ... except the one who had just forbidden him to touch it.

Chapter 4

Precisely at dawn the next morning, Cyral sat across the table from his Master and looked at him expectantly.

"Before a new Master is allowed to play the music of an element," Ferghus told him, "he must master a few new skills and remove any impediments he may have. We'll begin with the skills, the first of which is a new method of taking someone into an object with you." He took up his lap harp. "Allow me to demonstrate."

The Master glanced at his collection of seashells on the fireplace mantle. There was a periwinkle shell sitting in front ... a beautiful specimen, small and coiled in a conical shape, with a sharp point at its tip. The inner part of the lip was creamy white, the outer shell striated from light wheat and taupe to goldenrod and deep russet. Focusing on it, the Master began to play.

Cyral's senses were immediately taken into the shell, seeing it through his Master's eyes. He had only a moment to admire the outer layer of the shell from within before he was drawn swiftly back out again.

"That's what you've been taught to do," Ferghus said. "To focus *only* on the object. When you play its music, your listeners travel with you and experience it as you do. Now, I will do something different. I will focus on the shell *and* on my bond with you."

Once again the Master focused on the shell, then closed his

eyes for a moment before he began to play. Once more Cyral was pulled into the shell, but this time he saw more than the luminescent outer layer of the shell. He saw the shimmering song of his Master next to him and, to his astonishment, heard him speak.

Now I am no longer playing a solo, but a duet ... the song of the shell on my harp, and the song of our bond in my mind. You have now traveled here with your own song entwined with mine, and thus are experiencing the shell from your own point of view. We can see each other's songs, and we can communicate.

Cyral looked around in awe. *Why, everything is as clear as if I'd entered the shell by myself, except that I can't move around on my own. Is that because it's your energy being used, not mine?*

Exactly. But, although you can only move where I take you, you can look about in any direction you choose, whereas before, you could only see what I chose to look at.

The Master moved them deeper inside the shell, where pastel prisms reflected from above and below, their music warm and inviting. Moving even deeper revealed thin layers of hexagonal shapes laid out with the precision of a master bricklayer. The world around Cyral shone with iridescent beauty as the two of them discussed the things they were seeing. Then the Master drew them out and stilled the harp strings.

"That was marvelous!" Cyral exclaimed in delight. "I've never entered that type of shell before. And it's so much more fun to explore something new with someone else!"

"The reason this is the first lesson taught to a new Master is because it allows the experienced Master to teach the far more complex skill of mastering the elemental forces in tandem, with perfect clarity of vision and unbroken communication. Saves a great deal of time and cuts down on ... accidents."

"Accidents?"

Ferghus gave him an offended look. "You don't think I'd hurt my own student on *purpose*, do you?"

"How badly hurt are we talking about?" countered Cyral.

"Pish, tosh, my boy! Nothing to worry about. Why, only one new Master has ever died from—"

"Died!"

"Well, he wasn't *my* student!" Ferghus said indignantly. "The most painful things you'll experience at my hand will be over the next two days, and you certainly won't be dying from them."

"I can't wait," Cyral said without enthusiasm.

"Practice patience, then," Ferghus advised. "It's a virtue ... or so I've been told."

It was Cyral's turn to chuckle. Patience was indeed not one of his Master's defining characteristics. "What's next?"

"You're going to use your boundless energy to practice taking me into every seashell on the mantelpiece." Ferghus handed his lap harp to Cyral. "You'll be doing your practicing on this until I'm convinced you're ready to use a full-sized harp. When this incessant rain finally stops, you can pick up your own instruments from your cabin, along with anything else you need. You'll be staying here for some time, likely well into summer."

"That long?" Cyral asked in surprise. "I thought ... well, that time was in short supply."

"It is," Ferghus acknowledged, "but I've taken a few steps to ensure that I'll have the time I need to train you. And finish up a long-term project of my own," he added with a glint in his eye.

Cyral's eyes narrowed. *A few steps? A long-term project?* What, he wondered, was his devious Master up to now?

Ferghus looked pointedly at Cyral's lap harp, and the Bard pushed aside his curiosity. Focusing his attention on a different shell in the Master's collection, he began to play.

Three hours later, after entering and discussing every seashell on the mantelpiece, Ferghus brought the lesson to a stop.

"Well, that didn't hurt at all," Cyral said.

"And you're still very much alive, if a bit dizzy," the Master cheerfully pointed out. "Which means it's time for lunch." He shook his head when Cyral began to protest. "You must never expend so much energy with your Gift that you haven't the strength to bring yourself back out of an object."

"But why am I dizzy? It was barely a morning's work!"

Ferghus chuckled. "Accomplishing what takes new Masters a fortnight to do. A single connection requires little energy to maintain, but the added connection to the complex song of another person requires a great deal of it. With experience, you'll be able to tell how much of your energy is being expended, but until then, the first sign of dizziness or weakness is to be regarded as a direct command from me to get out of the object immediately. Feed yourself, drink plenty of water, and don't attempt to use your Gift again until you're fully rested. I will instantly know if you're about to go past the point you just reached," he warned. "Know that I can and will stop you from doing so, and it will not be pleasant. I won't allow your own curiosity to endanger you."

Taken aback by his Master's vehemence, Cyral stared at him for a moment, then solemnly promised not to overtax himself.

After lunch, Cyral demonstrated his ability to easily take his Master with him through various objects using the Master's full-sized harp. The larger harp enhanced the experience and required significantly less energy.

"Wouldn't it be easier," the Bard asked, "to learn these skills on a full harp to begin with?"

"Yes," his Master replied, "but it would also be more dangerous. Using a less powerful harp slows things down, giving me time to correct any mistakes." He looked approvingly at Cyral. "Not that I expect many of those. Your expertise in moving songs gives you quite an advantage. In fact, I think we can move on to your second lesson. It isn't a very pleasant one," he said as he handed Cyral his lap harp, "but it's necessary." He rose and fetched a bucket from the kitchen, then placed it next to his chair as he reseated himself. Ignoring the Bard's curious glance at it, he continued.

"I taught you long ago how to block a listener from following you when you play the music of an object. Thanks to the Stone, you are exceptionally good at it. Has anyone ever managed to break through one of your blocks?"

"No, they haven't."

"There is, however, one person who doesn't *need* to."

Cyral nodded. "You, Master. Your bond to me is enhanced; my bond to you is not. So, while I can't block my mind to you, if you blocked *your* mind, there's nothing anyone could do to enter it unless their Gift was a great deal stronger than yours or they teamed up against you."

"Exactly. The enhancement is put in place because we will not take the risk of allowing anyone but Masters to use their Gift in total privacy," Ferghus told him. "Just one rogue member could do untold harm by erecting an unassailable block and using his Gift for his own gain or to hurt someone else with none the wiser." He indicated the lap harp. "Now, then, you also know how to bring yourself back *out* of an object, gradually changing your focus to your own song and using it to withdraw your conscious awareness from the object and back to yourself. Then you would stop playing. Have you ever stopped playing *before* returning to yourself?"

"No," Cyral said. "I was well taught—by yourself—not to."

"Yes, and I know the apprentice I taught never disobeyed that stricture. The Bard who sits before me now, however, is going to do so. Use the harp to enter the sea glass on the table," the Master instructed, "then, stop playing."

After a single surprised look, the Bard picked up the lap harp and focused on the opaque piece of blue-green glass. He began to play its music and sent his awareness into the object. Then, giving himself no time to be distracted by the luminescent world he had entered, he stopped playing.

The next moment he was emptying the contents of his stomach into the bucket held in front of him, his stomach cramping uncontrollably, his senses reeling. He sat back into his chair as his Master, muttering something about the waste of a perfectly good lunch, took the bucket outside to rinse it.

"Now you know a second way to return from an object," the Master said when he returned with the bucket. "It's called being snapped out. Not a pleasant way to come back to yourself ... and anyone who's with you will experience the same thing."

Cyral grimaced. "Why would I want to use such a method?"

"If someone enters your mind uninvited while you're within an object, simply stop playing. Both of you will be snapped forcefully back out, and your antagonist will be in no shape to try a second time ... especially if you're using your own, considerably larger harp, and he's at a distance, making his disorientation and nausea far worse than your own." He indicated the lap harp lying on the table. "Take the harp and enter the sea glass again, but this time do *not* stop playing."

Relieved, Cyral set the lap harp in place. "Do you want me to take you with me?"

"No," the Master replied, pushing himself farther back in his chair. "I'm quite comfortable right here."

Unable to shake the uneasy feeling that this was some kind of trick, Cyral focused on the sea glass and began to play its music. Barely a moment after entering the glass, his Master's song appeared like magic next to him, startling him so badly that his hands left the strings of the harp altogether. The next moment he found himself in his chair, disoriented and dry heaving over the bucket Ferghus was once again holding for him.

"You *said—*" the Bard began indignantly.

"That I was quite comfortable where I was," Ferghus finished, setting the bucket down. "I didn't say I was going to stay there.

Now, why did you disobey my instruction *not* to stop playing?"

Cyral blinked. "You startled me! Intentionally, no doubt, but I wasn't expecting it."

"Exactly. You've just experienced being snapped out of an object twice. The first time you intentionally stopped playing; the second time you were startled into doing so. But regardless of whether it was intentional or not, the result was the same. Not a pleasant experience from inside a piece of glass, but here you are, safe and sound." The Master paused, then spoke with quiet emphasis.

"That will *not* be the case should you stop playing within an elemental force. Entering an element by playing its song is not like entering an object. For the elements have an awareness."

A tingle of dread went through Cyral. "Like the Stone?"

"Yes, which is why I warned you to never stop playing while within it. I've come to believe the Stone has far more in common with our elemental forces than it has with its rock cousins."

The Bard nodded in silent agreement.

"The song of an element is aware of your presence and has more power than you can imagine. You will have a brief moment of time before the element becomes aware of you, during which you can intentionally stop playing and return to yourself. Once that time is past, doing so will *not* snap you back. Instead, it will concede control to the element, which will take your awareness wherever it wishes. Finding you at that point," the Master said grimly, "will not be easily accomplished, if it can be done at all. Which is why you need to be ... startle-proofed, shall we say ... before meeting the elements. Once an element is aware of you, you must not allow *anything* to take your fingers from the strings and stop playing. Nor can you allow yourself to become so depleted of energy that you can no longer keep them there yourself."

The Bard's eyes widened. No wonder his Master had been so insistent that he never overtax himself while using his Gift.

"Your fingers flew off the strings when you were startled by my mere presence in the sea glass," the Master said. "I'll be doing a far more thorough job of startling you over the coming days. You won't know when it will happen, or how. But I won't allow you to enter an element until I can no longer startle your fingers off the strings of your harp."

Cyral grimaced and nodded.

"You'll experience fear in each of the elements," Ferghus warned. "Not the fear of being startled by your Master, but the bone-freezing, mind-numbing fear of imminent death. You will experience the horrors of burning to death ... of drowning ... of suffocating ... of falling to your death. You must counter this with the rational conviction that the overpowering fear you are experiencing has no power to actually hurt you. It is only an emotion, however intense, of a mind that can't conceive of being somewhere the body is not. Your body will still be sitting right here playing your harp, not burnt, drowned, suffocated, or plummeting from the skies above." He indicated the sea glass. "As you know, not all our senses go with us into an object. Our sight and hearing do, but our sense of touch does not, so although you can't hear the music being played on your harp, you can feel the strings under your fingers as you play it. The same is true when you're within an element. So remain acutely aware of the feel of the strings, for as long as you can feel yourself playing them, you *know* your body is right here, safe and sound. That awareness will help you master your fear ... and the moment you do, the intense physical sensation will leave." The Master paused for a moment before continuing.

"A Master's training is rigorous," he said quietly. "He must be able to control his emotions before he can hope to control an elemental force. And fear is not the only dangerous one. Even the thrill of riding the windsong can cause you to stop playing if you continue until your energy is depleted."

"Wouldn't it be better to suppress my emotions entirely?"

Ferghus shook his head. "Emotion is a powerful force and not to be dismissed as unimportant. Although acting *on* an emotion can be deadly, acting *with* it is a useful tool. Using your Gift with a strong emotion will increase its power in ways you can't imagine now. Remember that, for if ever you need more power than you normally have, fan the flames of *any* emotion attached to it. As, in fact, you did once before with Bryan. Your strong emotion of grief at that moment allowed you to do what you did, despite your utter lack of training in moving songs. Armed with only a lap harp, no less! I always knew your Gift was strong, but that day..." the Master shook his head, "that day I saw it for what it was, and knew it would become the Gift we would one day need."

"Then, what you did afterwards," the Bard said slowly, "bringing me back ... all those tests you gave me ... I thought you were ashamed of me for breaking my vow, that you were testing me repeatedly to decide whether or not to expel me from our Order."

The Master gave him a startled look and shook his head emphatically. "Never that, for not once in all these cycles have I ever been ashamed of you! I brought you back because I wanted you here," he said gently, "where you could grieve for your friend in peace and eventually find the strength to deal with what happened, as you're beginning to do now. As for the Bard Tests you underwent," he said reprovingly, "they're hardly given as a punishment."

Cyral's mouth dropped open. "Those were my *Bard* Tests?" The extensive series of tests were given to Bards who had finished rotations in at least three different territories, and passing them was a requirement for eligibility to become a Master.

"I gave them to you one at a time as you were prepared and ready for them. You can rest assured," Ferghus said dryly, "that when you earn a punishment from me, it will not be delivered with such subtlety as that."

Cyral chuckled softly.

They took a break for dinner, a savory lamb stew with toasted bread and chopped greens. The Bard's thoughts wandered as he ate, thinking how much better entering objects with a full harp was compared to a lap harp. How much better, he wondered, would it be with his dream harp? The longing for his harp was growing intolerable, and it hadn't helped that Ferghus had taken it from its case and repositioned it so that it was fully visible through the Master's open doorway. Seeing it there every night and morning was an exquisite torture, deliberately inflicted. *Why?* His Gift burned within him every time he passed his harp, as though demanding the full expression such an instrument could give it. Coupled with the greatest harp in all of Eire, what would his Gift be capable of? He cast a speculative glance toward the Master's bedroom.

"Careful!" Ferghus warned.

Cyral assumed an innocent expression. "Didn't you tell me that my never having considered breaking a stricture worries you? Surely, I should alleviate that..."

"Consider it all you like," Ferghus said, a glint in his eye. "Just don't *do* it." He pushed aside his plate and rose. "I have a stack of Bard reports sitting on the desk in my room. You can practice out here." He indicated the table by the fire. "Place at least six objects on the table and practice moving through all of them as quickly as possible, spending only a moment in each to decide which one will be your next target. Speed and quick reflexes will be needed in meeting the elemental forces. So if, during your practice tonight, someone should suddenly appear without warning, I suggest you continue to play. And if he begins chasing you through the objects, I suggest you avoid getting caught. Then spend some time exploring the effect your emotions have on your music."

Cyral glanced at him in surprise. "How am I to do that? Sit here trying to anger myself?"

"Anger is not the only emotion you can use, but if that's the one you want, just think of me," the Master said dryly. "I'm sure you can come up with something I've done to anger you."

Cyral frowned and said nothing, but the Master didn't miss the glance of longing the Bard sent down the hall.

It was late when Ferghus emerged from his room. Cyral sat by the fire, softly playing the Master's harp, oblivious to its owner's entrance. Ferghus stood in the hall for a few moments, struck by the poignant minor melody that filled his home, its sadness reflected in the tears tracing paths down the Bard's cheeks. The Master's senses were filled with memories of Bryan, a collage of poignant pictures from the past, and Ferghus was struck by the depth of what that single friendship had meant to his boy. *He had no friends before coming to me, and living out here in isolation from the seaport didn't bring any to him. I should have realized that and done something about it.*

The Master stood motionless until the wistful melody came to an end. Then, after a long pause, a few plucked notes seemed to lighten the room and the harpist's mood with it as they moved ever swifter up the strings. As Ferghus entered the living room, he was met by a fast, sprightly village piece, a veritable dance of notes that seemed to brighten every corner. The Master listened in admiration of his protégé's skill until the harpist deftly brought the music to an end.

"I trust it's my presence that has stimulated this burst of unrestrained joy," Ferghus said dryly.

Cyral's eyes flew open. "Why, of course, Master. What *else* could possibly snap me out of my charmingly reclusive nature? Not that you haven't been trying." He glanced at the bucket next to him. "Thanks to your efforts, I've emptied my stomach into it twice already, but have yet to notice an increase in my social skills."

Ferghus raised a brow. "You're developing quite the sarcastic wit for someone who is not yet a Master and entitled to it."

Cyral grinned up at him like the apprentice he had once been.

"I learned from the very best."

Ferghus chuckled. "So you did, my boy. So you did." He took the seat next to Cyral and closed his eyes, firelight casting flickering patterns of light and shadow over the creases in his face.

"Are you all right?" the Bard asked in concern.

"Just a bit tired," Ferghus murmured.

"If you need any help, you know that—"

"I'll be fine, my boy. Go get some sleep."

Cyral studied the Master's face for a few moments, then quietly put away the harp and retired to his room. His Master did not look just a bit tired. He looked utterly spent, more exhausted than Cyral had ever seen him. *After working at his desk? Who gets that exhausted reading Bard reports while occasionally taking a break to startle the wits from the harpist in the next room?* That would certainly not tax the indomitable Prime. Using his Gift to mentally speak with someone for over three hours, however, would exhaust anyone. *But who would he be talking to at such an hour, for so long a time?* Cyral shook his head, thinking of the Master's mysterious project he had taken steps to make time for. He shivered slightly as he tried to settle into sleep. One thing was certain. Whatever Ferghus was up to was taking a toll on his health. And apparently he wasn't going to accept any help from his Bard.

Chapter 5

The following morning, after breakfast had been cleared away, Cyral took his accustomed place in the armchair across from Ferghus. There was no table filled with objects between them, no harp in evidence, and he wondered what lesson he would be receiving this time. His Master didn't leave him wondering for long.

"Today we will deal with impediments," he announced. "Issues that would prevent you from being elevated to the rank of Master Bard and taking a seat on the Council. As you know, what a Bard does with his Gift is instantly known to his Master, but what about the Masters themselves, who alone can use their Gift in total privacy? If an unmonitored Bard could cause untold damage with his Gift, imagine what a rogue Master could do, armed with the power of the elements."

Cyral's eyes widened. He had never even considered such a thing before.

"Thus," the Master continued, "we suffer no weak links on our Council. Every Bard who has attained eligibility to become a Master must submit to having their mind scanned by two Gifted healers or a Master before being chosen. And every Master on the Council must submit to the same thing every cycle, to ensure their Gift has not been compromised by an unresolved emotional issue. A trauma they've repressed, perhaps. Or a problem they have with someone, a problem they don't want to admit having."

Cyral shifted uncomfortably. "So ... you're going to scan me?"

"I'm well aware of your two impediments, my boy. And the first one we're going to deal with is me."

The Bard opened his mouth to protest having a problem with him, but something he saw in his Master's eyes made him close it.

"There is more than one reason to remove this impediment," Ferghus said. "You've learned how to block an unwanted intruder when you're using your Gift. But in an actual battle, you won't *have* a block in place, for you will need the energy it takes to maintain it. The chance of a mental attack is admittedly low, but the possibility does exist and must be prepared for."

Cyral frowned. "What Bard or Master would attack me?"

"Who said anything about Bards and Masters?" Ferghus steepled his fingers and raised a brow. "Can you be absolutely certain there isn't a single Druid in Eire who is also Gifted? A Druid who knows how to ask questions and discover answers that might enable him to use the Gift in ways we would never consider doing?"

A sudden chill went through Cyral. "No ... I can't."

"And if such a one existed, and *I* were Odhran, I would place him near the battle, unbeknownst to either side, ready and able to create havoc in the minds of the Masters. You must be ready for such a one, able and willing to repel him ... even if he is *not* a Druid," he added pointedly, "but a member of our own Order. A Bard who was passed over in his bid to become a Master, perhaps. Or," he said in a steely voice, "a Master who has decided to take matters into his own hands and save *himself* instead of a Council that refuses to support him." Ferghus' face darkened. "A specific, renegade Master who can effortlessly enter your mind any time he chooses, through any block you care to set. A Master who can create more havoc in your mind than a dozen Gifted Druids ... unless you stop him."

The Bard's mouth went dry as his Master looked at him with

a fierce hardness he'd never seen before. Then Ferghus took up his harp, shut his eyes, and began to play.

The next moment Cyral found himself walking barefoot near the water's edge of a rocky beach. His boots were tied together and slung over his shoulder, and the cold water swirling around his feet and ankles felt wonderful in the heat of the day. He kept an eye on the encroaching waves, for the tide came in quickly on the western coast of Eire and the small cove would soon be underwater. Sidestepping away from a wave much larger than its companions, he inadvertently stepped between two rocks hidden in the sand. He cried out in pain and surprise as his foot drove into a deep hole below them, wedging his knee firmly between the rocks. He frowned and pulled his leg as hard as he could, but to no avail. Again and again he tried, using every possible angle, fighting to free himself before the tide took him under. Sitting on the sand with his back to the waves, he frantically dug around his buried leg, pushing out sand that the tide effortlessly returned, trying desperately to move the rocks and free his leg from its underground prison. Though clearly of the essence, time ceased to exist, his world a confused collage of sand and pain, bloodied fingers and panic as the waves crashed against his back with increasing force, twisting his leg painfully against the rocks with every blow. His boots were torn from his shoulder. The rising water reached his chest ... his shoulders ... his face—

A roar of panicked outrage split the air as Cyral leapt from his chair, his chest heaving, looking wildly about for the beach that wasn't there. His leg felt perfectly normal ... no pain from bloody scrapes inflicted by barnacled rocks. His trembling fingertips were not ripped to shreds.

"Did you enjoy the nightmare I sent you?" the Master asked grimly, setting aside his harp. "If not, you'd best sit back down," he advised. "For it is now your own, and I intend to enter your mind and trigger it again ... and again ... and again!"

"Wh ... what?" Cyral gasped, stuttering for the first time in over a dozen cycles. He fell back into his chair, struggling to control his ragged breathing.

"I've invaded your mind with a nightmare that's now a memory of your own," Ferghus stated. "If you want to be rid of it, you must get rid of *me* before I trigger it again with a mere touch."

"How do I do that?" the horrified Bard demanded.

"You must attack me, repelling me from your mind with the strength of your Gift." Ferghus closed his eyes.

Cyral had no time to utter a word of protest before Ferghus' song appeared in his mind. He froze, unwilling to attack his own Master.

The next moment he found himself once again walking along the same rocky beach, headed toward the hole between two rocks he couldn't see. Again, his foot drove into it, painfully trapping his leg; again the tide moved in, bringing the waves ever closer. Knowing it was hopeless, he clawed at the rocks in a futile attempt to save himself. Just before the waters closed over his head...

Cyral came awake, choking on nonexistent seawater. He glared at Ferghus, angrier than he could ever remember feeling.

"Stop this!" he growled.

"No," Ferghus said flatly. "It's a lesson you need to learn. And if nothing is the best you can do against me," the Master said disparagingly, "it will be a very long lesson, indeed."

Anger burned so fiercely in Cyral that he didn't trust himself to speak. The Master who had ruthlessly taken his harp away after Cyral had played it but once—and for *him,* no less—was now going to visit a nightmare on him repeatedly while mocking him for his unwillingness to repel him?

"You're angering me on purpose!" Cyral accused.

"Of course I am. Use it! I'm attacking you with a nightmare, and I guarantee you I will continue doing so until you stop me."

"I don't want to hurt you!"

"Ah ... so now we come to it. I'm hurting you, yet you won't hurt me back, even to keep me from doing something unconscionable. Is your Gift so weak?"

"You're the one who keeps telling me it's stronger than anyone else's!" Cyral shot back. "Do you really want to find out if it is?"

"I'm not the one who needs to! Prove me right, or around we'll go again ... over and over all night long, if necessary. For I have no such compunctions about hurting *you.* I will do what I must, and until you do what *you* must to thwart me, I will not stop."

The inflicted torture of seeing his dream harp held captive in the Master's room flooded Cyral's mind, and the hot anger nearly suffocating him transposed to solid ice, as impenetrable as any block he'd ever set against the Stone. He watched with narrowed eyes as Ferghus' eyes shut. The moment the Master's song appeared in his own mind, Cyral hurled the block of ice at it without hesitation, holding nothing back.

The Bard opened his eyes to see his Master slumped in his chair, unconscious, his face pale in the firelight. The remaining ice in Cyral instantly melted as he lurched to his feet.

"Master!" He grabbed a blanket and hurriedly tucked it around Ferghus, then feverishly rubbed warmth into the cold hands. "Are you all right?"

The Master stirred, then groaned and opened his eyes, gazing at his protégé with a mixture of admiration and pride. "Most impressive, my boy!" he said hoarsely. "Why, it took me six times to get angry enough at my own Master to blast him out of my mind. Congratulations!"

"With fifteen Masters in Eire," Cyral grumbled as he returned to his chair, "how did I end up with the one who congratulates me for knocking him out cold?"

"Sheer luck, my boy," Ferghus said with a glint of amusement in his eye. "But keep one thing in mind as I dish out these lessons to you. I'm not training you to live up to *my* Gift. I'm training you to live up to your own." He sat up and pushed the blanket off. "So, if I should decide, in my infinite wisdom as your Master, to visit yet *another* nightmare upon you—"

"I'll repel you with so much force," Cyral growled, "you'll have a chair-sized hole in your wall!"

"That's my boy!"

Cyral gave his Master an exasperated look and went into the kitchen to fetch some tea. He brought two steaming mugs back to the table and they sipped for awhile in silence.

"So," the Bard finally said, "that's why you said that *you* were my first impediment?"

"You were unwilling to hurt me, to fight back and stop an attack I was launching against you. So, despite the considerable strength of your Gift, if *I* went rogue, you would be powerless to stop me. Every Master must be willing and able to rise up against another Master—even their own—should the need arise."

The Bard turned his eyes away, staring sightlessly at the fire.

"You are not a warrior," the Master said quietly. "Yet you must become one. And just now you have proven that you can. Odhran will have a clan of warriors on his side, seasoned and armed for battle, able to attack from land or sea, on foot or horseback. I will have one warrior, armed with his harp and his Gift."

All color leached from the Bard's face.

"You will not be without support," Ferghus told him. "When the time comes, every Master will do everything they can, and our combined strength will not be negligible. But without you, it will not be enough."

For some time, only the crackling of the fire broke the stillness. Then the sound of Ferghus slapping his hands against the arms of his chair as he got to his feet startled Cyral from his gloomy thoughts.

"Time to work, not worry," Ferghus said succinctly. "And that requires sustenance." He marched off toward the kitchen.

The moment they took their seats after lunch, Ferghus got straight down to business. "You've convincingly proved that you can remove a Master from your mind," he said. "How would you like to try your hand at removing a nightmare?"

Cyral perked up. "Like this horrible one of drowning that's still there, waiting to visit me when I'm asleep tonight?"

"Unfortunately, we can't rid ourselves of our *own* memories or dreams. We can only face or suppress them. But we can rid others of them, so I propose a simple trade. I'll remove the dream from your mind, and then you'll remove it from mine."

"You have the same nightmare?"

"Where else did you think I got it from? It's the dream my Master gave me to learn the same lesson."

The Bard stared at him in surprise. "And ... he didn't remove it for you afterwards?"

"I asked him not to."

Cyral blinked. "You *wanted* to have a horrible nightmare like that floating around in your head?"

"I asked him to leave it there so I could give it to my own protégé someday. Learning to repel someone you trust requires a great deal of emotion the first time, and I've never had nightmares strong enough to be useful for the purpose. My Master taught me how to silence the nightmare so it didn't trouble my sleep. Now that the dream has served its purpose, I'd prefer it to be removed."

"How do we do that?"

"Very carefully, for if a Gifted person perceives you as a threat, they'll forcefully repel you. If they're strong in the Gift, they can even do it while asleep. Not a problem now, for both of us want the removal and will certainly not repel each other for the favor."

"Have you ever removed a memory from someone before?" Cyral asked curiously.

The Master was silent for a long moment. "Once," he finally said, "when I was a Bard, and only because it was necessary. A young girl was traumatized so badly she couldn't speak, couldn't sleep without nightmares waking her. I removed her memory of it and the nightmares it caused, and she slept the better part of two days, then woke up her normal, happy self, unaware of what had happened to her."

"Why didn't they summon a Master or healer?"

"They did, but the girl was too frightened of any stranger to allow them near her."

"Then how could you—" Cyral fell silent as he realized how. "You knew her." It wasn't a question, but the Master's silence answered it. For a long moment, neither of them spoke.

"She was my sister," Ferghus said at last. "So my Master taught me how to do what needed to be done. I've never seen a memory orb as black with terror as hers was," he said in a low voice, then gave himself a slight shake. "Fortunately, I had a Master who understood that my sister's welfare was more important than adhering to the strictures of what a Bard can or cannot be taught."

This time it was Cyral who broke the silence between them. "I think I'm also fortunate to have such a Master," he said softly.

Ferghus smiled. "I'll remove your nightmare first, then you can remove mine the same way."

Cyral glanced at him in surprise. "Using our bond to enter your mind? Are you going to remove your enhancement so I can travel it?"

It was Ferghus' turn to be surprised. "You still think that? No wonder you've never—"

"What? You mean, all this time I could have traveled our bond into your mind, just like any other?" The Bard gave his Master an indignant glare. "You may not have specifically *said* I couldn't, but you most certainly led me to believe—"

"Well, of course I did! Who wants an inquisitive apprentice constantly invading his mind, asking ridiculous questions he could answer himself if he used but half his brain?" Ferghus demanded. "*Most* apprentices figure it out on their own!"

Cyral laughed. "I suppose I did pepper you with enough of them the conventional way."

"So you did," Ferghus said wryly. "Now, speaking of dreams..." And with that, the Master closed his eyes.

Cyral quickly followed suit, to find Ferghus already there, the notes of his song shimmering with energy. The Bard turned his attention to the background of his mind and the myriad of memory orbs filled with their own music. Some were close, some barely visible, some bright, some dim. Colors of various emotions swirled through each. *There must be thousands of orbs,* he murmured, as though afraid they might hear and discover their plot to remove one. *How will we find the one we want?*

Think of the beginning of the dream, Ferghus instructed, *and hold the image of the beach and waves steady in your mind.*

Cyral did so and was amazed when one of the orbs emerged from the background, approaching until it was nearly touching them. The notes of the song were dull and dark, the emotions swirling through it black with fear and streaked with the charcoal grey of despair.

Easy to identify the bad memories, Ferghus said. *They never shine, and since we don't like to think of them, we push them to the back, where it's easier to ignore their presence until they disturb our sleep. If I left this one here, you might repress it so deeply that you could no longer remember it in the conventional sense, thus be unable to bring it forward, though it would still exert its influence. You might be walking the beach one day and find yourself reliving the nightmare or dreaming of it again that night. Or you might repress all memories of walking the beach, until you have a strong dislike of beaches that you can't explain or understand. That being said, repressing a memory can also be a useful tool. Healers often do it in order to calm an injured person so they can receive healing. Later on, they pull their full memory of the event forward and help them deal with it.*

Cyral looked at the darker memories farther back in his mind. *How is it dealt with?* He thought of Bryan and wondered if he really wanted to know the answer.

By facing it. You would bring the memory to the forefront of your mind, as you've just done with this one, then explore it to find out where it came from and what you can learn from it so you don't create others just like it. Which, as with most difficult things, is easier to say than do.

What would happen to it then?

It would lighten and eventually brighten, residing peacefully in your mind. You would no longer want to remove it, for you would value the lesson it gave. Now, then, since you're already an expert mover of songs, I'll only need to mention that taking hold of a memory is different than it is with the song of an object or a person. For the moment I trigger this memory by touching it, it will begin to play in your mind and in my own.

Cyral was astounded. *So, both times you sent me this nightmare, you experienced it, too? Not just the first time when you used your harp to play it in your own mind? And you were willing to do this over and over again—* He fell silent.

Of course I was, my boy. How else would you learn anything from me if I wasn't willing to teach? Now, I'm going to touch the song with mine, triggering it to begin playing ... and at the same time withdraw from your mind, releasing it to float away before returning to myself, just as you did with Bryan's song with the aid of your harp. Intently focusing on the destination of my own mind is extremely important when moving a memory, however. If I allow myself to focus on the dream, I will be unable to withdraw, and you and I will experience the entire dream again. Thus, removing the memory of someone who is suffering from a trauma must be done with skill and focus, or instead of alleviating their suffering, you will increase it.

Fascinated, Cyral watched as his Master's song moved toward the nightmare and touched it. The Bard shuddered as the beach began to form once again in his mind. Then his Master's song left, taking the dark song with it, and the vivid beach scene in Cyral's mind vanished. A few moments later, the shimmering song of his Master reappeared.

Tell me what I just did, Ferghus said.

You removed one of my memories.

Which one?

I ... don't know, Cyral replied in surprise. *I remember how you did it, and that I wanted you to ... that it was a terrible memory you used in order to teach me to repel even you from my mind if necessary. But I don't remember what it was.*

It wasn't a memory of your own.

Cyral pondered this. *So, you removed it as a mercy, just as removing the terrible memory from your sister was?*

Yes. What I did for my sister, however, created a memory of my own creation in my mind. It would have stopped me from becoming a Master if I'd kept and nurtured my anger and hatred against the one who had hurt her. My Master used this memory to teach me how to deal with such impediments.

Couldn't he have removed the memory from you instead?

He could have ... and I would have learned nothing. He knew I needed to learn how to use the hard things that happen to us in this life to grow and gain wisdom. So, many cycles later, when I had the same opportunity to remove a horrible memory of yours, swirling with grief and guilt, and darkening with anger and fear,

I also chose not to.

Cyral stared at his Master incredulously. *You could have removed it? And chose not to? So you allowed me to suffer for months to what ... teach me a lesson?*

I'm your teacher in many things, my boy, Ferghus sternly said, *but not in this. Your repressed memory is the teacher, and you can only learn the lesson it has to teach you by facing it. That, I can and will help you do. And there is no better place to do it than here in your own mind. For, just as I was one impediment to the full use of your Gift, Bryan is the other. Your experience that day was traumatic. You were filled with grief at what happened to your friend, anger that he had asked such a thing of you, guilt at what you thought was a breaking of your vow, and fear that I would cast you out of the Bardic Order for it. You did what most of us do with terrible memories. You pushed it deeply back in your mind in an attempt to avoid thinking about it. When you shut down my every attempt to discuss it with you, I brought the memory forward, far enough for it to enter your dreams, insisting that you think of it, that you learn from it.*

Cyral was aghast. *You wouldn't let me forget? Master or not, you had no right!* Anger took hold of Cyral with such unexpected force that he could barely speak. For a long, suspended moment, silence stood between them like an impenetrable barrier.

Get out of my mind! Cyral ground. *Get out, or—*

—you'll knock me unconscious?

Yes ... no. I don't know! Just ... leave! Please.

The shimmering song vanished. Cyral sat in his chair, his eyes tightly closed against the gaze of his Master.

"Can't you understand that I can't bear to think of it?" the Bard demanded. "I don't *want* to learn from it!" His jaw tightened. "I'm too angry to even look at you right now."

"But I'm not the only one you're angry with, my boy."

The quiet certainty in his Master's voice brought unexpected clarity to Cyral's turbulent mind, and his anger leached away with the realization that came with it. It was long before he spoke again.

"You're right," the Bard said in a low voice. "I didn't know until this moment how angry I am … with him." Unwillingly he opened his eyes, and the compassion in the amber eyes looking into his brought tears to his own. "How could you have known … what I didn't know myself?" Cyral whispered hoarsely.

"You have every right to your anger," Ferghus said gently. "Bryan asked a terrible thing of you. But holding on to your anger while refusing to admit it exists has been crippling you, my boy. And brought you within a hair of using your Gift unjustly against the one person who can help you. For anger, like all repressed emotions, must go somewhere. If we refuse to acknowledge its true target, it will choose a handier one. Do you see now why this is an impediment? Why no Master with serious, unresolved emotional issues can be allowed access to elemental forces? Indeed, if any Master suffers a trauma, he is forbidden their use until his mind is scanned to ensure that he is able to use those forces wisely once again. If he is unable to pass that scrutiny, his robe is forfeit and his Gift bound."

Cyral was shocked. "And … what about me?"

"Normally you would be subject to this scrutiny as part of your tests to attain Master eligibility. Not passing it, you would remain a Bard, ineligible to become a Master until you removed the impediment stopping you now."

"So … that's why you're doing this to me?"

"It's one reason, yes. For if I allowed you to meet an elemental force without resolving this, it would cause you to forfeit your robe and have your Gift bound by the Council." For a moment, emotion deepened the amber of the Master's eyes. "But … that's not the only reason I'm doing it, my boy," he said softly.

Cyral turned his gaze to the fire, looking into its flames as though searching for something in its crackling depths.

"I'll give you time to think," Ferghus said. He started to rise, but Cyral's hand on his arm stopped him.

"I ordered you to leave my mind," the Bard quietly said. "I apologize for that and humbly ask you to return to it, to help me face what I've refused to. For I can't do it alone."

The Master gave him an appraising look, then nodded and closed his eyes.

Cyral took a deep breath as his Master's song appeared again in his mind. *How do I face it?* the Bard asked unsteadily.

By releasing the emotions attached to it. You have acknowledged your anger with your friend. Can you forgive him for asking such a thing of you?

Cyral was silent. *Yes,* he said at last. *For if I had been in his place ... I would have asked it of him.* Something deep inside Cyral relaxed and melted away at the admission.

Can you forgive yourself for doing as he asked?

The Bard was silent, faced with the surprising fact that it was harder to forgive himself than it was to forgive his friend. *Yes,* he said at last, *because I know that if I'd asked the same of him, he would have done it for me.* He was astounded at the lightness he felt at this second admission.

You have just untangled your anger and guilt from a tragic circumstance that neither of you could have prevented, his Master told him. *There is no further reason for the emotions to remain. Their time is done. Release them, my boy.*

Perhaps it was only the trick of the light in his own mind from the shimmering song of his Master that produced the shadow that emanated from his own, swirling with crimson and a sickly pea green. Real or not, Cyral focused on it, using the energy of his Gift to repel it away from him, out through the walls of his mind to drift away on the wind. The light from his song flared with sudden brilliance. His Master spoke gently in his mind.

Take care that you do not recreate what you have just

released. For awhile, you might find you need to release the emotions each time you think of what happened, but that need will lessen with time until it's no longer necessary. The Master paused for a moment. *You were understandably angry with me for not allowing you to forget what happened,* he said. *Would you choose to forget it now?*

Cyral thought for a moment and discovered to his surprise that he wouldn't. *No. It was the last, best thing I could do for my friend, and I'm no longer ashamed of it.*

Then turn and face the memory of that day, for you have brought it to the forefront of your mind.

Cyral turned and was astonished by the song that shimmered before him, a song with a myriad of other songs connected to it, the prismatic orbs reflecting the many experiences he had shared with Bryan. And in that moment of clarity, he saw how close he had come to poisoning those precious memories by ruthlessly repressing one of them ... saw also that his unwillingness to make another friend had come from this single experience. He gazed and thought ... and learned, time passing unheeded. At last he turned toward his Master.

I don't know how I can ever thank you.

By passing the lesson on, my boy.

The Master's song faded from Cyral's mind, and they came to themselves, blinking at each other from their chairs.

"I think," the Master said dryly, observing the tears Cyral hastily brushed away, "I'd rather *not* have my nightmare removed by someone in a highly emotional state. After dinner will be soon enough." He stood up and began to move toward the kitchen but was arrested by a pair of strong arms that embraced him, and showed no signs of letting go. Ferghus held the young Bard tightly.

"Sit here and rest awhile," he said gently. "I'll get our dinner today."

Chapter 6

Winter, having apparently received the Prime's belated notification concerning the arrival of spring, blew itself out quickly within the next few weeks, and the grassy hills were soon dotted with golden patches of dandelions and buttercups. Ferghus was spending more time than usual in Aille-Mara. When Cyral questioned this as the Master prepared to leave again one evening, he said he happened to be a Bard or two short at the moment, then shook his head emphatically at Cyral's offer to help.

"You'll stay right here and practice," Ferghus told him. "Mere strength in the Gift, however impressive, is not enough when meeting an elemental force. You're going to need speed and quick reflexes, my boy." He stabbed a finger at the assortment of objects on the table. "The games we've been playing with those were designed to develop them. Your final test will be tomorrow morning. If you can catch me three times in a row before I've visited all six of those objects, I'll introduce you to your first element."

The Master left and Cyral grinned wolfishly at the objects on the table. If outmaneuvering Ferghus was the only way to move on to the elemental forces ... well, his Master was about to discover that his Bard had learned more from the Stone's awareness than creative ways to block it. For the mysterious black object had also grown in strength, becoming ever more clever in its attempts to breach Cyral's mind, and he had indeed needed increased speed and quick reflexes to block its attempts. He hadn't mentioned this to his Master, for he had detected no animosity or malevolence in the awareness that sought to connect with his own. It had felt more like a game of wits, his own pitted against that of an intelligent but alien opponent, a challenge he found himself missing since his Master had instructed him to curtail his use of the Stone.

He retired to his room before Ferghus returned, pausing long enough to give a longing look and murmured greeting to his harp. A few hours later, he woke to see the faint flickering of light under his door. He rose and walked into the living room, intending to gently chide his Master into getting some much needed sleep, but the words died on his lips the moment he approached him. An un-gifted observer would think Ferghus had fallen asleep in his chair, for his head rested unmoving against its back and his eyes were closed. The Bard, however, knew his Master was in a light trance as he used his Gift to speak to someone.

The Bard retraced his steps to his room, wondering who would be talking to his Master at such a late hour. He quietly closed his door and tried to get some sleep himself.

The next morning Cyral rose to find his Master gone. Shaking his head, he spent the morning whizzing in and out of objects, chasing an imaginary Master. When the real one came in a few hours later, Cyral looked up in concern. His Master's face was lined with fatigue and worry. Without bothering to remove his cloak, Ferghus headed straight for his chair and nearly fell into it.

"Master!" Cyral jumped up and brought Ferghus a mug of spiced cider. His Master's eyes were closed, his face drawn. Cyral gently touched his arm. "Drink this before you fall asleep in your chair. I'll bring you a meal, then help you to your bed."

"There's so much yet to do." The words were barely audible.

"And I'll be here to help you do it ... after you *sleep*." Ferghus barely nodded, and Cyral held the mug to his Master's lips. "Drink," he said sternly. "And that's an order ... sir."

Amusement flickered across the Master's face as he opened his mouth. After several swallows, some color returned to his face. Cyral set the mug within the exhausted Master's reach and brought him some food. After eating far less than Cyral thought he needed, Ferghus waved it away and attempted to get up.

The Bard hurriedly supported his arm and helped him to his bed. After a single sigh, the Master fell sound asleep. He didn't emerge from his room until dinner was ready.

"Excellent venison stew, my boy," Ferghus said as he took a second helping. "The vegetables aren't cooked to mush the way so many others do, and the balance of herbs is just right! Don't know when I've had better."

"Probably not since the last time you worked all evening, marched off late at night, stayed up even later talking to someone, then went off again without breakfast," Cyral said pointedly.

The Master set his fork down and looked at him gravely. "I received word last night that our mine was taken over by a band of fianna."

"*What?*"

"I don't think I need to elaborate on who funded it."

Cyral was aghast. "It's really happening ... just as you said."

"I would vastly prefer to be wrong. Fortunately," Ferghus added as he picked up his fork, "no one was hurt because no one was there." He took a bite of stew.

"But ... where were our three Bards?"

"I commanded them to leave a few days ago. I had Tadhg take horses to them, so they should get here the day after tomorrow, I'd say. I'll send them on their way back to Barrach after they deliver a few things I have need of."

"So now you're expecting a direct attack on our Order?"

"Not immediately," the Master replied. "They have a great deal of digging to do first, considering that every tunnel has been thoroughly blocked. And," he added with a grim smile, "The fianna aren't likely to do it for free."

"The Council blocked Glindar's tunnels? I'm glad they finally came to their senses and listened to you!"

"Oh ... did they?" the Master murmured.

Cyral's mouth dropped open as the reason for his Master's increasing exhaustion became clear. *"You've* been doing it—all on your own—instead of sleeping? The blocking of *all* the tunnels?"

"At times it's incumbent on the Prime to do what must be done. Fortunately, he happens to be a prodigious Master of Earthsong. Although," he added wryly, "using it at such a distance as this taxed me to the limits of my strength."

"It nearly *killed* you!" Cyral exclaimed, outraged on behalf of his Master. "And now what? You said there's still much to do."

Ferghus nodded as he took a sip of cider. "There is, but my little project is already well underway since I started preparations for it two cycles ago, and none of it will involve my use of the earthsong. Physically speaking, the worst of it is over ... at least, for me. All my Bards will be working hard, however."

"Are two of them the Bards you 'happen' to be short of?"

Ferghus glanced at him. "Tryg and Cormac are working offsite, and I would prefer you not to contact them. They are both under strict orders not to communicate with anyone but me."

Cyral nodded. "I assume you're going to call a Council session and give the Masters a large, pointed piece of your mind?"

"I won't trouble myself. Barrach will be calling a Council session himself the moment his Bards return and refuse to tell him anything concerning the mine. Convenient, at times, that a Prime's orders outweigh a Master's. We have less than a half cycle to prepare for a massive exodus ... or face annihilation." He pushed aside his plate and headed for the living room.

Cyral cleaned up and joined him. "What can I do to help?"

Ferghus looked meaningfully at the objects on the table. "You can *beat* me. Convincingly!" He cocked a brow in Cyral's direction.

"And I will *not* make it easy for you." They had scarcely readied their harps before the Master began to play.

Cyral didn't hesitate, launching himself after his Master and catching him in the third object. When Cyral opened his eyes, Ferghus was giving him a startled glance.

The second time, he caught his Master in the second object. Ferghus raised a brow.

The third time, he caught his Master before he left the first object. Ferghus smiled. "You've improved tremendously, my boy!"

Cyral grinned. "Am I ready to meet an elemental force?"

"We'll begin right now ... with firesong."

"How long will it take?" Cyral wanted to know.

"That depends entirely on the strength of your Gift and the determination of your spirit. We give new Masters three months for each of the four elements."

"We don't have a whole cycle!" Cyral exclaimed.

"Which is why you'll have but two weeks with each. One to gain command of it, one to practice using it. Then on to the next." He cocked a brow at his flabbergasted Bard. "As I said, *all* my Bards will be working hard."

Cyral closed his mouth as Ferghus settled back comfortably in his chair and began to lecture. "There are three stages in successfully commanding an element. The first is playing its song and entering it. During this stage the element is unaware of your presence, and your only focus will be on commanding yourself, for it's your own mind that will become your enemy. You know perfectly well that when your conscious awareness enters anything, your body remains right here, playing its song on your harp, for you retain the awareness of your fingers on the strings. You therefore know that if you play the song of water and enter it, your body is not going to drown; that if the windsong sweeps your awareness up, your body is not in any danger of falling to its death. You realize that entering the earthsong is not going to suffocate you ... and if I entered the firesong right now, you certainly wouldn't expect me to burst into flames." The Master stabbed a finger at the fireplace. "But the moment you enter that fire," he said emphatically, "your mind will turn on you, insisting that you're about to be burned alive. If you listen to it and give in to fear, you'll feel like you are, indeed, being burnt. Your own panic will take your hands off the strings, and you'll be snapped violently back out. When you manage to recover your wits—and stomach—you'll be surprised to find you haven't been scorched from head to foot."

Cyral's eagerness abated. "What will happen then?" he asked.

"Your ears will be scorched with a few choice reprimands from your Master, who will send you straight back in," Ferghus said matter-of-factly. "Something that is quite likely to happen more than once, for it's extremely difficult to enter the fire without fear the first time, or to ignore the sensation fear arouses that you're being burned alive. You must ardently *believe* that your song can be neither burned nor consumed by it, and that your body is quite safe. Fear will then have no foothold and there will be no sensation of being burned. Then you will enter the second stage, the battle with the element over the control of its song. For once you are free to move within the fire and do so, the element will be aware of you."

A shiver went down Cyral's spine, thinking of the awareness within the Stone that had not become apparent until he'd moved.

Ferghus paused, his amber eyes shining in the firelight as he gazed into the flames. "An elemental force," he said at last, "is exactly that—a *force*—an entity with incredible energy that will challenge you for the control of its song. Inanimate objects and living things make no attempt to assert dominance when you are inside them, but an elemental force can and will. As long as you are playing its song, you are in control of the element. The moment you are *not* playing its song, the element is in control of you, and you no longer have the option of snapping yourself back out. Each of the elements will attempt to halt your playing in a different way.

Fire will exert its force to pull you through its colors of red, orange, yellow and finally white, each of which are more intense and thus more difficult to free yourself from. Most first-time novices, aghast at feeling the force of an element's pull on their song, stop playing in the red portion of the flame; some make it to the orange. But all of them end up being dragged into the white center of the flame and must be rescued by their Master or perish there." He quirked a brow at Cyral. "To avoid that," he continued, "you must *command* the firesong. It will then subside and willingly obey your directives, which for now will simply be taking you where *you* wish to go within it. You are *not,*" he added sternly, "to give it any other command until you are trained to do so." He accepted Cyral's hasty nod and continued.

"Having gained command of an element, the third stage is *using* it, for you can do far more than merely move around within it. Increasing or decreasing its tempo and volume will have an immediate effect on its speed and strength. Various types of articulations will also have an impact, as will the phrasing you use. I will train you to use these techniques and apply them in the real world, but ultimately, your own dedicated practice will determine what you can do and how well you can do it."

Cyral nodded soberly and stared into the fire, his mouth suddenly dry. This wasn't the grand adventure he'd been envisioning since he'd become a Bard and was allowed to listen to the songs of the elements. His respect for the Masters, high to begin with, had gone up several notches since Ferghus began his dissertation. Like all Bards, Cyral had spent cycles listening to the elemental songs, envious of the Masters who alone were allowed to use them, whether to calm a violent storm or put out a village fire. Utterly ignorant of what that entailed, he had listened with an increasing desire to command the songs of fire, water, wind, and earth. Now, on the cusp of actually doing so, that desire had abruptly vanished.

"The first time I attacked you with a nightmare," the Master unexpectedly said, "you refused to fight back. The second time, you knocked me unconscious. How were you suddenly able to do that?"

"You made me angry," Cyral reluctantly replied, "and I knew you meant what you said and wouldn't stop."

"Exactly. Knowing how unwilling you were to fight your own Master, I intentionally goaded you. Not very sporting of me, perhaps, but it worked." The Master's brow lifted. "Do you require me to goad you into mastering the fire? If so, admit it now and I will save us both a great deal of time and energy we can't afford to lose. The Stone enhanced the strength of your Gift. Our games have taught you to use it without hesitating. Now you must use it with the full power of your *will*. For meeting an elemental force is no game and requires all you have within you to give."

Cyral thought of the coming invasion of Aille-Mara and met his Master's gaze without flinching. "I won't require goading."

"Then let's begin with a single flame." The Master rose and placed more wood into the fire, which was snapping merrily on the hearthstones. Then he fetched a thick candle and placed it on the table in front of Cyral.

"Set your harp in readiness," he instructed. "When I light this candle, play its music and enter the flame. I'll be monitoring you from our bond, leaving me free to use my own harp in the event that you need rescuing."

Cyral nodded wordlessly and picked up his lap harp.

Ferghus lit a splint and ignited the candle's wick, then tossed the splint into the fire and nodded to Cyral.

The Bard took a deep breath and focused on the solitary candle flame. He listened to its music, entranced as always by the fiery beauty of the notes, the burning intensity of its melodic line. He began to play its music, sending his awareness smoothly into the flame. Despite his resolve not to let it, fear consumed him as the red inferno surrounded him. Flames licked hungrily at his legs, his arms, his fingers. Perhaps the heat wasn't real, the flames not truly burning his body, but the pain he felt was excruciating. He lost his focus almost immediately, his burning fingers flew off the harp of their own accord, and he was snapped back out of the flame. He came to himself disoriented, nauseated, and furious. His Master opened his own eyes, took one look at his face, and said nothing. Cyral gripped his lap harp and glared at the candle. Then, playing the firesong across the strings of his harp with firm, sure motions, he stormed his way back into the flame.

This time the force of his anger kept fear at bay and there was no sensation of burning heat. But the moment he moved, he felt a strong pull on his song from the center of the flame, dragging him slowly toward it. Frantically, Cyral resisted, but still he moved forward, the color of the flame changing with every bit of ground he lost, from red to bright orange to yellow. Then he caught a glimpse of the blue-white center of the flame and the beautiful, shining song pulling him inexorably toward it, and was so astounded that he nearly dropped his hands from the strings. Countless times he had listened to and played the music of objects and living things, countless times he had entered them and seen the beauty of the shimmering songs held within them. He had taken hundreds of songs into the Stone to study them, then carefully returned them to their hosts. But never once had a song acted on its own volition to take *him,* and his anger hardened to icy defiance. He would not be taken by the firesong of this flame and trapped inside its center to be studied like a specimen. It was one thing for *him* to do it ... quite another for something to do it to *him.* Yet clearly, pitting his own strength against the strength of an element was a battle he would ultimately lose no matter how strong his Gift was. Advice from his Master replayed itself.

You must command the firesong.

Cyral stopped resisting the force pulling him inward and focused his attention on the firesong itself, flickering within the center of the flame. His fingers moved commandingly over the harp strings, increasing the dynamic level without changing the tempo.

These notes are mine to summon when I wish, and mine to direct! I will command my own movements!

The firesong flickered as though surprised at the pronouncement, and the pulling of the element stopped just as the yellow had lightened to white. In relief, Cyral commanded the firesong to take him back to the red periphery of the flame, where he wondered what he should do next. Then he heard music from another harp, playing in unison with his own. His Master's song shimmered next to him.

Nicely done, my boy! Look through the flame's perimeter. Do you see the fire beyond?

Coming from the fireplace? Yes, I see it!

We're going to transfer our awareness into that fire.

From here? How?

By listening to its song and playing it. The only difference is that you will continue to play this song until you clearly hear the other one, then make the slight adjustments needed to segue from this song to that one. You will find that they are almost, but not quite, identical.

Is that why you put more fuel on the fire before we started?

Of course. And the best part is that you will not need to regain command of the element, as you would if you returned to yourself.

Delighted with that news, Cyral did as instructed and found himself in a fiery world, speechless with wonder.

Together they explored the fire, traveling from flame to flame. They skimmed along logs blackening and crumbling to ash, moved fearlessly over craters where cauldrons of sap erupted in explosive pops. Vivid shades of orange, scarlet, and blazing saffron flared and danced around them, while beneath them the collapse of branches and sizzling of bark blended seamlessly with the firesong they played together. Every new flame burst into being with its own fragment of firesong shimmering at its center. Ferghus effortlessly manipulated individual flames, demonstrating the effect a change in dynamics or tempo produced. A flame would flare with an increase in the tempo of its song, or sputter and die when it slowed. When at last they returned to themselves, Cyral stilled the strings of his harp, filled with the exhilaration of the fiery world they had just left.

"That was completely … absolutely…"

"Indescribable?" his Master suggested.

"Yes!"

Ferghus smiled. "This afternoon you're going to head for the beach, where you'll practice building small fires of various sizes and traveling them on your own."

Cyral was startled. "You're not coming?"

"Someone who gained the command of firesong on his second try at the very brink of its center hardly needs a keeper. Build it well out of the tide's reach and don't sit too close to it," he instructed. "Restrict your experiments with dynamics and tempo to the fire-song of *individual* flames, as you saw me do. Slowing the tempo of the entire fire might put it out, and if you increase it too quickly … well, I'd rather *not* return from my engagements this afternoon to find my protégé burnt to ashes on the beach."

"I'll keep the tempo under strict control!"

Ferghus rose from his chair. "You have one week to practice. Then, if you pass my test, I'll introduce you to your second element." The Master's brow lifted challengingly. "Since you managed to avoid being roasted, we'll see how you handle drowning."

"Ha!" The Bard struck a triumphant chord on the harp. "No worries on that score, Master. I'm an excellent swimmer."

Ferghus snorted as he headed for his room. "Where you'll be going, my boy, that skill will be useless."

Chapter 7

Sunlight had barely begun to glint speculatively over the hills a week later when Cyral took the seat across from his Master. Elated at having passed his firesong test the night before, he grinned confidently at the bowl of water on the table.

Ferghus arched a brow and tapped the bowl with his fingernail. "Based on your experience with fire, what do you think will happen when you send your awareness into the water?"

"I'll have to enter it without giving in to the fear of drowning," Cyral promptly responded. "Otherwise I'll feel like I *am* drowning and be snapped back out, then subjected to a blistering lecture from my Master, who will order me back in. Once my fear of you is greater than my fear of drowning, the water will fight for control of its song, pulling me—" Cyral frowned. This element had no center, and no boundaries except those imposed by the bowl.

Ferghus smiled grimly. "Just as the firesong tried to pull you into the center of its flame, the watersong will exert a pull downward to its greatest depth, which in the bowl is limited. Out in the bay, open to the vastness of the ocean, however..." he said meaningfully, and the Bard paled.

The Master's brow arched. "You understand now why I'm not down on the beach, about to watch my impudent duckling get his wings wet for the first time in the bay of Aille-Mara?"

"I do," Cyral soberly replied.

"If my duckling gets swept away—and most ducklings do—I'd much prefer looking for him in *here,*" the Master said, gesturing to the bowl, "than out *there.*" He nodded pointedly toward the window facing the bay. "Can I trust that you won't even *consider* entering a larger body of water than what stands before you until I give you leave?"

"Consider it unconsidered!"

"Very well, then." The Master indicated the lap harp sitting next to Cyral. "Set a block and off you go!"

"You're not coming?"

"I'll observe from here. You'll either give in to fear and snap yourself back out, in which case I'll have the bucket and lecture ready for you, or you'll battle the watersong for control, a matter which can be somewhat ... explosive. If you fail to stop the watersong's downward pull, I will, of course, rescue you." Ferghus shrugged. "Eventually. A little seasickness might prove to be a better teacher than I and save me the trouble of having to rescue you a second time."

Cyral, feeling queasy already, picked up his lap harp and focused on the surface of the water. The fluid notes filled his mind, his fingers moving smoothly from string to string as his conscious awareness entered the water, slipping into it without a ripple. His world changed to a translucent sheen. His mind began insisting that he needed to breathe, then cried out that he had, in fact, taken a desperate, gulping breath. Cyral felt cold liquid rapidly filling his lungs, ensuring that this would be the last breath he ever took. The pressure became intolerable. His fear increased.

This isn't real! I'm not drowning, it only feels like it! Marshalling his will, Cyral forced his attention away from his burning lungs and toward the song his fingers were still playing. The sensation of drowning dissipated and the Bard looked around him in relief. In front of him, he could see a few tiny, iridescent bubbles clinging to the bowl, straining against its resistance. One of them broke free and floated upward, bursting open to release its captive air when it reached the top. All around him, the clear, legato watersong flowed with such entrancing beauty that he didn't realize at first that it was pulling him slowly downward.

Cyral quickly pulled back, but, as with the fire, he only managed to delay the inevitable. Below him, an undercurrent of power began to form, swirling around as though stirred with an invisible spoon. Alarmed, he pulled as hard as he could. Again, his downward movement slowed, but the current beneath him continued to build, spinning him around the perimeter of the bowl like a top, each spin bringing him lower than the one before.

Realizing he needed to focus on the watersong, not fight its pull, Cyral tried desperately to find it, but nowhere in front of him could he see the telltale shimmer of the song he could clearly hear. All he could see were tiny sparks of light flashing past, faster than he himself was moving, as if he were inside a piece of granite where a miniature whirlwind had blown the tiny flecks of mica loose. Could the lights whizzing past him be the notes of the watersong, each of them sucking him downward in the whirlpool his world had become? Desperately, he tried to focus on the shining sparks, but they were too fast. Was it only his fevered imagination, or were the notes laughing at him as they danced past, slipping away just as he thought he could make sense of them? He found himself growing angry with their mocking laughter, just as he had been incensed at what seemed to be the firesong's nefarious plot to trap and study him like a specimen.

As he spun his way inexorably downward, Cyral realized there was only one place the watersong could be. He twisted himself around and looked behind. And there it was, close on the heels of his own song, a beautiful, shimmering song with undulating ribbons of notes. Sparkling pieces flew outward from them, notes flung free of the song they belonged to, zipping gleefully past him. Behind the watersong, he could see shining flecks melding with the ribbons, prodigal notes returning home to their score. *No wonder the watersong is so fluid! Its song is constantly changing, shedding notes from the last measure and adding them back to the first.* As his own song came perilously close to the bottom of the bowl, Cyral focused his will on the watersong behind him and issued a command for it to stop pulling him and send him up. Without warning, his world exploded.

He spun, end over end, having no idea which way was up or down, chaotic bubbles boiling all around him. For a moment he had the strange sensation that the world of bubbles, water, and song had frozen in place, as if obeying a command he couldn't hear. Then the world turned black.

The next time Cyral opened his eyes, the bubbles were gone, yet the world still spun crazily around him. He heaved the contents of his stomach into a bucket held under his chin. A strong hand kept his head bent over it, and he heaved again. He shivered violently and heaved once more, then sat trembling until his breathing calmed and he was pressed back into his chair. His face was gently wiped, a blanket was wrapped around him, and gradually the world grew still. Cyral stared at the bowl of water sitting calmly in front of him, not a single bubble breaking the surface, and grimaced, wondering if he would ever be able to take a drink of water again. A deep-throated chuckle made him look up to find his Master observing him from the other side of the table.

"If you're about to blister your duckling's ears," the Bard said hoarsely, "he'll humbly listen to every word."

"I would only do that if you had given in to your fear of drowning and snapped yourself back out. You didn't. In point of fact, you did amazingly well for your first time. Clever of you to turn like that and see the watersong. I didn't think of that until my second trip."

Cyral frowned. "What caused the explosion?"

"You did."

"*I* did? But ... how—" The Bard stopped, trying vainly to make sense of what had happened in the bowl of water.

"Unlike the declaration of control you issued to the firesong, you commanded the watersong to send you up. You did *not* specify where. So it sent you up with all its force, and the watersong," he said meaningfully, "is just as full of power in a bowl of water as it is in the vastness of the ocean. It just has less to work with, fortunately for you."

Cyral stared speechlessly at his Master, then turned his gaze back to the bowl of water. "How did you bring me back?"

"I entered the water, commanded it to be still, and pulled my unconscious duckling out of it."

The Bard frowned. "Why didn't you *tell* me about the importance of details in commanding the elements?" he demanded.

"If every detail is explained to a duckling, he never learns to think for himself," Ferghus said tartly. "Knowing something because you've been told it, and knowing it by *experiencing* it, are two very different things. You'll be a far better teacher yourself if you teach from experience." Rising, he fetched two more bowls of water from the kitchen and placed them next to the one on the table. "Observe closely—but not *too* closely—what happens to the water in each bowl." Ferghus took up his lap harp and began to softly play.

The Bard watched intently as the water in the first bowl began to swirl gently around. The water in the second bowl began to churn, bubbles forming and breaking on the surface as though the water were simmering over a fire. Cyral had just leaned forward with interest when the water in the third bowl erupted without warning, drenching his surprised face. Ferghus rolled his eyes.

"Didn't I tell you not to look too closely?"

Cyral sighed and reached for the towel.

"Since you got such a good view of the action," Ferghus continued, "perhaps you can tell me what I did."

The Bard thought for a moment. "In the first bowl, you slightly increased the tempo of the watersong, causing the water to swirl around it. In the second bowl you increased its tempo even more, causing the water to churn and bubble. The third bowl, though..." Cyral frowned in thought. "You must have commanded it to rise without specifying how high, then brought yourself out *very* quickly, before the explosion could catch you," he said, impressed with the quick reflexes such a feat would require.

Ferghus nodded. "Very good. Practice gradually increasing the tempo of the watersong this afternoon and removing yourself before the effect reaches you. I'll be staying home today, but I have much to do and won't be pleased to be constantly interrupted by the need to rescue you. Once you can easily duplicate all three of the effects I performed in a row, we'll take a little trip to the beach."

Cyral stared out the window at the bay. "Oh, joy."

Ferghus chuckled. "The watersong is not something you feel an affinity for?"

"Not at the moment."

"You can nevertheless achieve proficiency with it, as all Masters must. Some have a fairly equal proficiency with all four elements. Some find themselves preferring one or two of them over the others. And some have an affinity for one or more of them, becoming Masters of them when the element's song, of its own volition, touches theirs."

"I imagine *you* have an affinity for them all?"

Ferghus' eyes glinted with something akin to amusement. "There's a reason I'm Prime of our Order, my boy."

⌁ ⸙ ⌁

Although Cyral had commanded the watersong in his first try, it wasn't easy to gain the finesse that Ferghus demanded of him before being transferred into the enormous and potentially deadly bay of Aille-Mara. His problem, as the Master pointed out to him more than once, was not a lack of power in his Gift or strength of his will. It was his inherent hesitation in decision-making. Cyral preferred to contemplate choices and outcomes before making up his mind. Acting quickly and decisively did not come naturally, but his Master seemed determined to instill the quality in him.

"*Use* the instincts you were born with," Ferghus told him. "Being a Master requires the ability to make quick decisions, sometimes with very little information. You won't always have time to pace back and forth, analyzing the situation from every angle. At such times, refusing to act is itself a decision and it's rarely the best one. You have good instincts ... trust them! You'll find that most of the time they'll steer you right."

"And the times when they don't?"

"Learn from them and let them go."

So Cyral had spent two days practicing for hours in the bowls of water, commanding the elusive watersong quickly and decisively. Then, altering the song's tempo, he sent it spinning in the bowl, churning up hundreds of bubbles and leaving so quickly that he was not caught in their turbulence again.

The next day, Ferghus was called to Aille-Mara, and Cyral doggedly continued practicing his skills with both watersong and firesong. When the shadows in the room lengthened, the Bard put away his harp and rose, intending to start dinner, but instead began restlessly pacing the living room. He cast a longing gaze toward his Master's bedroom, where his harp still stood in lonely captivity. His jaw clenched and he was swept with an intense desire to rescue it, to *play* it, to feel those marvelous strings under his fingers again and hear the sweet, rich tones he had only heard once. His knuckles turned white with the strain of keeping his word.

In all the cycles since you apprenticed me, you've never once imposed your will on me without giving me a reason ... until now! Are you trying to goad me into disobeying you? Or are you using anger once more to teach me some incomprehensible lesson?

Cyral would not break his word, whether he was ever given a reason for the restriction or not. But he was under no stricture not to feel angry about it. His fingernails dug painfully into his palms as he forced himself to walk stiffly to the kitchen. He had barely begun preparations for dinner when the front door opened and Ferghus walked in. Cyral did not so much as look up.

The Master stood observing the Bard's closed expression for a moment as the vegetables on the cutting board were chopped with unnecessary force. Then he approached and laid his weathered hand over Cyral's smooth one, stilling the motion of the knife.

"I'll finish this," he said gently. "Go take a walk along the bluff. Then return when you're ready."

Cyral lifted eyes filled with pain to his Master, then he nodded and left without speaking. Ferghus watched him go, his own eyes filled with regret.

"I'm sorry, my boy," he murmured as he turned his attention to chopping the remaining vegetables. "I'm truly sorry."

That evening Cyral passed the Master's three-bowl test and the next morning they sat on the beach with their lap harps.

"For this first tour of the bay, I'll take you with me," Ferghus told him. He began playing and they entered the water together with the smooth, effortless ease of a Master accustomed to issuing commands and having them instantly obeyed.

And so the watersong did, swirling gently around them as though anxious to please. Ferghus chose to follow the perimeter of the bay to the north, and Cyral gazed around in amazement as they glided smoothly through an underwater dreamscape. The surface above swelled in hypnotic waves, the light revealing thousands of aqua bubbles. Below him the seagrass swayed rhythmically with the tide, a scuttling motion within revealing a hermit crab changing locations. Here and there a few nudibranchs could be seen, splashes of red and orange among the dark green grasses. A school of mackerel swam through the two songs in their path, their iridescent blue-green backs with wavy black stripes creating hypnotic patterns all around them.

Can't they see our songs? Cyral wondered.

No, although whales, seals, and dolphins are apparently able to sense our presence.

They continued on, stopping for a moment where Easach Falls spilled into the bay near Cyral's cabin. The Bard was thrilled when Ferghus headed straight for it, the watersong tumbling them through a world of bubbles and foam. Then they continued on, pausing when they reached the opening of the bay. A seal darted around them, heading out to the open ocean beyond.

Take note of this place, the Master told him. *Do not travel farther than here unless your command and experience with the watersong is extensive and you have a harp to match it.*

Cyral gazed beyond the bay in awe. *Have you been out there?*

Many times. The first time was when I was a young Master, anxious to impress. I was lucky to have the strength to return. And, he added wryly, *my Master was indeed impressed—with my foolishness—and restricted me to bowls of water for a week. Stupidity aside, it was a fascinating trip. Though most think coral can only be found far to the south, there are coral formations west of here that stagger the mind. Some of them are complex structures taller than many houses stacked on top of each other.*

They crossed the opening to the bay and continued along the perimeter until they passed the wharf of Aille-Mara and came back to where they had begun.

Coming back to himself, Cyral looked at his Master with delight. "That was incredible!"

"And even more so to do it yourself." Ferghus indicated Cyral's harp. "This time we'll go in tandem, each of us using our own harp and communicating through our bond. Doing it that way will take more of our energy, but I'll be able to rescue you more quickly if you should need to be. We'll begin with circling the perimeter of the bay again, so you can get your bearings before experimenting. Keep in mind that if you stop playing, the watersong will swiftly pull you out to the open sea," the Master warned.

"I won't stop."

"The watersong will take you wherever you command it to, but you can also choose to simply move with its own current, so mind your location and the direction of the tide. The fact that you're in command of the watersong won't prevent it from tossing you against a cliff when it's coming in, or pulling you out to sea when it's going out if you're foolish enough to move with its flow without paying attention to where you are. And even that is easily corrected provided you do not panic and stop playing."

The Bard nodded thoughtfully, and the Master continued.

"Don't assume that, once you've gained command of an element, its awareness is no longer a factor. Inanimate objects do not act on their own, and plant life follows predictable growth patterns. Animals and people are not so predictable, following urges they don't always understand themselves. Elemental forces of nature seem utterly unpredictable. If they're following any natural laws, those laws are not clear to us, making it appear as though they have minds of their own, impressively powerful minds. I've found that it's best to treat them with respect and never let your guard down."

Feeling excited for the first time about handling the fluid element, Cyral focused on the watersong and began playing it, eagerly entering the bay with his Master and quickly establishing command over the watersong. They circled the perimeter of the bay once more, stopping several times for lessons. Ferghus taught him how to move rocks and shells against the tide. He showed him how to send a thin stream of water in any direction, even upward to shoot above the surface like the spout of a whale. The Bard enjoyed this, producing one spout after another. They followed a pod of dolphins for awhile, skimming along in a world of sunlit bubbles as fins and flippers broke the surface.

Altogether, Cyral had a marvelous time, and late that afternoon decided to prepare one of his Master's favorite dinners. He finished just as his Master returned from another outing. Ferghus sniffed the air appreciatively as he entered the kitchen.

"Is that fish stew I smell?"

"Your favorite kind."

"Excellent! Let's get busy demolishing it. Barrach has apparently given up trying to get information from the two Bards I sent back to him. He's called a Council session for next week to air his grievances and demand to know what I've been doing." The Master speared a dripping piece of cod. "Eat up, my boy!" he cheerfully advised. "You have a great deal of practicing to do before I'll allow you to meet the windsong."

Chapter 8

A week later, Ferghus took his time walking to his place at the head of the Council table, the eyes of fourteen other Masters following him as he did so. All of them remained standing until the Prime took his seat, the atmosphere in the Hall thick with silence. Ferghus dispelled it with a brisk tap of the mallet on each of the three chimes.

"This Council is now in session," the Prime said with a nod toward the Scribe, who hastened to pick up his quill. "Much has happened since we last met. As you all know, our mine was taken by a band of fianna a fortnight ago. You also know there is nothing we can do to regain possession of it, short of retaliating in like kind." Ferghus turned to Barrach, seated to his right. "Since the Second of the Council called this meeting, I will turn it over to him." Ferghus settled comfortably back in his chair and gave the Second his attention.

Barrach's expression was grim as he met the Prime's eyes. "Last week both of my Bards returned from Glindar empty-handed. They told me they had left a week earlier—at *your* command to leave for Aille-Mara—on horseback. From there they were told to return to their *Master* on foot. I want to know why."

"Well," Ferghus said with a shrug. "They were *my* horses, after all. I saw no reason to send them all the way to you and then have to retrieve them ... or did you expect me to gift them to you? Aille-

Mara was a bit out of their way, but given that our territories are adjacent, the use of my horses still saved them a full day's time."

"Blast your horses!" Barrach growled. "I want to know why you commanded them to leave the mine and answer no questions from their own Master about what's been going on up there!"

Ferghus' brow lifted with surprise. "The horses? I gave no such command to them, I assure you."

A spluttered laugh came from the Scribe's desk as a ripple of amusement circled the table.

Barrach scowled. "Stop side-stepping, Ferghus! You know perfectly well what I mean."

The Prime sighed. "Must I truly remind the Second of the Council that, as Prime of our Order, I have every right to give any command I see fit to *any* Bard—*or* horse—without answering to anyone for it? Your ire seems quite misplaced, considering the fact that Glindar was attacked three days after I commanded your Bards and mine to leave." His brows arched into stiff peaks. "Surely you don't wish that I had *left* them there, do you?"

"Of course not! That's hardly the point—"

"Then what *is* the point?" Ferghus demanded. "Should I have informed *you,* a Master who did not believe there was any threat, of the imminent danger to his Bards? Would you have done anything if I had?" He arched a brow at the silent Masters. "Would any of you? I informed this Council more than once that Glindar would be attacked. And in return, whose support did I receive to thwart it?" He looked inquiringly around the table, but not a single Master would meet his eyes.

"So," Ferghus continued, "I did what was necessary to alleviate it. I kept in close contact with my sources in the Connemara Territory, and the moment I heard the attack was imminent, ordered our three Bards to leave, thus saving their lives. You're welcome, by the way," he said pointedly to Barrach, who dropped his eyes and did not reply. "I also provided them with horses so they would not be followed and apprehended, as they likely would have been on foot. You must pardon me for not thinking to gift them my horses as well. And all this has upset you? If *this* is the reason we're here, I believe I'll leave you all to it and go home. I have far more important matters to attend to there ... not the least of which is my lunch." He picked up the mallet.

"If the two of you will stop sparring for a moment," came the Third's measured voice, "perhaps we can get to the issue we need to discuss." Liam looked at the Prime, who set the mallet down. "But first I will assure you that we are all *very* grateful to you, Ferghus, for saving three lives ... for acting when none of us would have believed it necessary. If Barrach will not thank you for it, I will."

"Do not think me ungrateful, my friend," Barrach put in. "You have my most fervent, if belated, thanks for acting in time."

Echoed thanks came from every Master at the table.

"That being said," Liam doggedly continued, "you sent Barrach's Bards back to him empty-handed, and he claims there was a full cache left at Glindar. Something he would know, for he was the one mining it this month and thus the one who receives the proceeds from it. Surely his Bards would have taken that cache with them. Yet they refused to answer to their Master, saying they were under oath to their Prime not to speak to anyone about the mine." He glanced at Ferghus. "None of us will dispute your right to give any command you like to any Bard, but under the circumstances, will you not give us an explanation?"

"If I told you that the threat is not yet past," Ferghus countered, "would you believe me?"

Silence, broken at last by several affirmative voices from around the table.

"At least most of you are now willing to admit that much." Ferghus glanced at the Scribe and shook his head, whereupon Diarmuid nodded and pushed aside his parchment. The Prime turned to Barrach. "If I asked you not to send your Bards to Lóis, that our alternate mine must remain undisturbed, would you do so?"

Barrach frowned and said nothing.

The Prime's eyes swept the Masters. "How many of you would be willing to help me prepare for a full-scale exodus from our homeland?"

A gasp and the clatter of a quill came from the Scribe's desk. The silence that followed remained unbroken.

"The takeover of our mine, I see, has changed nothing," Ferghus quietly said. "You still do not believe."

Liam shook his head. "It's not that we don't believe the Druids might still be a threat. Certainly we're willing to admit you were right about them attacking Glindar. But that's past now ... they have what they were after, and as you said yourself, there's nothing we can do to get it back. It's time to move on, not move *out*."

"Well said," agreed Fionn. "There are steps we can and should take—more *cautious* steps—without overreacting like this."

"The 'overreaction' that just saved three of our Bards from certain death?" the Prime shot back. He turned to Liam. "Until such time as I have the full support of this Council," he said in a steely voice, "I will not answer your questions regarding the steps I've taken to ensure our survival. What I *will* tell you is that we've been given more time for me to do what I must apparently continue to do alone. One of my sources says Odhran has become increasingly upset over the last two weeks, too touchy for any to dare approach him. Perhaps this is because he recently learned that the mine he took over has had every last tunnel of it solidly blocked."

Exclamations of surprise came from all around the table.

Barrach stared at him in shock. "You did all that—in a month's time, and at the distance of Aille-Mara—by *yourself?*"

"Lacking any support from this Council, yes ... I did it alone. It will be an expensive, time-consuming undertaking for Odhran to get them open again, not knowing which tunnels lead to wealth and which lead to dead ends, especially with my addition of several more bogus tunnels. He can hardly have his Druids open them, who have no idea of his perfidy. That leaves him haggling with the fianna to do it for him. And that," the Prime said with satisfaction, "will cost Odhran dearly. The fianna know he can't let any word of the takeover reach the ears of the Ard Rí, who has turned a blind eye to *our* ownership of it, but will not suffer the Druids to have it, who are amply recompensed by the Rí they serve. With such leverage as that, I imagine the fianna's terms for opening the mine will be appropriately outrageous. This is why our alternate site must remain closed. Odhran is not likely to attack our Order until he has a productive, lucrative mine under his control. Until then, any Bard traveling through the Connemara mountains will be followed."

"You've done a superb job of inconveniencing him," Conall said, "but why should Odhran attack us at all now? As Fionn already pointed out, he has what he wants."

"And every reason to think we're going to want it back! He will expect us to do to him what he just did to us. So he will strike first, the moment he knows Glindar is a productive find."

"Then open up Lóis!" Liam exclaimed. "Show him we have no need to attack him."

Ferghus smiled thinly. "And what makes you think he will not take that one as well, putting us in the same position we're in now and giving him the means to rid himself of us all the sooner? Greed is a relentless taskmaster that does not listen well to reason."

He gave them a moment to digest this, then spoke with all the authority of the Prime of the Bardic Order.

"I can't command your belief, but I can and will command your obedience. No one is to go to, or send anyone else to Lóis Mine, on penalty of having their Gift bound and being demoted in rank. Our Order can afford to wait and let Odhran stew in the dilemma he now finds himself in." He looked at every Master in turn until they nodded in acquiescence."

Barrach drummed his fingertips against the arm of his chair, "How long must we wait?" he demanded.

"Until the Spring Council in May," Ferghus replied, "when I will reassess the situation."

The rhythmic fingers stopped. "And where are the contents of my cache?" Barrach gave Ferghus a hard stare. "My Bards did not have it, so it's either in Odhran's hands ... or yours."

"Are you charging me with theft?"

Thirteen Masters and a Scribe froze in shock.

"I have no proof until you free my Bards to speak." Barrach said levelly.

"Ah, the issue of proof rears its head again, in my favor for a change," Ferghus said mildly. "I promise you I will free them after the Spring Council. Will that satisfy you?"

The two of them regarded each other for a few moments, then Barrach nodded. "I can cover my Bard's stipends until then."

Ferghus picked up the mallet and gave each of the three chimes a firm tap.

"This Council session is adjourned."

Cyral spent the rest of that week practicing his ability to command the elements of fire and water. His skill with fire was such that his Master said he was fast developing an affinity for it, and his skill with water was improving daily. Indeed, the Bard's enthusiasm for producing waterspouts was causing a rumor to spread among the fishermen that a mischievous spirit inhabiting the bay was scaring fish out and bringing whales in.

Given his Master's permission to use his Bardic harp, Cyral expanded his knowledge of the fluid element with pleasure. If the watersong in a bowl was the basic theme, the watersong in the bay and open sea was a complex variation. Streams and waterfalls were yet other variations, and Cyral spent some exhilarating time riding the Easach river and tumbling down the falls into the bay. He had never had so much fun, and at the end of the week he sat next to his Master and prepared to meet the windsong.

"Wind is the most autonomous of the elemental forces," the Master instructed. "Fire is restricted by its need for fuel and air. Water is restricted by the earth itself, which gives seas, rivers, and lakes their boundaries. This gives both elements a physical structure that is reflected in their music." He nodded toward the large, covered bucket on the table. "It is not so with wind."

Cyral looked at his new practice arena doubtfully. "How can there be windsong without any wind?"

"Well," the Master allowed, "technically I suppose we should call it 'airsong', but that doesn't have the same ring to it. And, as you'll soon discover, air is never completely still, even if it seems so to us. There is always a song running through it, however slowly." He indicated the doorway, open to the warm spring air. "It's admittedly easier to hear the windsong out there. But the music in the bucket is the same song and can be heard if you listen closely."

Cyral eyed the bucket. "What do you want me to do in there?"

"Play the song you hear and enter the air in the bucket. You'll feel like you're entering it at a great height and will need to ignore the accompanying fear of falling. Once you've gained command of the windsong, direct it to take you where you wish within the bucket. Don't experiment with the windsong's tempo or dynamics."

The Bard nodded and set his lap harp in place. He eyed the bucket again, wondering how he was supposed to focus on something he couldn't see. He closed his eyes, but found it difficult to visualize the invisible air within the bucket. He could hear the wind outside the Master's home, though, blowing from the bay, and something deep within him yearned after it. Music slipped into his mind with the fluid ease of the watersong, music he had heard before while sitting on the bluff listening to it. Much to his surprise, however, it didn't come from inside the bucket or from outside the house. It came from all around him. Indeed, he was breathing the music in with every breath he took. It danced through all the pores of his skin and sang in his ears ... how could he possibly *not* hear it? Why, the windsong was everywhere! Fleetingly, he wondered why he had never heard it like this before. It didn't occur to him that he was supposed to be conquering his fear of falling, for he felt no fear of anything. There was only wonder at the incredible music that filled his soul.

The windsong was raw and wild and utterly unpredictable, flitting from one pitch to another in joyful abandon, unrestricted by the boundaries placed on things of material substance. How, Cyral wondered, could he play a song without form, one that followed no underlying chordal cadence? With difficulty, he abandoned his preconceived ideas of music composition, his expectations of where each note should logically go next, and opened his mind to what simply was. And in that moment, the concept of music structure vanished, and the Bard saw the device for what it was ... an aid for the minds of men that helped clarify music the way grammar clarified language.

The windsong was refreshingly free of such trappings. There were no measures lines or time signatures confining the rhythm, no key signature defining the tonal path. There was simply music, a song that followed its own nature. In burgeoning joy, Cyral began to play the windsong and felt his own song reach out to it. For one long moment the two songs seemed to regard each other as though pausing to remember a familiar face. Then, in an indescribable moment of wonder, the windsong moved forward and touched Cyral's own song. Freedom flooded through him, and the strictures of his life simply melted away. There was nothing confining him, nothing defining his path, no preconceived ideas restricting his thinking. There was only Cyral. In an ecstasy of release, he effortlessly took command of the windsong and soared upward with it, oblivious to the strong wind that instantly arose in the Master's living room.

He was vaguely aware of a series of crashes and what couldn't possibly be muttered expletives from his Master, but such unimportant things fell away as he directed the windsong to take him away from the intolerable confinement of walls. Out through the open door and the freedom of the wind sweeping over the cliffs from the bay. He was one with the windsong, united in the intense desire to fly without restriction, and in that moment the entire Council of Masters could not have stopped him.

He flew blissfully over the bay that he knew so intimately from below its surface, outpacing the puffins with their bright orange and yellow beaks. He careened through a flock of gannets, scattering them like giant snowflakes caught by an errant breeze, delighted to discover that apparently birds could sense his presence. One of them made a spectacular dive toward the ocean, slicing through its azure surface and bringing up a fish, then flying with deep, rhythmic wing strokes toward its nest. Cyral swiftly followed it, flying along cliffs filled with nests hidden from bluff or beach. Then he directed the windsong to take him out to total freedom from the obstacles the earthsong was forever putting in his path. And although the prevailing wind was blowing in the opposite direction, the windsong obeyed him instantly, speeding him out to the open sea on what seemed to be a wind current of his own.

Come back, my boy.

The whisper in his mind was annoying. Cyral ignored it, hoping it would leave, but still it spoke, soft and insistent.

Turn and fly back to me, my fledgling. The size of your harp is too small for where you are headed.

He frowned, not understanding what a harp was, knowing only the glory of flying, at one with the wind that blew under his command and having no desire whatever to turn back. And why should he? He knew where he wanted to go. Out and away. Nothing would bind him; nothing would stop him. So on Cyral flew, but the insistent voice would not be silenced, and something remained in him that could not ignore it.

You must turn back now! I promise you will fly again.

Soon? Memory and utterance of the word came with effort as his energy began to weaken.

Soon. But return to me now before you fly beyond my reach! I need you, my boy. We all need you.

With an effort that used most of his remaining strength, Cyral commanded the windsong to take him home, though the meaning of the word leached away with its utterance. Back toward the bay he flew, back to the constraining walls on the bluff he had flown from ... back to the voice that continued to whisper in his mind, urging him to hold on, to not let go of something called strings.

He opened his eyes to stare long and sightlessly at someone who was clasping his hands between his own, stilling the thin strands of a foreign object on his lap that his mind struggled to remember. After a long, vacant moment, it came to him.

Harp.

Yes, it's a harp. And who am I?

Cyral thought for an even longer moment, trying hard to remember. He stared at the amber eyes looking into his, bright with concern ... or was it tears? Wondering at the strangeness of tears in the eyes of an unfamiliar face, he hunted vainly for a word that would describe it. At last one came to him.

Master.

Cyral was enfolded in a hug that trembled with an emotion he couldn't understand. Then he was gently but insistently pulled to his feet. He took two shaking steps, leaning heavily on the arm that supported his. The arm guided him downward until he knelt on something soft. He sank onto the comfortable surface and something warm was placed gently over him. Then his eyes closed and he fell instantly and deeply asleep.

When next he opened his eyes, the room was warm and lit with the flickering flames of a fire. The same unfamiliar Master sat smiling at him and rose to bring him some water. Cyral's head was gently lifted, and he drank slowly, content to do nothing more than obediently swallow one welcome mouthful after the next. His head was eased back, and he slept again. Then he awoke to the wondrous smell of sizzling bacon and the warmth of sunlight slanting through the window. He pushed the blanket aside and struggled to prop himself up on the bedroll he was lying on.

"I knew the smell of bacon would rouse you, if anything could," came a cheerful voice from the kitchen. The Master emerged with a steaming plate of bacon, scrambled eggs, and honey-glazed biscuits. He set it on the table, then helped the Bard rise from the bedroll and sit in front of the mouth-watering meal.

Cyral concentrated on eating, surreptitiously watching the Master's every move. After devouring five slices of bacon, memories began to surface. This man had taught him how to make the harp he had seen on his lap. He attacked the eggs on his plate and remembered more. By the time he had polished off the biscuits, he knew. This was not just some random Master. This was *his* Master.

Ferghus beamed approval as he refilled Cyral's empty plate. "Another helping should be enough to bring you back to speech."

The Bard frowned as he struggled unsuccessfully to command his own tongue.

Ferghus shrugged. "Or not. Take your time. And have some tea ... I made your favorite kind."

Cyral emptied another plate of food and drank three mugs of tea. Then he sat back and made another attempt to speak.

"Soon," he managed to say.

It was the Master's turn to frown. "If you're referring to your next flight with the windsong, it will be *my* definition of 'soon', my boy, not yours. You need to recover your full strength before you fly anywhere farther than your own bed. You overtaxed yourself badly and were nearly lost to the wind."

"Sorry."

"You couldn't help what happened and couldn't have stopped it if you'd tried."

"You ... stopped me."

"No one could have stopped you. I could only keep asking you to return to me. Fortunately, you did so before it was too late."

Cyral frowned, struggling to remember. "What happened?"

"Do you remember anything?"

"I remember ... music..." He sat lost in the memory of it for a moment. "I was breathing it. It ... touched me. I'm not the same," he said wonderingly. "And I wouldn't want to be."

"The windsong has touched your song," Ferghus told him. "An affinity with the windsong is rare, and it usually takes cycles to develop. I've never known it to happen spontaneously at the first meeting." He shook his head, marveling. "Congratulations, my boy! You have just become a Master of Windsong. It is yours to command, and will obey your will instantly."

Amusement flickered in Cyral's eyes. "Like when you apprenticed me ... and your song touched mine? I became yours to command?"

"Absolutely," the Master replied tartly. "And my expectations of instant obedience have not changed a whit since then, Master of Windsong or no. So, off to bed you go, or suffer the consequences!"

～ ३ ～

Nearly a week passed before Cyral was allowed to use his Gift for anything at all. The one time he dared to grumble about his Master's dubious definition of "soon" earned him a ringing reprimand.

"You will *not* call the windsong to you," his Master told him sternly. "Not until I'm completely convinced your own song won't disappear with it, never to be seen again, and that's the end of the matter!"

"I'm truly sorry. I just ... I don't know what's wrong with me."

"You're enamored, my boy," Ferghus said in a gentler tone.

"As enthralled with the windsong as any lovesick youngling in the throes of his first crush. Give it time and distance, and turn your attention instead to the last element you must meet."

"The earthsong," Cyral said, in the same tone of voice he might have said "the dirt" with.

The Master of Earthsong chuckled. "I suggest you show a bit more respect for what you're about to wake up," he advised.

Despite himself, Cyral's interest was aroused. "Is it sleeping?"

"In a manner of speaking. The earthsong is the most powerful of the elemental forces, for it is the song this world was created with … the song that provides the foundation for everything else. It resides deep within the earth's core and has many variations, the most obvious being the mountains and other formations on its surface. There are many underneath as well, such as the stones and gems we mine from it."

The Bard perked up even more. "I'll be able to *see* them?"

"How else do you suppose we locate them to bring them to the surface?" Ferghus asked reasonably. "We'll spend a few days reviewing the elemental skills you've learned thus far—*except* the windsong—and then I'll teach you how to move through the earth, beginning with a crawl."

Cyral grimaced. Crawling did not sound appealing to one who had so recently flown.

"You might keep in mind," Ferghus added pointedly, "that some things that begin life crawling end up soaring."

The Bard looked up with amusement. "So, your duckling is now a caterpillar?"

"A good enough analogy," the Master agreed. "You'll spin your cocoon in the earth, and we'll see how long it takes you to develop your wings."

Chapter 9

A few mornings later, Cyral sat surveying the wooden bucket filled with earth that his Master had placed on the table. "Must I crawl through *that?*"

Ferghus narrowed his eyes. "Successfully navigate your way through this and perhaps we'll discuss other possibilities. Off you go, and don't forget..."

"To keep my hands on the strings and not stop playing."

"And?"

"That I'm not going to suffocate or be buried alive." His own assurance notwithstanding, Cyral took a deep breath as he set his lap harp in place. He had never cared for closed spaces. He positioned his fingers on the strings and focused on the earth. Powerful music filled his mind, complete with fleeting fragments of the songs of the many rocks he had studied within the confines of the Stone. Of course, he reflected, that's what the earth below was made of ... at least, for as far down as anyone had dug. He took a deep breath, thankful that for now the earthsong would be restricted to the depth of a bucket. Then his fingers moved in unison with the majestic song of the earth itself.

To his surprise, he didn't travel into the individual particles of rock and soil that made up the earth, as he had expected to. Instead, he seemed to travel *between* them, each grain so close together he felt suffocated. Yet, even as panic reared its head, he realized it wasn't the miniscule space between the particles that he traveled. It was the energy holding those particles together.

His mind insisted there wasn't enough air to breathe here, that his body would be crushed between the rocks like Bryan's beneath the tree. He needed air and space, and he needed them now or he would certainly die, no matter what his Master had said to the contrary. The urge to fly took him, intense and overpowering. Panic froze his will and fingers, stopping the strings and snapping him back out of the earth with bone-jarring force, barely aware of the bucket he violently threw up into, or the towel that wiped his face afterwards. He sat gasping for breath, unaware of anything except the overwhelming need to fly, to rid himself forever of the earth's intolerable, suffocating weight. He rose to his feet and staggered to the open door. Something pulled him backward. He shrugged it off, gasping lungfuls of air as he lunged over the threshold, out and away from confining walls.

As if it had come at his bidding, he saw what he craved ... the gloriously open air stretching out over the bay to the horizon beyond. And it was filled with the marvelous sound of the windsong, beckoning him forward as though inviting him to join it. In a burst of pure joy, he hurried toward it. Irritated when something once again pulled him backward, he yanked himself free. It pulled more forcefully, but still he resisted, dragging it forward with him.

Whoa, my boy! Let's not be thinking you can fly without the aid of the windsong and your harp! Nor can I, so if you go over the edge, we will perish together.

Cyral frowned, then came to a stop as the meaning of the words registered in his panicked mind. He sank to the ground, trembling, his Master's hand tightly grasping his arm.

"Can I let go of you and trust you won't leap to your death?"

The edge of the cliff became clear to the Bard's stunned perceptions. He gasped and scrambled away from it, his chest heaving as the intense panic gradually left him. Ferghus released his arm and sat silently next to him.

Cyral hugged his knees to his chest until the trembling stopped, then looked gratefully at his Master. "Thank you ... again. How can something I have an affinity for nearly kill me twice?"

"The windsong means you no harm and can't be blamed for your infatuation with it. Nor can you be, which is why your ears are not ringing with reprimands at this very moment."

Cyral managed a wry smile. "You won't summarily order me back into the earth, then?"

"Of course I will. But not right now, and certainly not up here."

"Yes ... I think I'd prefer a lower elevation, myself."

"What's happening to you is not that unusual for someone with a windsong affinity, although the intensity of yours has taken me by surprise." He chuckled softly. "Who would have thought that the windsong, the most unpredictable of elemental forces, would instantly bond with the most predictable of Bards? You might well find that the trait of unpredictability is now part of *you*, as well."

The Bard frowned. "Are you saying that I can no longer be trusted not to do something outrageously stupid at any moment?"

"Only for awhile. You'll soon be your normal, dependable self again, but you might find yourself more willing to think ... flexibly."

"So, when I'm not trying to hurl myself off a cliff, I'll be breaking rules left and right?"

"Is that not what we've been doing for these many fortnights?"

Cyral conceded the point with a shrug.

"We'll take the bucket down to the beach this afternoon."

The Bard looked up in surprise. "I thought you were going to Aille-Mara to help mediate a dispute."

"I've changed my mind. I won't leave your side until you have successfully entered the earthsong and are no longer in danger of attempting to fly from it without a harp. The earthsong is the most willful of elements, which is why I saved it for last. I would not have done so had I known you would have such a strong affinity for the windsong, which is in many ways its opposite. It's little wonder you panicked at the constriction of the earth and fled to the freedom of the skies. The earthsong will help ground you and give you control over your need to fly again. And right now," he said with a pointed look at the edge of the cliff, "I have no confidence whatsoever in your ability to stay grounded."

That afternoon they headed for the beach. Cyral was convinced he could overcome his fear of the suffocating constriction, but to his chagrin, he panicked in the bucket of sand even more quickly than he had before. It wasn't until the morning of their third trip to the beach that Cyral finally overcame his fear and kept his focus on the earthsong as he began to play. The next moment, he was yanked down with a force that nearly ripped his lap harp from his hands. Stunned at the power that had him in its grip, his senses hurtled down through the sand to the bottom of the wooden bucket, then straight through it into the moist beach sand below. A multitude of shapes filled his mind as he was inexorably pulled through sand, rocks, and sediment, down to a bedrock of the same reddish gold sandstone the cliffs of Aille-Mara were made of. The sensation that he was moving between objects changed. For now he was moving through *stone,* surrounded by its striated colors, yet traveling through *space,* though he could not fathom its existence here. The earthsong, he perceived, could move as fluidly through the earth as the watersong could through the sea, the windsong through air, the firesong through flames. A strong desire to command it filled him.

Grasping the notes with his will, not just his fingers, Cyral directed them to slow down, to follow *his* tempo. The music began to slow, and his descent into the earth with it ... but then the tempo was yanked out from under him, as if an angry earth maestro had stormed back onto the stage and confiscated the baton, wielding it once again at his own furious tempo.

Cyral would likely have yielded control to the earthsong in that moment, but the Master of Windsong refused such cowardice and rose to the challenge. *You want to fly, do you? Fine. Let's fly!*

Instead of fighting against the earthsong to slow the tempo, he increased it. Plummeting faster through the layers of sandstone, his fingers flew with lightning speed over the strings. As though taken by surprise, the earthsong hesitated, and Cyral triumphantly took control and directed the earthsong to take him where *he* wanted to go ... north, to the Connemara Mountains. His plunge into the earth stopped, and for a single, incredible moment, time was irrelevant. The notes of the earthsong gleamed all around him, filled with what seemed to be the power of creation itself, the power that held everything together. His song—indeed, his very soul— quivered as the earthsong moved closer and touched it.

In that moment, willpower was forever redefined for Cyral. He had thought of it as another word for stubbornness, but now he understood willpower for what it was ... the focused ability to bring into being whatever the mind could envision. It was a quality that resonated with Cyral, for had it not brought into existence the most incredible harp in all Eire? If there was one elemental force that would wholeheartedly agree with his Master's assertion that there were no such things as impossibilities, it was the earthsong.

And then Cyral was flying, as he had longed to do since the windsong touched him, flying with abandon through seemingly solid rock as the earthsong took him steadily north in obedience to his will. The vivid red and gold of sandstone changed to beige and tan. He passed caverns filled with wonders, with massive, rocky roots protruding from their ceilings ... walls that glistened with moisture as though sweating from the effort of bearing the weight above them ... pale, translucent creatures under the mirror-like surface of underground pools. Light browns gave way to brittle lay- ers of dark rock, then to the sparkling granite he'd spent so much time studying. He marveled at huge veins of clear quartz, the beau- tiful mossy greens of marble, and a small cavern glinting with blue, lacy crystals that he recognized as connellite from the collection of rocks and shells on his Master's hearth.

Then a thoroughly unwelcome voice entered his mind. *You're beginning to tire, my boy. Turn back now.*

No! I won't go back to you, to have you take this away, too! If you won't allow me to fly with the windsong, I'll fly with the earthsong.

If you overtax yourself, you won't be able to fly at all.

I'll decide what I'm able to do!

Well, my boy, you'll have a great deal of time to review your decision once your strength gives out. You'll be trapped somewhere in the earth until I can find you ... if, that is, I can find you.

For a long moment, Cyral hesitated, his frustrated desire nearly overwhelming him. Then he commanded the earthsong to take him back. He came to himself on the beach, his hands stilling the strings, his anger leaching away as he realized what he had said.

"I deeply apologize, Master."

"Becoming a Master of Earthsong is a heady experience," Ferghus said quietly. "One that removes your inhibitions and enables you to say how you truly feel."

"I have no right to feel angry with you!"

"Haven't you? I've taken the harp of your dreams away from you and placed it where its presence tortures you. I've forbidden you the windsong you long to fly. Your anger at such restrictions is understandable. Indeed, it may well have facilitated your affinity with the earthsong that freed you to express it."

"You have every right to restrict a child from what he can't handle," the Bard said roughly.

"I haven't restricted you because I think of you as a child," Ferghus said sternly. "If *you* see yourself that way, then I strongly advise you to take a better look. You may lack the robe and the Council's approval, but you have just now attained the level of a fully trained Master!"

The Bard's eyes widened, but the Master continued, his voice laced with incredulity, as though astonished he needed to point out the obvious. "Must I define you to yourself before you believe in who you are, in what you have so magnificently become in just two seasons' time? You are a superlative thinker, able to ask questions that lead you to answers that expand your knowledge and excite your curiosity to know and discover more. You are a harpist without parallel, with a harp that has no equal in all of Bardic history. You are a Master of Songs, of hearing them, playing them, untangling them, moving them where you wish, no longer requiring the Stone to do so. You have gained expertise with the songs of fire and water. You are a Master of Windsong and now a Master of Earthsong as well." His brows lifted challengingly at the astounded Bard before him. "Do these titles sound like they belong to a *child?*"

"No."

"Then stop thinking of yourself as one!"

Bard and Master regarded each other over a bucket of sand. Memories washed through Cyral's mind like waves over the beach, leaving every grain of sand in a different place. His point of view shifted as his vision turned deeply inward. He saw his abilities as a thinker, a Bard, a Master of Songs, a Master of two elemental forces. He felt the pressure of their collective weight, pressure he instinctively shied away from, just as he had the intolerable weight of the earthsong. And, just as he had needed to turn his focus away from that pressure in order to be free of it, he turned his focus away from the pressure of his own abilities to look at them clearly and dispassionately, to hear their music. For, he perceived, there was indeed music coming from those acquired abilities, music he had created himself with hard work and perseverance, wondrous melodies that had woven themselves into his song and become part of who he was. He stood struck by the awareness that the song he had been created with had not remained the same in endless repetition. For indeed, he had been composing it himself with each of life's many experiences, developing the theme, embellishing it, giving it shape and contour, depth and meaning. *He* was the composer of himself, and it was time he took ownership of, not just the song of his conscious awareness, but of his soul ... the song that was Cyral.

Deep within, he felt his song flare with brightness, dispelling the heavy shadows he had increasingly felt himself under. For there was no need whatever for him to live up to being a thinker, Bard, or Master of anything. He simply *was* those things, and they fit him comfortably, like oversized clothing he had been wearing for a long time without realizing how well he had grown to fit them.

Why have I never understood this before? And how have I done so now?

The moment he asked it, he knew. He had seen his innermost being with the depth of the earthsong, and flown free of its weight on the wings of the windsong. For a long moment he stood humbled by the gifts they had given him. Then he blinked and saw his Master smiling at him as though fully aware of the mental transformation that had just taken place.

"I don't suppose I need to say anything," Cyral said.

"No ... but if you'd like to, I'll listen."

"In that case, since you so clearly defined me, I think it's only fair that I define us."

The Master's brow lifted, though he said nothing.

"You are the Master of a fully grown Bard with the abilities of a fully trained Master, who will not hesitate to use them when needed. You are no longer my Master by right of your enhanced bond, for I've outgrown that Master and require the monitoring of my Gift no longer. You are my Prime and I owe you my obedience, but you are also my Master by my own choice, and always will be. I love and respect you, but if ever you do something I do not agree with, I will challenge you, knowing that you'll always listen to me and give what I say a fair hearing. You have my complete trust in forbidding me my harp and the windsong, and though I cannot fathom your reason for it, I choose to accept those restrictions until you decide to lift them."

Ferghus stood motionless for a moment, then touched his right palm to Cyral's forehead and closed his eyes. The Bard felt a jolt of energy as something deep within him was removed.

Ferghus lowered his hand and opened eyes filled with pride and sadness. "I've removed the enhancement to our bond that was made when I became your Master and my song touched yours. I will no longer be instantly aware of what you do with your Gift. What you do with it now is your own concern from this day forward, and you are accountable only to the Council for your actions with it, as are all Masters. For you have *my* trust in knowing that you will always use it for the good of our people."

For another long moment they looked at each other, acknowledging their new relationship without the need for further words. Then Ferghus broke the contact and motioned to the bucket of sand between them.

"Would you care to explain to me how you escaped from that bucket to go gallivanting off with the earthsong to the Connemara Mountains? For I've been a Master of Earthsong far longer than you, and I could not have pulled off such a feat."

Cyral shook his head. "You'll have to ask the earthsong, for I have no idea. It took me straight down and through the bottom of the bucket into the earth. There was no time to argue with it."

Ferghus frowned at the wooden bucket as though deeply offended by its unorthodox behavior, then picked it up and emptied it. Walking a few steps to the water's edge, he rinsed out the bucket, then used it to scoop up some water. Holding it still for several moments until the dripping had subsided, they could both see a place near the middle where water continued to steadily drip through.

"This bucket was fine when we used it yesterday," the Master said thoughtfully. "I'll inform the Council that all receptacles should be thoroughly checked for cracks before being used to train new Masters. Retrieving a terrified novice in a bucket of sand is a simple matter; bringing him back from the depths of the earth is not." He turned his attention to Cyral. "Apparently you made enough of an impression with the earthsong that it touched your song in your first meeting! I stand impressed, my boy."

Cyral smiled at such praise from his Master, though he found himself wondering why the earthsong had done so. Was it because he had unexpectedly responded to it as a Master of Windsong, and not as an intimidated Bard?

"You'll need to work hard with the firesong, watersong, and earthsong to attain true proficiency with their use," Ferghus told him. Every Master can use the earthsong to mine what we need to support ourselves, or the watersong to bring fish into our bays. The windsong can calm what would otherwise be a devastating storm, and slowing the tempo of the firesong of a burning house can save an entire village from suffering the same fate. You are a Master of Windsong and a Master of Earthsong because their songs have touched yours, so you can call these two elements at will."

"You're the Master of all four elemental songs. How many other Masters are?"

"None. Barrach is a Master of all but earthsong. Liam and Fionn are Masters of Firesong and Watersong, five others are Masters of Watersong, six of Firesong. And," he added, "just as harp is your primary Bardic instrument, if you're a Master of more than one element, one of them will be your primary element. Mine is the earthsong. Yours is the windsong."

Cyral digested this in silence for a moment. "Does becoming a Master of an element give you anything more than the convenience of effortlessly calling it?"

"It gives you greater power with it, and the dominant trait of the element becomes part of you as well, similar to the way the Stone takes on the dominant trait of a song placed within it."

Cyral smiled wryly. "So now I'm unpredictable and obstinate

... and soon to become what? Wishy-washy and hot-tempered?"

The Master chuckled. "I'd prefer to say that you'll enjoy the traits of being flexible, strong-willed, creative, and passionate, for such are the elements of wind, earth, water, and fire." His brow quirked. "Do you not find all four of those traits in your Master?"

"I certainly do," Cyral said with a grin. "Which makes me wonder what sort of creative punishment he will devise for the Bard who dared to fly in his face and defy him." Ferghus glanced at him in surprise, and Cyral looked at him with affection and respect as he quietly continued. "For, whether that disrespectful Bard has the abilities of a fully trained Master or not, he is still a Bard, and has no right to act the way he did to his Master and Prime."

Ferghus pursed his lips thoughtfully, then turned and headed toward the steep path leading to the top of the cliffs. The tall Bard scrambled to follow his agile elder.

"I was thinking," the Master said conversationally, "that breakfast in bed tomorrow sounds good."

"You?" Cyral said dubiously. "Stay in bed that long?"

"I'll expect it to be served immediately upon my awakening."

"But you're up before the birds!"

"And I will allow you to do it again the following day."

"But—"

"*And* the day after that."

The silence that fell after this was broken by Cyral's soft chuckle. "Yes, Master. Three days of breakfast in bed, served the moment you awaken."

"Ah ... the welcome sound of obedience fills my ears."

"As well it should. You are, after all, the Master of four elemental forces ... and me."

"So I am. Let's not be forgetting that again, my boy."

Chapter 10

Six weeks later, the day of the Spring Council dawned bright and clear. Inside the Council Hall, however, the atmosphere was heavy enough that the Cailleach, hag of winter storms, could have comfortably taken a seat at the table. None of the lively banter that usually accompanied the first session of this auspicious event was in evidence. Each Master silently took his place in order of his strength in the Gift, beginning with Barrach, Second of the Council.

Ferghus took his seat at the head of the Council table and surveyed them, his expression grim. He picked up the mallet and hit each chime once.

"The Spring Council is now in session. There have been a number of tragic events that you're all aware of by now, although perhaps you have yet to grasp their implications. Every one of our territories has suffered a loss over the last month except the two most southern ones: mine and Barrach's. The lives of thirteen Bards have been lost to seemingly random accidents, most while traveling, four by sudden illness, three by unexplained fires in their cabins. Obviously, these were *not* accidents!"

The Masters looked at each other uneasily. "Come now," Barrach said. "These were tragic occurrences, certainly, but every one of their Masters has conducted a thorough investigation, and nothing has come to light that would point a finger at Odhran."

"No *proof* has come to light, you mean? The Prime asked icily. "Did you expect to find written confessions hanging on their charred cabins, or on their broken bodies at the bottom of ravines our Bards have suddenly developed a habit of falling into?"

Silence.

"Odhran is thinning the herd," Ferghus said sternly. "And, with no more intelligence than the cattle of Eire, you continue to graze, undisturbed."

"We're *not* undisturbed," Liam countered. "We're simply not yet convinced that—"

"—these were anything more than *accidents?*" the Prime said incredulously. "What does it take to make you understand?"

"We understand that something is terribly wrong," Liam retorted. "And yes, you're probably right in thinking it's the Druids who are to blame. But it's a huge leap from that to leaving our homeland, so let's explore alternatives!"

The silence that fell over the Hall this time was palpable. It was broken by Ferghus himself.

"Perhaps this will convince you that there *are* no alternatives." The Prime's eyes swept the Council commandingly. "Open your minds to me!"

"*All* of us?" Barrach exclaimed. "Ferghus, you can't—"

"Open them."

The implacable command hung in the air for a moment, then Barrach shrugged slightly, sat back, and closed his eyes. Every Master at the table did likewise. The Scribe's quill dropped to his desk as he slumped there, his own mind swept with the Masters' into the vivid memory coming from the Prime of the Bardic Order.

The blurred image of a window took shape, the glass pane slightly ajar. Cold wind buffeted the watchers from behind. Several large tables took shape through the window pane. The room was empty except for two men who sat across from each other, one in Druidic garb, the other in warrior leathers. Two belt knives lay on the table between them, each of the blades pointed at one of the men. Between the knives was a mug, a small pot of what looked to be sea salt, and a shallow bowl of dried oak leaves. Smoke curled up from the leaves, and the earthy fragrance of sap and bark filled the air. Fragmented speech reached the listeners through the crying of the wind as the two men sheathed their knives.

...send you the information ... to reach the specified port.

...needing an estimated time ... to prepare for an attack of this scale.

Not this season ... Fall Council, when most Bards and Masters ... don't have a definite date...

The horrified listeners watched as the Overdruid leaned over the table and whispered words they couldn't hear, then reseated himself. A few more fragments of speech reached them.

How many boats...

... enough for eighty warriors. ... larger one to take them there.

The image faded and the Masters opened their eyes. Ferghus sat slumped in his chair, his eyes closed, his face ashen. Barrach and Liam surged to their feet, each of them taking one of the Prime's ice cold hands in their own and rubbing it brisking.

"You old fool," Barrach muttered savagely. "You should only have shown two or three of us, not fourteen plus a Scribe!" The Prime opened his eyes and the Second glared into them. "The others would have believed us! No need to half *kill* yourself—"

Ferghus frowned and waved him off. "I'm perfectly fine," he rasped. He reached for his mug, but Liam whisked it off the table and held it to the Prime's lips himself.

"As fine as a snowflake in August," growled Barrach.

Ferghus pushed aside the mug. "I'm *fine*. Now, take your seats, the both of you," he ordered. He sat up straight and motioned toward the Scribe, still slumped over his desk.

"Conall, see to Diarmuid. I doubt he's used to having his wits taken from him without warning."

The young Master hurried to the Scribe's aid, gently shook his shoulders and offered him some water. Diarmuid sipped it gratefully as the Masters erupted with questions.

"What in the name of the Maker himself—"

"How could you *possibly* have seen—"

"Where was that? And *when?*"

"Faolán? Isn't he the warrior who's taken over—"

"The island of Carr, I believe."

"On the *west* coast? Celtic warriors have never—"

"My sources say that Faolán is a renegade who's leading Celtic raiders and fianna alike—"

"Well, *I've* heard—"

"It's what we heard just *now* that concerns me!"

This last statement caused all eyes to turn toward the Prime.

"Perhaps, Ferghus," Barrach said levelly, "you can explain where this memory of yours came from."

"It isn't my memory," said the Prime. "It's the memory of one of my informants in Gaotha, who agreed to let me take it from his mind to provide you with the proof you insist upon having. He also recognized the voice of the other man. Cathair, Overdruid of Connemara, who, young though he is, has the ear of Odhran."

Horrified silence fell. Ferghus drank deeply from his mug, then set it down with finality. "I would vastly prefer to be sitting here apologizing to you all for delusional behavior unbefitting a Prime," he said. "Instead, I must add a few more unpalatable truths for you to absorb." He turned to Barrach.

"I told you I would release your Bards from their silence regarding the mine after the Spring Council. I released them this morning, and you will find that their account to you will fit with what I'm telling you now. I was indeed doing more at Glindar than blocking its passageways," he said. "I was mining as well, bringing up four more caches of precious stones over the winter months and another two in the weeks leading up to the attack. I had three horses delivered to Glindar in readiness for a sudden departure of our three Bards. When news came to me that our mine would be attacked within the week, I commanded them to remove all six caches, along with your own substantial one, and bring them to me here. Then I completed the blockage of the mine. After they arrived here with its wealth, I sent your Bards on their way back to you, under oath not to speak of it."

Fourteen flabbergasted Masters stared at Ferghus. Barrach's mouth worked soundlessly for a moment.

"You ... mined half a *cycle* of gems? *How?*"

"Alone during the winter, then with a great deal of help from Brenach's muscles and your Bard's Gifts, and Fionn's before them." Ferghus smiled tightly at Fionn's surprised and Barrach's horrified expressions. "Your Bards did not use the earthsong and broke no strictures," he continued. "They simply joined me, allowing me to use the power of their combined Gifts. They did so willingly," he added, "although, had they not been willing, I would have commanded them to do it. I needed the help, and my other Bards were needed elsewhere."

"And then you took all this wealth for your own?" Barrach stared at the Prime, whose gaze did not falter. "This isn't merely theft," he said in a stunned voice. "It's theft on a scale unprecedented in all of Bardic history! *Why?*"

"To pay for the ships we need to take us to safety," Ferghus calmly replied, to the startled gasps of everyone at the table. "And procure a willing Shipmaster and crew for each of them. Such things do not come cheaply. Which is why," he said with a shrug, "if you had disobeyed my order not to visit Lóis Mine, you would have discovered that it has been emptied of its resources, something I was doing with the help of two of my own Bards for the last two cycles. I would have returned all this considerable wealth to the Council if it turned out I was wrong about Odhran.

Unfortunately, I wasn't."

The table erupted in a confused babble of voices, some of them excited, others outraged. Barrach sat motionless in his chair.

"Of course," the Prime said with a clarity that cut through the voices and brought silence back to the hall, "if you prefer to stay here and deal with Faolán and his currachs full of Celtic warriors and fianna from our own shores, you certainly may. I've given you time by sealing both mines. I've given you the possibility of escaping by pillaging their wealth. Our Bards and all of us at this table are known to Odhran; we will not be able to disappear into the anonymity of village life, the way those of lower rank will be able to," he warned. "Odhran will leave them alone, for they are no threat to their lucrative positions with the Rí, nor will he harm our healers who serve his Order as well as our own. He knows nothing of the Gift's existence, for we have kept it strictly out of our records and quite secret for the last several centuries. And if he *does* know, he knows it's the possession of Bards and Masters, not found in those of lower rank, who know little to nothing about the Gift themselves. So every Bard and Master will be given a choice to stay here and hope for the best, or join us in leaving, along with their families. My Bards have all chosen to leave and have been diligently helping me with the prodigious job of having ten ships constructed without anyone being aware of it. Five of them will be completed before the summer solstice, the other five about a month after."

"Ten—" Barrach lost all power of speech.

Ferghus sat back and let thirteen Masters go at it, listening to the fierce debates that broke out, while next to him Barrach stared silently at the Council table.

At last the Second of the Council turned toward his Prime. "Clearly, your parents misnamed you," he said dryly.

Ferghus raised a brow. "I'm admittedly not as 'vigorous' a man as I once was, but you needn't rub it in. Taller and stronger you may be, but last I checked, you weren't all that many cycles younger."

Barrach snorted. "Oh, you're strong enough still, never fear. But I think "Sionnach" would be a more fitting name for you."

The Prime's mouth quirked in amusement. "A fox?"

"*Sean*-Sionnach ... a *wise* old fox."

Ferghus chuckled. "Tell me, then ... will you stand with this 'wise old fox'? Or will you stand against him?" He nodded toward the others when Barrach glanced at him in surprise. "You hold more power here than you know," the Prime quietly continued. "For what lies ahead, I would have that power with me."

For a long moment, Barrach was silent. "Then let me make it clear where I stand," he said at last. He leaned over, picked up the mallet, and gave the largest chime a firm tap. As the sweet sound died away, every voice died with it. All eyes turned to the Second of the Council as he set the mallet down.

"This is not the time for talking about events none of us can change," Barrach told them. "This is the time to take action, either for or against our Prime. For *he* has clearly taken action on his own that is unprecedented. If we stand against him, we vote him out as our Prime, take back the remainder of what he has stolen, finish the ships with it and sell them in Armorica ... for using them here is tantamount to gifting them all to the Ard Rí, then being punished with immobility for the favor. We hold our Fall Council somewhere inland, far from any seaport Faolán can reach. And we stay alive and alert, hoping that the *next* time Odhran makes a move against us, we'll know about it in time to evade it again ... and yet again." He arched a brow at the silent Masters. "Is that the kind of life we want for ourselves? For our families?" His eyes swept the Council. "Each of you must make up his own mind, but as for me..." and Barrach pushed his chair back and stood, tall and strong. "I stand with my Prime, the Sean-Sionnach of our Order, who has single-handedly given us the chance of a *new* life. Who stands with us?"

A broad grin lit Liam's face as he rose to his feet. "*I* do!"

"And I!" said Fionn a heartbeat later.

As one, the Masters erupted from their chairs, cheering.

Ferghus sat immobilized for a long moment. Then Barrach and Liam held out a hand each, and Ferghus, laughing, let them bring him to his feet. A mighty shout filled the hall.

"Sean-Sionnach!"

For two days, Ferghus did little but sleep and eat the meals Cyral prepared for him. "I'll be fine, my boy," he said in response to the Bard's worried expression. "Barrach, Liam, and Fionn have things well in hand for now, giving me a chance to regain my strength. Indeed," he added with an indignant frown, "the three of them banded together, had the nerve to insist that their joined ranks out-weighed my own, and forbade me to go anywhere near Aille-Mara for at least three days." The Master gave his chuckling Bard an exasperated glare.

Ferghus spent the third day assessing Cyral's progress in all of the elemental forces except the windsong. "Excellent," the Master said with satisfaction. "Your strength in all three is already far greater than any other Master, myself included. And we will need every bit of that strength. The Stone came to this particular beach for a reason. Perhaps it was simply attracted to the closest Master of the element it was submerged in. Perhaps not. But regardless, it was never meant for me. It was meant for you, who alone had the strength to withstand the increasing strength of its awareness and who used it to increase his own strength just when we desperately need it." The Master picked up his harp. "Come, let's spend the evening playing duets. It's been too long since we played for the enjoyment of it, and tomorrow I must go back to work."

Cyral lost no time fetching his Bardic harp—having long since stopped thinking of it as Bryan's—and together they launched into one duet after the other. He had nearly forgotten how satisfying it was to play with another highly skilled harpist, both of them so closely connected that every note was rich with meaning.

Then his Master set aside his harp and took up his flute. "Let's see how well we can compose something together," he said challengingly. "Improvise me an introduction!"

Cyral chuckled, strongly reminded of his composition lessons as an apprentice. "Major or minor?"

"Both," the Master decided. "For all entwined songs have elements of happiness and sadness."

"A song of us, then … as we once were, or as we are now?"

"As we are now, my boy," came the quiet reply.

The Bard looked steadily into his Master's eyes, and for a moment it seemed to him that every experience they'd had together since he'd been called back to Aille-Mara was reflected in that amber gaze. Not trusting himself to speak, he set his fingers in place on the strings and began to play.

The music began in the minor with a gentle melodic line that seemed to ask a question, then sadly answered itself. The flute drew the harp upward, yet remained in the minor mode with it, as though to reassure the harp that the minors were not to be avoided or refused … that without them, the majors wouldn't sound as sweet. Indeed, the flute whispered, the minors were the deep wellspring from which the majors would one day emerge.

The flute beckoned, encouraging the harp to climb higher and leave the minors behind. Together, they modulated to the major, and for one brief, incredible moment, the harp flew joyously upward toward a sky as clear and bright as an early spring morning. Then, just as the rays of the sun touched it, the flute took the harp inexorably back to the minor theme it had arisen from, as though saying there was more to be learned from it before it could fly free.

And so the minor theme played itself again, this time by the harp alone, the music almost, yet not quite the same … changed, perhaps, by its brief moment in the sun. Right at the end, the harp music modulated to a sad, softly spoken question. And the flute answered it in a strong and vibrant voice that resonated with certainty, leaving no room for doubt that one day, the minor bond the harp suffered would be loosened and fall away ... and it would fly free at last, this time without restraint.

The room fell silent as the music died away. The Master lowered his flute to his lap, his gaze taking in the deep emotion evident on the harpist's face as the Bard stared toward the Master's bedroom.

"I have indeed taken you back into the minors after helping you out of them," Ferghus said gently. "But never," and the Master's voice resonated with all the certainty of the flute, "never will I leave you there alone."

Cyral nodded wordlessly. He cleared his throat, then set his Bardic harp aside and looked appraisingly at the flute. "Such a beautiful tone ... a shame it hasn't a bigger range."

A faint smile crossed the Master's face as he glanced at the flute. "One day it will," he murmured.

Before Cyral could respond to this cryptic comment, Ferghus gasped. His eyes became unfocused, his head fell back against his chair, and his flute slid from fingers that could no longer grasp it. The Bard lunged forward and caught the small instrument before it fell. He set the flute on the table, then studied his Master's face, perceiving that someone was communicating with him. He took his seat and silently waited. Whatever was happening in Ferghus' mind was tearing the Master apart, alternating waves of resolve and grief visibly aging his face in the flickering firelight.

The Master moaned, reaching out as though to recapture something precious that had escaped his hand. Cyral leapt to his feet and caught him as he fell forward, the amber eyes opening into his with such naked grief that the Bard held him tightly to himself and remained kneeling there as his Master trembled in his arms. Then Ferghus was weeping, a passionate storm of anguish that pushed Cyral back on his heels. The Bard silently pulled him close.

At length the travail of grief stopped and Ferghus sagged in Cyral's arms. The Bard picked him up and carried him to his bed, then, with a brief glance of longing at his forbidden harp, he went to fetch his smaller one. He sat down on a stool near the bed and waited. The moment Ferghus grew restless and moaned in his sleep, Cyral began to softly play and the Master relaxed and fell into a deeper sleep. Thrice more during the night the Bard calmed the Master back into sleep. A few hours before dawn, when Cyral's eyes were beginning to close on their own, Ferghus spoke. The Bard came instantly awake.

"Thank you, my boy, for what you did for me." The Master's voice was raspy, as though sorrow's blade had scored it raw. I don't know how I would have made it through the night without your music, or survived such grief if you had not held on to me."

"I'm truly sorry for whatever happened, Master. Will you be all right now if I leave you?"

Ferghus nodded, and Cyral wearily rose to leave. He stopped at the threshold when Ferghus spoke again.

"You haven't asked me what happened."

"You'll tell me if you think I should know."

"I'll tell you all of it, my boy ... but later will be soon enough, for it's a long story that began last winter in the Grove of Gaotha. Get some sleep now. We'll speak of it in the morning's light."

Cyral nodded and left, wondering what tragic story could possibly have begun in a Druid's Grove so far to the north as Gaotha.

Movement Two

The Grove of Gaotha

on the day the Stone was found

Chapter 11

Sixteen hundred furlongs north of Aille-Mara on the Connemara coast was the windswept village of Gaotha, and thirty furlongs into the wooded hills to the east of it was a grove of trees. Not that there was anything remarkable about that, for the hills were wooded with stands of oak, ash, and an occasional splash of silver birch. This particular grove, however, was special, for it was a Druid's Grove, and a rare, fine one. It measured a full eight furlongs in diameter and contained an inner ring of rowan trees, with an outer ring of hawthorns around its perimeter. Both types of trees were revered by the Druidic Order.

The rowan was a tree of many legends. One tells that the goddess Hebe lost her chalice of youth, and an eagle fought to recover the cup and return it to her. Wherever the great bird shed a drop of blood or a feather, a rowan tree sprang up. Accordingly, the bright green leaves, perfectly symmetrical on either side of their stem, unfurled every spring bearing an uncanny likeness to feathers. The bright red berries symbolized the drops of eagle blood. The power of the rowan was enhanced by a pentagram, an ancient protective symbol, embedded in the bottom of every rowan berry.

Legend also claimed that the first human woman was created from the rowan tree, and thus the Aes Sidhe, faery folk of Eire, blessed it with delicate, creamy-white flowers. When the moon was full, folklore had it that the faeries might be seen dancing around the rowan trees. Thus the trees were looked after with the greatest of care by the Grovetenders, and the deadfall collected from the rowans was considered sacred. Indeed, it was known across Eire that the best rune staves, walking staffs, and divining rods favored by the Druids came primarily from the Grove of Gaotha. Accordingly, the Grove was protected around its perimeter by hawthorn, the faery tree of Eire. The white flowers of this tree grew in clusters, hiding their thorny branches. Their small red fruits joined in the deception, bearing poisonous seeds within. No one would trespass on ground guarded by such a tree. Indeed, few would even dare speak of them for fear of upsetting the faeries.

The elderly Druid limping his way between the hawthorn trees in the Grove on this cold winter morning, however, seemed to suffer from no such inhibitions. Despite the slight grimace of pain on his face, his uneven steps were confident, supported by a runed walking staff of polished oak. His forest green robe with the insignia of an oak tree on the front of the right shoulder, bound at the waist with a silver cord, proclaimed him to be no ordinary Druid, however. For this was the garb of a Grovekeeper, only one rank beneath a Council Member, the highest rank in the Druidic Order. There were but nine Grovekeepers, one for each of the nine sacred Groves of Eire. Daithi, Grovekeeper of Gaotha, the largest of these Groves, had tended the trees here for twenty-five cycles and had, he thought, little to fear from the faeries. And, though he had kept a lookout, not once had he ever seen them dancing around any of the rowan trees ... or the hawthorns either, for that matter.

Although, there was that one night... A tingle ran up his spine at the memory, and he shrugged it off. Surely that had just been a trick of moonlight and shadow. *It couldn't possibly have been—*a memory of his older brother instantly appeared in his mind, insisting there were no such things as impossibilities. Daithi sighed. *Yes, yes, I know ... I just don't necessarily agree.*

He smiled at the thought of Ferghus, whom he still missed

sorely and thought of every day. Their parents had expected Daithi to join the Bardic Order like his brother had and at least one family member in every generation before them. Daithi had dutifully taken lessons on harp, lute, and lyre until the day he turned of age at fifteen. He had done well, but he wasn't Gifted. Not like Ferghus, whose amber eyes practically guaranteed him admission to the Order. Daithi's eyes were an equally rare bi-color, a rich cinnamon brown near the pupils, radiating outward from light mint to a deep emerald around the perimeter. Not acceptable for the Bardic Gift, apparently. Nevertheless, he would likely have followed in his brother's footsteps if Druid Cillian hadn't come into his life when Daithi was ten. Unbeknownst to anyone, even Ferghus, Daithi had taken lessons with the Druid for five cycles. Becoming Cillian's acolyte when he turned of age and no longer needed parental permission to do so was what Daithi had wanted, and he had never regretted that decision, though it had cost him his family.

As Daithi continued limping through the hawthorns, he sternly told himself to stop such sour conjectures. Regardless of the reason, he wasn't Gifted ... at least, not in any way the Bardic Order or his family would understand. It was hardly Ferghus' fault, and his older brother had always stood up for him, though Daithi knew he hadn't understood his decision to train with a renegade Druid who had abandoned his own Order. The rest of his family had been shocked, considering Daithi's action a betrayal of family tradition, but if Ferghus had felt the same way, he had never shown it and had defended him against their condemnation, though Daithi had seen the confusion in his eyes.

Perhaps it was simply in Ferghus' nature to be a defender. For he had also staunchly defended Daithi against the bullies who had done their utmost to make his life more miserable than it already was. Without Ferghus, there would have been no way to outpace his tormentors since the sickness that had stunted Daithi's growth when he was seven, leaving his right leg shorter than the other and consigning him to limp his way through the rest of his life. And deal with three of the boys who had been jealous of his prowess in krebit, a game demanding both speed and strategy, and who now considered him easy prey. The village of Ganach became a place of torment for the boy who had once been as quick and nimble as his name implied. Daithi had stopped believing in his brother's assertion that nothing was impossible, and perhaps his belief in the faeries had disappeared along with it. For certainly his fervent prayers to the Aes Sidhe had gone unanswered, and the healers of the Bardic Order had been unable to help him. A memory surfaced of limping home with his brother after yet another attack and crying out in bitterness at Ferghus' oft-spoken belief.

If nothing is impossible, brother, then why were the healers unable to heal my leg?

Their inability doesn't make it impossible. Someday, when one of them asks the right questions and discovers the right answers, they'll be able to.

"Not in time to help me," Daithi murmured, but without the bitterness that statement had been infused with when he had hurled it at his brother those many cycles ago.

I must check the oak leaf collection, he reminded himself to dispel the past from his mind. The festival of Imbolc was only a few days away, bringing with it the promise of spring. Hopefully the weather would be wet and stormy so the Cailleach, hag of winter storms, would be unable to collect wood for her fire and thus go to sleep, bringing winter to an official close. Tossing a small handful of oak leaves into the fire on the day of Imbolc provided strength and healing from winter ailments, so on this day their fires would remain lit throughout the night. The villagers could easily obtain their own oak leaves, but the ones originating from the mighty Oak standing in the center of the Grove were considered to have much stronger magical properties. Though the pain from his own infirmity had never been eased by his Imbolc fire, Daithi tossed some oak leaves into it anyhow and kept his reservations regarding its efficacy to himself. If such things provided comfort and hope to those too poor to afford a healer, who was he to deny them? As Cillian had sternly told him when Daithi rashly expressed his doubts, hope was a powerful healer that charged no fee, and he would be well advised not to rob anyone of its services.

The Grovekeeper smiled as he limped through the rowans, ignoring the pain running through his right hip and knee. His hand reached out to gently touch bark or branch as he went, enjoying the energy that came from them, which would increase in strength with the arrival of spring. He loved his work here, work no one could interfere with. Even Cathair, the Overdruid in charge of the territory of Connemara, whose rank was equal to his own, must defer to Daithi in matters that pertained to the Grove and Celtic festivals. The Grovekeeper, in turn, must defer to the Overdruid in matters that pertained to the towns and villages of Connemara, but there was little reason for the two of them to clash. Indeed, Cathair came to the Grovekeeper's home once a week to play a game or two of Stones, though Daithi mistrusted his motives for doing so and was careful not to let his guard down. Cathair was not quite as circumspect, letting slip his jealousy of the Council members' higher rank.

Of course, Daithi had taken care that no one knew his own brother was Prime of the Council of Master Bards. Bardic apprentices and Druidic acolytes cast off their surnames when they took their vows, so unless someone knew both of them from before that, there was little chance of their relationship being discovered. He and Ferghus had grown up in Ganach, on the east coast of Eire, far from Aille-Mara or Gaotha, and his family had kept his Druidic ties secret, simply saying he'd decided to leave and make his own way in the world. Nor had anyone in his Order asked, for regardless of his advanced skills and robe, he'd been known as "Cillian's acolyte" for cycles. Now, secure in his position, he kept silent because of Cathair. He distrusted the Overdruid's ambitions and his avowed subservience to their Order, knowing it for the thin veneer it was. Cathair, he knew, would do whatever served Cathair. The man was sincere enough in his beliefs, but Daithi would not allow his relationship to the Prime of the Bardic Order to be manipulated.

Nor did he wish anyone to know that Ferghus spoke to him on the first of every week, using the bond between them the Master was adept at traveling. Daithi couldn't see this bond himself, but Ferghus had described it to him as two cords of sparkling notes twined together, creating a song his brother assured him was one of the most beautiful songs he had ever heard. Ferghus told him that if they ever met in person again, he would play it for him. *I would like that,* Daithi reflected, but the chances of him ever traveling to Aille-Mara at this point were slim to none.

Daithi entered the center of the Grove, where a single white oak spread its branches unhindered, towering over its rowan companions. He bowed before it as he always did, for the oak was the sacred symbol of strength and longevity and this one, possibly the oldest in all Eire, was deserving of his reverence. Said to attract the lightning of the gods, this particular oak was well protected by the surrounding rowans, trees believed to deflect such lightning. The staff in his hand flared with energy, as if recognizing the tree it had come from, for it had indeed been fashioned from one of its deadfall branches. Beneath him, Daithi could feel the flow of energy moving both directions through the ancient tree.

All Druidic acolytes were trained to sense energy lines, their own first, then that of the trees their Order revered. Even after receiving their robe as a full Druid, most could do little with this except enjoy the sensation, using it as a focal point for meditation and to enhance their health. Those who were skilled became Adepts, able to perceive energy lines as scintillating pathways and use them. Some Adepts became teachers, employed by the Rí to educate their children. Others, depending on their affinity, rose higher in the Druidic hierarchy by becoming a Stoneseer, Diviner, or Arborist, able to use energy lines in specific ways.

An accomplished Stoneseer could draw from the energy lines of the earth itself to move stone. Most of the bridges, causeways, celestial observatories, and sacred sites, not to mention their own Meeting Hall at Uisneach, were built with their aid. They also oversaw the construction of many of the castles and homes of the Rí.

Adepts who became Diviners had an affinity for the energy of the weather. They used cloud formations and the behavior of birds to foretell the future, determine auspicious times for events, and interpret omens. Some Diviners could pull energy from their staffs, lending further credence to their divinations. For what was more convincing than making a pronouncement to the accompaniment of a flash of light from their divining staff? A strong Diviner could produce vivid flashes of colored light, each color adding a specific meaning to the divination and giving him an honored position in the household of a Rí. The strongest of all the Diviners was employed by the Ard Rí himself, King of all Eire.

Though all Adepts, Stoneseers, and Diviners employed by the Rí were free to enjoy the status it brought them, not to mention the fine accommodations and food, the coin they earned was returned to the Order's coffers, while they themselves continued to live on the stipend of their rank, just as all Druids did.

As an acolyte under Cillian's tutelage, Daithi had mastered many of the energy skills of those employed in the Ri's households. When his mentor had taken him to the Council for formal admittance to the Order, Daithi had followed his advice and said nothing of it to anyone, having no interest in divination or manipulating stone. Nor had he said anything about his ability to see more than energy lines. For he could also see what Cillian called energy fields, the spectrum of colors that emanated from the energy lines of all objects and living things, reaching outward in unfurling ribbons of what seemed to be living light. Daithi had chosen to reveal just enough of his abilities to become an Arborist, known for his ability to travel every branch and leaf of several adjacent trees in a single session. This had played a key role in his rise to Grovekeeper of the most treasured Druid's Grove in all Eire at the age of thirty-five cycles, the youngest Arborist to ever be so honored.

Daithi stood now before the ancient Oak, aware of the energy line flowing beneath him toward the tree, moving quickly in the spring and summer and slower in the fall and winter, as it was now. There was energy moving down the tree as well, a misty energy coming into its leaves from what seemed to be the air itself and moving through every branch downward to the roots. Daithi never failed to thrill at the movement of pure energy, feeling the flow of it now through the soles of his boots. He bent over and removed them, letting the full force of the Oak's energy fill him as he dug his bare feet into the cold, rich soil.

Daithi stood facing the tree, his feet planted directly above a large root, and concentrated on his own energy field that flowed outward in colors of predominantly emerald, honey gold, and cerulean blue to overlap the tree's. Then he sent his awareness through his field and into the Oak's. Behind him six figures came from between the trees, five of them Grovetenders in robes of moss green, bound with umber cords, the insignia of an oak leaf on the right front shoulder. They formed a half-circle behind Daithi and stood silently waiting for his weekly assessment of the Grove.

The Grovekeeper was unaware of their presence, his mind already traveling quickly through the energy field of the ancient Oak, critically inspecting it from roots to crown and finding nothing needing attention. A few minutes later he was traveling through the energy fields coming from the rowan trees, enjoying the freedom of unimpeded, pain-free travel. He spent a few extra minutes scanning the hawthorns as well, the fleeting thought that surely the faeries must appreciate his concern for their trees putting a slight smile on his face. For if, despite their unwillingness to heal his leg, the faeries did exist somewhere, surely it would be here in this most ancient of Groves. Finishing his assessment, he sent his awareness back through the colorful paths and returned to himself, keeping his eyes closed until the slight dizziness left him. Then he turned to his Grovetenders.

"Rowan four," he announced, "has a widow-maker in its upper branches. I could have freed it, but since I had a youngling standing right behind me who can climb it like a squirrel," and he smiled at the red-haired boy grinning up at him, "I decided to conserve my energy and let him exercise those muscles and free it himself. Mind yourself, lad," he warned. "Certainly no one will be made a widow should the branch fall on you, but that's no reason to tempt fate."

"I'll be careful, Grovekeeper Daithi!" The youngster of eight cycles, dressed in village garb of woolen breeches and a loose-fitting tunic, bowed and turned to leave.

"Shaylor," Daithi said mildly, bringing the boy to an abrupt halt at the use of his full name.

"Your two months of tutelage with each of the Grovetenders ends today, so after you complete any tasks Grovetender Dorrean has given you, come to my home. You'll be staying with me for awhile so I can assess your aptitude for becoming an acolyte."

"Yes, Grovekeeper," came the hushed response.

"Have you studied the list of seventeen trees and shrubs I sent for you to memorize before your first lesson with me?"

The face that turned toward Daithi was flushed with color that matched his hair. "I've studied it every day ... I promise!"

"Then you'll do well in the testing I'll give you this afternoon."

Shay's face paled. "I'll do my best, Grovekeeper." The boy hurried off, to the accompaniment of a few chuckles.

The Grovekeeper turned to Dorrean, a short, stocky man with thick black hair. "How has Shay done in his studies with you?"

Dorrean frowned. "Well, there's no doubt the lad works hard and tries to please. He can read and cipher fairly well for a village boy. And he has an uncanny knack with gardens, the like of which

I've never seen before." He gave Daithi an exasperated look. "But the boy hasn't the memory needed for becoming an acolyte, much less a Druid, who must memorize the entire history of Eire."

Daithi glanced at the others. "Do the rest of you agree?"

A round of reluctant nods answered him.

"He might do well with history, for he can remember stories well enough," piped up Eoin, the youngest of them. "Well, he can," he said defensively when Dorrean frowned at him. "When my sister and her daughter came for a visit, I asked Shay to entertain the wee thing for awhile. The lad soon had her spellbound with the stories I'd told him in the evenings, and he repeated them to her word-for-word. He'd only heard each of them once."

"That's true enough," Dughan said, unexpectedly taking Eoin's side. "I think the only thing he can't remember is a list. Of anything. Even food supplies from the village, which the Maker knows he enjoys *eating* well enough."

Ronán, second eldest and tallest of the Grovetenders, nodded agreement. "Getting him to memorize a simple list of ten conifers nearly drove me out of my mind," he groaned. "He *still* can't recite them accurately, not even after a switching to encourage him to study harder. I'm sorry to say it, for I like the lad, but I don't think any of us will want him as an acolyte."

Daithi nodded thoughtfully. "And what do you say, Alben?"

Alben cocked a head nearly bereft of hair, then straightened his back, wincing a bit. "We all know the lad excels at growing things. Would be a shame to see such talent wasted in the village when it could be serving the Grove. He needn't become a Druid for that, and I'd gladly train him as a gardener."

Approving nods greeted this offer.

"I'll teach the lad myself for a few weeks before making my decision, as I do for all potential acolytes," Daithi said. "Now, continuing with my assessment, rowan eight's energy flow has become disrupted from a blockage in its upper trunk. Although it appears healthy to the eye, its vitality is ebbing within. Perhaps, Eoin, your youthful energy could find that blockage and remove it."

"I'll see to it right away, Grovekeeper." Eoin bowed and left.

Daithi continued giving instructions until only Alben stood there, the oldest Grovetender at seventy-five cycles, fifteen cycles older than Daithi. The Grovekeeper gave him a nod of respect.

"Alben, I'm afraid hawthorn twelve has weakened significantly. The other trees are doing what they can to support it, but I could use your experience and advice on the matter."

The old man's face lit up. "Certainly … a pleasure to be of help. Soon enough I expect I'll be passed over as too old to be of use."

They began walking toward the afflicted tree. "Explain to me how the other trees are supporting the weakened hawthorn," Daithi unexpectedly said.

Alben glanced at him, surprised at such a basic question, but answered readily. "A weakened tree can't take in energy as well as it used to, so the trees nearby send it some through their roots."

"So any acolyte could tell me. But how do you, an experienced Grovetender, *know* this to be true?"

"I can tell by traveling its energy line, for it moves slower in a weakened tree. And I can sense the energy lines coming from the other trees' roots and entering the old one's where they touch."

"And why should the healthy trees do this? Isn't it better for a weakened tree to die and make room for a young, strong one to take its place?"

Alben shook his head. "No, for it will be a long time before a young sapling can grow big enough to replace it, and during that time the surrounding trees will be more open to the wind and weather." Alben's voice strengthened as he warmed to his favorite topic. "And the older tree can provide protection from more than the weather. When insects start feeding on its leaves, it sends out bright, fast energy. Then the trees 'round about send out a slower energy that must attract predators that feed on the leaf-eaters, for the very next day there they are, saving the Grove!" He gave an approving nod to the tree he was passing. "The trees of the Grove need each other, and they know it. I've seen them support each other time and again, and know, just as the trees do, that it's better to strengthen the weakened tree than let it die."

"One might say, then, that the weakened tree is still valuable because of its wisdom. Wisdom it uses to benefit the Grove. Wisdom the young sapling will take cycles to obtain."

"Why, yes, Grovekeeper ... that's it exactly."

"And so are you valuable to us, for precisely the same reason."

The old man came to a surprised halt.

"I will follow the Grove's example and strengthen my weakened tree, who has more wisdom than all the others," Daithi told him. "Not cut him down and replace him with youthful brawn, an easy thing to obtain. My Grovetenders all need each other, and they'd best know it, just as the trees do. If any of them don't, let me know and I'll take care of it."

The old man nodded. He straightened a bit and headed purposefully toward the ailing hawthorn, Daithi limping along behind.

Chapter 12

Surrounding the Grove of Gaotha were six domiciles, five of them made of stone with thatched roofs for the use of the five Grovetenders. Each of these was abutted by a woodshed on one side and a small garden on the other. Inside was a small but serviceable kitchen, a living area with a fireplace, and a bedroom. The Grovekeeper's home on the west side of the Grove, however, was made entirely of split-ash. It had a large kitchen with a table big enough to seat eight people, a huge living area with a fireplace and several comfortable chairs, a spacious bedroom, and three guest rooms. The front of the house faced the hawthorns that encircled the Grove. A grassy clearing with a single ash tree stood between the trees and the home, bisected with a path that wound its way through the trees into the Grove, and a side path that led behind the house and on west to Gaotha.

Daithi had been taken aback by the size of his home when he first came here, for his needs were simple, and this home was far too rich for his tastes. His protest to the Council, however, had fallen on deaf ears, and he soon came to see the necessity for such a home, for the Grovekeeper of Gaotha had many visitors. Most were there to pick up their orders of staffs, rune staves, or divining rods, and appreciated staying the night before heading back home. His other visitors were either Council members, Arborists, or Grovekeepers, who came to discuss various problems with the most respected Grovekeeper in all Eire and expected comfortable accommodations.

At the moment, Daithi was seated at his large table, regarding its only other occupant ... a crestfallen youngster who had just failed his test. "I believe you told me you studied this list."

"I did, sir ... every day," Shay said miserably. "I just can't remember it." He'd come at the Grovekeeper's bidding ten months ago, and it was just his bad luck that his first lesson was memorizing a list. As much as he loved learning about living things, Shay hated lists, for he couldn't remember them, something his hand had already borne stinging witness to, courtesy of Grovetender Ronán. He closed his fist in anticipation of more strokes, devastated that the punishment would be administered by the Grovekeeper himself. He fervently hoped he wouldn't be sent away afterwards. He liked the kindly Grovekeeper, who treated everyone in his domain with equal courtesy ... even him, a simple village boy. That, he knew, was a rare thing.

The Grovekeeper was silent for a few moments, fingering the silver ring on his finger as he often did when thinking deeply. Shay looked at it curiously, liking the interlocking leaves carved into the beautiful band.

"Tell me the name of the faery tree," Daithi unexpectedly said.

Shay looked up in surprise. "Hawthorn, sir."

"And if I changed two of the letters, making of it a funny name like 'Bawshorn', could you remember that?"

"I don't know," the lad said doubtfully.

"What does a sheep say?"

Shay blinked. "Baa."

"Which can easily be misspelled as "b-a-w," can it not? And what happened to the poor thing if all its wool was cut off?"

"Well, it was shorn—oh!" the lad grinned.

"Can you remember it now?"

"Bawshorn," Shay said confidently.

"Now, imagine poor little Bawshorn out in the pouring rain, hunting for shelter in a field that has seventeen different trees and shrubs in it. Each of the ones you recite from the letters of his name will disappear from the field. There are five for B, two for A, and four for H—yet another way to misspell 'baa'—and all the rest have only one. Think about what I've just said for a moment, then repeat it back to me."

The boy did so, then slowly repeated it.

"Excellent. So, tell me five trees and shrubs that start with B."

"Birch, blackthorn, broom, buckthorn ... and bramble."

Two that begin with A, and one each for W and S."

"Ash and alder for A. Willow and spindle for W and S."

"Four for H."

"Hazel, hawthorn ... holly and honeysuckle."

"And one each for O, R, and N."

"Oak, rose, and, um ... nettle."

The Grovekeeper smiled. "And now sixteen of the seventeen trees and shrubs have disappeared from the field, and the only thing you had to remember was a sheep with the misspelled name of 'Bawshorn', and that B, A, and H—yet another misspelled version of 'baa'—have five, two, and four items, the rest having one. Now, what do you suppose is the last, twisted tree you overlooked that poor Bawshorn huddled his miserable wet self under?"

Shay grinned. "A juniper. Not a good choice for cover, that."

"Well, you made everything else disappear, so it's all the poor fellow could find. Now, tell me exactly what you need to remember in order to recite the entire list of seventeen."

"Bawshorn, whose name rhymes with hawthorn, is out in the rain, looking for a tree to huddle under." He thought for a moment. "Another way to spell "baa" wrong is b-a-h, which have five, two, and four items from the list. All the rest have one, and once I make those sixteen disappear by reciting them, all he'll find left to huddle under is a juniper." He grinned. "It's almost a story!"

"You have a perfectly good memory, lad, or you couldn't have recited that back again so well. You just needed a method to organize a list in your mind, so it doesn't become a confused jumble. You don't need to memorize seventeen different things if you make a story from it, leaving blanks for the listed items. Your familiarity with the trees and shrubs easily filled them in."

Shay nodded thoughtfully.

"Tomorrow morning, at our meeting in the Grove, I want you to recite your list to the Grovetenders. And the next time you're given a list to memorize, use your good imagination to organize it into a story, no matter how silly. Indeed, the sillier it is, the easier it will be to remember."

"I will," Shay promised.

"Now, I believe we're about to have an unexpected visitor. When he arrives, open the door for him, welcome him in, then bring him some of my elderberry tea. You can get it ready now."

Shay had barely finished filling a mug when the distinctive sound of approaching hoofbeats was heard. Wondering at the Grovekeeper's acute hearing, Shay opened the door to a tall Druid who pushed past him without glance or greeting. His black hair fell unbound past his shoulders. His forest green robe and silver cord were a match to the Grovekeeper's, for the two men were of equal rank, but the insignia of a walnut staff proclaimed him to be an Overdruid in charge of a territory. Shay blanched and quickly bowed to the imposing visitor.

"Welcome, Overdruid Cathair," the boy said nervously and quickly brought the tea.

"Grovetender Alben is at the shed on the east side of the Grove," Daithi told Shay, "sorting through the deadfall you collected last week for good branches to make into staffs and divining rods. In fact, since it's not the day Overdruid Cathair and I play Stones together, perhaps he's here for a new staff himself." He lifted an inquiring brow at his visitor. "Unless, of course, you no longer have need of one with your new mode of transportation."

"Connemara is a large territory, and a horse is far more efficient," Cathair said. "However, I still use my staff, and it *is* showing signs of wear."

Daithi smiled at Shay. "Well then, lad, be on the lookout for the best staff material you can find. If nothing is suitable, we'll await the next storm. Be sure to return in time for dinner. I'll want to hear that list you memorized, so be thinking on it."

"Yes, Grovekeeper." The youngster bowed and quickly left.

The two men regarded each other silently for a moment. "I wasn't expecting you," Daithi said. "Has something come up that I can help you with, besides a better staff?"

Cathair leaned back in his chair, his dark eyes never once leaving Daithi's. "I was wondering ... just how far can you travel the energy lines of the trees?"

"Throughout the Grove, of course," Daithi said expressionlessly. "I have no need to travel outside its boundaries."

"But you could?"

The Grovekeeper pursed his lips, considering. "For a short distance perhaps, though I see no reason why I would want to." He smiled wryly. "The older one gets, the less energy one has to expend on foolish displays that serve no one."

"Rumor has it that your ability to travel the energy lines is still the greatest in all Eire." The Overdruid gave Daithi a tight smile that failed to reach the dark eyes above it. "Surely one with such talent can travel farther than a short distance from the Grove."

Daithi's mouth quirked. "As I'm sure you're aware, rumor has a way of distorting the facts, and I haven't corrected the misconception. Allowing people to believe I'm powerful engenders greater respect for the Grove, and less likelihood of trespass."

Cathair's eyes narrowed. "Another question, then. If you were to stand in the center of the Grove and I were to stand among the hawthorns, quietly speaking, could you travel the energy lines to where I was and hear the verses I was reciting?"

Daithi's eyes lit with interest. "A fascinating idea ... but if we were to test it, you'd be standing there reciting for a long time. The energy of tree roots travels extremely slowly, as I'm sure you've discovered from traveling energy lines yourself."

Cathair shifted uncomfortably. "Of course."

"And gives one a terrible headache if traveled too long."

"Indeed. How slowly do the energy lines in the Grove travel?"

"From the center of the Grove to the hawthorns is about four furlongs. So, if you began reciting at dawn, I wouldn't reach you until mid-morning of the following day."

Cathair's brows lifted. "And how long from here to Gaotha?"

"That's about thirty furlongs, so ... a bit over eight days, I'd say. I could reach the hawthorns, but it's doubtful I'd have the energy to return, for traveling an energy line quickly depletes the traveler's own. There's also the problem of hearing you once I arrived. The energy line of a tree is not silent, as I'm sure you know."

"Yes, it has a ... peculiar sound."

"And there's no way you could hear someone speaking, quietly or otherwise, through a sound that can cause a terrible headache."

"I see." Cathair looked at him appraisingly. "How, then, do you manage to assess the Grove each week, if it takes so long to travel their energy lines?"

"I don't need to travel them for that purpose. The trees may look separate from each other, but they can communicate quite effectively, even if in ways we don't understand. If something is amiss with a tree, they all know about it. I merely send my awareness into the roots of the Oak and listen."

"And you can understand such speech?"

"There's a reason I was selected as Grovekeeper of Gaotha," Daithi said mildly.

"Fair enough," Cathair rose to leave. "This has been an interesting discussion," he said, flicking a piece of dust off the sleeve of his robe. "We should have more of them."

"May I ask what precipitated it?"

Cathair paused on the threshold. "Certain information that only I am privy to has been going astray from Gaotha over the last few months. I'm interested in finding out how ... and where it's been wandering off to."

Daithi steepled his fingers and quirked a brow. "I'm flattered you think me so powerful, but I'm afraid you'll have to look elsewhere for your eavesdropper. Closer to home, perhaps. My Grovetenders haven't the time to be listening at doors or spying through peepholes. This is the most prestigious Grove in Eire. Keeping up with the incessant orders for staffs and divining rods keeps everyone quite busy, not to mention seeing to the needs of the Grove itself and preparing for the seasonal festivals and rites we take an active part in. As for me, I've no interest whatever in the doings of the village. There's quite enough on my plate."

"Good to know," Cathair said as he opened the door. "Do keep it that way." He gave the Grovekeeper a sardonic nod and left.

Daithi sat still for a long moment, listening to the receding hoofbeats. How, he wondered, had a Druid with no ability to travel an energy line—none of which emitted peculiar sounds or caused the slightest headache—ever managed to become an Overdruid? There must be a connection between him and Odhran after all, as Ferghus suspected. The Grovekeeper frowned. He would have to be more careful. Rumor had indeed painted a distorted picture of his own abilities, but not in the way he had led the Overdruid to believe. Daithi chuckled at the thought of understanding the speech of trees from within their roots. A necessary misdirection, for it wouldn't do to let Cathair find out just how powerful the Grovekeeper of Gaotha actually was. He sent his awareness through the energy field of the floorboards to push against the door Cathair had left open. The door closed with a satisfying thud.

No ... it wouldn't do at all.

Chapter 13

A fortnight later, Daithi stood with Shay in the center of the Grove, deep in a discussion about the intelligence of trees.

"I've always liked trees," Shay said doubtfully, "but I've never thought they were smart. They can't even talk!"

"And how do you know they can't? Is it because they don't use words, like you and I do?"

The youngster frowned. "How else could they talk?"

The Grovekeeper nodded toward a young rowan. He made a scampering motion with his fingers toward the tree, twirled his forefinger around three times, then made another scampering motion toward himself. He glanced at Shay and nodded meaningfully toward the tree.

The boy grinned, ran over to the tree, circled it three times, then ran back to the Grovekeeper.

"It seems to me," Daithi said, "that I just gave you perfectly clear instructions you obeyed without a single word being spoken by either of us. Does that mean we're not intelligent?" He smiled at the boy's surprised expression. "Words are a convenience, lad, but they're not the only way living things can communicate. Trees have been around for thousands of cycles and have many ways of communicating with each other. Ways that seem like magic to us."

Shay's face lit with interest. "Magic?"

"Magic is the word we use to describe what we can't explain." Daithi indicated the trees with his walking staff. "Look around and you'll see the world is full of magical mysteries. And the exciting thing about solving them is that the magic doesn't disappear ... it moves to another layer. He limped over to a young rowan and laid a hand on its trunk.

"This rowan," he said, "needs its bark to survive, just as we need our skin. We know this because if a deer tears its bark off all around a tree, the tree will die. And yet the deer will only attack *one* tree before moving on, leaving the others untouched. Why?"

"It's a magical mystery!" Shay eyed the rowan with interest.

"So it seems. But what if I told you that a tree afflicted in this way sends a fast-moving energy through its bark. And when that energy reaches the trees near it, they send out a slower-moving energy. As soon as this reaches the deer, they leave."

Shay shook his head. "No one could know that unless they could *see* it," he said with certainty.

"Which is exactly how I know it. For Druids are trained to sense energy lines, especially those of trees," Daithi told him. "And Adepts who become Arborists can travel those lines."

Excitement banished disbelief and newly acquired pronouns. "Ye can travel *inside* the tree?"

"How else do you suppose I know what the needs of our trees are when I assess them each week?"

Shay glanced at him in surprise. "Well, yer ... you're the *Grovekeeper*," he said, as though that explained everything.

Daithi chuckled. "This robe gives me no special powers, lad. I know the needs of our trees because I can see their energy lines and am trained to repair and replenish the ones that are deficient, as are all my Grovetenders."

"What do the two energies the trees send out look like?"

"The fast-moving energy looks like silver magic; the slow-moving energy like dark grey magic."

Shay gave him an impish grin. "Because you can't explain them yet?"

Daithi nodded. "In solving the mystery, its magic moved a layer deeper, giving rise to more questions. What are these two energies I see coming from the trees and how are they produced? That's the new magical mystery that has taken its place, and I have yet to solve it. Perhaps one day *you* will."

"And if I do, a new magical mystery will take its place?"

"There is no end to magical mysteries." Daithi pointed his walking staff at the Oak and Shay caught his breath.

"There's colors!" the boy exclaimed in excitement. "Shining colors coming from yer staff! Greens and browns and golds!"

"Yes," Daithi said, "for my staff was made from the deadfall of the Oak and responds to it." He lowered his staff and leaned on it.

"They're gone," Shay said in disappointment.

"The colors are still there, lad, and with training you'll soon be able to see them whenever you wish. For everything has energy lines in it that emanate a colorful field all around it that some of us can see, as you just have from my staff."

"Around everything?" Shay asked incredulously. "Even me?"

Daithi chuckled as he glanced at the swirling colors of emerald, indigo, and burnt orange coming from the youngster. "Most definitely you. Yours are telling me you have a deep connection to nature ... and that you're fairly bursting with curiosity and a love of adventure. Which," he added dryly, "explains why you've been a bit of a handful for my Grovetenders."

The boy stared down as though hoping to catch a glimpse of colorful magic leaking out of himself.

"So, then," Daithi continued, "you might say the trees can communicate with each other using their energy."

The youngster looked with new appreciation at the rowans.

"Can all trees talk like that?" he wanted to know.

Daithi nodded confirmation. "They can talk in other ways, too, especially through roots that touch the roots of another tree."

Shay stared at the ground, fascinated by the idea of interconnecting roots chattering away right under his feet.

"Take off your boots and socks now and follow me."

The boy quickly did as instructed and padded barefoot after the Grovekeeper, who had moved close to the Oak.

"Stand next to me and concentrate on what you feel coming through the ground into your feet," Daithi told him.

After several moments, Shay shook his head. "I don't feel a thing but the grass and dirt," he said anxiously.

"Place your feet exactly where mine are and try again." Daithi stood aside.

Wonderingly, Shay did as he was told. After a few moments of concentration, he looked up in excitement. "I feel a tiny tingling in my feet!" he exclaimed. "What is it?"

Daithi smiled. "That's the energy coming from the Oak's root you're standing over. It usually takes several weeks for an acolyte to detect a tingle. You're very sensitive, which isn't surprising since you could see colors coming from my staff."

"I can just barely feel it," Shay said in a hushed voice, "and you can feel it through your *boots?*"

"I've had a few more cycles of experience than you have, lad." Daithi motioned toward the tree. "Collect a handful of stones, then walk slowly around the Oak, for it's the oldest and most powerful of the trees in the Grove. When you feel the energy of a root, place a stone there, then follow it away from the tree to the point where you can no longer feel it and mark it with another stone."

Shay nodded and began eagerly collecting stones.

Daithi watched, shifting to ease the soreness from his hip. Most Grovekeepers tested a few acolyte candidates each cycle. If accepted, they were assigned to one of their Grovetenders, with the most promising ones kept by the Grovekeeper himself. Daithi had trained several acolytes over the cycles, but for the last ten cycles he had been looking instead to find someone with a Gift like his own. And at last, after looking everywhere he could find an excuse to travel to, he had found one where he had least expected to ... in the garden of a tumble-down shack on the outskirts of Gaotha.

Daithi had been preoccupied when he left the village that early summer afternoon or he would never have taken the path that led to the cove. When he finally looked around, he was surprised to discover how far he'd traveled. The last shack that could lay claim to being part of Gaotha stood to his right, and he stared at it, struck by the contrast between the unkempt hovel and the flourishing garden next to it. Neat rows of cabbage, leeks, turnips, and onions were laid out with precision. Leafy carrot tops swayed gently in the breeze. A bed of parsley, mint, and rosemary was flanked by several rows of strawberries and a trellis of peas. Not a weed was to be seen. As the Grovekeeper studied the garden appreciatively, a head popped up from behind the trellis, and a young boy stared up at him. His unkempt hair was nearly as red as the ripening berries.

Well, now, Daithi said with a smile, *I was just wondering who was responsible for such a beautiful garden, and right before my very eyes, he pops up like one of the faery folk of old!*

A smile flitted across the boy's freckled face. His eyes, Daithi was startled to see, were as brown and emerald green as his own.

Did you plant all this yourself, lad?

The boy nodded, studying the Grovekeeper's robe in awe.

Well, you've certainly done a wonderful job ... especially if they taste as good as they look.

Oh, they do, sir! the boy said eagerly. *Would ye like to try?* He picked up a basket of strawberries and held it out.

Daithi limped over and selected one. *Thank you.* He bit into the ripe berry and his eyes widened. *Why, this is delicious! I don't know when I've tasted better.*

The boy's face lit, and he watched his unexpected guest finish the strawberry with pleasure.

What is your name, lad, and how old are you?

I'll soon be eight and my name is Shaylor, but most everyone calls me Shay. Unless I'm in trouble, he added ruefully.

Daithi chuckled. *It's a pleasure to meet you, Shay. I'm Grovekeeper Daithi.*

Ye take care of the trees in the Grove and all, the boy said reverently. *I've seen 'em ... from a distance,* he added hurriedly. *I wouldn't never intrude. They're wonderful things, is trees.*

The Grovekeeper's smile deepened. *I can understand your liking for fruits and vegetables. Why do you like trees?*

They're good fer climbin'! came the enthusiastic response. *Ye can see all sorts of interestin' things from the top of a tree.*

Daithi nodded gravely. *Indeed you can. Tell me, how did you manage to grow such a lush garden so early in the season?*

Shay shrugged. *I just like growin' things.* His hand reached out and gently touched a leaf. *Don't ask fer much, do they? Just water, air, sun—all of it free—and they likes to be touched and sung to, and that don't cost nothin' but time.*

The Grovekeeper arched a brow. *Sung to?*

Just hummin', really, the boy mumbled. *Not much to brag of, but I think they listen and grow the better fer it. Sounds crazy, I s'pose...*

Will you show me?

Shay gave him a startled look, then shrugged again and set down the basket. He looked critically around the garden for a moment, then moved toward the row of carrots, and a green, feathery top that was shorter than the ones on either side. *Ye aren't doin' as well as the others, then, are ye?* he murmured as he knelt down beside it. He stroked the leafy top gently, then began humming tunelessly, unaware of the Grovekeeper, who had moved silently behind him.

Daithi watched intently as the boy hummed. Beneath him, the

Grovekeeper felt a small surge of energy flow into the roots beneath the plant. The carrot top moved against the breeze toward the boy's hand. Daithi's eyes widened. After all these cycles of searching far and wide, he had found the one he was looking for less than thirty-five furlongs from the Grove? The Maker above was surely chuckling. Daithi laid a hand on Shay's shoulder.

Can you read? he asked, knowing it wasn't likely.

Mam taught me my letters before she took sick, Shay said proudly, *and I read every book I can borrow. I love stories,* he said wistfully. *They take ye places.*

How would you like to come work in the Grove, lad, read all the books you like, and learn all about the trees there?

The boy scrambled to his feet. *Do ye mean it?*

I certainly do.

Shay bit his lip and glanced worriedly at the shack. *Well, but … Mam needs me to look after her, like. She 'asn't no one but me.*

Perhaps we can strike a bargain, then, Daithi said. *We'll go talk to her, and if she agrees to let you go, I'll see to having someone look in on her every day, bringing her whatever she needs. You'll be given a small allowance that you can spend on yourself, or on her, as you like, and I'll also see that you have enough free time to come visit her every other day and see to your garden here.*

The hope that lit the boy's face needed no interpreting.

The Grovekeeper came back to the present to find Shay looking at him anxiously.

"Are you okay, sir?"

"I was just remembering the day I first met you."

"'Twas a lucky day for me." A shadow crossed the boy's face. "And for my mam. She'd never have lasted so long or been so comfortable if it hadn't been for you." He frowned slightly. "I've been wonderin' … you told me you'd keep me for a cycle before deciding, and it's gettin' close..." his voice trailed off. "Are you going to send me away?" he asked anxiously. "I don't want to leave the Grove."

"Now, that," the Grovekeeper said quietly, "isn't quite the whole truth, is it?"

The youngster flushed. "I don't want to leave *you*. Nor the Grove, neither. And it's not just because I've got nowhere else to go ... you know how much I like the trees and all."

"I do, and you needn't fear being sent away." He smiled into the boy's hopeful eyes. "You have a Gift, lad, one very much like my own. I intend to train you in it. Therefore, if you want to stay in the Grove, it will be as my protégé, not as a Druidic acolyte. Unless, of course, you *don't* wish to..." he staggered back a step as Shay launched himself into his arms.

"Oh, thank ye, sir!" the ecstatic boy cried. "I'll work the hardest ever, and I'll do whatever ye say ... and memorize all the lists in the whole world. I promise!"

Daithi chuckled and held the boy close, knowing for the first time what Ferghus must have felt like on taking Cyral as his only apprentice so many cycles ago. "Now, then," he said, ruffling Shay's hair and making it stand up like a torch, "you've set out your stones and haven't missed a single root. You've also followed their energy lines quite a bit farther out than I expected. I have some daily assignments for you that will hone that ability." His voice became stern. "You're not to miss a single day, mind. Repetition is critical for gaining the mastery of anything worthwhile."

Streaks of golden joy shot through the boy's energy field. "I won't miss a one!"

Late that evening, long after his tired protégé had gone off to bed, Daithi sat before the fire wishing he could do the same. He sighed wearily. Ferghus was supposed to visit tonight and he had yet to come. *A shame I can't contact him.* Not that he hadn't tried, but all he'd ever received for his efforts was a headache.

Daithi had just risen to bank the fire for the night when his brother's voice startled him so badly that he fell back into his chair.

Hello, brother. Sorry to be so late, but something came up. I was surprised to see you were still awake.

How did you see that?

If you're asleep, your part of our bond is quiescent and lacks its usual sparkle. Ah ... I see that you've recently met someone who's important to you.

Really, Ferghus? Is nothing in my mind private?

Ferghus laughed. *Don't worry, your thoughts are still your own, though at the moment they're fairly obvious. You could forbid me access to your mind, of course, but then we'd have to resort to the tedious method of writing letters ... and who wants that?*

In spite of himself, Daithi chuckled. He'd never been able to stay irritated with Ferghus for long. *Definitely no letters. No one must ever find out that we're brothers.*

All humor left Ferghus' voice. *I've told no one, and the only person in the Bardic Order who knows is Brenach. I asked him to keep it confidential, and you know he would betray neither of us. Why the sudden worry?*

Cathair is suspicious that I've been spying on him.

I take it he's correct.

Of course he is. How else can I find out what he's up to in time for you to thwart him in his endless search for your mine? The man is obsessed with finding it.

And knowing exactly where he's sending his spies to search has been extremely helpful.

Well, you're welcome.

It's none of my business how you get your information, but please be careful. I would never forgive myself if something happened to you because of me.

Daithi sat for a long moment in indecision, finding it hard to cast off his customary reticence about his abilities. *You've never asked me how, which I appreciate,* he said at last. *But there's no danger of Cathair catching me. For I'd be standing in the center of the Grove with my eyes shut ... hardly a crime for a Grovekeeper expected to travel the energy lines of the trees to check on their welfare. If I should travel elsewhere—to an open window of our esteemed Overdruid's home, perhaps—who would ever know?*

You can see ... and travel ... energy lines?

Daithi smiled, enjoying the rare surprise in his brother's voice. One generally had to get up before the crack of dawn to startle Ferghus. *All acolytes can detect energy lines, and all Adepts can travel them within a tree and provide healing. The reason Cillian took me as his acolyte is because I could also see the colorful energy fields they emit. He taught me how to travel them as well.*

I never knew ... I thought— Ferghus seemed strangely flustered. *Well, never mind what I thought. It hardly matters now.*

You thought I had betrayed our family by running off with a renegade Druid.

Silence fell between them. *I thought you had run off with a renegade Druid, yes,* Ferghus said at last. *I did not think you had betrayed our family by doing so. It's not a betrayal to follow your own path.*

And so you defended me. Thank you for that. I might have grown quite bitter if you had abandoned me, too.

I would never have done that. But tell me about these colorful energy fields you can travel.

You believe that all things are created with music. From my perspective, all things are created with energy. You hear it as a musical song and send your awareness into it by playing it. I see it as a field of colors and send my awareness into it by traveling through my own overlapping field.

But ... this is amazing! True to Ferghus, he immediately began exploring the possibilities. *I wonder what would happen if we both entered the same thing at the same time?*

That might be a bit difficult, Daithi said dryly, *considering all the furlongs between us.*

But Ferghus would not be put off. *You must admit it's a fascinating idea! And it raises the question of why you can't enter your own mind and see our bond there. I travel my own song to enter my mind; I should think you could do the same with your own colors. Or can't you see your own energy field?*

Well, yes, I can. Daithi frowned, considering this. *It's never occurred to me to immerse myself in … myself.*

If it works, you'll be able to contact me when you need to!

So you can tell me to get lost, you're too busy with big important matters to listen to a pestilent little brother?

Ferghus chuckled. *No promises. But come now, try entering your own mind! I promise not to make a peep.*

The next instant, Daithi's mind was as silent as if Ferghus had left it completely. Excited by what he was about to do, the Grovekeeper settled back into his chair and concentrated on what he could only call a different way of seeing. Colorful energy fields surrounded him, soft earthen tones from the wood of his furniture and floor, more vibrant, swirling ones from the flowers on his table. His own colorful energy field overlapped them all, and he could have effortlessly entered it and traveled to one of the others by focusing on it. This time, however, he focused inward, to his own mind, then closed his eyes and allowed his awareness to flow into it.

The next moment he was staring at shimmering colors he didn't recognize, and wondering where they had come from. To his surprise, his brother's voice spoke from them.

Well, then … there you are. Welcome to your own mind!

Incredible! Is that bubble of colors actually you?

Is that what you see?

Yes. What do you see when you look at me?

A sparkling sphere, each pinpoint of light a note in the song of your awareness. To your right is the bond we've created over the cycles. To me, it's a brilliant twining together of two songs, one composed by me, the other by you. What do you see?

I see a twining of our colors. Mine is emerald, honey gold, and cerulean, with a few traces of silver. Yours is an unusual mix of burnt umber, honey gold, indigo, and a hefty dollop of silver. The first time I've seen it, actually, for you left home before I gained the ability."

Interesting! We see colors of emotion in memory orbs and know their meaning. The colors you're seeing must be different, though, for those don't reflect my emotions at the moment.

They're personality colors, different from emotion colors, which for you right now is a rather euphoric bright yellow.

A match to the meaning it has for us in a memory orb! And you understand the meanings of personality colors as well?

I do, indeed. Yours means you have an uncanny ability to be a pain in the rear end.

Ferghus' song sparkled with his laughter. *Apparently chromafields are brutally honest.*

Chromafields?

Better than calling them colorful energy fields, don't you think? And, like a chromatic scale, comprised of every possible note one might choose to compose from, these chromafields of yours can be composed from every possible color.

Chromafields ... I like that.

You're welcome. Is the color of an object's chromafield the same as its actual color?

Most objects emit several different colors, but their actual color is not often one of them. I don't know why.

And what about plants or trees?

An object's colors rarely change. A plant's or tree's colors do, depending on the time of day and how healthy it is.

Fascinating! And a person's?

That's as complex as the people themselves are, Daithi told him, *for their personality colors can change throughout their lives, and their emotions create streaks or swirls of colors that constantly fluctuate.*

Similar to the songs we hear, Ferghus mused, *for a person's song can change over time, and their emotions quickly effect its tempo and sparkle, which we learn to interpret like you do their* colors. Ferghus fell silent for a long moment. *No wonder you followed Cillian,* he said at last. *It must have been wonderful, the first time you moved freely and without pain through a chromafield.*

You understand, Daithi said softly, seeing a mix of lavender and indigo reflect the compassionate sadness in his brother's voice.

What I understand is that my brother is as Gifted as I am, just in a different way. A way that brought him freedom of movement and unfair judgement from our family and made his path far harder to follow than my own. If I had known— Dusky blue regret stopped Ferghus' voice.

You could have done no more than what you did, not knowing, Daithi told him. *And perhaps that's why I never told you.* He hesitated, having never spoken of that time to anyone before. *Losing my family was devastating, especially at that age. I wanted Cillian to be that for me, but he rebuffed my efforts to make him so. When he took me to the Council and left me there, I felt ... abandoned. Again. It meant everything to me that, even though you didn't understand, you were always there for me anyhow.*

The least I could do, considering I was enjoying the accolades of climbing the Bardic Order hierarchy while you were unfairly ostracized as the follower of a renegade Druid. And now, he added wryly, *here you are, a perfectly respectable Grovekeeper, and I'm a renegade Master. I'm sure the irony is giving the Maker endless entertainment.*

You? A renegade? Daithi chuckled. *If only our parents were alive to hear that. How have you become a renegade?*

One of my informants is on the Druidic Council.

What? Daithi exclaimed in mock indignation. *You have a spy of higher rank than me?*

He told me that Cathair had a long meeting with Odhran a fortnight ago.

Daithi's levity vanished. *He's found your mine?*

Nice to know my little brother has more sense than my Council, who won't act without proof. So I've taken matters into my own hands. I'm teaching Cyral everything I know, things forbidden to all but Masters. That alone would shock my Council out of their collective wits, he said wryly. *But even worse, I'm thieving from my own Order. The first is a breaking of strictures; the second a breaking of Bardic Law, not to mention being morally reprehensible. Thus thoroughly qualifying me as a Bardic renegade.*

Daithi was too stunned for a moment to speak. *I'll increase my vigilance in watching Cathair,* he said at last. *If at all possible, I'll get you the proof you need.*

Thank you. You can travel any strong bond you've made with another into their mind, but if you need to contact me, it's best to simply focus on our bond and call to me, so you don't abruptly appear in my mind when I'm using my Gift. Oh ... and be sure to tell your red-headed, freckled youngling that his uncle said hello.

By the Maker! Daithi exclaimed. *I hope that someday someone comes along who knows more than you do and can cut that ridiculously large ego of yours down to size!*

Ferghus chuckled. *One can always find someone who knows more than they do, little brother. Some of us just have to search harder than others.*

Chapter 14

A fortnight later, the windswept fishing village of Gaotha was living up to its name. The winds were even more fierce than usual, battering the coast and sending sprays high over the stone jetty extending into the small bay. Not that anyone was there to see it, for not even the most intrepid fisherman had ventured forth this day, and all fishing boats had been taken as high up on the beach as possible. So there was no one to see the currach rounding the southern point in the late afternoon light. A witness would have gaped in disbelief, for the Celtic sea clans preferred raiding the northeast coast of Eire, seldom rounding the tip of it to reach the west. For a warrior currach to come from the south was unprecedented in living memory. A witness would have run to sound the alarm and warn the village of the boat being masterfully rowed through the tempestuous sea by eight strong men. Not a large raiding party, to be sure, but Gaotha was small and undefended, easy pickings for Celtic warriors, though little of value was likely to be found in the small fishing village. Yet the currach headed purposefully toward shore, bringing its load of eight warriors and a ninth Celt who plied no oar of his own. Faolán, Chieftain of the clan.

As the son of a prodigious Celtic raider on the eastern coast of Eire, Faolán had absorbed the skills of leadership at a young age. Chafing in his father's shadow as he grew older, he began spending time with Lorn, a captured fian on board his father's ship, who had willingly joined the crew but was not yet trusted to join a raiding party. The fianna, he learned, were land warriors, many of them having fallen out of favor in the armed forces of the Ard Rí, or the household of a lesser Rí. Unable to find employment, they had banded together in small groups that were rapidly becoming a serious thorn in the sides of those who had dismissed them. From Lorn, Faolán had also discovered which members of the crew would happily swap his father's leadership for his own ... a dozen men and Lorn himself, enough to start a warrior clan. So one night, when his father had drunk himself into a stupor, the fourteen of them had taken two currachs and left. Not for shore, where they would be expected to go, nor did they head south. They went north, the least likely direction to head in the winter.

Young though he was, Faolán had led them well enough to gain their respect, and all of the men had stayed with him, augmented by Lorn's northern band of fianna. Not daring to cross paths with his father, Faolán had taken them clear around the northern coast to the western one, in search of a secluded place of their own. The uninhabited, rocky island they'd found off the Connemara coast, with a sheltered bay facing west, was perfect ... for now. He'd spent the last two cycles growing his band and his fleet of currachs. And one day, Faolán promised himself, he would return to the eastern coast, unafraid to meet his father.

Now, as the currach glided toward shore, Faolán studied the village disparagingly. *I could leave my warriors on the beach and take this village myself! Foolish of Cathair to meet me here, where Lorn told me he grew up and has a decent sized home. He'd best hope we strike a deal, or there'll be nothing decent left of it.*

Faolán waited until his warriors had drawn the boat clear of the waves before he left it with three of his crew and strode toward the village with the other five, his leathers flapping slightly in the stiff wind. His name suited him well, for he was a short, wiry man with piercing green eyes ... as fierce and feral as one would expect a "little wolf" to be. His long, tangled red hair, refusing the confines of the thong binding most of it, blew wildly in the wind, and the sand crunched under his studded boots. A short sword was strapped across his back and two sheathed knives adorned his hips. He strode through the village to the only tavern, a weatherbeaten building with a sign clanking hollowly on its chains proclaiming it to be *The Pipit's Nest*. He threw open the door and entered as though he owned the place and fully expected every inhabitant within to acknowledge the fact.

In this he was not disappointed, for the fishermen fell silent at his entrance. The Chieftain scanned the room, then cocked his head and raised a brow at the two men seated at a large table against the far wall with a clear view of the room and door. The two men seated there blanched, abandoned the food and drink Réiltín, the serving "girl" of forty cycles, had just set there, and scuttled over to a different table. No one else moved as the six armed warriors strode to their chosen table and seated themselves. Faolán took a swig of ale from the abandoned flagon and smacked it back on the table with a curse.

The tavern keeper, a stout, elderly fellow who'd been called the Keeper for so long he'd nearly forgotten his own name, emerged from his kitchen and scowled at Réiltín, standing frozen against the wall. The words of annoyance on his lips vanished as he followed her frightened gaze and saw the table of Celtic warriors. He swallowed hard and nervously approached.

"And what might I be gettin' ye?" he asked deferentially.

Faolán glanced at the two meals in front of him. "I've plenty right here ... and already paid for as well," he said meaningfully, "but bring full meals for my men. Take this swill away and bring ale that hasn't been watered down." He stared at the man as though daring him to dispute the inferior quality of his ale.

The Keeper bowed acquiescence. "Right away!"

"And send a message to Cathair. Tell him Chieftain Faolán is here to see him … and he'd be well advised to be gettin' here before my meal is done."

The Keeper nodded and glared at Réiltín. "Ye heard the man! Get yer cloak and deliver the message, since yer of no use here."

She nodded and hurried to the kitchen, the Keeper on her heels.

"Get out the back quick, now, and don't be comin' back this night," he warned her in quite a different voice as she grabbed her cloak. "I don't want ye anywhere near the likes of them, and it's certain no one else'll be orderin' anythin' more 'til they move on."

She gave him a grateful glance. "I'll be here early tomorrow."

"There's no need to—"

"I'll be here," she said firmly and slipped out the garden door.

In the common room, the fishermen silently fortified themselves with sips of ale and directed sidelong glances at the warriors. Not even those closest to the door made a move to leave, tethered by their own curiosity and unwilling to draw attention to themselves. When the warriors ignored them and dug into the fried fish and potatoes the Keeper delivered with all haste to their table, hushed conversations began to circulate as the fishermen returned to their own interrupted meals.

It wasn't long before the front door blew open and Overdruid Cathair entered, a look of annoyance on his face. Chieftain and Overdruid locked eyes like two alpha wolves as Cathair slammed the door shut, strode to the table, and took the empty seat across from the warrior. All conversations in the room died.

"I would have preferred," Cathair said tightly, "to speak with you in *private*."

"And I'd have preferred to be dealin' with a *Council* member," Faolán said pointedly, glancing at the Overdruid's green robe with disdain. He glanced at his warriors. "See to our privacy."

The warriors immediately rose, unsheathed their swords, and advanced on the fishermen, one of them jerking his head toward the door. The room was speedily cleared as utensils clattered to the table and unfinished meals were abandoned. The warriors separated, two of them slipping through the front door, two out the back. The last one pushed a heavy table against the kitchen door and headed for the back rooms.

"You have your precious privacy," Faolán said levelly. "Now, explain to me why I traveled here from Carr in such weather."

"I sent an ample recompense for your trouble."

"The only reason I'm here. I don't leave my island unless I'm assured of making a profit. You've promised me a rich payment." The feral eyes bored into Cathair's. "To do something you apparently wish to keep secret. You'd best be telling me what it is without further delay, Druid. It's a long trip back, and if I don't accept your terms, I'll be sending a signal for the rest of my crew to join me and take what profit we may from this storm-cursed village of yours." His lips curled in a slight smile and his eyes lit, as though anticipating the pleasure razing the village would be.

"You'll do no such thing!" Cathair hissed.

"And who's to stop me?" Faolán's eyes glinted dangerously as he leaned back and fingered the long knife at his side.

"No one. But perhaps this will." Cathair reached into his robe and brought out a well-filled drawstring bag, which he tossed on the table in front of Faolán. "Consider it a down-payment."

The warrior's eyes narrowed. He opened the bag and slid a handful of stones and two nuggets onto the table. The stones were connemara marble of the highest quality and several amethyst crystals. The larger of the nuggets was galena with streaks of silver in it, the smaller was gold. He shrugged noncommittally.

"Very pretty, but its value is no more than I can gain from razing this village and a few others on the way back. Is there more where this came from?"

"A great deal more ... *if* you leave the Connemara coast untouched and succeed in your task."

Faolán leaned back. "And what, exactly, *is* this task?"

Cathair leaned forward intently. "To take the mine those stones came from."

"And who controls it now?"

"The Bardic Order."

Faolán snorted. "I may be a sea-faring Celt," he said, "but I'm not ignorant of matters on land. The Bard's mine is worthless!"

Cathair raised his brows at the stones on the table. "Do those look worthless to you?" He let that sink in for a moment. "The Bardic Order has to be getting their funds from somewhere, and it certainly isn't from the Rí, who only pay coin to their Healers and give the Order freedom of movement. The Bards have been very crafty in seeding the mountain with abandoned mines to make it look like the area is devoid of wealth, but I've finally tracked the real one down. My man waylaid one of the Bards coming from it." He stabbed a finger at the stones. "That's what he carried."

The warrior grunted. "Not much of a take."

Cathair shrugged. "It is when you multiply it by how many trips are going back and forth from it. Carrying small amounts minimizes the risk of anyone finding out how productive the mine is."

Faolán sat back down with an appraising look. "And what would prevent me from takin' control of this mine myself?"

Cathair snorted. "You haven't the knowledge to run it, much less do it without attracting attention. Bards and Druids can move freely through the Connemara mountains. Your warriors can make a single strike and disappear, but they can't take up residence without the Ard Rí's considerable forces showing up to push them back into the sea." He leaned back. "Far easier to sit comfortably on your rock of an island," he said, his voice intensifying as he leaned forward, "and receive a steady percentage of the profits of a well-run mine. A mine containing veins of everything on that table, and more." he smiled. "Do I have your attention now?"

The gleam in Faolán's eyes belied his nonchalant tone of voice.

"Perhaps. Tell me, Druid ... what do you hope to gain from this?"

Cathair's brow lifted. "Is control of such a mine not enough?"

The warrior rolled his eyes. "Don't be trying to outfox a fox. We both know it's your Order that will control it, not you. What do *you* stand to gain?"

Cathair frowned and said nothing, but Faolán's sharp eyes caught the glance the Overdruid gave his forest green robe.

"Ah," Faolán said knowingly. "It's a robe of a different color you're wanting, then. A darker robe with a lighter cord to offset it, I'll wager. Emerald and silver, perhaps ... with a silver staff insignia?" He crossed his arms and looked speculatively at the silent Overdruid, as though imagining him garbed thus. "I must admit, you'd look quite fine dressed as a member of the Druidic Council, young though you are. Of course, you'd have to move all the way to the Druid's Hall in Uisneach, wouldn't you? But perhaps you wouldn't mind trekking over eight hundred furlongs to get away from here." He looked around in distaste. "*I* certainly wouldn't."

"I want a place on the Council," Cathair said evenly. "You want coin. Working together can give us both what we want. I have the sworn oath of the First of the Council to give a half percent of the mine's profits to the one responsible for their takeover."

"And would that be me, Druid ... or you?"

"It will come to me," Cathair admitted reluctantly, "and I will, of course, hand it over to you."

"Will you, now?" the warrior asked idly.

"I know perfectly well what would happen to me if I didn't."

"Make it two percent and I'll consider it."

"Two!" The Overdruid exclaimed. "Do you have any idea how long it took to get an agreement for a *half* percent?"

"Your problem, Druid, not mine. Two percent."

"Would you consider—"

"No. Two percent and we have a deal. Not otherwise."

Cathair sat fuming in his chair for a moment, then sighed.

"Very well, then, two percent it is. I'll get his agreement somehow." *So, he thinks himself a fox and me a fool, does he?* A vision of the Council Hall came to him, with its open walls and ceiling, its trees, expertly pruned to be kept small. He could almost smell the scent of flowering shrubs and the lush carpet of grass leading up to the immense Council table of connemara marble.

Outside, a heavy rain began to fall. A flutter of wings announced the arrival of a small whinchat, who perched on the narrow ledge just under one of the partially opened windows of the tavern, ruffled its feathers and hunkered down as though grateful to find a dry perch. Neither man paid the bird any attention.

Cathair arched a brow at Faolán. "After the takeover of the Bard's mine is successfully accomplished, your men will remain there to ensure our safety as we assess its value. Once that's complete, they'll be sent back. From then on, you'll be paid two percent of the mine's profits each quarter-cycle, for as long as our Order retains that control."

"I'll expect my men to be bringing back a full report of the mine's productivity," Faolán said, his eyes boring into Cathair's.

"Of course. They can verify its accuracy."

"One of them will return each quarter to receive our two percent ... and ensure its *continued* accuracy."

"I would expect no less," Cathair said. "I also expect you to send two of your fianna to me after you're satisfied with the first report. They'll remain with me until I get what *I* want."

Faolán's brows lifted. "Do you not trust Odhran to keep his word?"

"Let's just say that I'll trust him more after he keeps it. Until then, I'm an expendable liability. The presence of your men will make it easier for him to keep his word than to rid himself of me. So ... do we have a deal?"

Faolán gave him a look bordering on respect. "We do."

The two men clasped arms across the table, then rose to leave.

"And next time," Cathair said, "have the sense to come to my home, not here."

Faolán snorted as he tied the bag of stones to his belt. "If you give me cause to seek you out on my own, Druid, you won't live long enough to care where you are." He gave a shrill whistle to recall his men. "How many rooms?" he asked one of them.

"Four, none of 'em occupied."

The Chieftain nodded and his men headed toward the rooms. Faolán glanced at Cathair. "Tell the fool in the kitchen we'll be leaving at dawn's light and will expect to be fed before we go." Without waiting for a reply, he followed his men.

Outside the window, the whinchat took flight.

Next to the Oak in the center of the Grove of Gaotha, Daithi collapsed in exhaustion. Never had he traveled for so long in a bird before, and it felt like his mind was still part avian, free to fly the skies and reluctant to return to the body it belonged in.

Transferring his awareness from a hawthorn into a nesting bird was a skill that, to Daithi's knowledge, no other Druid had or even knew about. A costly skill in energy and risk, which was why he had not divulged this ability to anyone else. Traveling an energy line drained one's own energy, and although he could replenish it from a tree's chromafield without harming it, he couldn't risk depleting the energy of a bird in flight.

Contrary to what he had led Cathair to believe, he could have traveled to the village almost as quickly as the whinchat had flown there, using the chromafields of trees, roots, and even the soil itself. Then he could have transferred into the chromafield of a bird that could take him wherever he wished. He had used this method many times before to keep himself abreast of the doings in Gaotha, particularly Cathair's. This time, however, the storm prevented it, for the birds were hunkered down in their nests, and it would have taken too much time to find one. Here in the Grove, he knew the location of all of them, so he had chosen one to fly him all the way to the tavern and back through the storm. Too tired now to pull energy from the ground, he lay motionless. His mind wandered as he rested, remembering the first time he had seen an energy field.

Daithi was ten cycles old when Ferghus left to join the Bardic Order. The first time he ventured out without his brother's protection, one of his tormentors spotted him and ran off with a whoop of victory. Panicking at the thought of what would happen when he returned with his two friends, Daithi left the road for the woods, limping along as quickly as he could. When no one pursued him, he slowed his gait and wandered aimlessly for awhile, enjoying the peace and solitude ... until he heard the taunting calls of the boys as they searched the woods for him. He stumbled through the trees, the boys hooting and yelling as they spotted him and closed in. He looked back in terror, then slipped and fell, sprawling at the feet of a Druid who had apparently appeared out of thin air. The imposing man was garbed in a robe of rich chestnut brown with the insignia of a twisted branch on the left front shoulder, bound at the waist with a beige cord. His wiry grey hair was tied back with a thong, and his eyes flashed with cinnamon and emerald brilliance. Daithi gasped, seeing for the first time someone with eyes like his own. The three boys came to an abrupt halt.

Why do you chase him? demanded the Druid.

No one said a word.

The Druid's face darkened. He stared at each boy in turn, holding his staff out toward them as he intoned their full names. *Every action sends the energy of your intent out from you,* he said sternly. *And what you send out will return. Watch for it, and when it comes, remember this day and all the others like it, when you took pleasure in tormenting someone weaker than yourselves.* He struck his staff on the ground three times. *If ever you do so again, harm will return to you threefold before the cycle is over, for you are three against one. So I have said it. So it will be.*

The boys, their eyes wide with fear, turned and ran. The Druid held out his hand and helped Daithi to his feet.

Thank you for your help, sir.

When the opportunity to help another comes to you, the Druid told him, *do the same.*

Daithi solemnly nodded. *You ... knew their names?* he hesitantly asked.

I know the names of most of the inhabitants of Ganach, though few of them know mine. I'm Druid Cillian.

Will they really be hurt themselves if they keep hurting me?

The Druid's brow quirked. *Are you asking me if I lied to them? A Druid does not lie. Take care of your thoughts, to keep them bright and positive. For what you think emanates from you and will return to you in the circulating flow of your own energy. Brightness begets brightness. Darkness, more darkness. Thus, you are creating yourself with every thought you think.* He gave Daithi a keen look. *You still have brightness within you, youngling. Do not let the darkness of others overshadow it.*

Daithi considered this. *Hurting me would come back to them eventually, then. But ... you told them that harm would come to them threefold before the cycle is up.*

The eyes so like his own flickered with amusement. *Ah, now you're asking me if I used magic to curse them with details. If so, it was with their own belief.* He leaned on his staff. *Look around you, Daithi. There is magic in everything you see. But the most powerful magic is what you believe in your soul to be true. If they believe the harm they inflict will return to them threefold—and their own belief will indeed bring it about—they will not risk harming you again.* He turned to leave.

But if it wasn't magic— Daithi gathered his courage. *Then what were the colors that came from your staff when you pointed it at each of them?*

The Druid froze. *Colors?*

Daithi nodded, looking wonderingly at the rowan staff. *They're still there. Swirling golds, mostly. Some browns and greens. I've never seen anything like it before.*

The Druid turned and looked at him appraisingly. *Perhaps you and I should talk. Come along.*

They walked together the rest of the afternoon, through woods dappled with sunlight, and meadows filled with wildflowers. Druid Cillian showed Daithi hidden, shadowy places near hardwood trees where chanterelles were plentiful, telling him the mushrooms would continue to grow in the same place every cycle.

Daithi looked at the chanterelles with interest. *The mushrooms I collect for my Mam grow on stumps and logs.*

Most do, but not chanterelles. And unlike other mushrooms, which grow quickly within a week or two, chanterelles grow slowly for half a season, so only pick the large ones and let the others continue to grow. The Druid taught him how to identify the tasty mushrooms by their appearance and their slightly fruity aroma. *There are no other mushrooms that look the same in all Eire, so you needn't fear being poisoned. If it lacks the aroma, however, you have a different type of chanterelle. It will do you no harm, but it's bitter to the taste.*

They collected edible roots and berries, Cillian telling him fascinating things about them. Finally, Daithi reluctantly said he needed to finish his chores before his father came home.

Would you let me come to see you again? he asked hopefully.

I'll be in this area for a time, the Druid told him. *Do you see the rowan over there? Sit against its trunk and I'll come.*

But, how will you know I'm there?

The Druid pointed his staff at the tree. *Tell me what you see.*

More colors! Daithi exclaimed. *Going from your staff to the tree.* He stared in wonder at the shimmering flow, then the Druid lowered his staff and the colors faded away.

This staff was made from the deadfall wood of that same tree, Cillian told him. *It has an affinity for it, so its energy field, which is what you're seeing the colors of, is pulled toward it. You might say the staff is aware of the tree it came from. If you're sitting against the tree, youngling, I'll know.*

Daithi studied the staff. *Can all Druids do that?*

No. I left my Order to travel alone for two reasons, one of which was to find someone else who could. The Druid cocked an eye at him. *I believe I'm looking at him now.*

From then on, the two of them met frequently. Under the Druid's strict and often gruff tutelage, Daithi absorbed and memorized information on flora and fauna, herbal remedies, and the entire detailed history of Eire. He learned how to detect and travel the energy lines of objects, plants, and trees. But the most important thing the Druid taught him was something no one else could have ... how to travel the colorful fields such things emitted, giving him a freedom of movement his own body would not allow. And the day after he turned of age, Daithi left home and followed Cillian with the firm conviction that this was where he belonged.

At the moment, however, soaked to the skin and lying exhausted with his face against the wet ground, one could perhaps pardon Daithi for having second thoughts. Yet he knew he would go to far greater lengths than this to help Ferghus. And trips to the tavern to collect the gossip of fishermen were seldom necessary since the day Réiltín, the serving-girl at *The Pipit's Nest,* had come to his door begging his help for her dying mother five cycles ago. He had snagged his satchel of herbs and tonics and gone back with her. He could not halt the progression of her mother's illness, but he had bolstered her energy with his own and left Réiltín with herbs to ease her mother's pain and give her a few more months of life before the end. Since then, Réiltín had brought him information on anything of importance that happened at the tavern, and kept a window there slightly ajar at his request.

Earlier today she had arrived at his home in the pouring rain, breathless with excitement, to tell him that warriors had come to the tavern and were meeting with Cathair that very moment. As soon as she left, Daithi had gone straight to the Grove. Once he had transferred his energy into the whinchat, it had been a simple matter to direct the bird to *The Pipit's Nest*.

He had made it to the tavern in time to see the face of the warrior through the slightly open, rain-spattered window and easily recognize Cathair's answering voice. He'd heard enough to realize a bargain had just been made to take over the Bard's mine, the Overdruid having apparently discovered its location. The moment the warrior left, Daithi had returned with the whinchat back through the wind and rain to its nest. Once the bird's energy field overlapped the hawthorn's, Daithi had transferred his energy into the tree, and from there back through the Grove to himself just as the rain finally stopped. Daithi lay against the ground, the wet grass tickling his face, and dug his fingers into the moist earth, letting its energy flow into him. Partially restored, he rolled over onto his back with a fleeting wish for the rain to resume, for he could not remember ever being so parched.

"Better, Grovekeeper?" The concerned face of Alben looked anxiously into his.

"In a moment," Daithi rasped.

Alben unslung a skin of water, then supported Daithi's head and helped him drink. The Grovekeeper thirstily drained it.

"Much better now," Daithi said. "Thank you." He sat up and gratefully accepted the dry blanket the old man offered him. "What are you doing here at such an hour?"

"I often take a walk through the Grove of an evening," Alben said. "An old man like me sleeps all the better for it."

"Walking around in the pouring rain with a pack containing a full water skin and a blanket helps you sleep?"

A brief smile crossed the old man's face. "Wasn't raining when I left, though I could smell it coming, and I like to keep an eye out."

Daithi's mouth quirked. "For me? Or for the faeries?"

"Now, then," Alben said reproachfully, "No harm in looking out for both, is there? Us old trees like to make ourselves useful."

"You've seen me here before, then, yet you've said nothing."

"Not my business what the Grovekeeper does of an evening."

"And the faeries?"

Alben shrugged. "I suppose that's none of my business either ... but there's been a time or two I've heard something."

"Really?" Daithi looked at him with interest. "Such as?"

"Singing. Beautiful, it was." Rapture removed several cycles of age from the old man's face. "One of these days I'm going to see them," he said with conviction.

"I'm sure you will." Daithi cleared his throat. "I would appreciate you keeping my ... evening activities ... confidential."

"Of course, Grovekeeper, of course, as I've always done."

"And if anyone were to ask?"

"Why, I'd tell them the Maker's own truth." Alben's eyes held not a particle of guile. "I took a walk, as I often do, and came across the Grovekeeper taking a bit of a nap in the grass, so I did. It's not for me to be questioning why, so I asked no questions." He shook his head disapprovingly, as though the Grovekeeper were a rebellious child caught out of bed. "Perhaps you should head for your own bed now. You're sure to sleep well for all the night air you've taken." He held out a hand.

Daithi chuckled and accepted the old man's hand to help him to his feet. "You're a good man, Alben."

The old man snorted. "Not to hear my wife tell it."

"Is that why she refused to live in the Grove with you?" Daithi asked in amusement.

"She didn't want to live out here in what she called 'the wilds'.

Always said I'd be the death of her, and I guess she was right, for though she was the younger of us, she passed away ten cycles ago."

Daithi chuckled, thanked Alben for his help, and headed home. He checked on Shay to be sure the boy was sound asleep, then quietly closed his bedroom door and built up the fire. He stood near it for awhile, welcoming its drying warmth, and thought about what he had overheard at *The Pipit's Nest*.

Having found the mine, Cathair would have gone straight to Odhran, hoping to curry favor with the First. Odhran would see it as a golden opportunity to arrange the takeover with no risk to himself. If the venture failed, a single renegade Overdruid could be turned over to the Ard Rí with apologies and no harm done to the Order.

Daithi snorted. He trusted Odhran no more than he had Bran, Odhran's predecessor. The dusky blue and shadowy purple of the current First's chromafield showed him to be cold and highly manipulative, and the charcoal black of deceit did not improve the blend.

It's difficult to deceive someone who can see the colors of an energy field. Trust what you see, Daithi, not what you hear.

His mentor's words spoke clearly in his mind, and Daithi turned his thoughts back to the Overdruid. Disposing of a single renegade Grovekeeper wouldn't pose any moral dilemma for Cathair. If the ambitious Overdruid found out that the Prime of the Bardic Order was Daithi's brother, his life would be forfeit.

Daithi took his seat, distractedly feeling the interlocking leaves of his ring. Ferghus had sent him the ring when Daithi became a Grovekeeper and it had never left his finger since. His brother had a similar one, engraved with tiny notes on a swirling music staff, that Daithi had sent him when he became a Master Bard. As he turned the ring on his finger, he closed his eyes. Ferghus needed to know what he had overheard.

A moment later he was looking in awe at the colorful bond

with his brother, one that emanated a chromafield of its own. He pushed aside the temptation to travel it and spoke.

Ferghus!

His brother's chromafield appeared only a moment later, smoky grey worry swirling through it. *What's wrong?*

Cathair has discovered where your mine is! He met with a warrior named Faolán at The Pipit's Nest a few hours ago. In return for taking over your mine, Faolán's to receive two percent of its profits. He's returning to Carr in the morning to lead his warriors to the mine's location. For a long moment, Daithi's mind was as silent as if Ferghus had left. At last his brother spoke, his voice tightly controlled.

I've picked up quite a bit of information on Faolán, and none of it is good. How did you find out about this?

I was told of the meeting in time to catch a ride with a whinchat to an open window of the tavern ... in a rainstorm, I might add. I got there in time to hear their agreement.

A bird? Ferghus asked in surprise. *I'm going to want to hear about that later, brother. Right now there's much to arrange and no time to bother with my Council. I must act immediately. Thank you for letting me know ... you've just saved the lives of three of our Bards.*

And with that, Ferghus was gone.

Daithi blinked. The Bardic Order's mine was manned by only three Bards? He filed the question away for later and turned his attention to more immediate concerns. Cathair's suspicions of him were already aroused. It was likely the Grove was being watched. Perhaps it would be wise to tire of Shay's cooking and take a meal or two at *The Pipit's Nest*. Réiltín must not make any more trips to the Grove, or she might well be reunited with her mother sooner than she'd like.

Chapter 15

Spring had just begun to decorate the hills with primroses, blue-bells, and bright yellow celandine when Daithi decided it was time to introduce his protégé to traveling energy lines. The boy had exceeded all his expectations, eagerly absorbing everything he was taught. Detecting energy lines and actually traveling them, however, were two quite different things. Daithi had planned on waiting until he was a bit older, but had reconsidered. For Shay was ready, and it certainly wouldn't do for the boy to start experimenting on his own. Most of their lessons were held in the center of the Grove when no one was likely to disturb them. So, early one evening, the two of them stood near the Oak.

"You've done well in learning how to sense the energy lines of everything in the Grove, especially the tree roots," the Grovekeeper said approvingly. "I think it's time for you to begin learning how to send your own awareness toward an energy line. We'll start by eliminating all distractions. This is training we give to all of our Druids, and the Masters of the Bardic Order give to all their Bards. They call it a sense-deprivation test, which enhances their sensitivity to music. We call it energy training, which enhances our sensitivity to energy lines. Their Bards must endure it for a week; we do it in several sessions of an hour or so." He glanced at the Oak.

"Sit between those two roots with your back against the tree."

Shay positioned himself accordingly and watched with interest as Daithi withdrew a drawstring bag from his robe.

"I'm going to shield your eyes," the Grovekeeper told him. "Your ears will be plugged with wax, and you're forbidden to speak until the session is over. I'll be here with you the whole time. Concentrate on feeling the energy of the roots on either side of you, and the trunk of the tree against your back. Your own energy will respond to the tree's energy and you'll feel it as a tingle, just like the tingle in your feet when you're standing directly over one of its roots. See if you can take your awareness closer by focusing on the halfway point between yourself and the tingling energy, then imagine yourself flowing toward it. If you're successful, you will no longer be aware of your own body or the sounds of the woods. You'll hear only the pulsation of the energy lines, and see them as two scintillating streams. You might even be able to detect which one is flowing toward the tree and up the trunk, and which is flowing away. Go no closer, just observe them for a few moments, then visualize yourself flowing back. Practice doing this several times. During the session, I might silently approach you and attempt to touch one of your shoulders. If you sense this as a third energy line, stop me by grasping my arm. If I touch your hand, that will indicate the session is over. Do you understand?"

Shay nodded.

Daithi suppressed a chuckle. There was no fear on the face that looked expectantly into his, only the excitement of a boy about to go adventuring. The Grovekeeper brought out a pair of eye shields, which he placed over Shay's eyes and bound with several layers of cloth. Then he took a small portion of wax and softened it by infusing a small portion of his own energy into it to produce warmth. Shay sat against the Oak, motionless and tense.

"Relax, lad. Tension will keep you from sensing anything. The tree does not see or hear in the same way we do, and yet it's open and alive to everything around it. For just a little while, don't be Shay. Be a tree." Then he firmly plugged the youngster's ears with the softened wax and stepped back.

Shay expelled a deep breath and leaned his head back against the tree. After several moments, the Grovekeeper silently approached him. The boy stiffened slightly, as though fully aware of his presence. Daithi waited for several moments, then reached out toward his shoulder. Shay's hand shot out, grasping the approaching arm and preventing his touch. The Grovekeeper smiled and moved silently behind the tree. Shay relaxed.

Without warning or sound, Daithi reached around the trunk to touch the boy's other shoulder, but once again found his arm gripped by Shay's hand. The Grovekeeper's brow lifted. *This youngling is Gifted, indeed!* He moved out from behind the tree and watched as Shay practiced detecting the Oak's energy lines and sending his awareness halfway to them, his body going limp as he succeeded, then moving restlessly as he returned to himself. The Grovekeeper's brow lifted again, impressed with how well Shay was doing. He had almost decided to end the test when the hand he was about to reach for tentatively moved toward the exposed root and touched it. The small fingers lightly stroked it, reminding Daithi of the way the youngster had touched the feathered top of a carrot when they first met. Shay made no sound, but Daithi knew he was humming tunelessly in his mind. The Grovekeeper's eyes narrowed as stood back, folded his arms, and watched.

After awhile the boy went limp again. His head fell to the side and the small hand resting on the tree root slid slowly to the ground. Daithi stood looking down on what seemed to be his peacefully sleeping protégé. The Grovekeeper, however, knew the look of someone traveling an energy line; the youngster's eyes moved rapidly behind their lids, his breathing was fast and even. Shay hadn't fallen asleep from the boredom of repetitively traveling halfway to the Oak's energy lines and back. Guided by the connection his touch and humming had produced, he had not only moved *toward* an energy line, he had immersed himself *in* it.

Daithi closed his eyes and instantly perceived the energy of the boy's awareness moving tentatively and somewhat furtively up the tree trunk, as if expecting any moment to be dragged back to the body it belonged in. Daithi chuckled, not surprised that Shay had disobeyed him for the first time. Enthralled with his discovery of the two flows and quickly bored with practicing what was apparently easy for him to do, Shay had been unable to resist exploring. And the tree-climbing boy had not chosen the flow of his own energy, but the far more powerful upward flow of the Oak's.

Ah, youth! Not the slightest idea where they're going half the time, but blundering on ahead anyhow. Ferghus always said most discoveries are made by young fools who have no idea what they're doing. This particular young fool, however, needs to be taught a lesson.

Daithi sent his awareness into his own chromafield and from there into that of the Oak's, where he easily caught up to Shay, who was traveling the energy line of the upward flow of sap like a glistening bubble. Staying far enough back to remain undetected, Daithi followed the youngling up the trunk to the crown of the tree. Shay ignored the many turns he could have taken, climbing straight up toward the highest branch. He moved smoothly with the flow now, as though confident he would not be intercepted, and traveled it to where the energy line, now much narrower, split off to the right. Deciding to take this, the youngster followed it to where another decision had to be made. He could continue on course or take an even smaller flow to either side of him. Here he hesitated for a moment, then again took the one to the right. This flow branched off twice more, but the boy kept to the main path this time until it abruptly came to an end.

Still the Grovekeeper kept his distance, watching as Shay floundered, trying unsuccessfully to return the way he had come.

When Daithi was certain the youngster understood he was trapped, unable to move against the current that had taken him there, the Grovekeeper moved forward. Coming close to the panicking boy, Daithi touched Shay, who recoiled in fear. Having expected this, the Grovekeeper pressed harder, pushing the bubble against the wall of the channel and keeping it firmly trapped.

It's me, Shay. Stop fighting. As long as our energy fields overlap, we can communicate.

The boy surged against Daithi so hard that the Grovekeeper found himself pressed against the opposite wall, Shay clinging frantically to him.

Please help me! I can't get back ... I don't know how! I'm sorry! I'll never disobey ye again, only please get me ba—

Hush! The Grovekeeper's command cut the hysterical cries off. The bubble clinging to his quivered, and Daithi spoke with quiet firmness. *Panicking will use up your remaining energy all the faster, making it even harder to get back. Calm yourself, Shay, and listen to me. If you do exactly what I tell you to, you'll make it safely back again. Do you understand?*

Y-yes.

Very well, then ... while we're here, you might as well learn a few things besides obedience. The trunk of a tree has five layers of energy, Daithi instructed. *The two that are strong enough for an acolyte to detect are the ones made up of flowing channels of sap, one of them going up, the other going down. Not surprisingly,* he said dryly, *you chose to enter the one going up. And where do you suppose the first turn you took led you?*

To one of the branches ... I think.

Yes, the highest one, in fact. And the turn you took after that?

I'm not sure. A smaller branch, maybe?

Yes, then to two much smaller twigs, and that's where the flow came to its end, having successfully traveled from root to leaf, bringing a disobedient youngling along with it.

Fear gave way to intrigue. *I'm trapped inside a leaf?*

Specifically, in the tiny nodule of what will soon become a bud and eventually a leaf. And what do you suppose would happen if the wind were to rise and tear this tiny twig off its branch, to go twirling down to the ground ... or perhaps be blown clean out of the Grove?

Intrigue fled as fear surged anew. *I ... I would...* The frightened voice fell silent.

Die? Yes. Without the knowledge of how to return to your body, you would indeed die, just as you would have surely died right here if I hadn't followed you. Regardless, whether on the ground or still attached to the tree, you would last only as long as the leaf bud. As it dried out and fell apart, or leafed and eventually did the same, you would be released from it to return to the Maker ... who would hopefully install a better set of ears for instructions before sending you onward or back again. Your body, sitting against the tree, would be unresponsive to anyone's attempts to awaken or feed it. Your breathing would slow—bit by bit—and eventually stop altogether. The Grovekeeper briefly paused. *We would, of course, hold a service for you here in the Grove, where I would extol your virtues and not mention the disobedience that led to your untimely demise.*

Fear gave way to utter horror.

Do you understand now why I told you not to go farther than the halfway point?

Yes, sir, came the chastened whisper.

Listen well this time, then, and do exactly what I tell you to. As you've already discovered, you can't fight against the powerful flow of an energy line in the Oak. Fortunately for you, even the nodule of a leaf has channels of sap flowing in both directions. We need to transfer into one that's going down.

But I don't know how!

Well, you shouldn't know how, that's certain, Daithi said

dryly, *but you've already demonstrated that you do, whether you understood what you were doing or not. The day we met, you hummed to a carrot that wasn't doing as well as the others. That carrot wasn't getting as much energy from the soil. By touching and humming to it, you matched the vibrational speed of your energy to its own. Since your energy field is much stronger than the carrot's, that exerted an upward pull, bringing more energy from the ground into the carrot and enabling better growth. And, after hearing about your uncanny gardening abilities from my Grovetenders for the last three seasons, I suspect you've been humming away in their gardens as well. And afterwards, you're tired, aren't you?*

Sometimes I fall asleep right there in the garden.

Now you know why. That's nothing, however, compared to how exhausted you're going to be after this little escapade. For you treated the Oak exactly like the carrot, moving your hand to touch the root next to you and humming to it in your mind. This most ancient of Oaks, however, is hardly an ailing carrot, and matching its energy is not to be done lightly. Once the speed of your energy matched that of the Oak's, its stronger energy pulled yours all the way toward it. Still, had you stopped humming and followed your own energy back to yourself while it still overlapped the Oak's, you would have come to no harm. Instead, you foolishly allowed yourself to be pulled into the Oak's upward flow and away from yourself with no knowledge whatsoever of how to bring yourself back. Open your awareness now, just as you did with the carrot and the Oak, and tell me what you sense.

For a moment, all was silent except for the fluid movement of the sap. When Shay spoke again, his voice was raised with panic.

I don't sense anything!

Relax, lad. Fear is the great paralyzer. If you allow it to dominate your mind, you won't be able to extricate yourself. I'm going to push you back against the other wall. He waited for a moment until the boy stopped quivering, then moved him to the other side. *What do you sense now?*

The youngster answered almost immediately. *Tingling!*

That's the downward channel running alongside this one. Since humming works well for you, hum exactly what you hear, then send yourself into its flow. It will move much slower than the one you followed up, as if the sap is encountering invisible barriers that slow its downward path. Don't panic at the sensation, for none of them will trap you, and I'll be right behind you.

Shay obediently began humming, soon matching the vibration the Grovekeeper could clearly hear next to them. The bubble moved slowly through the wall of the channel and disappeared.

Daithi followed and found the lad clinging to the wall of the other channel, as unwilling to move downward as a cat up a tree. Daithi gently touched him. *I'm right here, Shay. Can you see me?*

You look like a bubble filled with green, gold, and blue. What do I look like? He asked curiously.

A bubble filled with the same emerald green as mine, and more burnt orange and indigo than any youngling ought to be allowed ... which explains the adventuring curiosity that got you into this mess. Right now, it's time for you to head back down to where your energy overlaps that of the tree's, Daithi said sternly. *No deviations, and you're to do precisely what I tell you.*

I promise!

When at last Daithi opened his eyes, wind and moonlight were chasing shadows around the Grove. He looked down on Shay, who was just beginning to rouse, his face pale with exhaustion. The Grovekeeper removed his eye shields and ear plugs.

"That was awesome," the youngster breathed. He glanced up at the Grovekeeper and lowered his eyes. "I guess I'm in a lot of trouble," he said morosely.

"That would be an excellent guess."

"I'm sorry, sir," Shay said miserably.

"You and I will have a thorough discussion about this tomorrow," Daithi sternly promised. "For now, suffice it to say that there are other dangers besides the ones you encountered today. You are not to hum or travel *any* kind of energy line without my permission and presence. Am I understood?"

Shay quickly nodded. "Yes, sir. I won't disobey you again."

"Now, then, have you recovered enough to get to your feet?" Daithi held out a hand.

The youngster gave him a grateful look and grasped it, but once on his feet, swayed and would have fallen if the Grovekeeper hadn't steadied him.

"Let's sit here awhile," Daithi suggested, and Shay sank gratefully back against the trunk of the Oak.

"Sorry," the boy mumbled, "I'll ... be okay ... in just a bit."

Daithi sat down next to him and pulled him close. Shay stiffened in surprise, then relaxed and nestled his head against the Grovekeeper's shoulder.

"By tomorrow evening, perhaps," Daithi murmured.

Shay sighed and fell sound asleep. The Grovekeeper sat there for a few moments, wondering how he was going to get the youngster back home, when a tall figure emerged from behind a rowan.

"Alben?" Daithi asked in surprise.

"Aye, it's me."

"A bit late for a walk ... I doubt even the faeries are still up."

"Plenty of moonlight tonight, so I thought I'd take a turn around the Grove." Alben glanced at Shay. "I can see the lad's exhausted, and you must be tired yourself, late as it is and all. Perhaps you'd let me carry him back for you?"

Daithi nodded gratefully. "I'd appreciate that."

Alben hoisted the sleeping youngster over his shoulder, and a tired sigh escaped Daithi as he stood up and leaned on his staff.

"You have an uncanny knack of knowing when I need someone," the Grovekeeper said.

Alben was silent as they began walking, then he abruptly cleared his throat. "I'll tell you what I know," he said. "I know you didn't bring the lad here in order to produce another Druid out of him, a boy all of us like but none of us wanted as an acolyte. I know you have an affinity with trees that far surpasses anything I've ever seen, and I know Shay has one with gardens. Doesn't take deep thinking to realize you've found a protégé you can teach everything you know to. And I know the teaching of things no one else likely knows is best done in private, late like. So, I've stepped up my evening walks." He glanced sideways at Daithi's astonished expression. "Beyond that, I know nothing, except that you can count on me to always be here in the Grove when you or your lad need me." He shrugged. "You're a superb Grovekeeper ... always looking out for the Grove and for us, and we all know it. Now you have a youngling to look out for as well. Wouldn't hurt, would it, if someone looked out for you?"

Daithi chuckled softly. "No, Alben. It wouldn't hurt one bit."

They walked on, their conversation turning to the coming Bealtaine festival, marking the day the cattle were driven out to the summer pastures. Whereas at Imbolc all hearth fires were kept lit day and night, at Bealtaine they were all put out, then relit from bonfires set in the center of the village. Every family put a handful of oak leaves into the bonfires, most of them from the Grove.

"The shed is full of oak leaves we collected last fall," Alben said in satisfaction, "so there'll be plenty of smoke for the villagers and cattle to walk through."

Daithi nodded approval. The smoke would provide strength and protection for those who walked through it, ashes smeared on hide and hands for good measure. Yellow flowers symbolizing the flames would adorn every home, and oatcake dough would be braided and baked in the bonfires. Many of those loaves would find their way to the Grove in appreciation for the powerful leaves.

"And our supplies of rowan wood?" Daithi asked. "Orders for

staves and rods are beginning to come in."

"We've a goodly supply, properly sorted," Alben assured him. "Wasn't a hard winter, but we've had plenty of windstorms to give us a nice stockpile of deadfall, and we've already made a few dozen staves and a dozen rods from them."

"Excellent."

"Have you any dried mistletoe leaves left for tea?" Alben asked. "You and the lad could use some, and the mistletoe from the Oak is especially strong. Eoin climbed up and cut it himself, and Dughan made sure and certain it never touched the ground."

"I've still some left," Daithi assured him. He limped up to his front door and opened it for Alben, who carried Shay to his room and settled him comfortably into his bed. The boy didn't stir.

Alben turned and found Daithi standing at the open door, his eyes fixed on the sleeping youngster, and an unguarded expression on his face that made the old man smile.

"There's something else I know," Alben said softly.

The Grovekeeper tore his eyes away from the sleeping young-ster and glanced at him. "And what would that be?"

"I know that you'd make an excellent father."

Chapter 16

Six weeks after Faolán's first visit to *The Pipit's Nest*, Cathair sat glaring at him over the same table that had hosted their first meeting. "I told you to come to my home, not here!" he stated angrily.

"If I come to your home, Druid, you won't be expecting me and it won't be to talk," Faolán said meaningfully. "My men cleared the room the moment you arrived. If you want it more private than this, we'll leave and you can row yourself to Carr."

The Overdruid scowled. "Did you bring the men I require?"

"No."

"You agreed to bring two of them!"

"When the mine was proven *viable*," Faolán retorted. "It's taken your men six weeks just to know it's likely the right mine ... and all the time my men have been kept there, clearin' it for you! Can't your Druids," he asked bitingly, "use their magic to clear it themselves?"

"Your men have been generously paid for the trouble!"

"But *I* have not! I'll send your henchmen in three weeks' time, not before, and only if I'm given clear proof that the mine's viable. Four bags like the last one might convince me. Otherwise my men stay with me, and you can take your chances with Odhran."

"You'll get your proof." Cathair leaned back in his chair and gave Faolán a sly look. "In the meantime, you can begin planning an attack that will ensure that your earnings not only continue, but increase to three percent of the mine's profits as well. Don't bother trying to get more," he warned, "because I can't give it."

The Chieftain's eyes narrowed. "*Now* what do you want?"

"I want you to break the Bardic Order."

Faolán stared at him for another long moment. "You want me to wipe out an Order whose members are scattered all across Eire?" he asked incredulously, then threw back his head and laughed. "And here I thought I was dealing with a man of reasonable intelligence." He got to his feet.

"I didn't ask you to wipe the Order out," Cathair said evenly. "I asked you to break it. It will wipe *itself* out after that."

"You have their mine, Druid. Why destroy them?"

"They're going to want it back again and are surely making plans to do to us what we just did to them. Your fianna are not the only ones for hire. And if the mine leaves our control, your earnings vanish with it. Three percent of nothing is nothing."

"Even if I were to be riddin' you of every member of the Bardic Order on the western coast," Faolán growled, "there would still be hundreds of them elsewhere. Do you think the rest of them will line up on the beach for my convenience? Whatever else they may be, the Bards are not fools!"

"You need only make a single strike," Cathair said. "One that will decimate all the Masters and most of the Bards. The few that are left will be demoralized and unable to revive their Order."

The Chieftain's eyes narrowed as he sat back down. "There are more than just Masters and Bards in the Bardic Order."

Cathair waved a dismissive hand. "Harpists, Pipers, Lutists ... teachers of their instruments, of no interest to the Rí, and thus no threat to our positions with them. It's the Bards and Masters that are the true threat. With them gone, the others will swiftly remove their robes and blend into the common folk of Eire. Traveling minstrels will soon be all that's left of the mighty Bardic Order. And every village and town that has given them their allegiance will change their tune and give it to us."

"And what of the Ard Rí?" Faolán demanded. "I have no more desire to run afoul of him than Odhran does. An occasional raid on coastal villages or towns is tolerated; a strike against the Bardic Order will not be!"

"And a single raid on a coastal town is all this will be," Cathair assured him. "A shame there happened to be an unusual number of Bards and Masters there at the time. If they got themselves killed in the pillaging..." He sighed. "A truly tragic coincidence."

Silence fell over the tavern's common room, the only sounds the clatter of dishes from behind the blocked kitchen door. Then the Chieftain slapped his belt knife on the table, the sharp point aimed directly at Cathair, who threw him a startled glance.

"You want an oath?"

"I do."

"Druids do not break their word!"

"Nor do sea warriors. An oath," Faolán growled, "or no deal."

Cathair slapped his belt knife two handspans away from the Chieftain's, pointed directly at him. "What do you swear by?"

"The salt of the sea. And you, Druid?"

"The sacred oak leaves of the Grove."

Faolán's brow lifted sardonically. "You carry them with you?"

"The Keeper is sure to have some dried oak leaves from Imbolc to use on the festival of Bealtaine next month." Cathair strode to the kitchen and soon returned with a mug of water, a small pot of sea salt, and a shallow bowl of dried oak leaves. He placed the items between the two opposing knives. Faolán spooned salt into the water and stirred it while the Overdruid took a taper from the mantelpiece and used it to ignite the leaves. Tendrils of smoke drifted into the air like the release of ancient wisdom, redolent of earth and sap, bark and leaf. Both men breathed it in deeply, then drank from the mug of salted water. Cathair looked directly into Faolán's eyes as he spoke his vow.

"*If* you're successful in eradicating all Bards and Masters from the port of my choosing on the day I specify, your percentage of the mine's profits will be adjusted to three percent. You will continue to receive your payment every quarter-cycle until the mine plays out or is taken out of our control. No further commitment will be asked of you *except* for leaving the Connemara coast unmolested. All raiding must be done elsewhere."

Faolán's green eyes gleamed. "I'll eradicate the Bards and Masters from the port you choose, on the day you specify. I'll leave the Connemara coast alone as long as I receive the agreed upon three percent of the mine's profits. If ever I'm cheated of my full payment, Druid, my sword will find you and hold you accountable, and the Connemara coast will be raided without mercy ... with special attention paid to Gaotha."

Still holding each other's eyes, they sheathed their knives. "I'll send you the information you'll need," Cathair said, "with enough time for you to reach the specified port."

"I'll be needing an estimated time now, Druid, for there's much to prepare for an attack of this scale."

"Not this season or the next. Their Fall Council, when most Bards and Masters will be there. I don't have a definite date on that yet." Cathair stood up. Leaning across the table, he whispered something that brought a startled look to the Chieftain's face.

"Just a small bit of information you'll keep to yourself," Cathair murmured as he reseated himself.

Faolán raised a brow. "An exceedingly careful man, I see."

"That I am. How many boats do you have?"

"The currach I've just arrived in, and four others besides. Enough for eighty warriors. And by the time we set sail I'll have a larger one to take them there."

Cathair nodded and Faolán gave a shrill whistle. His warriors quickly joined him, and they left, leaving the door open to the wind.

The Overdruid pushed aside the table barring the kitchen

door. The Keeper emerged and glanced around in relief. He paled a bit when he saw the smoking oak leaves. "Surely ye didn't..."

"Make an oath? I would do far more than that to protect Gaotha," he assured the shaken man. "This day I've struck a bargain with the devil himself, my friend, in exchange for leaving the Connemara coast free of his pillaging ways. He'll take his warriors elsewhere from now on."

The Keeper's face lit with awe and admiration. "Bless ye, Overdruid! Such a kind soul ye are!" He frowned. "I hate to think what the scoundrel wanted from ye in return."

Cathair gave him a pained look. "I will gladly pay it for the protection of Gaotha." He squared his shoulders bravely. "After all, is it not my home as well as yours? For I grew up on this very coast."

The Keeper nodded fervently. "So ye did. And lucky we are to have ye here."

Cathair smiled and left. He untethered his horse, mounted, and rode toward home. On the way, he crossed the road leading east to the Grove and saw Réiltín trudging tiredly toward him. Cathair narrowed his eyes. There were no homes in the direction she had come from ... only the Grove. He shook his head. Even if she had run straight there with news of his meeting with a Celtic sea warrior, Daithi certainly couldn't have traveled to *The Pipit's Nest* in time to overhear anything. He shrugged and rode on.

～ ❦ ～

That night the Grovekeeper contacted his brother once again.

Daithi ... dare I hope this is just a social visit?

If it were, I would leave and let you sleep, for you sound exhausted. I'll be brief. Cathair made an oath with Faolán today. I wasn't in time to hear it, but the setting of their belt knives, the pot of sea salt, and smoking oak leaves made it plain enough. And despite the infernal wind, I heard most of what they said afterwards. Faolán is going to raid a port of Cathair's choosing on the day of your Fall Council!

There was a long silence as purple turmoil and streaks of crimson anger shot through Ferghus' chromafield. *It will be held in Aille-Mara this cycle,* the Master said grimly. *The exact day hasn't been set yet.*

Can you move it somewhere inland?

That would only delay the inevitable, for Faolán has fianna and Celts under his command and can strike from land or sea. And next time we might not have the advantage of being warned. Thanks to you, I now know how much time we have. And the only way to save Aille-Mara and our Order is to leave Eire before then. Odhran won't pay for an attack that doesn't benefit him.

The Grovekeeper went cold. *But ... where will you go?*

I have no idea.

Daithi was silent, stricken at the thought of losing his brother to some unknown, faraway place, unable to talk with him again. They could both make the connection between Gaotha and Aille-Mara, but the farther the distance, the more energy it took. At some point the distance would be too great to make the connection at all.

You've done much for me, Ferghus said quietly. *And yet I would ask of you one more thing. For I am indeed exhausted. Without the Council's support, I've had no choice but to do nearly everything on my own. I can't continue doing so much longer.*

Your own Council has still refused to back you?

People do not willingly leave their homeland unless there is no other choice, and I've had no proof to offer them. You do.

Daithi was stunned. *You want me to travel to Aille-Mara?*

I know you can't do that, and it would take too long to get here, regardless. But a memory of yours can travel here in a mere moment, held in my own mind. Will you let me take it?

You can take a memory? Daithi asked, astonished. *My memory of what I just heard at The Pipit's Nest?*

I can not only take it, I can trigger it to play in the minds of the Council so they experience it just as you did. That's better than any other proof I could possibly offer them, for a memory cannot be fabricated. And, though reluctant to act, my Council knows their Prime is not delusional.

Will I still remember it?

No, but I can return it to you if you wish.

Take it. Use it as you will.

Daithi watched in fascination as his brother's song moved toward the colorful orbs Ferghus had told him were his memories. The largest one was the closest, swirling with the grey anxiety and black fear Daithi had felt for his brother as he listened to Cathair and Faolán, deep crimson streaking an angry path through both. His brother's song touched it and for a brief moment Daithi caught a glimpse of the common room at *The Pipit's Nest* through the eyes of a whinchat. Then both song and orb disappeared from Daithi's mind. As the Grovekeeper puzzled over what it was that his brother had just taken, their bond flared with sudden brilliance.

Thank you.

Chapter 17

A week later, Shay went about his chores with less than his usual attention. He had replenished the woodpile, but not the woodbox inside the house. He had taken the Grovekeeper's clothes to the stream to clean them, but forgotten to take his own. Most telling of all, he had weeded the entire garden behind the house without once breaking into a tuneless hum. Distractedly, he wandered out to the ash tree that stood at the beginning of two paths, one heading east into the hawthorns and the Grove beyond. The other path led around the house and continued west to the village.

Shay sat against the trunk, trying to decide what to do. His own mind, he thought bitterly, wasn't helping. Nor, apparently, did it care a fig for proper pronouns.

Ye have to tell him!

He won't let my disobedience pass this time ... he said so! I don't mind anyone else punishing me, but not him. Never him.

He didn't say ye couldn't—

He didn't say I could! I'm not supposed to do anything he hasn't given me permission to do. He sighed heavily and headed slowly back to the house. *Better get it over with.* Arguing with himself was only driving him crazy.

He opened the door, both relieved and dismayed to find the

Grovekeeper still at his desk, reading. Shay pushed the door silently closed behind him and stood chewing his bottom lip as the parchment was laid aside and the eyes so like his own were turned in his direction.

"Is there something you need to talk to me about?" Daithi asked quietly.

Shay went to stand before the last person in the world he wanted to disappoint and stared intently at the floor. "I think I might have disobeyed you again."

"You don't know?"

"I'm not sure."

"Perhaps you should tell me what you've done—or not done—and then we'll decide together."

"Well, I've been practicing sensing energy lines, like you said, but—" Shay took a deep breath. "Remember when I saw color come out of your walking staff?" Without waiting for an answer, he rushed on. "Well, I've been seeing color come out of a lot of other things ... and people, too. You didn't tell me I could, so I guess I shouldn't have looked at them, but they just ... happened. I should have told you right away, but..." his voice trailed away.

"Did you think that I would punish you for it?"

"Yes," Shay admitted in a low voice. "But mostly I just didn't want to disappoint you."

"Look at me, Shaylor."

His full name dragged the boy's unwilling eyes upward.

"The colorful energy fields you've been seeing are called chromafields. There's certainly nothing wrong with seeing them, unless you disobeyed me by *traveling* them," the Grovekeeper told him gravely. "Did you do so?"

He shook his head emphatically. "No, sir, not even once. I just looked at them and tried to figure out what the colors meant."

"Then you haven't disobeyed me. And I'm glad you trust me enough to come to me about anything, even something you might have done wrong. Okay?"

Relief flooded Shay. "Okay."

The Grovekeeper's eyes lit with interest. "Now, tell me about these chromafields you've seen."

"I've seen earth-colored ones from all the trees," Shay began eagerly, "and the ones from the garden plants and the Grovetenders, and *yours,* sir, with shining gold and—"

"Hold on, lad," Daithi said with a laugh. "You've been seeing chromafields everywhere, it seems. But have you figured out what it is you're seeing?"

Shay was silent for a moment, considering this. "You told me everything has energy lines, like the trees, and that they send out a field of energy that can be seen. Is that what the chromafields are?

"It is."

"Can the Grovetenders see them, too?"

Daithi shook his head. "They can sense the energy lines, and they can travel them to provide healing, but they can't see the chromafields. In fact, you and I might be the only ones in Eire who can."

Shay stared at him. "Just ... us?"

"We can't know for sure, but anyone else who could would almost certainly be in our Order, likely a Diviner, and would have had no reason not to tell the Council about his ability. It would have brought him a great deal of honor and prestige."

"But, then ... why didn't you tell them *you* could?"

It was a moment before Daithi answered. "Many cycles ago, my mentor didn't trust the newly elected First of the Council. When I joined the Order and saw his chromafield, I understood why. So I followed his advice and told no one of my abilities.

"Except ... me?"

"Except you and my brother. Now, then, have you any questions about the chromafields you've seen?"

"Well, I've been wondering about their colors. Why is there no color in an energy line, but chromafields are filled with them? And how come the colors of object's chromafields never change, but plants' colors do? And some of yours do, too, though some of them stay the same."

"Excellent questions," Daithi said. "If the energy lines have colors of their own, it's color we can't see. I believe what we do see is the energy's shimmering vibration as it provides the supporting framework that holds a crystal together, or travels from one place to another, like the sap up or down a tree. The emission of that energy, however, *is* visible in a spectrum of colors unique to it. This is its chromafield, which in objects is faint and does not move or change. The chromafields of living things, however, are brighter and they move, flowing outward and back into their hosts in a never-ending cycle. Chromafields of animals and people have two different types of colors: personality and emotion. Personality colors emit light, from a soft glow to a scintillating sparkle. These colors don't generally change, although they can if we change in some fundamental way ourselves. Colors of emotion move in streaks or swirls and fluctuate with our feelings."

"And every color means something?" Shay asked in wonder.

Daithi nodded. "And the same color can have different meanings. Crimson, as a personality trait, denotes strong-willed leadership. As an emotion, however, it indicates anger. And because emotional energy moves quickly, they have a profound effect on us and those around us. Positive ones are warming, increasing the speed of our energy and radiating outward to others, affecting them in a positive way. Negative emotions are cooling, slowing our energy and drawing it inward, making us perceptibly colder to others. Have you ever reacted strongly to a total stranger before seeing their expression or hearing them speak?"

Shay nodded ruefully, thinking of the Overdruid.

"Now you know why. The positive emotion that speeds our energy up the most is joy, and the negative one that slows it down the most is fear." Daithi turned and indicated the door behind him.

"You usually come through that door with the cheerfulness of a normal, carefree boy, and your chromafield is wide open, reaching me all the way over here at my desk. That tells me that all is well with you. A few moments ago, however, you came in with very different emotions, and your chromafield was shrunken, nowhere close to reaching me. I immediately knew you were upset about something, so I put aside my work to find out why." He smiled into Shay's astonished eyes. "The chromafields can tell you a great deal about those you know ... or think you know. If someone lies to me, for instance, their chromafield shrinks with the lie, and lets me know they do not believe what they're telling me."

"Then ... that's how you knew, when I told you I didn't want to leave the Grove—"

"That, even though it wasn't a lie, it wasn't the whole truth, for your chromafield, though it didn't shrink, faded slightly. One who masters the chromafields," he said ruefully, "is difficult to deceive."

"Isn't that a good thing?" Shay wanted to know.

"One would think so, but sometimes ignorance is a more comfortable companion." He turned a threatening scowl upon his protégé. "Now, what has *my* chromafield to say to the youngling who has been observing it without my express permission?"

Shay laughed. "It's big and open clear to the door and beyond with no red in it, telling me you aren't angry a bit, however you might growl."

Daithi chuckled. "Continue to study the chromafields of myself and the Grovetenders. Understanding the meaning of what you see will save you a lot of trouble. And mind what I told you before about not telling anyone else of your abilities. You'll find that no one will thank you for being denied the freedom to lie to your face."

They spent the rest of the afternoon outside in the shade of the ash tree, discussing various aspects of chromafields, particularly their usefulness for traveling inside objects, plants, and especially trees. Afterwards, Shay stood grappling with the implications of what he had just learned.

"When you check the Grove each week, then," he said slowly, "you aren't just sensing the trees, you're traveling them?"

"Yes."

Shay frowned. "But it takes me half the afternoon just to travel up *one* tree and back, and I end up exhausted!"

"And yet I've traveled the entire Grove in less than an hour for twenty-five cycles. And, since my chromafield is not informing you I believe any differently, what does that tell you?"

"That you're not traveling the energy lines inside the trees, like I've been. You must be traveling their chromafields."

"Very good. And how would that be different?"

Shay's brow crinkled. "You could go a whole lot faster than sap. You could go wherever you wanted, to every branch and leaf, so quickly..." His voice died away, his eyes round with imagining.

"And when I wanted to move to the next tree?"

"You'd just transfer yourself into its overlapping chromafield and go right on your way."

"A simple enough matter here in the Grove," Daithi said, "where the chromafield of every tree overlaps at least one other. What if I wanted to go to a solitary tree whose chromafield didn't?"

This took some thought. "You told me once that every handful of dirt had tiny fibers in it, like a root system we can't see with our eyes. Do those have chromafields, too?"

"They do, but don't rocks as well? And the earth itself, which is nothing more than finely crushed rock?"

Shay stared at him, astounded. "But then ... is there anything you *can't* travel?"

"Not as long as it has a chromafield, and so far, the only thing that doesn't appear to have one is the wind. My brother believes that's because an element must have a physical manifestation in order to have energy lines that project a chromafield ... at least, one that we can see. Earth, water, and fire all do, but if the wind does, it's one we can't detect."

Shay's mouth dropped open. "Have you traveled them?"

"No. I can pull energy from them, in the same way Stoneseers can pull it from the earth's energy lines to move heavy stones, but I have not yet attempted to immerse myself in such power as that, power I might not be able to control. Nor did my mentor, who cautioned me not to attempt such a thing until others with the same Gift were found and more knowledge gained. He believed that this aspect of the Druidic Gift is just beginning to emerge in Eire, whereas the Bardic Gift has been around for centuries. You're forgetting one very important thing, however."

"What's that?" Shay asked, feeling dazed.

"The exhaustion you feel after traveling an energy line up the tree and back. What keeps an old, crippled Grovekeeper from collapsing after traveling the entire Grove in a single session?"

Shay's brow furrowed. "You must be getting more energy from the chromafields." His eyes widened. "But doesn't that take energy the trees need?"

"It would if I took it from an energy line inside it, which is why I seldom take it that way. Taking it from the chromafield it emits, however, has little impact on the tree itself, making traveling that way much safer for us both. Which means I can move all the faster, the effect on the trees is negligible, and my Grovetenders don't need to carry me home."

Shay was silent, digesting what the Grovekeeper had told him. Of all the amazing things he had learned, the most incredible one was knowing that he could experience all of this himself. He glanced at the hawthorns ringing the Grove and saw their enticing chromafields. He wondered what it would be like to travel so freely through every branch and leaf, heedless of the thorns. For one glorious moment, he felt intensely, vibrantly alive, quivering with possibilities waiting to be explored.

"Remember what I told you, lad," the Grovekeeper warned.

Shay glanced guiltily at his mentor. "How did you know what I was thinking?"

Daithi chuckled. "It's what I thought when I first learned what I just taught you. And the indigo of curiosity and burnt orange of adventurousness in your chromafield have gotten disturbingly bright," he added. "I strongly suggest you keep them toned down."

Shay's brow creased. "How do I do that?"

"Try thinking of the list of deciduous shrubs I'm going to quiz you on tomorrow."

Chapter 18

Two weeks later, *The Pipit's Nest* was filled, every fisherman eager to celebrate his fine catch of the day. Spirits were high, voices rose to match them, and ale flowed freely from the kitchen as Réiltín went back and forth with flagons and mugs.

The sun had just dipped below the horizon, leaving the tavern in shadows, when the door opened and a tall young man walked in. His blue robe, bound with a silver cord, proclaimed him to be a Bard. His dark brown hair was tied back, and his grey eyes were alight with good humor. Across his shoulder was a Bardic travel bag whose shape clearly outlined the harp within.

"Ho, then, if it isn't Garvyn!" one of the fishermen called out. Friendly greetings came from the tables, for Garvyn was one of their own. Glynda, Garvyn's mother, had been born and raised in Gaotha and had fallen in love with Brenach, a Bard who'd been passing through on his way to visit his family in Ganach. Three days later, the two of them had circled a handfasting bonfire. Brenach had remained in Gaotha long enough to sire Garvyn, who hadn't seen much of his traveling father during his childhood. The boy had excelled in musical instruments and had apprenticed to the Bardic Order when he was sixteen. He was the first from Gaotha to ever do so, for the fishing village had a long history of alignment with the Druidic Order, with the Overdruid making his home there and the most prestigious Grove in Eire located in the hills above it.

"A Bard now, are ye?" a heavyset fisherman asked with a sniff. "Where've ye been, that kept ye from comin' back till now?"

"I was assigned to one of the eastern territories first, then sent up north," Garvyn replied. "But my father asked Master Conall to send me to him for a visit last week. The Master was willing, so I'm on my way to Delbna."

The man snorted. "If ye came from t'north, ye went well outta yer way fer a drink. An extra few hundred furlongs, or I'll eat 'em!"

"Eat as many of 'em as ye like, Paddy" came a mocking voice from one of the back tables. "For it's no more weight they'll be puttin' on ye." Everyone but Paddy laughed.

"Let the Bard come an' enjoy 'is ale in peace," an old fisherman admonished. "The Maker knows he 'as reason to need it."

Garvyn scanned the suddenly silent room, frowning slightly at glances that shifted elsewhere. "Anyone have room for a weary traveler at their table, then? And perhaps a drink to spare?"

"Room enough right here," drawled the old man, indicating the empty chair across from him. "But if it's a free drink yer wantin', it'll cost ye a song. I doubt ye've had much time fer music lately, and it's a healin' thing, to be sure."

Before Garvyn had a chance to do more than cast him a puzzled glance, the room erupted.

"Song! Song! Give us a song!" Wooden mugs thudded against the tables in rhythm to the chanting.

The Bard grinned and unslung his harp. "A song for a drink."

A chair was hurriedly brought and set in the corner of the room next to a chair that had a flute lying across it.

Garvyn glanced at it in surprise. "Is there a flutist here?"

A young man gave a yelp as he was hustled from his chair by an encouraging fisherman.

"Aye, though he'll never tell ye so," the fisherman said. "Not much fer speech, is Ruairí, but he's good with fishin' nets and flutes. He'll play anythin' ye ask." He gave the reluctant flutist an exasperated push. "Go on now, Ruairí, no need to be shy of a Bard who grew up right here, just like ye did yerself!"

Garvyn picked up the flute and handed it to its nervous owner. "Not likely they'll appreciate a song of Bardic Lore," he murmured. "So let's give 'em a sea song introduction. Then I'll sing a tune I composed called 'The Mermaid's Net' in alternating stanzas of six and four. Have some fun and improvise whatever you like between the verses. He grinned conspiratorially. And, since no one's heard the song before, no one will know if we hit a sour note or two!"

A shy smile lit Ruairí's face as he lifted his flute and began to play a sea song intro to the harp's accompaniment. Then Garvyn launched into a rollicking song sure to please a fisherman's ears.

Oh, once upon a sunlit day,
A mermaid came within the bay.
And there a lad with face so fair
Was in his boat, a-fishin' there.
Alone in his boat, so unaware…
A pity he was a-fishin' there.

She caught his eye and smiled at him.
She flashed her scales and silv'ry fin.
"Come hither, lad, I'll treat ye well!
'Tis down in the depths below I dwell."

His eyes grew wide, he stared aghast,
But 'twas too late, her net was cast.
"Come follow me out from the bay.
Fear not! My songs will lead the way."
Oh, foolish lad, to leave the bay…
Hark not her songs that lead the way!

She sang for him the mornin' long,
Beguilin' him with verse and song.
And out he went... Beware, ye men!
For never the lad was seen again.

So, if ye hear a mermaid's song,
While on the sea a-fishin' long,
Plug yer ears and keep them so,
Or down in the depths ye'll surely go!
Down in the depths, way down so low...
'Tis down in the depths ye'll surely go!

And if yer boat returns alone,
Yer widow's sure to weep and moan.
But if she finds out where ye lay (ha-ha!),
Then down in the depths (take my advice!)
Down in the depths 'tis best to stay!

The room rang with laughter and splashes as mugs thumped the tables. "Now *that's* worth a drink, so it is!" declared the old man, beckoning the Bard with his mug and sloshing a fair amount of its contents onto the man sitting next to him. "Bring 'em both a drink, lass," he told Réiltín. "'I'll pay fer 'em both."

A blast of cold air heralded the arrival of Cathair, who made his way to a secluded table in the corner, as he often did in the evenings. The Overdruid rarely spoke to anyone and seemed content to nurse a single drink for an hour or so before returning home. None paid him any attention except for Réiltín, who gave the old fisherman a smile before hurrying over to Cathair's table.

The old man's gaze followed her for a moment before turning to the young Bard. "Name's Seamus. Wasn't expectin' such a cheerful song from ye, all things considered."

Garvyn frowned. "What do you mean?"

The old man regarded him thoughtfully. "If ye don't mind me askin'," he said at last, "where are ye plannin' to spend the night?"

"At home, of course. That's where I'm headed, and thought I'd stop in for a drink or two first." He smiled. "Haven't seen my mam for three cycles."

"Nay, lad," Seamus said quietly, "ye can't be goin' there."

The Bard looked up sharply. "Why not?"

"Yer mam's been gone for nearly a fortnight, taken in sickness so sudden not even yer father could have returned in time to say goodbye." His voice softened at the Bard's stricken expression. "Naught there but memories ye might not be wantin' to face this night. It's sorry I am to be the one to tell ye. I'm sure Brenach would have wanted to tell ye in person and keep ye by his side fer a bit. Doubt he'd expect ye'd take an extra day or two to stop here first."

Garvyn closed his eyes. "Was she in pain?"

"No, and she went peaceful at the end."

The drink arrived, Réiltín placing it before the Bard with a sympathetic smile that faded when she caught sight of his face. She glanced at Seamus and moved on to serve the Overdruid his ale.

"Drink up," the old man advised Garvyn. "Won't change a thing, but 'twill help fer tonight. I only 'ave the one drink m'self most nights and act the tipsy fool fer the sheer fun of it." He glanced fondly around the room. "These drunken sods will pay fer the rest of yer drinks tonight, and never know it. Least we can all do. And ye'll be stayin' the night at my place," he added.

The Bard looked up in surprise. "I'm beholden."

"Nay, lad. I owe yer father for many a thing he's done fer me."

Garvyn stared at his mug for a moment, then lifted it and drank deeply.

Behind them, Cathair's shrewd eyes rested on the Bard. The Overdruid waited silently until the night was late and Garvyn had taken in several drinks and caroled as many increasingly bawdy songs to go with them. Then Cathair approached.

"Good to see you, Seamus," the Overdruid said affably. "Kind of you to help our young friend here drown his sorrows."

"'Tis no trouble."

"Getting him to your home in his condition might be. I rather doubt he'll make it that far ... perhaps you'd allow me to help. You go on home to your rest, and I'll arrange for a room here for our inebriated friend." He raised a hand. "Won't cost him a thing, not even for his meal when he wakes up. My word on it."

Seamus glanced at the Bard staring owlishly at his empty mug. "Well, then, I thank ye." He called Réiltín over and settled his bill. Then he rose, squeezed Garvyn's shoulder, and left.

Cathair settled himself in the old man's place and glanced around the room. Only a handful of men, well in their cups, were still there. "I believe your father has recently been posted to Delbna," he said pleasantly.

The Bard peered up at him. "So what if 'e 'as?"

"As you can see by my robe, it's my responsibility to keep informed about all those in my jurisdiction," Cathair said mildly. "Where was he posted before?"

"Wouldn't tell me," Garvyn said, poking his finger owlishly at a knot in the wooden tabletop. "Important place ... was in charge of Gifted Bards," he said proudly.

"Gifted," Cathair repeated blankly. "Talented, you mean?"

The Bard frowned and shook his head. "Not talented. *Gifted.*"

"Ah ... and these gifted Bards are ... gifted in what, exactly?"

"Hafta ashk them," came the resentful reply. "The Gifted don't favor the ungifted with that infer ... infro ... inframation." The Bard made a valiant attempt to drink from his empty mug.

"Surely you know, or at least suspect, something." The Overdruid reached over to snag a flagon of ale that hadn't been emptied, and poured what remained into the Bard's mug.

Garvyn yawned. "They talks to each other," he murmured.

"Well, of course they talk—"

"No, no," the Bard said impatiently. "They talks up *here,*" he said, tapping the side of his head. "But my father was in charge," he said defiantly. "At leasht," he added in confusion, "he was."

"I'm sure he did a wonderful job. But—not to denigrate your father's abilities—one would expect a *gifted* Bard to have been placed in charge. One who could ... talk up there."

Garvyn took another swig of ale, then cast a sly glance at the Overdruid. "Father hash a connecshun," he said conspiratorially, "He's Mashter Ferghushes childhood friend. With a connecshun like that," he said, waving his mug and sending a splash of its contents Cathair's way, "who needsh t'be Gifted?"

The Overdruid stared at him for a moment, then fastidiously blotted his stained robe. "Who, indeed?" he murmured. He looked thoughtfully at his inebriated companion. "What do you know about Ferghus? Did your father ever speak of him?"

Garvyn shrugged. "No. But I overhearse ... overhearshed him talkin' to my mam 'bout him once."

"I see. And what did he tell her?"

"Said Ferghush had lotsa talent. Kind. Defended hish younger brother from bullies."

"Commendable," Cathair murmured. Then he frowned. "And who is this younger brother of Ferghus?"

"Dunno." Garvyn's head drifted slowly toward the table.

"Did he mention why he was bullied?"

The Bard sighed and closed his eyes. "Got shick."

Cathair's brow raised sardonically. "With an illness that attracted bullies?"

Garvyn barely managed to shake his head. "Left him witha lump ... limp." His head fell forward, his eyes closed, and he slept.

It was late when Cathair left the tavern, having seen to Garvyn's room and safe conveyance there. He headed back home, thinking furiously. Daithi was hardly the only person in Eire who limped ... but could it be? Was Daithi's older brother the Prime of the Bardic Council? A Gifted Prime who could communicate mentally with his brother all the way from Aille-Mara? He thought of seeing Réiltín trudging along a path that only went to the Grove. Had the woman gone there right after giving Cathair the message that Faolán was once again waiting for him at the inn? Had she done the same thing at their first meeting as well? It would explain why Faolán's warriors had found the mine deserted! Cathair had no idea how Daithi had made it to the tavern in time to hear the deal he'd made with Faolán to take the mine, and later, the plan to attack Aille-Mara. But given the possibility, everything began to make sense. For if Daithi could make it to *The Pipit's Nest* in record time, he could travel the shorter distance to the Overdruid's home even faster. And if he could overhear a conversation in a closed and guarded common room, he could certainly overhear the ones in Cathair's study. The Overdruid's anger burned as he thought of the information that had been trickling all this time out of his private meetings straight into the ears of the Prime of the Bardic Order.

That cunning little snake! Cathair fumed. *I thought him an honorable Druid, and he's been passing information to his brother all this time ... why, he probably joined our Order to spy for him!*

It wasn't until he entered his home and closed the door behind him that his anger chilled to icy resolve. In the morning he'd make sure the Keeper knew he was taking a trip down the coast for the day. Then he'd circle back through the hills in the afternoon and pay a little visit to the Grovekeeper of Gaotha.

Chapter 19

Shay spent the following morning memorizing the detailed list of chromafield colors and their meanings Daithi had given him. Then he practiced seeing and unseeing the chromafields close to the Grovekeeper's home, and explored the energy line of one of the ash tree's roots. He'd ached to travel a chromafield since his mentor told him about them, but he hadn't disobeyed, traveling them only on those occasions when the Grovekeeper took him along. Though the wonders Daithi showed him were tempting, the dangers that were pointed out to him quickly curbed any inclination the youngster had to venture off on his own.

After lunch, Daithi joined him under the ash tree and taught him how to enter his own mind to see the twined colors of their bond. He explained what the many translucent memory orbs were, and how they could be replayed with a single touch, all of which fascinated the listening boy. When they returned to themselves, the Grovekeeper glanced at the lowering sun.

"Enough, lad. There'll be time enough tomor—" Daithi abruptly broke off, frowning at the ground in consternation, then turned his attention to the path leading behind the house and closed his eyes.

The question on Shay's lips died, knowing his mentor was flying along that path from one chromafield to the next.

"Go!" The Grovekeeper erupted from his trance with a voice

of thunder. He whirled upon the frozen youngster next to him. "Go now!" he commanded fiercely. "No time to make it into the Grove. Up into the ash, as far as you can get before he arrives! Make no sound, and don't show yourself, no matter what you see or hear … do you understand me?"

"Y-yes—"

"Quickly, now!"

A brief flurry of leaves fell as Shay scrambled up to an upper branch he often sat on to study. He had barely settled himself in place before the sound of hoofbeats informed him that the Grove-keeper's unwelcome visitor had arrived. A horse and rider trotted into the clearing and stopped in front of Daithi. The tall rider quickly dismounted and tethered his horse to one of the tree's low branches. Shay's mouth went dry as he recognized the voice of the Overdruid.

"Courteous as ever, I see," Cathair said. "Coming out to save me the bother of knocking on the door! One might think you knew I was coming."

"I was merely on my way out," Daithi said calmly. "Is there something I can help you with? Shay delivered your new staff some time ago. Didn't it meet with your approval?"

"Surely you already know that it did … or weren't you eaves-dropping at the time?"

"What are you talking about?"

"You know perfectly well what I'm talking about, traitor!"

Daithi's voice turned steely. "How am I a traitor?"

"Stop the pretense! I know perfectly well who your *brother* is."

"I'm hardly to blame for who I'm related to."

"He's the Prime of the Council of Master Bards!"

"Did a declaration of war with the Bardic Order go out that I failed to receive?" Daithi asked icily.

"You've been feeding him information that isn't yours to give! Some of which I actually gave you myself over a game of Stones, a game I thought I was enjoying with a *friend*."

"Ah, so apparently this war is being waged by you alone. If we were friends, you would know I'd never do anything to put either Order in danger, any more than my brother would. I can't, however, say the same of *you*, who is actively seeking to destroy the Bardic Order for your own gain."

Cathair's blow caught the Grovekeeper full in the face, sending him to the ground. He got back up and wiped the blood from the corner of his mouth. The slightest of trembles came from high in the ash as Shay looked on in mounting horror.

"You have no right to question *my* honor," Cathair growled. "But I have every right to deal with traitors I find within my territory, and your lofty position won't save you. I don't know how long you've been spying on me to feed information to the Bardic Order, but it stops *now*." He withdrew a leather thong from his robe, then grasped the Grovekeeper's hands and tightly bound his wrists. Daithi did not struggle.

"Not even going to give me the pleasure of a fight?" the Overdruid asked contemptuously.

Daithi shrugged. "I'm hardly your size, and there's nowhere I could limp without you quickly overtaking me. If you wish to take me before the Council, there's little I can do to stop you. Nor," he added pointedly, "is there any reason I should fear to face them. You've no proof I've done anything wrong, and they're certainly not going to believe I've been spying on you from the distance of the Grove. The fact that you don't happen to like my brother, whom you've never met, is hardly incriminating."

"I've no intention of involving the Council in this. Where's the boy?" Cathair demanded, glancing around the clearing.

"Shay has many chores, which includes helping the Grovetenders with theirs."

"A pity. I'm sure you would have enjoyed watching what I intend to do to him. I'll deal with him after I deal with you."

"He knows nothing!" Daithi hissed. "What reason would I have to tell a youngling anything that would put his life at risk?"

Cathair snorted. "It's what he might have *heard* that concerns me. Judging by his fear of me, I'd say he's heard far more than he should have. Now, move!" He shoved Daithi toward the house. "I'll see for myself if the boy is inside, and then you're going to tell me every word you've ever said to your brother for the last cycle."

The moment the door closed behind the two men, Shay began moving down the tree as quietly as he could. His mind furiously berated him, telling him to obey the Grovekeeper, but he refused to listen. He wouldn't stay here, shivering with fear in a tree, while the one who meant more to him than anything else in the world was taken inside and likely tortured.

He didn't fight back because he knew I might make a sound and be discovered. Maybe there's nothing I can do, but if I can just get close enough to his chromafield...

The boy reached the ground and moved toward a slightly opened living room window as stealthily as a cat. From inside the house came the sound of something heavy skittering across the floor, followed by several crashes and an oath from Cathair. Shay hastened his steps and peeked through the window.

Daithi stood silently facing the door, his eyes closed, his hands still tied. A second oath from Cathair brought the boy's eyes to the bizarre spectacle of the Overdruid pinned between the door and the heavy oak table. Broken pieces of crockery littered the floor, and a stone vase lay toppled on the table.

"How did a Druid who has no power with energy lines attain such a high rank?" Daithi taunted. "Any one of my Grovekeepers could defend themselves better! Apparently this isn't the first deal you've made with Odhran."

"After I kill your brat, I'll torch your precious Grove!" Cathair threatened as he struggled to free himself. "Every tree, every branch and leaf of it burned to the ground! Does the traitor who travels the trees know if they scream when they're burned? Tell me, Daithi ... do the trees scream? Will you hear them in whatever traitor's hell you end up ... *ahhh!*" He broke off, his face turning nearly purple with rage and his frantic efforts to push the table away. "Isn't being a traitor enough for you?" Cathair gasped. "This is *murder!*" He groaned in pain as he strained to reach the vase, lying just out of his reach.

"This is *justice,*" Daithi retorted, his brow furrowing with the strain of keeping Cathair trapped. "If I wanted you dead, you already would be! I don't need to kill you to bring you to justice. I only need to keep you trapped until my Grovetenders arrive."

Shay! Bring the Grovetenders as quickly as you can! Hurry!

Shocked at hearing Daithi's commanding voice in his mind, Shay's gaze snapped back to the Grovekeeper, whose eyes were still closed in concentration, his focus split between keeping Cathair trapped and sending a mental directive. A mere moment, but it was enough. Shay never saw the Overdruid's hand reach the vase, didn't see the hurtling object in time to utter a single cry of warning before it hit the Grovekeeper. Shay gasped in horror as Daithi was thrown backwards to the ground and lay there unmoving. Blood trickled slowly from a gash in his forehead and dripped to the floorboards. Cathair uttered a curse as he managed to push the table away, then slumped to the floor, breathing raggedly.

Shay stood rooted in place, aghast at the change he saw in the Grovekeeper's chromafield. It was small and quiescent, not the open, vibrantly moving field it usually was. His own chromafield, heightened by his turbulent emotions, easily overlapped it. Running for the Grovetenders would take far too long to bring help in time. The only thing that could help was ... *energy,* Shay realized. *Healing energy.* Could he travel into the Grovekeeper's chromafield to give his own energy to him? But how? *Maybe I can enter his mind and wake him up! He can take energy from chromafields, so he should be able to take it from mine and heal himself with it! It should work ... it has to work!* Taking a deep breath, Shay focused on the Grovekeeper's chromafield and began to send his awareness into it at the very moment that the Overdruid stumbled between them, his stronger chromafield superseding Daithi's weakened one.

Shay gasped as the world changed, utterly unlike the way it had when the Grovekeeper had taken him into the chromafields of objects and trees as a passive observer. Though he had never entered the chromafield of a person before, he knew instantly that this one belonged to the Overdruid, not the Grovekeeper. For there was darkness here, rife with malicious intent, and he froze in its embrace, unwilling to make any move at all that might announce his presence. And yet, he realized in fresh horror, he *was* moving, inexorably carried along with the chromafield's flow toward the one who emanated it, as helpless to change direction as he had been when caught in the flow of the Oak's sapwood. Emotions seethed around him. Crimson anger and burnt orange distrust carried him through a scintillating landscape of burgundy's powerful drive, tainted by the rust brown of selfishness and the veridian green of ambition, and he shuddered to think of the mind it was taking him to. Would Cathair become aware of him there?

Think! How did you get out of the tree? You listened ... and heard a flow of energy going the other way!

There was nothing to listen to here, but there was plenty to *see*. He looked frantically around for his own chromafield, but it had already fallen behind him as the Overdruid apparently moved farther away from the window. The flow he was in moved inexorably toward Cathair, but he could see a different stream of similar colors that was flowing the other way. Words the Grovekeeper had said to him not long ago returned vividly to his mind. It was the first lesson, Daithi told him, he had learned from his mentor.

Take care of your thoughts, to keep them bright and positive.

For what you think emanates from you and will return to you in the circulating flow of your own energy. Brightness begets brightness. Darkness, more darkness. Thus, you are creating yourself with every thought you think.

Shay stared at the two chromafields, one flowing outward from the Overdruid, one flowing in, and was filled with revulsion. *He's feeding himself his own darkness and doesn't even know it!*

Shay concentrated with all his might on the path flowing outward, willing himself to move toward it, but nothing happened. Panic reasserted itself, urging him to scream—but he had no voice. Flee—but he couldn't move. Do something, *anything*—but he had no idea what. And bit by bit the colors he was trapped in were taking him closer to the mind of the one who was emanating them and feeding them back to himself in a never-ending cycle.

And then he was there, in a mind like and yet utterly unlike his own. Twisted cords of color rose around him, a few gleaming, most dull and lifeless. And all around him, without sound or substance, was something akin to speech, though he heard nothing that could be called words. Fragments swirled around him, each of them with a spark of color that was gone before he could identify its hue. Streaks of reddish black hatred and the burgundy of self-righteous anger cut through the mental landscape. Bewildered and appalled by what seemed to be the Overdruid's thoughts, he frantically searched for a way out of the nightmare his world had become. Before him was a myriad of translucent memory orbs, each swirling with colored emotions. And the chromafield was taking him slowly but inexorably toward them.

As Shay stared at the orbs, remembering the Grovekeeper's lesson on them—could it possibly have been just a few hours ago?—his fear was replaced by an idea ... a crazy, insane idea. Hiding in the ash tree, he'd been shocked—and proud!—to discover that the Grovekeeper had been spying on the Overdruid, putting himself in danger for the good of Eire like the heroes of legend ... like Fionn mac Cumhaill himself, perhaps, whose exploits Shay delighted in reading about. And now, right here in front of him, was a chance to spy on Cathair's own memories! Who knew what he might discover? The idea was irresistible. And all he had to do was touch one of the orbs. Shay ignored the voice in his head screaming at him not to be a fool, and focused on a large orb he was about to pass. Experimentally, he leaned toward it.

The next thing he knew, he was shaking uncontrollably, disoriented to find himself still slowly moving along like a boat that had drifted nearly to the end of its impetus from oars left idle in their oarlocks.

Wh ... what just happened? For a moment he thought he felt a comfortable chair under him ... caught a glimpse of a large desk Then the wisps of memory broke apart and disappeared like the last tendrils of a forgotten dream. He knew time had passed, yet had no awareness of how much. He was confused to see he was coming to the last of the orbs ... hadn't he just entered them a moment ago? Relief swept him when he realized he was slowly changing direction, that the inward flow was becoming an outward one. Around him the chromafield began to seethe and gain speed as it swept him back out of the Overdruid's mind. He steeled himself to ride it, keeping his focus on the brightness he could see in the distance. As he approached it, he recognized it as the outer edge of his own chromafield, but the Overdruid was still too far from the window for their chromafields to overlap. The only way back to himself was to ... *jump.* He froze at the thought.

Fear is the great paralyzer. If you allow it to dominate your mind, you won't be able to extricate yourself.

The truth of this lit his mind, and he calmed himself by turning his thoughts to the most comforting memory he had of the Grovekeeper. The moment when, exhausted and slumped against the trunk of the Oak, the Grovekeeper had sat down next to him and pulled him close. The boy relaxed with the memory of nestling his head against the Grovekeeper's shoulder. As he neared his own chromafield, he realized the gap would not get any narrower than it was at this moment. Pretending with all his might that his mentor was right behind him, he jumped.

Shay opened his eyes to find himself sprawled on the ground, nauseated and disoriented. He stared at the window above him. He remembered looking through it, remembered the pinned Overdruid struggling to free himself, remembered the Grovekeeper falling to the floor, unconscious. He remembered deciding to enter the frail chromafield of his mentor and frowned. The next thing he remembered was opening his eyes a moment ago.

The sound of repeated blows came from within the house. Shay cautiously peeked through the window, horrified to see the enraged Overdruid wielding the Grovekeeper's own staff on its inert owner, who had been bound hand and foot and was groaning in pain with each blow. Impotent rage filled Shay as he glared at the misused staff. He trembled with a fierce desire to pull it out of the Overdruid's hands.

Cathair uttered a startled oath as the staff flew from his grasp and hit the wall just beneath the window Shay stood at. For one horrified moment, the boy froze in terror as dark eyes stared directly into his. Then he defied the Grovekeeper's assertion that fear was the great paralyzer and ran like he had never run before.

No squirrel ever scrambled as fearlessly into the protection of the thorny hawthorn trees as Shay did in the next few moments, ducking his head and scuttling behind the trunk of one just before the door flew open and the Overdruid appeared, glaring about the empty clearing. His horse whinnied and moved restlessly under the ash tree. The youngster huddled against the hawthorn's slender trunk and closed his eyes. There was no hope of remaining hidden here unless Cathair didn't bother looking toward the trees. *Be a tree. Just ... be a tree. And maybe—*

When no cry of discovery came from Cathair, Shay opened his eyes a fraction and stared in disbelief at the hawthorn branches that were suddenly shielding him from view. He was certain there had been no branches low enough to shield him when he had scurried under them. Yet several branches now bent low to the ground, their foliage intertwining in an effective shield. He breathed a slow sigh of relief.

The Overdruid, grimacing with pain, walked to the ash tree and peered suspiciously up into its branches. Frowning, he calmed his horse and scowled at the hawthorns and the Grove beyond. Then he headed purposefully to the woodpile. Shay, surreptitiously peeking through a slight break in the branches, saw him pick up the kindling box and take it into the house. He returned a few moments later and took the emptied box into the peat shed. A short while later he painfully lugged the box of dried peat into the house and returned empty-handed. He gathered a few straight branches from the woodpile and took them into the house, then reappeared awhile later with three burning brands.

"No," Shay moaned. "Please, no..." Helpless to do anything, he watched the brands flare as they were tossed through the open door of the Grovekeeper's home.

The Overdruid walked back to the ash and untethered his horse. He stood there silently watching as smoke began to roll out through the open door. The house began to burn, the windows lighting up with a macabre dance of flames and shadows.

"*That's* justice," Cathair growled. He withdrew a small silver object from one of the pockets of his robe and idly inspected it.

"A pretty thing," he murmured, his words barely reaching the boy not ten paces away. "And now it can grace the hand of someone who deserves to wear it." He slipped it back into his pocket.

Shay barely clamped his mouth shut in time to prevent the outraged cry in his mind from emerging. *You'll never deserve to wear his ring!*

Cathair said nothing further until the roof of the house began to collapse. "So, not going to give me the pleasure of hearing you scream, Daithi?" he said as he mounted his restless horse. "Well, I'm sure your brat will make up for it." He snapped the reins and rode out of the clearing, taking the path that led to the village.

Crouched under the branches of the hawthorn, Shay shivered and stared unseeing at the collapsed home. Flames and thick curls of smoke rose eerily into the darkening sky. He heard a single cry of grief resound through the clearing, but was unaware it had come from him. The hawthorn's branches lifted, releasing him to run ... run fast and hard. He never saw Alben's surprised face as he raced past the Grovetender, who was hurrying toward the burning house, never heard his shout to stop. He ran without awareness or thought, straight into the heart of the Grove.

Chapter 20

Daithi had been past all feeling when the beating stopped and Cathair abruptly left the house, then returned twice to scatter kindling and dried peat around the room. The Grovekeeper felt strangely uncaring about his fate, which he had known was sealed the moment he had groggily come to himself under the feel of his own staff, his arms and legs securely tied, his strength all but depleted. No, it wasn't his own death that disturbed him. It was the knowledge that Cathair would hunt Shay down and kill him as well, then put the Grove to the torch for pure spite.

As though the mere thought had brought them, three flaming brands flew one after the other through the open doorway. Daithi groaned. He didn't fear death, but to leave this life enveloped in flames, with Shay within hearing—

No. Not like that. He wondered briefly if he had the strength left to travel the chromafield of the floor and the ground beneath it, leaving his body to burn without him. But then—

Not like that, either. He needed Ferghus. And he needed more time than the flames were going to give him. Marshalling his remaining strength, Daithi opened his awareness of the floor's chromafield and pulled energy from it, then pushed the energy toward the kindling and peat. It scattered as if blown by an errant wind, most of it toward the kitchen. One of the burning brands rolled with it, but the other two wound up against the living room wall. Daithi closed his eyes, utterly spent. His home would still be forfeit to the flames, but he had bought himself some time. Opening his awareness to his own mind, he instantly perceived the sparkling bond he shared with his brother.

Ferghus, he managed to say.

Daithi? What in the name of—

Listen to me! For a wonder, Ferghus fell silent at the whispered command. *Cathair knows you're my brother. He set my home on fire, leaving me inside, tied and barely conscious. Shay is hiding outside within hearing, and I don't want his last memories of me to be screams of pain. Free my song, Ferghus! It won't be long before the flames reach me.*

His brother's voice was shaken. *Why not escape through the chromafields?*

And then what, brother? Would you choose such a life for yourself? Your conscious awareness inhabiting chromafields not your own, your soul left behind, unable to release itself to the stars? I'll do it if I have to, to spare Shay, but please, Ferghus ... release me and spare us both.

Ferghus' energy flared suddenly with a force to rival the flames that even now were licking at the walls. Daithi closed his stinging eyes, coughing in the smoke that was beginning to fill the room. *Hurry ... there's little time.* Ferghus' chromafield moved toward him, and Daithi felt the pull of it in his soul as it touched his.

And then he was moving away from his body, out through his burning home and up into the clear air above, held firmly in the powerful embrace of his brother's song. Below them, the wind changed direction, blowing the smoke toward Gaotha and away from the Grove. And though he could not fathom how, he knew Ferghus had done this for him, and murmured his thanks. Above them stars flared against the dark canopy of the sky, though it was still daylight below. The pull from the light of those unworldly stars was irresistible, and his freed awareness burned with the desire to travel that path up and away from this world to wherever it might lead. Ferghus, however, was still holding him fast, loath to let him go. And in that moment of clarity, Daithi saw his brother's song entwined with his own and heard the beautiful music coming from it ... felt his brother's sorrow as keenly as he felt his own burgeoning joy.

Thank you for releasing me. Daithi didn't say what he knew Ferghus already understood. Though his brother had released him from his body, he had not yet released him from himself.

You know ... how much I— Ferghus' voice broke off.

I know. I love you, too, brother.

The next moment Daithi was free, rising up like an iridescent bubble from the surface it had clung to. He thrilled at the wondrous sensation of freedom, of the many impressions and thoughts that flew to him as though returning home after being gone for a lifetime. He absorbed them effortlessly as he rose euphorically upward toward the beckoning stars.

Then something brought him to a stop, as if an invisible cord was holding him to the earth he had risen from. He glanced down, curious to see what was keeping him from the Chromafield of all chromafields above, begging to be traveled.

Far below him Daithi could still see where his home had been, its roof and walls collapsed. He saw the frantic movements of his Grovetenders and men from the village as they labored to keep the fire contained. None of this, however, was tethering him in place ... instead, it was a solitary Oak that had stood for untold centuries in the center of the Grove. Its immense chromafield bathed the entire Grove in its light, and a golden tendril streamed upward to reach his own, touching it as tenderly as though he were a wayward child needing to be coaxed back to where he belonged. The Oak's golden chromafield beckoned him from below, the silver starlight from above, both streams of energy far more powerful than his own. Marveling at forces he knew could coerce him, but would not, he hesitated, uncertain which path to take. He glanced at the Oak and, though the distance was far for mortal eyes, perceived a young boy sobbing convulsively against its bark, high in the uppermost branches.

Shay! Daithi held himself where he was. Every particle of his being strained to answer the stars and move away from the cares of this world, which he no longer needed or wished to concern himself with. But if he did, what would happen to his Grove? To Shay? Who would ensure their safety if Daithi did not? Held in a single tendril of the Oak's vast chromafield, he gazed at the shrunken one of the youngster he dearly loved ... a boy who had just witnessed his mentor being burned alive in his home. Shay was not an acolyte. In the morning, he would leave the Grove for the village and walk straight into Cathair's hands. It took no intuition to know what would happen to him then.

Yet, inexplicably, intuition came to Daithi in that moment, in a silver vision so clear, so profound, that his senses reeled in the shock of it. He saw the role the Grove would one day play in the Druidic Order if he but claimed it as his own. More, he saw the role the boy he loved would play in the Bardic Order if Daithi but let him go. In anguish he glanced at the stars. There was no judgement in their clear light. He could go or stay, claim or not claim, keep for himself or release. The choices he made were his own, the myriad paths that would follow trickling off into time like rivulets into streams, streams into rivers, all of them emptying into the same vast sea.

Refusing to answer the call of those incredible stars, Daithi followed the pull of the Oak's chromafield straight to Shay's trembling one, its usually vibrant colors nearly eclipsed by the chaotic swirls of ash grey grief and black fear. The moment he touched it, he found himself in a mind raw with pain.

Shay.

The boy froze.

Shay, it's me. I'm not in my home, nor did I ever feel a single flame. I'm here with you, and I won't leave you until you're safe.

The youngster erupted in a fit of incoherent babbling.

Hang on to that tree trunk, Shaylor, Daithi said sternly. *I'm in no fit state to pick you up if you should fall.*

Babbling was replaced by hysterical laughter. "Are you really … but I saw … how could you be … I must be crazy!"

Follow your chromafield into your own mind and tell me what you see there by simply thinking your words, not speaking.

There was a moment of silence at the unusual command, then Shay took a deep breath and obeyed it. *It really is you! But … your colors! They're amazing!*

Perhaps because I no longer have a body complaining that it needs its energy replenished … like you clearly do.

I don't know where to go. Maybe Grovetender Alben?

You can go there for a few hours to get some food and sleep, but you must not stay in the Grove. Cathair will be looking for you here, likely first thing in the morning.

The boy shuddered. *Couldn't the Grovetenders stop him?*

All of them put together couldn't stop the likes of Cathair.

Shay was silent for a moment. *Can you?*

As long as I'm with you, he will not touch you. First, you need to get to Alben's, then out of the Grove well before dawn. I'll take you to Réiltín. You can stay safely there until we set out for Ferghus. It's a long way to Aille-Mara. To Daithi's surprise, black fear once again shot dark tendrils through the boy's chromafield.

Aille-Mara? I … think I've heard of that before, Shay said.

You have? From where?

I can't remember, but I don't think what I heard about it was good. His voice tightened with anxiety.

Aille-Mara is just a seaport far south of here, Shay, Daithi said reassuringly. *Much larger than our fishing village is, but nothing to fear. My brother Ferghus is Prime of the Bardic Order and lives a bit north of the town, along the coast. He can keep you safe. There's no safe place for you here in Gaotha.*

Shay absorbed this in silence. He knew the Grovekeeper had told him the truth. He also knew it wasn't the whole truth. *Will ... you come with me?* he asked uncertainly.

I'll be with you every step of the way.

The whole truth of that burned brightly in Shay's mind.

～ ⚜ ～

Late that night Alben returned home, exhausted and heartsore, to find his living room flickering with soft firelight, revealing a small figure sleeping soundly on a mat.

"Well, there you are, then," the Grovetender said softly.

For awhile, Alben.

The old man jerked upright at the familiar voice in his mind. "Grovekeeper?" he gasped. "Is it you?"

It's me, and I need your help once again. Perhaps you should sit down and we'll talk.

"Yes ... yes, I think I will," Alben murmured and sat on the floor right where he was. "Can you talk to anyone you want to ... like this?" he asked wonderingly.

"No, only those I've created a strong bond with. My Grovekeepers, Shay ... a few others."

Alben nodded. "We put out the fire and found you. Or, well, your body, as is, and Eoin fetched an urn. I thought you might like your remains to rest by the Oak. Ronán has it now. I looked for your ring, thinking you'd like Shay to have it, but I couldn't find it."

If it wasn't on my finger, Cathair must have taken it.

"The Overdruid was there?" The old man frowned. "Shay was terrified when he ran past me ... are you saying that Cathair..."

Cathair set the fire, leaving me bound inside. He'll be coming to find Shay and kill him, for the youngling is the only witness to the murder he committed against me.

All color drained from the old man's face. "What! He ... *dared* ... we thought the fire a terrible accident!"

It was no accident. Cathair discovered that my brother is Prime of the Bardic Order and is convinced I was spying for him.

"Nay, don't be telling me more. None of my business what the Grovekeeper does."

Daithi chuckled. *You can be sure that it was for the good of both Orders.*

"Oh, I've no doubt of that. No doubt at all." The old man glanced at Shay. "Is there something I can do for him, or for you?"

You can watch him for me while I tell the others to be at the Oak by dawn's light. Cathair will be coming for Shay, and he's threatened to set fire to the Grove. He must be stopped.

Alben was speechless for a moment. "He will be," he growled. But Daithi was gone.

When the Grovekeeper returned, he found Alben asleep in a chair next to Shay. Daithi roused his old friend enough to see him to his bed, then turned his attention to Ferghus, wondering how he would take the shock of hearing his dead brother's voice in his mind. As it turned out, Ferghus' exasperated voice spoke the moment Daithi entered it.

Well, brother, it certainly took you long enough!

I didn't want to interrupt your grieving, Daithi said dryly. *How long did it last? All of five minutes?* To his surprise, it was a long moment before his brother replied.

More like five of the worst hours of my life, Ferghus said in a low voice. *Until Cyral left my side and I could bear to look at our bond again. Instead of being dull and lifeless, it was more vibrant than ever ... I suppose your youngling kept you here?*

For a moment Daithi was silent. *I was following the light of the stars—such incredible stars, Ferghus!—when the Oak stopped me. I looked down and saw Shay. He was high in its branches, dousing it with tears. He heard the beating, saw the house go up in flames ... and he's barely nine. Cathair intends to find and kill him. So I followed the Oak's pull back to him.*

A defenseless youngling? Ferghus was outraged. *No wonder you stayed! What are you going to do?*

I'll claim the Grove for my own and deal with Cathair. But first I'll take Shay to someone I trust, where he'll be safe until we set out.

Set out for where?

For you.

Me? Ferghus was astonished. *I'd welcome the lad, certainly ... but Aille-Mara is hardly a safe harbor right now, and wouldn't he rather go to someone in his own Order?*

I never took him as an acolyte, and he's taken no oaths. He's Gifted, Ferghus, able to see chromafields and travel them, the only one I've found in all these cycles of searching. Cathair wants to kill him, and Odhran would exploit his Gift. He'll be safe with you.

Get him here before the Fall Council and I promise he'll be with me on one of our ships ... but not as the youngling of a Grove-keeper. As my orphaned nephew he'll be beyond the suspicion and distrust that is otherwise sure to fall on him.

I can't thank you enough for this.

It's the least I can do for my own nephew. I feel ... responsi—

Never say that, or even think it, brother! What I did was done, not just for you, but for both our Orders, and the only one responsible for my death is Cathair.

Ferghus was silent for a long moment. *Thank you for telling me that.*

I can get Shay past the sentries between our territories, Daithi told him, *and stay with him until he reaches you. And,* he added with a chuckle, *I can entertain him with stories of his uncle that will make the transition easier for him.*

Hmph! Embellished to the hilt, no doubt ... but why leave him at all, Daithi? You could come with us, too, in the mind of a boy who loves you. What a comfort that would be to Shay ... and you know how much I would welcome your presence among us.

It didn't seem that his brother would answer at first. When at last Daithi spoke, his voice was low with regret. *I wish I could, but I will not. For the good of Eire, I must stay and claim the Grove as my own. For his own safety and for the good of your new land, Shay must go with you.*

The silence this time was broken by Ferghus. *I won't press you, then ... I well know the power and pull of an intuition.*

How did you know it was an intuition?

What else could make you leave him, if the stars could not? You're doing what you've seen is best for Shay.

As you always have for Cyral, Daithi said softly. *I'll speak to you only with need until I see Shay safely in your hands. We can say goodbye then.*

No one can count on 'then' ... the only certainty is 'now'. I regret not being able to finish the last sentence I spoke to you. I love you, brother. Whatever happens then, know that now.

Blended colors and a song entwined, shimmered for a moment, then slowly moved apart.

Daithi turned his attention to Shay. The boy was moving restlessly, moaning as a dream began to take shape in his mind ... a dark chromafield taking him where he clearly did not want to go, dissolving in flames and the ashes of shattered hopes. Daithi moved to cover the boy's shrunken chromafield with his own, gently drawing it outward, away from the fear and terror the dream was arousing. The nightmare faded, and Shay sighed and fell into a deep, peaceful sleep.

Chapter 21

Réiltín, the serving girl at *The Pipit's Nest*—a title she laughed at, for her days as a girl were long since over and done—had spent most of the night tossing and turning in her bed, unable to sleep for thinking of the tragic events of the previous day. She kept seeing the smoke rising from the Grove, and hearing the hoofbeats pounding past her doorstep as every man who had a horse galloped east to help put the fire out. Then the horrifying news that the Grovekeeper was dead, his house a smoking ruin. At last, well before dawn, she sighed and got dressed. She brought the fire back to life and hung a kettle of water over it by sheer habit. Then she sat down at the kitchen table and gave in to the desire to have a good cry.

A light tapping at the door startled her. She brushed her tears hastily away and went to answer it, wondering who in the world would be calling at such an hour. To her astonishment, a bedraggled, red-headed boy stood on the step.

"Well, now ... and who might ye be?" she asked.

"I'm sorry to disturb you so early and all," the youngster said nervously. "I'm Shay. Grovekeeper Daithi's boy? He told me to come to you."

Réiltín gave him a puzzled glance and motioned him in. "Have a seat at the table, then. Ye can tell me what he said after I get ye somethin' to eat. How does that sound?"

Shay smiled and slipped comfortably back into the village

speech he had grown up with. "I'd be beholdin' to ye."

Réiltín put some dried bramble leaves into two mugs and poured hot water from the kettle into them as Shay took a seat at the table. Then she took a loaf of bread from the breadbasket and sliced two thick pieces from it, slathered them with honey, and laid both on a single plate in the center of the table. "Wouldn't anyone in the Grove take ye in, then?"

"They would've, but the Grovekeeper told me not to stay there. Too dangerous, he said." He looked hungrily at the bread.

Réiltín sat down across from him. "Because of the fire? The men who rode up there with the wind at their backs, when they saw 'twas the Grovekeeper's home that was burnin', thought they'd be too late to save the Grove, but the wind suddenly began blowin' t'other way, toward Gaotha. 'Twas strange, but a good thing fer the Grove. 'Tis safe enough to go back now." She pushed the plate of bread toward him. "Go on, eat up," she said. "I'll not send ye away hungry." She frowned slightly. "The Grovekeeper told ye that?"

Shay nodded. "Wants me to stay here while he goes back to the Grove fer a bit." The boy snatched up one of the slices of bread and took an appreciative bite.

Réiltín stared at him incredulously. "Are ye sayin' he's alive? Because sure enough 'twas his body they found there."

The boy hurriedly swallowed. "He wanted to tell ye himself, but didn't want to scare ye by speakin' in yer mind with no warnin'. 'Tis kind of strange and all, the first time. He said to ask ye if it's okay first, and if ye agree, he'll explain it all to ye there."

Réiltín blinked. "He'll explain it all ... where?"

"In yer mind. Is that okay? It doesn't hurt," he assured her when she frowned. "And he can explain things better than me."

Réiltín's frown deepened. "Where is Grovekeeper Daithi right now?" she demanded.

"He's in my mind."

Réiltín gave him a disbelieving look and pushed one of the

mugs of tea toward him. "I think ye should finish up this tea and bread, lad," she said kindly, "then get yerself back home again, or wherever ye'll be livin' now, and have a good long sleep."

Shay stared sightlessly at the tabletop for a moment. Then he looked at her earnestly. "The Grovekeeper wants ye to ask me a question nobody could answer but him."

She sighed and went along. "Fine, then. What did he give me fer my mam five cycles ago?"

Shay appeared to commune silently with the table again, then blinked and carefully recited a list of herbs. "Ginger, St. John's wort, feverfew, devil's claw, and valerian root ... and he told ye she shouldn't have much milk and bread, cuz it would make her worse." He grinned, flushed with success in repeating everything correctly, then caught sight of Réiltín's stricken face and dropped his eyes. "I'm sorry I've upset ye. I know what it's like to lose yer mam ... and to be grateful to the Grovekeeper fer being kind to her."

Réiltín scarcely heard him. "His very words," she said in a hushed voice, "and ye couldn't possibly have known. No one could." She gave Shay a brisk nod. "All right, then. Tell him he can speak to me any way he wants. I'm listenin'." She glanced somewhat nervously around her, then her mouth dropped open as vivid colors filled her mind. The last thing she remembered seeing was the grin on Shay's face as he began wolfing down the second piece of bread. Then she had ears only for the Grovekeeper's welcome voice, though what he told her filled her with a rising fury.

When at last Réiltín blinked a few times and came to herself, Shay was staring at the empty plate morosely. He glanced at Réiltín's face and blanched.

"To think," she practically spat into his face, "we were taken in by 'is lies!" She stormed to her feet and paced angrily back and forth. "Actin' so nice and friendly, he was, claimin' to care for Gaotha, for wasn't it his own home, too?" She stood still and glared at Shay as though he were personally to blame for this duplicity. "I tried to warn them!" she declared as the boy shrank in his chair. "*No* one meets with the likes of a Celtic warrior unless they're up to no good ... but they wouldn't listen!" She collapsed into her chair and burst into tears. "That *arrach*—that *monster*— murdered him!" she wailed. "Burned him alive in his own home!"

Shay pushed her mug of tea tentatively toward her, but Réiltín rose and began pacing again, frowning in thought.

"The Grovekeeper said ye need to get to Delbna as quick as ye can, as far south as we can take ye before the border. Whilst I make arrangements fer that, ye mustn't stay here, fer that sorry excuse of a Druid saw me comin' from the Grove and might come here to look fer ye when he can't find ye there." She stopped pacing. "I know someone I can trust ... has a cart and pony and makes deliveries out of Gaotha now and then. 'Twill get ye there much quicker than on foot. Ye'll be safe with him." She removed her apron. "Come along, then, we'd best be goin' now."

Shay nodded and rose, giving the basket a regretful glance.

"Don't worry, lad," she said dryly. "He has a kitchen and there's sure to be food in it." She grabbed her shawl and they left as the first rays of sun peeked over the horizon.

⁓ ⚘ ⁓

As the flush of dawn began to filter through the Oak's canopy, the Grovetenders began to arrive in unaccustomed silence, exchanging quick, sideward glances as they approached the tree. Ronán placed Daithi's urn against the trunk as Alben entered the clearing.

"Ah, I see the Grovekeeper asked you to bring it," their elder said approvingly, "and you're all here, just as he instructed."

Ronán glanced up in surprise. "He spoke to all of you, too?" The others stared at him for a moment, then a collision of voices filled the clearing.

"I woke up and thought it was a dream—"

"I couldn't believe my own ears when I—"

"You had the same dream?"

"Did he tell you what hap—"

"How he was *murdered* by Cathair?" Alben demanded, overriding the cacophony. "How our friendly Overdruid is now looking to do the same to Shay for witnessing it? Not to mention burning the Grove to the ground for spite and to be rid of us all!"

Four astonished pairs of eyes blinked. This was not the mild, elderly Grovekeeper who had always allowed Ronán to lead them.

"This was no shared delusion of a dream!" Alben said, so fiercely that not even Ronán dared to speak. "Look to the rowan!" he commanded, pointing at the very largest of the protective trees.

Four pairs of eyes fastened on the tree. For a moment, all was still, hardly a breeze stirring. The silvery trunk reached up into branches filled with clusters of creamy white flowers set against a background of feathery leaves. Then the branches began to sway, undulating back and forth, though no other tree's branches were stirring. A white blossom flew from the tree and stopped in mid-air in front of Ronán, who reached out a trembling hand and accepted it, holding it to himself in awe. Three more blossoms came to a stop before three equally flabbergasted Grovetenders. The tree once again stood as immobile as all the others.

Alben cocked an eye at his stunned companions, all of them holding white blossoms like attendants at a handfasting. "Ready to listen to me?" He accepted their hasty nods. "Now, then, here's what the Grovekeeper wants us to do."

~ ❧ ~

An hour later Cathair rode alone from his house to the Grove. He had slept well the previous night, knowing that Daithi was no longer going to be feeding information to Ferghus. He skirted the ruins of Daithi's home, somewhat surprised the Grove hadn't caught fire as well, considering the direction of the wind when he left. He hadn't meant to actually torch the Grove when he'd angrily hurled the threat at Daithi, for Cathair's belief in the sacredness of the Grove was genuine. But the nosy Grovekeeper would be replaced with another one ... unless there was no Grove to keep. Best to come back tonight, accidentally drop a torch or two on the outside perimeter, and hopefully the Council would need to find a new location for their ninth Grove.

He continued on to each of the Grovetender's cabins. None of the Grovetenders were there, and he searched each cabin in vain for the wretched boy who knew far more than was good for him. The two men Faolán had promised him were due to arrive tomorrow morning, and Cathair was determined to have the boy securely trussed and gagged in his home, ready for them to dispose of. Ridding his Order of a known traitor was one thing; killing a boy who had done nothing yet to deserve it was another, his words to Daithi notwithstanding. He'd go to the Grove looking for him out of deep concern and take him away with him, then claim the boy had run off on his own. Far better than having two fianna storm through the Grove and likely kill him on that sacred ground. His own mind rose up to accuse him.

And didn't you do the same to Daithi?

Daithi wasn't in the Grove! he fiercely answered himself. *And the Maker knows he deserved to die. He's a traitor, and he tried to kill me!* He finished his circle of the Grove and tethered his horse to the tree in front of the ruins of Daithi's home.

"I'll find that brat if I have to search the entire Grove to do it," he muttered savagely as he strode through the hawthorns. But, though he searched through both hawthorns and rowans with grim determination, he could find no trace of anyone. *Aren't Grovetenders supposed to be here, tending their Grove?* Then, hearing voices, he followed them to the center of the Grove and came to an abrupt stop. All five Grovetenders were facing the ancient Oak ... and an urn that nestled against its trunk.

Alben turned toward him. "How fortunate!" he said affably.

"You're just in time for the Grovekeeper's service."

"My apologies for interrupting you." Cathair glanced around the clearing. "I was concerned for Shay's welfare, the poor boy, and came to offer him my home to stay in until I can find a couple who are willing to take him in. As Overdruid of this territory, it's my responsibility to see that he has a family."

"It would be if he were an acolyte," Alben said, "but the boy has taken no vows, nor did our Grovekeeper have any intention of having him do so."

"All the more reason for me to take him off your hands," the Overdruid said smoothly. "Your Grovekeeper and I knew each other for many cycles, and the least I can do for my friend is to take care of Shay for him, as Daithi would want me to do."

"Perhaps we can discuss that after our service," Alben said. "All of us have already made our eulogy speeches. Would you like to make one?" He motioned Cathair forward and the Overdruid reluctantly took his place next to him. Eoin and Dughan silently moved behind them.

"I won't delay your service more than I already have," Cathair said. "Shouldn't Shay be here?"

"As I said, the boy is not a member of our Order. Now, be still, everyone, and focus on the Oak."

All eyes turned to the ancient tree, its leafy crown lit with sunlight. After a few moments of silence, Cathair shifted restlessly. *What on earth are they wait—*

A gasp came from Eoin as the sunlit leaves above seemed to liquify, golden drops of light, iridescent with sheens of emerald, cerulean, and silver, rained down from the tree and into the earth below. Cathair froze in horrified disbelief as the clear, powerful voice of the Grovekeeper entered his mind.

I, Grovekeeper Daithi, claim this Grove as my own by right of the foul murder Cathair committed against me, who is here to hunt down Shay, the sole witness to his deed. Take him!

Cathair backed up as accusing eyes turned to him. He paled at the realization that his wasn't the only mind who had heard the Grovekeeper speak. "This is some kind of trick!" he cried, but not a single expression changed. Every one of the Grovetenders, he knew, could manipulate energy lines. He was uncertain of the power each of them held on their own, but when added together with the power of Daithi's angered spirit—

He turned to flee, but it was too late. Eoin and Dughan grabbed his arms and turned him to face the Oak ... and Alben.

"Is that how you treat your 'friends'?" Alben demanded. "By burning them to death in their own homes?"

The Overdruid glanced fearfully at the Oak. "Let me go! You haven't the right to lay hands on me!"

"We've the right to do far more than that," Alben growled. "You stand accused of murder and will face the Council for it!"

Anger banished Cathair's fear. "How *dare* you threaten me! You can't take me to the Council without proof ... which you don't have, because I've done nothing wrong!"

"We know what you did to him," Dughan declared, his brows bristling. "We know you beat him nearly to death with his own staff, then set fire to his house ... with him in it!"

"Where's that young brat?" Cathair snarled. "Bring him to me, and I'll teach him not to lie!"

"If you're speaking of Shay," Ronán said coldly, "we haven't seen him, and have no idea where he is now. Unless there's a *second* murder you'd like to confess to."

"You've no proof of *any*—"

"I saw the lad during the night," Alben cut in. "Grovekeeper Daithi told me you likely took his ring, but 'twas Shay who told me where it is now. For he saw you take it out of the left pocket of your robe, saw you stand and admire it while the Grovekeeper's home burned ... ah," he said, observing Cathair's horrified expression. "I see you forgot to remove it. Foolish of you. Tighten your hold," he commanded Eoin and Dughan. "Search his robe," he told Ronán.

"No!" Cathair tried to break free, but the two Grovetenders held him fast. "Let go of me! You've no right, I tell you!"

"We have *every* right to do as our eldest Grovetender commands," Ronán said with a respectful nod to Alben. He reached into the left pocket of Cathair's robe, the Overdruid twisting in vain to stop him.

"Well, well ... what have we here?" Ronán withdrew a silver ring and held it up for all to see. Dappled sunlight caught it, revealing the intertwined leaves of Daithi's ring.

"The brat lies," Cathair ground between clenched teeth. "Daithi *gave* his ring to me! A token of our friend—"

"Murderer!" Alben accused Cathair. "You'll answer for it to—"

Alben got no further. Cathair jerked his arm out of Eoin's loosened grip, then swiveled toward Dughan and drove his fist into the Grovetender's surprised face. Instead of trying to evade Dorrean, who was standing behind him, he lunged forward and shoved Alben out of his way as hard as he could. The Grovetender fell heavily backwards, his head connecting hard with one of the roots of the Oak. Blood spread slowly, trickling over the massive root to fall onto the earth below. For a single, horrified moment no one moved or spoke, then everything seemed to happen at once.

Eoin leapt forward with an anguished cry. "You've *killed* him!" He dropped to his knees by Alben's side.

Cathair was already running as fast as he could to the rowans, Dughan and Dorrean in pursuit, while Ronán dropped down next to Eoin to see what he could do for Alben. The pursuing Grovetenders abruptly stopped at the rowans, stared at each other for a moment, and returned to their colleagues. Dorrean shook his head when Ronán threw them a questioning look.

"The Grovekeeper told us to go back and help Alben ... that he would fetch Cathair himself."

Deep within the rowans, Cathair came to a stop as he realized he was no longer being pursued. He stood gasping for breath, winded from the unaccustomed run through tangled underbrush. Above him a wind began to stir, sending a moaning dirge through the trees. The two lowest branches of the rowan he was standing next to reached out toward Cathair like groping arms. He backed off hurriedly, staring at the tree in renewed fear. Behind him the low branch of a young rowan scraped across his back, dragging its feathery leaves across his neck. Cathair screamed.

The next moment he was running again, beset on every side by reaching rowan branches that clawed his face, and roots that unearthed themselves before his stumbling feet. He tripped in the thick underbrush and fell, then scrambled to his feet as the very earth beneath him surged. Weeping in fear, he ran, and the Grove whipped him soundly as he fled, the thorny branches of the hawthorns tearing his robe and raking his flesh. Then, to his utter horror, he broke out of the underbrush straight back into the center of the Grove. He froze, staring around him in confusion.

The Grovetenders, kneeling at Alben's side, barely glanced up as a vine whipped out from the rowan next to the Overdruid and entwined itself around his legs. He fell to his knees, screaming for help as the vine bound his arms tightly to his sides and gagged his mouth. Outraged, muffled oaths came from behind the leafy vine.

The Grovetenders paid him no attention, their hands firmly placed on Alben, their faces set in concentration as they gave him their energy.

"We can't save him," Eoin murmured in grief.

"No," Ronán said sadly, "but we can give him a chance to say what he wishes before he goes."

A single sylvan drop fell from the tree onto Alben's forehead.

"Grovekeeper," the old man whispered.

I'm here, Alben. I'm so sorry I didn't anticipate his attack.

"Nothing to be sorry for ... too old to be transplanted. Glad to be going like this, having helped you one last time." He sighed.

"Would have liked to have seen just one of the faery folk."

You've been the truest of friends. Go in peace, Alben, and follow the stars when you see them.

The oldest Grovetender opened his eyes and stared up at the impenetrable canopy of the Oak. "Why, there *are* stars ... in the morning's light!" he marveled. His head fell slowly to the side, his eyes closed, and Alben breathed his last.

A rumbling sound came from the earth below, and the four Grovetenders scrambled hastily back. Between the two roots where Alben lay, the earth began to crumble inward. The Grovetender's body and the urn containing the remains of the Grovekeeper slid gently into the opened cavity. The grave closed. The rowan trembled and clusters of snowy blossoms floated from its branches over to the Oak, covering the dual grave completely.

Before anyone had a chance to speak, Ronán gasped and closed his eyes. After a long moment, he spoke.

"Grovekeeper Daithi commands us to leave the Grove with all our possessions. We will not be returning. Because of the sacrilege committed here and at the Grovekeeper's home by Cathair, the Grove is closed to all and may not be trespassed upon." He shook himself slightly, then opened his eyes and gave them a haunted look. "And," he added in a hushed voice, "he told me..."

"Told you what?" Dughan asked.

"He didn't do ... that," Ronán whispered, nodding at the grave.

For a moment they all stood there looking uneasily around them. Then Ronán gave them a decisive nod. "We'll obey his last command to us. Pack up, each of you, and meet me at my cabin in the morning. We'll leave together for Gaotha, to spread the word that the Grove is off limits to all, and that Cathair is a foul murderer. Then we'll travel to Uisneach to report to the Council." His face hardened. "Cathair will be going with us. The Council won't take the murder of a Grovekeeper and Grovetender lightly."

Chapter 22

The next morning, a series of tangled events occurred in the village of Gaotha. The first of them happened down at the cove as the sun's rays were beginning to lighten the sky. High up on the beach, Seamus was wrestling the last of three barrels into his cart while his pony snorted with impatience. Down at the jetty, the fishermen preparing to launch their boats stopped and stared at a sailed currach that rounded the point from the south and headed swiftly over the calmer waters of the cove toward the beach. Six rugged men were on board, four dressed in leathers, their beards braided. The other two were dressed in village attire. Frightened whispers came from the watching fishermen as many of them recognized some of the warriors as the same ones that had twice visited *The Pipit's Nest*. None of them paid the fishermen any attention as the boat's sail was lowered and the men took to the oars and wielded them with synchronized strokes. They headed purposefully toward the western end of the cove, where the water was calm. Then, dripping oars held above the surface, they allowed the currach to glide in and expertly brought it to a halt just shy of scraping the bottom.

"There's nothing to be afraid of."

The startled fishermen glanced toward the beach, where a cloaked and hooded man stood at the ramp to the jetty, though none had heard him approach. He carried a large pack on his back and leaned on a runed staff as he spoke.

"They're here for me, and the two that leave the boat won't be staying in the village."

"Overdruid Cathair!" gasped the fisherman closest to him. "'Tis a relief these men are known to ye, but ... yer face!"

"Mere scratches, nothing more," Cathair said brusquely, then strode across the length of the beach to the currach, where the two men dressed in common garb had splashed their way to the shore. Unable to hear them, the fishermen went about their business.

"Nice to know Faolán is so punctual," the Overdruid said as he approached.

One of the men in the currach scowled. A black braid dangled on either side of his face; the rest of his hair was bound tightly back with a leather thong. "He sent word we'd be here today to give you two of his men, and today it is. We weren't expecting to be greeted." He indicated the two men standing on the beach. "The fianna know where your house is, Druid."

"*Over*druid," Cathair pointedly corrected. "And plans have changed since I last contacted Faolán."

"How have they changed?" the warrior growled.

"Who's asking?" Cathair asked icily.

"Ragnar, and you'd best answer, *Druid.*"

"I don't answer to you ... but I *will* be going with you." Cathair stepped toward the water's edge, then stopped when knives suddenly appeared in the hands of every man aboard.

"Hold there," Ragnar commanded. "You'll answer, or you'll be staying here. We've no orders to be taking on a passenger."

"I found it necessary to get rid of a traitor who was feeding information to the Bardic Order. My colleagues foolishly tried to detain me, but I escaped them during the night."

Ragnar snorted derisively. "And who was this traitor of yours ... a cat? By the look of your face, I'd say you lost the battle."

The men's laughter died at the level stare Cathair gave their leader, but Ragnar didn't back down.

"And just how did a tree-loving Druid rid himself of a traitor?"

"I burned him alive in his home." Ignoring the murmur of surprise that greeted this, Cathair continued. "So, unless you want the one who is paying your expenses to be unable to continue doing so," he said pointedly, "I suggest you take me with you."

Ragnar's expression had gained a measure of respect. He motioned to a seat. "A Druid with blood on his hands is welcome."

"I had every right to rid my Order of a traitor who tried to kill me," growled Cathair. He turned to the two men standing next to him. "Your names?"

"Murrogh and Dunnal," one of the men said, indicating himself first and nodding toward his companion.

"Go to my house and pack supplies into the bags you'll find ready for you," Cathair ordered. "You can have the use of my horse, and there's coin enough in one of the bags to purchase another and cover your expenses. Don't be taking anything else from my home," he warned, "or you'll answer to me for it, and then to Faolán."

"Why are we being left here?" Murrogh asked. "Do you want us to go after these Druids of yours?"

Cathair shook his head. "You're to stay out of the Grove and well clear of my colleagues, but there's a young witness who saw what I did to the traitor. Shay is eight or nine cycles, thin and freckled, with hair redder than yours, and he knows he's being hunted. I've checked the places he might have gone in Gaotha. He probably headed south, thinking to find help from the Bards in Delbna, since that's his only chance of getting across the boundary of my territory. If he isn't there, check the coastal road on the way back. He can't have gotten far yet."

The warrior frowned. "You're wanting this boy killed?"

"Is that a problem?"

"Killing a man in battle wouldn't be. There's no honor in murdering a defenseless youngling."

"Keep him, then, to give to Faolán and make a warrior of him. Once the boy has blood on his own hands, he can't accuse another.

Take him south with you until you pass the estuary, then west to the coast. We'll be dropping off warriors there in three weeks. Join them after getting Shay onto that ship." Cathair fastidiously lifted his robe and cloak and waded out to the currach, where two burly warriors grabbed his arms and hoisted him in.

"Do as he told you," Ragnar ordered the men on the beach. He cast an eye at the lightening horizon, blushing with tinges of red. "And you, Druid," he growled, "will be taking an oar and pulling your weight 'til we catch some wind. "The weather won't be improving this day, and we're two men short. The sooner we get back to Carr, the better for us all."

⁓ ❧ ⁓

Scarcely three hours later, the common room at *The Pipit's Nest* was more occupied than usual for mid-morning. The sight of two burly strangers entering the Overdruid's house and leaving with full packs and his horse not long after dawn had caused a flurry of speculation, and there was no better place in Gaotha to speculate than the tavern. The joint conjecturing, however, had brought nothing further to light until old Maude, who had noticed the men and tracked their movements, came bustling in with the news that the Overdruid himself was not at home. She had knocked and peered through every window, she said with a satisfied nod. When no one answered, she had searched the premises.

"'Twas my duty to check on the man, now, wasn't it? Could've been lyin' dead in his bed! *Murdered* by those very men, no doubt!" Her eyes widened as her voice dropped to a conspiratorial whisper. "But nay, I'm tellin' ye true, t'were no body to be found anywhere in t'house ... no, not a speck of him anywhere! And unless he left before dawn's light, there's no way he could've left without *me* seein' it." She threw a challenging look around the room, but not a soul disputed this statement. "And where d'ye suppose they came from—on foot!—if 'tweren't the sea?" she demanded. "Warriors they be, dressed as such or no. We're all of us likely to be murdered in our own beds this very night!"

"Well, now," Seamus drawled from a table in the back, where he was finishing up his breakfast. "That's sure to be givin' ye plenty to gossip about, then, isn't it? Here or in t'afterlife."

The men laughed and Maude glared at Seamus, who raised a placating hand.

"I've no time to be getting' in a fuss with ye, Maude," he said. "But don't be wastin' yer own time lookin' fer our Overdruid. He left with the dawn in a currach of warriors, who exchanged two of their men fer him. Saw it with my own eyes when I was loadin' my cart. 'Twill be long, I'm thinkin', before we set eyes on him again." He rose and slapped a copper on the table. "Well, then, I'm off to Delbna to make a delivery—why, what's amiss, lass?" he asked in surprise as Réiltín burst from the kitchen in a fit of tears, clutching a scrap of parchment.

"It's me mam's sister, taken serious ill!" Réiltín wailed. "And no one there to care fer her. Word just came to me now as I was gatherin' herbs in the garden."

"Won't the Keeper let ye go?"

"He will and all, for young Shannon can take my place whilst I'm gone, but I 'aven't the time fer walkin' all the way to Creel!"

"Creel? Well, if ye don't mind my cargo, ye can come along with me. 'Tis only a few furlongs west o' Delbna, after all."

Réiltín brightened. "What cargo is that?"

"Barrels of rotten fish. Been collectin' what the fishermen would throw out otherwise, as I always do, and store it down near the beach where I can take my cart to collect it. Good food fer the soil, that, and not many willin' to transport it."

Sympathetic looks turned to the grimacing woman.

"I'm leavin' as soon as may be," Seamus added. "Wagon's packed and waitin' fer me outside. Is my order ready?"

"'Tis set to go. I'll fetch it and my pack, then."

Seamus nodded agreeably, and the moment Réiltín returned, the two of them headed for the door. No sooner had Seamus opened it, though, than the noisy arrival of ponies and wagons was heard coming down the dirt road.

"What now?" Seamus exclaimed. Behind him, the occupants of the common room pushed their way past as they vied for a glimpse of the unusual disturbance. Within moments they all stood outside, staring at the small caravan of four Grovetenders. One of them climbed down from his wagon and walked over to them.

"Now, then, Grovetender Ronán," Seamus said mildly. "Is something amiss at the Grove?"

The Grovetender shook his head. "Not since Cathair left it."

"The Overdruid?"

"The *former* Overdruid. He forfeited his rank the moment he murdered our Grovekeeper."

Even Maude was rendered speechless. Then the Keeper stepped forward, frowning.

"The day of the fire?" he exclaimed. "Why, I know fer a fact that the Overdruid headed south late that mornin'! He stopped in here fer a bite and told me so himself."

"I'm sure he did ... then doubled back and beat our Grovekeeper near to death before setting his house on fire with him in it," Ronán said, to gasps of horror. "Alben told us Shay witnessed it before he fled the Grove. And yesterday morning Cathair killed Alben before our very eyes! He escaped during the night, or he'd be coming with us to answer to the Council."

Stunned silence fell over the yard.

"He speaks the truth about the Grovekeeper's death," Réiltín suddenly declared. "Shay came to my house early yesterday mornin' and told me what happened."

The Keeper frowned. "And ye said nothin' of it 'til now?"

"Would ye have believed me if I had?" she shot back.

"So where's the boy now?" he demanded.

"Runnin' fer his life," she said angrily, "with no more'n a few days worth of food. Took off sometime durin' the night. He's the only one saw what happened, and I doubt he's comin' back. Was askin' me where Derry was, up north where his Mam come from. Hopin' to find family to take him in, no doubt." She turned a worried gaze to the northeast. "The Maker help him," she murmured.

Ronán nodded to Réiltín. "We're headed to Uisneach to report to the Council and be reassigned. If we come across the lad, we'll see he gets to Derry safely."

"Yer not returnin' to the Grove?" Seamus asked in surprise.

"It's been desecrated with a foul murder and wrongful death ... and the Grovekeeper isn't gone," he added with a meaningful look at the wide-eyed villagers. "His spirit has claimed the Grove, and all of us and Cathair himself are witnesses to it. We heard him proclaim it from the sacred Oak and confirm his death at Cathair's hands. The ground opened of its own accord and accepted his ashes and Alben's body at its very trunk! Then a sacred rowan covered the grave over with its blossoms." He paused as murmurs of wonder circulated the gathering. "The Grovekeeper's spirit will protect and take care of the Grove as he's always done," he gravely told the hushed gathering. "If you're wise, you'll not trespass on the Grove, or do anything to hurt it. Cathair himself could tell you why, for the trees of the Grove whipped and tripped him with branch and root, then dragged him back when he tried to flee."

"And so they must have," said Seamus, his voice filled with awe. "For the fishermen I spoke to after Cathair left told me his face was marked with deep scratches. They'll be tellin' ye so when they come back from fishin'."

The villagers looked uneasily in the direction of the Grove. The shadows in the east were growing, though the sun was still shining brightly. Seamus nodded decisively as he helped Réiltín into his wagon. Noses wrinkled at the smell of rank fish coming from the three barrels in the back. The old man nodded to Ronán.

"Daithi's Grove it is, then, and we'll not be intrudin'," Seamus said, unknowingly giving the Grove its new name. He pulled himself into the cart and took the reins. The villagers lost no time heading back into the tavern, talking excitedly amongst themselves.

"A moment, please." Ronán walked up to Réiltín and handed her a small package. "I've something for you from the Grovekeeper. Give it to the one who'll treasure it most." He turned, then paused for a moment. "And tell him we'll all miss him," he said in a low voice. He walked back to his wagon, and the caravan turned around to head back east on their way to Uisneach.

Seamus gave the reins a brisk slap and they headed south.

"Aren't we goin' to yer place to get Shay?" Réiltín asked.

"He's right behind ye," Seamus said with a chuckle. "Got me two barrels of rotten fish back there ... and one barrel of boy. After the stench he's been sittin' in, though, I doubt I'll fetch much of a price fer him."

Réiltín laughed, and a muffled voice came from the barrel behind her. "Can I come out now?"

"After we're well clear of Gaotha, lad, and find a stream to wash ye in." Seamus cleared his throat. "Clever of ye," he murmured to Réiltín as they left the tavern behind.

Réiltín glanced at him. "To spread the notion that Shay headed northwest?"

"To spread the notion that yer mam had a sister."

She laughed, but Seamus shook his head. "'Tis dangerous goin' with us, lass."

"Ye might be needin' me, old man," she said crisply. She looked down at the small package she held in her lap, then opened it. Inside was Daithi's ring. She caught it to her breast, tears filling her eyes.

Chapter 23

The journey by cart to Delbna took three days along the coastal road. Thanks to Réiltín's presence and the liberal application of boiled walnut hulls to darken his hair, Shay was able to sit up front between his elders after leaving the vicinity of Gaotha. Until they reached Delbna, Réiltín told him, he was the brown-haired son of an unlikely looking couple, a matter which spurred the new couple's first argument.

"More likely an old man with his daughter and grandson!" Seamus snorted. "What old codger like me would be handfasted to a young lass like yerself?"

"I'm forty if I'm a day," Réiltín retorted, "and ye well know it! Never called a lass fer over twenty of 'em ... exceptin' by yerself."

Seamus sent a sidelong glance over Shay's head. The boy kept still, only his eyes moving back and forth as he followed the conversation going on above him.

"And ... have ye minded?" the fisherman asked.

"Don't ye think I'd have told ye if I had?" Réiltín demanded. "And," she sniffed, "yer not such an old codger as ye'd like everyone to believe. Fifty-five ye are, and not a day older!"

"Hmph!" Seamus turned his attention back to the road.

"A mere fifteen cycles," Réiltín loftily informed the pony, "is nothin' worth mentionin' ... and if anyone does," she warned it darkly, "they'll be dealin' with me."

Shay's widened eyes swiveled back to Seamus.

"Nay, lass, they won't," the driver contradicted, a smart snap of the reins emphasizing his words to startled beast and boy. "Fer anyone givin' ye the least bit of trouble will be dealin' with *me*."

"Even Maude?" Réiltín asked archly. "She once set her sights on ye, as I recall."

"*Especially* Maude," Seamus growled. He sat frowning for a long moment, the reins going slack in his hands. The wagon came to a stop, then lurched forward a bit as the pony made for the side of the road to crop the grass. A long silence fell over the wagon, broken at last by Seamus.

"Why do ye think I've been comin' to the tavern every night fer all these cycles?" he asked the preoccupied animal. "Not fer the single drink," he assured it, "nor the company of half-soused fishermen." He glanced at Réiltín. "'Twas fer you. Was all I ever expected to have, those moments when ye come to my table and smile at me like ... like I mean somethin' to ye." He turned his attention back to the pony.

"And so ye do."

Another silent moment stretched forever to the listening boy.

"I never thought," Seamus said in a low voice. "Not fer a single moment all these cycles ... I just—" He broke off and stared at the grazing pony as if he'd never seen one before.

"Well, then," Réiltín said softly. "What is it we've been waitin' fer ... all these cycles?"

Seamus turned and reached over Shay's head to gently touch Réiltín's cheek. "Fer this," he said, and leaned toward her.

Shay let out a yelp and wriggled his way out from between them, then scrambled over Réiltín's feet to escape from the wagon altogether. "Think I'll be, er ... takin' a moment or two to relieve myself," he muttered as he headed for the bushes.

The chuckles coming from the wagon were echoed by the

Grovekeeper's chuckles in his mind.

⤳ ❦ ⤲

That night, Shay lay on his mat by the diminishing flames of the campfire, unable to sleep for the memories that seemed to grow more vivid with his every attempt to forget them. He saw a flying object strike the Grovekeeper ... saw him lying on the floor of his home ... saw a dark shadow fall across his vision that scared him to his bones. The flames of the campfire became the flames of the Grovekeeper's home, rising eerily into the sky above. He lay shaking, unable to stop the terror of it from taking over his mind. He pulled his blanket over his head, grasped the thin leather cord around his neck, and drew out the engraved silver ring that lay underneath his tunic. He clutched it in his trembling fist. Light spilled out from between his fingers, sparkling emerald green, honey gold, and cerulean blue with a streak of silver, the colors of the Grovekeeper's chromafield. His breathing slowed and he relaxed as a feeling of protection and safety flowed into him from the ring. The welcome sound of the Grovekeeper's voice filled his mind.

I've infused some of my chromafield into my ring. Whenever you feel afraid, hold it close and think of me, not as I was then, but as I am now—more alive than I've ever been, able to tell you freely how much I love you—and let it comfort you.

Shay nodded, unable to speak. The darkness in his mind lifted.

Perhaps you'd like to hear about some of the youthful exploits of your new uncle. Amusement laced the Grovekeeper's words.

Is he truly my uncle?

Yes, indeed, and it will please him if you call him so.

Uncle Ferghus. Shay frowned, trying it out. *Sounds strange. I never had an uncle before.*

Then we'll both call him 'Uncle Ferghus', and by the time you get there, it won't seem strange at all. Now, let me tell you the absolute truth about the idiotic stunt Uncle Ferghus pulled when he was about your age.

Shay grinned and slipped the ring back inside his tunic. It lay warm against his chest as Daithi began his tale, and the youngster soon fell asleep to the comforting presence of both.

A few moments later, he woke in terror, gasping with fear made all the worse for not being able to remember the lurking nightmare. He clutched the ring and the Grovekeeper's voice spoke soothingly.

It's okay, Shay. It was just a bad dream.

Can ye keep me awake? he cried. *Please?*

What did you dream about?

I don't know! It always begins with a shadow on the floor—and then I can't remember. I think it's somethin' that happened when I looked in the window of yer house.

Silence fell over his mind, broken at last by the Grovekeeper. *You left the tree after I told you not to?*

I ... I just wanted to be there for you, Shay said in a small voice. *The way you've always been for me. So I came down and looked and saw the Overdruid trapped behind the table ... and the vase hittin' you. I wanted to touch yer chromafield with mine so you could use my energy to heal yerself. But then I saw the shadow ... and somethin' happened, but I can't remember!* Shay cried in growing panic. "Then I looked again and he was beatin' you with yer staff. I was angry and wanted to take it from him ... and it flew from his hands and almost hit the window! He saw me and I ran—and the hawthorn protected me!—and he got kindlin' and peat and ... threw brands inside ... there was smoke and flames. He left and the hawthorn let me go and I ran ... and then I was up in the Oak, but I don't remember climbin' it.* The boy curled up tightly as silent sobs shook his body.

It's all right, Shay, you don't have to remember anything. Just relax and hold my ring close. I'm going to have a talk with your uncle and see if he can help.

Shay turned away from the fire's glow and lay awake, staring into the darkness and clutching the ring to his chest. It wasn't long before the Grovekeeper returned.

Your uncle can help you, but he says it's best done by someone you know and trust. Are you willing for him to enter your mind while you're sleeping and remove the nightmare?

Shay's anxiety soared. *But if I fall asleep, I'll have it again!*

Only the first few moments until your uncle identifies and removes it. When you wake up, you won't remember what it was and you'll never have it again. He removed a memory of mine once, and it didn't hurt at all.

Can ... can you be there, too? Please? I can do it if I know you'll be there.

I'll be there every single moment.

Okay. I'll try. Shay closed his eyes, but couldn't relax until he heard the gentle strains of a harp in his mind. He'd never heard music like this before. Bards played at *The Pipit's Nest* on occasion, but this music was nothing like the rollicking songs he'd heard from beneath the tavern's open windows, or the lively village dances at festivals. As peaceful waves of music filled his mind, he sighed, his head fell to the side, and he slipped into sleep.

And the nightmare began as he fell with two silent watchers into a dark shadow against the floor of the Grovekeeper's home.

Seething emotions of crimson anger and burnt orange distrust swirling through a dark chromafield embraced him, carrying Shay into the mind of someone he was so terrified of that he could barely think. The need to flee and the panic of realizing he couldn't overwhelmed him. Dull, ashen cords repulsed him. And everywhere, thoughts without words sparked burgundy and crimson streaks of self-righteous anger. Then he saw the memory orbs and an idea took hold of him...

The dream abruptly stopped. Harp music began to softly play again, dispelling the nightmare and sending the boy deeper into sleep. Daithi had no time to wonder at finding himself alone in Shay's mind before his brother's voice spoke.

Follow our bond into my mind.

The Grovekeeper did not hesitate, and the next moment his brother's sphere of colors shimmered before him, a dark memory orb right next to him. *You kept it?*

It's a nightmare I think we should both see to its conclusion, Ferghus said grimly, *and I wasn't about to make Shay experience it again. Cathair's is the only mind he could have possibly traveled into, for it certainly wasn't yours. The youngling decided to touch one of his memory orbs, so we're about to experience one of Cathair's memories as Shay saw it.*

Play it, Daithi said. He watched as his brother moved toward the orb and touched it.

Once again the shadow took the watchers into a dark chromafield. Once again they were nearly overwhelmed by the same panic Shay felt as he was taken against his will into the mind of someone he was terrified of. They felt the boy's thrill of excitement as an idea took hold of him, an idea worthy of the heroes of old. He leaned toward one of the memory orbs and touched it.

The next moment he was sitting in a comfortable chair in the most luxurious, spacious room he had ever seen. And sitting across from him was a tall, imposing Druid in an emerald robe with the insignia of a gold staff on the right front shoulder, cinched at the waist with a gold cord. His hair was iron-grey, his brows thick, his face lined with wrinkles. Cold blue eyes looked sharply into his as the First of the Council spoke with stern authority.

As I told you at our last meeting, there will be no place for an Overdruid with little power of his own on the Council until the mine is viable! You didn't tell me it would be deserted and all the tunnels would be blocked!

I had no way of knowing!

They must have known about the attack beforehand, and that betrays a lack of vigilance on your part, the First retorted.

I've been extremely vigilant! came the outraged protest. *The meeting was only a week before the attack, and quite secure. Nor was a mere week time enough to block all the tunnels.*

Yet blocked they were! Have you any idea how much it's going to cost to get them unblocked?

I'm sure the mine's proceeds will more than make up for it.

You'd better hope they do, the First warned.

In the meantime, a strategic raid on Aille-Mara during the Bardic Order's Fall Council would leave the mine securely in our possession.

Silence fell between them, broken at last by the First. *And if they arrange a retaliatory strike against us before then?*

Not a problem, for only the two of us and Faolán will know that the real attack will occur on the Summer Solstice festival day, when the majority of their Bards and Masters will be there.

Not as many as there would be at the Fall Council—

But enough to strike a fatal blow to their Order! A blow they couldn't possibly expect and will be utterly unprepared for.

Faolán will hardly do it out of the goodness of his heart, the First said with a snort.

He has a vested interest in seeing the mine remain securely in our hands. And I'm sure that, once the venture is successful, a slight increase of his percentage of the mine's profits would more than compensate him.

The silence that fell this time was a long one.

I warn you again, the First growled, *that you are solely responsible for paying Faolán. If anything is ever traced back, you will be accused and convicted of thieving from our mine and executed before you have the chance to even utter my name. With that clearly understood, I will agree to increasing your percentage from three to four percent. Will that suffice?*

Silence.

And I will send you a new robe. Emerald, with a silver cord and an insignia of a silver staff, perhaps? A sardonic brow lifted.

That would be greatly appreciated.

The scene faded, replaced once again by fear as the dark chromafield carried him onward and out of the mind he was in. On to where he would either return once again to the Overdruid's mind, or take the chance of leaping the gap between this chromafield and his own. Concentrating with all his might on his mentor to stave off his terror, he jumped.

Daithi came to himself to find his brother's chromafield colors shot through with streaks of crimson anger.

By the Maker! Ferghus hissed. *We haven't three months to prepare to leave ... we have but three weeks! We have ships, but only five are nearing completion. The other five won't be ready...* Ferghus' voice faded, and Daithi knew he was already formulating plans and discarding ideas as he worked through every possibility.

I'll try to get Shay to you in time, Daithi told him, *but if something goes amiss, don't wait! Every Bard and Master in Aille-Mara will be killed if you stay. You must get away before then.*

Shay will make it in plenty of time if he's with a Bard who can pass unchallenged through the border between our territories. I'll have Tadhg, a Bard currently assigned to Delbna and strong in the Gift, wait for you at The Wayfarer's Brew with full provisions and an extra horse. Let me know when you're close and I'll have him leave the tavern and wait for you behind the stables. He's a lean man of average height with sandy hair, and as a precaution, will not be dressed as a Bard. He won't put his robe on until they've left Delbna and are nearing the sentries.

Thank you for doing this for Shay, Ferghus.

There is little I wouldn't do for this nephew of mine, who worships my little brother as if he were Fionn mac Cumhaill himself.

Daithi spluttered an indignant protest and Ferghus chuckled. *I'll take his dream with me for the Council to see. It will silence any remaining doubts and ensure that every Master works doubly hard to complete our preparations in time. Your youngling will sleep deeply and wake up with no memory of ever having traveled into Cathair's dark mind. Little wonder he suppressed it ... the boy was terrified beyond belief! And we'd all have perished if it weren't for his determination to help you. I must go. Get Shay to Delbna as soon as possible.*

We're but two days away, Daithi said. *We'd travel even faster if Seamus would unload the fish,* he added in an aggrieved tone.

Fish?

As rotten as Balor's own soul. All Seamus would tell Shay was that it was 'a last line of defense'.

As Ferghus had promised, Shay woke up in the morning refreshed. He lay there for a moment, puzzled. He remembered his uncle was going to remove a nightmare from him, but couldn't remember what it was, though he was sure it had something to do with the Grovekeeper's window. He remembered leaving the ash tree and looking through it. He remembered seeing the trapped Overdruid ... the flung vase ... his decision to enter the Grovekeeper's weakened chromafield ... then, opening his eyes to find himself crumpled beneath the window. *I guess I fainted.* He rose to help make breakfast and break camp, but when Réiltín waited for him to get into the wagon before she did, he balked.

"I'm not fer bein' squished between the two of ye again," he grumbled. "I'll sit on the outside, or I'll be walkin'."

"And let yer poor old Mam be squished instead?"

"From what I saw yesterday, I doubt ye'd be mindin' any if ye were," Shay said, rolling his eyes.

Réiltín laughed, then climbed in and settled herself close to Seamus, who wrapped an arm around her and pulled her even closer. With half the seat to himself, Shay grinned and climbed in.

They traveled the rest of the morning, seeing few travelers on the road. But early that afternoon, just as the wagon was nearing the top of a grassy hill, Shay cried out for Seamus to stop.

"Two armed men are ridin' from the south!" he told him. "The Grovekeeper says I need to hide … the men are in a foul temper and if the Overdruid sent them to find me, mightn't care that my hair's been darkened and all."

"The *Grovekeeper?*" Seamus asked with a startled look, but Réiltín laid a hand on his arm.

"I'll explain later," she said urgently. "Do as the boy says."

Seamus stared at her for a moment, then brought the pony to a halt. He turned and flipped the edge of the tarp up. "No place to hide on this hillside, lad. Best place fer ye is back in the empty barrel. Doubt they'll be wantin' to open all three, and I put that flat-topped boulder in there to steady the barrel and make it 'bout the same weight as t'others. Brace yerself in case they shake it." He removed a flat tool from his pocket and, kneeling on the seat, pried open the lid. "Quick, now! Make no sound or movement, mind, no matter what ye hear, nor how bad it smells."

Shay stood up on the wagon seat and, grimacing, dropped nimbly inside the barrel. Seamus pounded the lid shut, pulled the tarp into place, and they continued on their way. As they crested the hill, dust rose from the south and two riders came into view, increasing their pace as they spotted the wagon. They soon pulled up in front of it, forcing Seamus to haul on the reins. One of the men pulled a sword from his back.

"Somethin' I can do fer ye?" Seamus said affably.

"Where'd you come from?" the man growled. "And what's under the tarp?"

"Come from up north, and ye can smell for yerself what I'm haulin'," Seamus said, gesturing to the back of the wagon. "Three barrels of rotten fish. If that's what yer wantin'," he added, "I can be sparin' a few."

The man snorted and gave a curt motion toward the wagon. His companion grimaced, then dismounted and handed him the reins. The mounted man gave Réiltín an appraising look.

"A bit young for you … or is she your daughter?"

Réiltín glared and Seamus gave her an exasperated glance. "There, now, what did I tell ye? No one's goin' to believe we're handfasted, now, didn't I say as much?"

The glare found a new target in Seamus. "I don't care a whit! 'Tis none of their business, to be sure, and anyone thinkin' different is goin' to have *me* to deal with, be they armed or not!"

Seamus sighed. "A woman's tongue is a weapon to reckon with. Wouldn't advise tanglin' with this one's."

The mounted man laughed. The other one was wrinkling his nose in disgust as he neared the back of the wagon.

"Ach, who'd be wanting rotten fish?" he muttered as the odor settled around the wagon in the summer heat. "Or her?" he added disparagingly. "Both of you stink to the heavens."

Seamus laid a quelling hand over Réiltín's. "The fish is good fer feedin' the ground," the fisherman said with a shrug. "Or so they say. If they're willin' to pay fer it, I'm willin' to cart it. At my age, ye take the work ye can find."

Shay, braced inside his barrel, froze as the man flipped the tarp up, gagged, and hurriedly stepped back."

"What a stench! Let's get out of here before we pick up any more of it."

"Give 'em all a shake first," the mounted man ordered. "Make sure none of 'em are the light weight of a boy."

Muttering under his breath, his companion obeyed, giving each a good shake. "About the same, all three. And a boy hiding in there would be dead already with no help from us." He spat into the dirt and remounted.

The first man was still staring at Seamus. "Have you seen a boy? Eight or so ... hair redder'n mine ... freckles?"

Seamus rubbed his chin thoughtfully. "Can't say as I have."

The second man snorted as he remounted. "If the boy has a nose, he'd have smelled this coming a furlong away and gotten well off the road." Reins snapped, and the two rode off, heading north toward Gaotha.

Seamus snapped his own reins, chuckling softly. "They'll be askin' at *The Pipit's Nest,* no doubt, and thanks to ye, lass, that'll send 'em northeast, givin' us plenty of time to get to Delbna."

"Can I come out now?" came a plaintive query behind them.

"Not just yet, lad," Seamus cautioned. "Before we're out of sight, they'll be turnin' to check there's still only the two of us."

A few minutes passed with no sound but the steady tread of the pony and the creaking of the wagon. Réiltín sent a questioning glance at Seamus, for the riders were well out of sight behind them, but Seamus merely smiled at her and pulled her close for a lingering kiss. She settled her head against his shoulder and blissfully closed her eyes.

A few moments later the sound of retching came from the back as Shay emptied the contents of his stomach.

"Now ye can come out," Seamus said mildly as he pulled off the road.

~ ❧ ~

They unloaded the noxious barrels at the next farmhouse they came to, the landholder delighted to get them at such a good price. Then, after a thorough scrub-down of the wagon, themselves, and their clothing at a stream Daithi led them to, they traveled on.

"The lass has been tellin' me about the Grovekeeper talkin' to ye," Seamus said to Shay. "Is he in yer mind all the time, then?"

The boy shrugged. "Mostly so. If I'm asleep, he leaves some-times to talk to his brother. He says to give both of ye his thanks for what yer doing fer me. And ye have mine, too," he added. "Not many would've done what the two of ye have."

"Yer both welcome, lad." Blue eyes twinkled into his. "Quietest passengers I've ever had ... considerin' my cargo keeps most away."

"That's because the Grovekeeper's been keepin' me busy with lessons every chance he gets." The boy grinned up at the old man's astonished face. "Not that I mind," he added. Indeed, Shay found his continuing lessons about chromafields fascinating. He loved everything about them. The Grovekeeper had greatly expanded Shay's knowledge of the colors he saw, which were different for each object or species of plant he looked at.

But the chromafields of people were the most interesting of all, and with three people to study, Shay soon became adept at in-terpreting them. Though he could only see his mentor's chromafield in his mind, the colors were the same as the ones he knew so well, though they were more vivid than before. The emer-ald green reflected the Grovekeeper's strong connection to nature. Honey gold bespoke kindness, cerulean blue a gentle spirit. Traces of silver revealed an ability to see that which is hidden, though his mentor had laughed at this, saying his brother had by far the lion's share of that color, and that his own silver ability was hidden at best. Shay didn't question the Grovekeeper about the grey grief that streaked his chromafield, or the way it sometimes seemed to make all its colors darken with sadness.

Seamus, on the other hand, had a chromafield that glowed with heather's quiet wisdom and the empathy of teal. Violet and burnt orange showed the fisherman to be an independent soul who loved a good adventure. The perfect colors, Shay thought, for this man he instinctively liked and trusted.

Réiltín's chromafield fairly sparkled with ruby red, showing her to be a passionately determined individual; forest green and sage explained her talkativeness and desire to care for those around her. *Too bad she never had a child she could have bossed around and fussed over,* he thought with a grin. Not that he'd minded finding himself in that role. Being fussed over was not, he thought, such a bad thing. His Mam had been too sick to fuss over him, and certainly the Grovetenders never had. Though, he thought ruefully, they'd certainly had the bossing part down pat. *Except Grovetender Alben never bossed me. And the Grovekeeper can be stern, but he treats me like—* He stopped abruptly.

My son.

Shay caught his breath. He waited for a long moment, but the voice didn't speak again.

～ ❧ ～

The following morning Réiltín clipped Shay's hair short and handed him a brimmed hat. Shay put it on and grinned up at her.

"Not bad," Réiltín allowed, giving him a critical look. "Best wear it 'til you arrive where yer goin', for the dye's beginnin' to wash out and there's no tellin' where those men are now."

Early that afternoon they rolled into Delbna. After winding their way through the busy marketplace, it wasn't long before a crooked wooden sign with burnt lettering told them they had arrived at *The Wayfarer's Brew.* Seamus drove the cart into the stableyard and around to the back, where a lean man with two horses was waiting for them. Shay nervously pressed himself closer to Réiltín, who took his hand in her own reassuringly.

"Now, then," Seamus said quietly, "go on with ye. Ye'll be all right now."

Shay nodded, extricated his hand from Réiltín's, then surprised her with a hug, not seeing the tears in her eyes for the ones blurring his own. He hopped down off the wagon, then turned and stood there, biting his lip for a moment.

"Thank ye," he said at last, "and ... well, if you really *were* an 'unlikely couple' ... I wouldn't have minded bein' yer son fer real."

At that, Seamus handed the reins to Réiltín and met the boy halfway as Shay ran around it and straight into the fisherman's open arms.

Seamus held him tightly for a moment, then ruffled his hair and smiled. "If 'twas safe fer ye in Gaotha, that uncle of yers would 'ave to fight us fer ye," he murmured.

Shay gave him a grin and walked toward the man with the horses, then turned and silently watched as Seamus slapped the reins and left.

Three days later, a pony and wagon with two weary travelers in it rolled up to Réiltín's door.

"Was thinkin' of takin' a drive tomorrow mornin'," Seamus said casually.

"Haven't ye had enough drivin' to last ye awhile?" Réiltín asked as she gathered her things and climbed down off the wagon.

"Thought I'd find me a special place fer a handfast bonfire."

"And who would ye be findin' it fer?" she challenged.

"Fer you. If ye'll come with me when I stop by to get ye."

Grey eyes and blue held each other. "Tell me then, old man," she said, her voice a bit unsteady. "Should I wear the dress I'm wearin' now, to help you find it? Or the blue one my Mam wore to her own handfastin', to light the fire and circle it together?"

"Ye'd look beautiful in the blue one, lass."

Her eyes grew bright with tears. "I've no handfast gift fer ye," she murmured. "But I can bring a lunch fer us to eat."

He smiled and nodded.

"And what will ye be bringin', then?"

"Flowers," he replied. "Fer your hair."

"What kind?"

"Any kind ye like."

"I favor the sea asters growin' wild amongst the rocks in the cove," she told him. "But they'll not bloom 'til midsummer."

"Stars of the sea, they're called."

She looked at him in surprise. "Not many men would be knowin' that."

"'Tis a flower matchin' a lass whose name means 'little star'," he said, surprising her yet again. "Been a bit more sun than usual, though, so surely there'll be some to find ... blue ones, perhaps, to match yer eyes."

He grinned, looking for a moment like the young, adventuring man he had once been. "Come with me, wearin' the blue dress, and we'll hunt 'em down together. Then we'll build ourselves a handfast bonfire on the beach ... where ye like to walk, keepin' an eye on yer old man, and I like to fish, keepin' an eye on my lass. I'll fasten the sea asters in yer hair and make a string of 'em to tie our hands together. Ye'll be the brightest star the cove has ever seen."

She laughed in delight and nodded. He tipped his hat to her, snapped the reins and left, the music of her laughter warming him all the way home.

Chapter 24

As the wagon rumbled away from *The Wayfarer's Brew*, Shay stood motionless for a long moment. Behind him, the Bard dressed in common village garb and a hat much like Shay's spoke.

"Come along, lad. Do you know how to ride?"

Shay turned toward the man and shook his head.

The man smiled. "I'm Tadhg ... not Bard Tadhg, mind. Just Tadhg will do until we've left Delbna.

"I'm sorry I don't know how to ride, sir," Shay murmured, worriedly biting his lip.

"You'll learn fast enough." Tadhg pulled an apple from his pocket, sliced a piece from it, and handed it to Shay. "The larger gelding is named Dorcha for the dark color of his coat. The brown gelding is Sásta, for he's a happy fellow and will give you no trouble. Introduce yourself to him with that apple slice and he'll follow you to the ends of the earth. We'll lead them to a field where I can show you how to ride him." He sliced another piece of apple. "Dorcha is not above stealing, I'm afraid," he said, looking fondly at his horse, who snorted in apparent disagreement, "so I'll keep him occupied while the two of you get acquainted. Then we must be off."

Shay held his apple slice out to Sásta, who unhesitatingly took it out of his hand and ate it, then nuzzled his tunic for more.

The Bard chuckled. "Sásta would like you to believe that he's starving, but he's had an ample breakfast and now a treat besides. Take hold of his reins now and come along."

They walked along the road for awhile in silence, then Tadhg cleared his throat. "Master Ferghus told me his nephew is being hunted by someone who would do him harm. I've no idea who's trying to find you, or why, but I'll get you to your uncle as quickly and safely as possible."

He needs to know who's hunting you, Shay, but not why.

"It's two fianna sent by Overdruid Cathair."

The Bard's eyes widened. "We'll take special precautions while still in his territory, then," he said gravely. "I'll ask no questions about it, but you can ask me whatever you wish."

Shay looked into the Bard's friendly eyes, amber in the growing sunlight, and his own widened as well. The Grovekeeper had told him what eyes of such a rare color meant in the Bardic Order. This was a Gifted Bard, able to see the songs of everything around him, just as Shay himself could see their chromafields.

He is very Gifted indeed, Daithi verified. *Now, look at his chromafield and see what it has to tell you.*

Shay focused on the Bard's chromafield, its deep blue and rosewood colors showing him to be intelligent and friendly, the mint green giving him a refreshing, healing energy Shay hadn't seen before, but immediately responded to. The Bard's chromafield radiated freely out from him. This, he saw clearly, was a man he could trust. "There's something I'd like to ask you," he said tentatively, "but it doesn't have to be now."

"Ask away," the Bard said cheerfully. "If I can't answer it right now, I can think it over while you practice riding."

"It's about my uncle. I've never actually met him, and ... well, I don't know anything about the Bardic Order. So, I was wondering if maybe..." His voice trailed off.

Tadhg gave him a smile. "Lessons on the Bardic Order will be no problem at all." He nodded toward a track leading off to their right. "There's the path leading to the field. Let's see how you and Sásta get on together, and then I'll tell you all about the Bardic Order while we ride. We've five or six days of traveling ahead of us. By the time you meet your uncle, you'll be as knowledgeable as any Bardic apprentice."

"I don't know if I can learn as quickly as that," Shay said doubtfully, "but I'll do my best."

The amber eyes looking into his lit with amusement. "Impossible, you think? Then here's the first thing you need to learn about the Bardic Order, lad. Our Prime is quite insistent that there are no such things as impossibilities. Best not to forget that."

Inside Shay's mind, Daithi chuckled.

～ ❧ ～

That evening, Daithi listened with interest to Shay's ongoing lessons on the Bardic Order. Tadhg had taught the youngster several things Daithi didn't know, for he and Ferghus had rarely spoken of the hierarchy of their respective Orders. They had, however, enjoyed many a conversation comparing the lessons given to Adepts and Bards, surprised to discover the two Orders had more in common than not. *A shame Ferghus never met Cillian,* Daithi thought. He could imagine the lively discussions between the two men who had so much in common, though Cillian had abandoned his Order, and Ferghus had become Prime of his.

Thinking of Cillian, Daithi's thoughts strayed from Shay's lesson to memories of his mentor.

After five cycles of intermittent instruction, followed by five more cycles as his acolyte, Daithi had been overjoyed when Cillian told him he had earned the robe of a full-fledged Druid at the age of twenty.

You can't, however, receive your robe from me, his mentor

said, *for I left the Order that alone has that right.*

Daithi froze.

Therefore, tomorrow we will leave for the Council. I will present you to them, and they'll spend several days testing you to verify your ability and knowledge. This is necessary for you to be accepted into its ranks and receive your robe.

And then ... we'll leave together?

No. I will leave immediately. You will stay for the testing ... and afterwards, go wherever the Council assigns you.

No! Daithi's cry echoed around the cavern.

Cillian quirked a brow. *No?*

I didn't work this hard just to lose you!

You were never meant to keep me, Cillian sternly told him.

I won't leave you!

You aren't leaving me. I'm leaving you.

Daithi turned away, his eyes blurred with tears of anguish and betrayal. First his family ... and now Cillian?

The two people in all of Eire who can travel the colors of energy fields found each other, Cillian said. *There's a reason for that, and it wasn't just to give me company in my chosen solitude. You have your own path to follow and must discover what it is. You won't find it by my side.*

Silence fell between them like an invisible wall.

Do you want me to go? Daithi asked.

No ... but I will not allow you to stay. One day you will understand.

Daithi turned at this. *No, I won't,* he said bitterly. *I'll never understand!*

Cillian gestured to a small chest at the back of their shelter, a chest he had forbidden Daithi to open. *Open the chest.*

Tears stinging his eyes, Daithi walked woodenly to the chest and opened it. He had often wondered what mystical or magical items might be hidden inside, but what met his eyes was a pile of

Druidic robes and cords. He blinked in confusion.

You are wearing the acolyte's tan robe and cord I was given many cycles ago, for a Druid with over ten cycles of experience can take an acolyte of any age. The Council will be giving you a Druid's chestnut brown robe with the insignia of a twisted branch and a beige cord, like the one I'm wearing. This is a rank earned by passing ones tests and thus is mine forever, as yours will be. Take my other robes from the chest now and identify them.

The first robe Daithi removed was a rich cinnamon brown with the insignia of a twisted leafy branch. A beige cord was coiled on top. *An Adept's robe,* he said.

The next robe was umbar, its insignia a single autumn leaf. The cord was beige. *An Arborist's robe.*

The third robe was forest green with an insignia of an oak tree, paired to a silver cord. *A Grovekeeper's robe,* Daithi said in awe.

The last robe was a rich emerald green with the insignia of a silver staff that matched the silver cord. For a moment, Daithi couldn't speak. *You were a Council Member?*

Does it matter if I was? Does anything I've taught you change because of it? Would you have learned more from Council Member Cillian than you have from Druid Cillian?

For a moment they regarded each other over a pile of robes and cords. *No,* Daithi said at last. *I learned from you, not your title.*

Remember that when you join the Order, and do not let the color of anyone's robe influence you.

In the morning they left for the Council Hall at Uisneach, four hundred furlongs to the southwest. And three days later they walked up a grassy hill to the standing stones at the top and the impressive building in front of them, if indeed a building it could be called. For the Council Hall of the Druidic Order stood more like a framework of nature. Daithi stood motionless in wonder.

Cillian pointed out the hall's unique features with his staff. *Each wall has three equal sections, the middle one fixed in place and housing two stone panels that can slide out from it to enclose the open sections on either side. The roof is similarly constructed, with each quadrant having a fixed center section and crossbeams, and moveable panels for the open sections between.*

How many Stoneseers did it take to set such heavy panels of stone in place? Daithi asked. *And how many to move them?*

It took two Stoneseers to place them there, and takes but one to move them.

His protégé gave him a startled look and Cillian raised a brow. *Have you not moved a rock yourself by moving its energy?*

Well, yes ... but not like those!

You moved far less heavy ones because you were using your own energy to do so. A Stoneseer uses the energy from the earth to move it, and there is no stronger source of that energy than here. For it isn't just objects and living things that were created with energy. The earth itself was as well, with vast, incredibly powerful energy lines that run through it like a framework. Lines that can be sensed ... and used by those trained to do so. He leaned on his staff and gave Daithi a keen look. *Open your awareness and see for yourself.*

Daithi glanced at him in surprise. *I've never thought to look into the earth,* he murmured.

That hardly makes it impossible, his mentor said dryly.

A grin flitted across Daithi's face as he thought of Ferghus. He held his rowan staff firmly in front of him and closed his eyes. Then he opened his awareness for the first time, not to an object, plant, or tree, but to the earth beneath him. His eyes flew open.

There's dozens of energy lines!

Why so surprised? We're not discussing a pebble or a bit of seaweed from the beach. We're discussing the very earth itself. Of course there are dozens of energy lines crisscrossing each other, traveling the length and breadth of Eire and far beyond. Some think of them as faery lines that the Aes Sidhe could travel. Our nine Groves were strategically placed where there are many such lines. But each and every one of those lines intersect right here, he said, thumping the ground decisively with his staff. *At Uisneach.* He watched as understanding lit Daithi's face.

So, Cillian continued, *the ancients constructed our Council Hall here, the 'Place of the Hearth', where the energy of Eire is the strongest, and where it can be used to move what would otherwise be far too heavy to lift.* He motioned toward the open-air hall.

I've timed our arrival to coincide with the Council's monthly meeting. You're about to enter a dangerous place, though it was not so until Bran became our First. I told you that I left the Order for two reasons, one of which was to find you. The other was to avoid having my Gift manipulated by him. Be wary, Daithi. If you are wise, you will only reveal your power with energy lines, not your ability to see and use the energy fields they emit. And, unless you have a desire to become a Diviner or Stoneseer, keep your ability to draw energy secret as well.

The two of them approached the Hall and spoke to the Hallkeeper, who told them to wait until he returned. Daithi looked around with interest at the woodland scene before him. The floor of the Hall was uncropped grass, gently swaying in the breeze that wafted unimpeded through the open panels. Dozens of junipers, rowans and hawthorns, pruned to keep them small, provided both privacy and shade. Judging by the bird calls coming from within, they provided avian nesting sites as well. Here and there a gardener wandered by, intent on his own business.

The Hallkeeper beckoned to them, then led the way through the trees. As they followed, Daithi heard the sound of flowing water. The path soon led them along a small brook that twisted its way around the trees and disappeared amongst the foliage. Crossing an arched bridge, Daithi saw a long marble table positioned in the center of a clearing. He whistled softly under his breath; the table could seat over a dozen people and must have cost a fortune.

At the moment there were ten Council members seated there, some casting curious looks Daithi's way, others leveling hostile ones at Cillian. Bran, First of the Council, looked up from his seat at the head of the table and spoke derisively.

So ... the prodigal Druid returns. How long has it been, brother ... fifteen cycles? Not long enough, I'm afraid. Leave us! I have no intention of reinstating you.

Daithi was stunned. The First of the Council was his mentor's brother? A brother who likely knew about Cillian's Gift. A brother Cillian did not trust.

I have no interest in reinstatement, Cillian said coldly. *I've come on behalf of Daithi, my young protégé and acolyte. He is here to be confirmed as a member of the Druidic Order and receive the robe he has earned.*

And why would we be interested in someone trained by a renegade who left our Order out of spite and jealousy?

You know perfectly well why I left, Cillian said sternly. *Daithi has no reason not to join and receive what is his due. It's the Council's responsibility to accept him for testing.*

Don't lecture me on responsibilities you abandoned!

Cillian held his brother's smoldering eyes for a moment, then turned and began walking back toward the footbridge.

And if we refuse him? Bran called after him.

Cillian stopped without turning. *The table you sit at is marble and cold to the touch. Warm it for them, Daithi. Very warm.*

Bran barked a laugh. *Traveling the energy lines of a marble slab like this one would take the best of us an hour to traverse its length, considerably longer to excite its energy lines.* He irritably tapped the manuscript in front of him with his quill. *I haven't got all day to give to your so-called acolyte!*

Cillian ignored him. *Daithi?*

Daithi shook himself from his numb state and focused on the table. Colors only he and Cillian could see flared from its surface.

He immersed his awareness into them and traveled into the marble. Unhampered by the need for its slow-moving energy lines, he moved swiftly through the table's length, exciting its energy as he went. Startled exclamations came from the Council as the marble began to heat under hands that were quickly removed from it. Bran uttered an oath and snatched up his manuscript as the edges began to curl and smoke. Daithi broke his focus and the marble cooled.

Cillian stood unmoving. *Still think you might refuse him?*

Silence fell over the Council table.

No, the First finally replied. *No, I don't believe we will.*

Then I suggest you treat him well. Cillian crossed the footbridge and disappeared among the trees.

Daithi shook off his memories and returned to the present, surprised to find how late it was. Shay was in his bedroll, drowsily listening to Tadhg's flute music. The Bard played every night, alternating between his harp, flute, and lyre. Daithi had been impressed by the healing effect the music had on Shay. Whether it was the music itself or the Bard who played it, the Grovekeeper wasn't sure, but he was beginning to think it was both. For it seemed to him that the music was a conduit, carrying the healing color of mint directly to the listening boy, soothing the tendrils of grey anxiety and smoky blue sadness that lingered in his chromafield. Tadhg, he thought, would have made an excellent healer. He wondered if that's why Ferghus had chosen this particular Bard to bring his traumatized nephew to him.

Daithi watched as Shay fell asleep to the flute's gentle melody. As the music came to an end, the memory of Cillian's words, spoken so long ago, came forcefully back to the Grovekeeper.

One day you will understand.

A streak of charcoal grey sorrow rippled through Daithi's chromafield as he gazed at the sleeping boy. *I understand now. I understand all too well.*

Chapter 25

Nine days after leaving Gaotha behind, Shay rode with Bard Tadhg up to Master Ferghus' home. He whistled softly in admiration of the stunning view the Master's home commanded, the waves of the bay below sparkling in the early morning sun.

"I'm going to miss you, Shay," Tadhg said as he dismounted and tethered his horse to the porch railing.

Shay gingerly dismounted and tethered his horse next to Dorcha. "I'll miss you, too, sir. And Sásta," he added with a fond glance at his horse. "Even if he made my backside as sore as if I'd been paddled every day since leaving Delbna."

The Bard laughed. Shay gave him a rueful grin, then cast a nervous glance toward the door.

"You've nothing to fear from your uncle," Tadhg told him. "He expects much from his Bards, and that's no bad thing, but a kinder man you'll not find anywhere in Eire."

"Will you come with me?" Shay asked hopefully.

"I'm not about to leave without greeting the Prime of my Order," Tadhg said with a chuckle, "but I'd go with you, regardless." He led the way up the steps and knocked firmly on the door. "And, so as not to break a Bardic custom the moment you arrive," he added, "let me greet Master Ferghus first."

Shay nodded, feeling his mouth go dry.

Speaking of paddlings, came a welcome voice in his mind, *Master Ferghus is the same person who hid in the pantry from our father's ire, made a racket stumbling over the flour bin, and when Father opened the door, came out floured from head to toe. Father sneezed the whole way through the paddling he gave him!*

Shay choked back a laugh just as the door was opened by the tallest man he'd ever seen, dressed in a blue robe and silver cord. This was a Bard, then, not his uncle, the boy thought in relief.

"Cyral!" Tadhg cried, stepping forward to clasp his arm. "I didn't expect to see you here. How is our Prime?"

"Master Ferghus recalled me to Aille-Mara a couple of cycles ago," the Bard said with a broad smile. "And he's doing as well as can be expected for someone who's been working non-stop for months on end," he added with an exasperated glance toward the heavens. He nodded toward the horses. "Truly, he could use one of those horses, though I doubt I could talk him into keeping one." His eyes, an even deeper amber color than Tadhg's, turned toward Shay, who stood frozen at the top of the steps.

At Tadhg's encouraging nod, Shay blurted a greeting. "I'm Shay—I mean Shaylor—that is, well ... it's an honor to meet you, sir ... er, Bard Cyral!" He floundered to a stop.

The tall Bard smiled. "Welcome to Master Ferghus' home, Shay. Or Shaylor, if you prefer."

"Shay's good," came the barely audible response.

"Then 'Shay' it is. I understand you're his nephew."

Shay had barely managed to nod before the Bard stood aside to make way for the Master, who had just come up behind him.

Tadhg immediately swept a deep, formal bow. "Master Ferghus. It's good to see you again! I've brought Shay to you."

The Master's eyes fastened keenly upon Shay for a moment before he answered. "I appreciate what you've done for me, Tadhg. Your family arrived safely a few days ago and are awaiting you in

Aille-Mara at your brother's home."

Tadhg smiled, then cast a worried glance at the horses. "They have room there for me to keep Dorcha, but not Sásta. If you wouldn't mind keeping him in your shed for awhile, sir, I'll see that hay and feed is sent to you this afternoon."

"You've a cart in there as well, Master," Cyral helpfully inserted before Ferghus had a chance to refuse. "Would come in handy when it's time to move ourselves and all our luggage and instruments to the ships," he said expressionlessly.

"And Shay is a fine hand at caring for him," Tadhg added.

Shay brightened. "Oh, I'd be hap—" he began, then fell silent when the measured look the Master was giving his Bards was suddenly turned on him. The boy stood rooted in place, transfixed by the golden regard. This, the boy knew, was not just a Gifted Master who stood before him. Though Tadhg was nearly a handspan taller, and Cyral a full handspan beyond that, his uncle's sheer presence easily dwarfed both men. The Master's chromafield, vibrant with the dynamic leadership of burnt orange and the lively curiosity of indigo, sparkling with intuitive silver, stretched out over the porch and halfway to the bluff beyond. But it was the kindness of honey gold, so prevalent in the Grovekeeper's chromafield, that calmed Shay enough to remember his manners. He made an awkward attempt to mimic Tadhg's formal bow.

"Uncle Ferghus. I'm—" He swallowed hard, forcing moisture through his suddenly dry throat. "I'm honored to meet you, sir ... and, well, I really would be happy to take care of Sásta."

The Master's eyes twinkled with humor. "The honor is mine, to be greeted by such a polite young nephew. But there's no need to greet your own uncle with such formality. Why, I don't even allow Cyral here to do so, unless some parochial old fool is watching." He frowned at the bushes near the porch, as though a few such fools might be lurking there. "Cyral, my boy, why don't you take my nephew inside and get him something to eat. If he's anything like you were at that age, he'll be hungry. I'd like a few words with Tadhg before he leaves. And," he added dryly, "Sásta can stay here in my nephew's excellent care."

The Bards grinned at each other and Cyral beckoned Shay inside. Taking a deep breath, the boy followed him into the house.

"Come, I'll show you where you can put your pack," Cyral said as he headed toward a long hallway.

Shay followed, glancing around in awe. The comfortable, spacious living room, with a huge open dining room and kitchen to his left, was even larger than the Grovekeeper's had been. The hall led to five rooms, two on the left, three on the right, and the first door on the left was wide open. He glanced in and stopped, staring in wonder at the most incredible harp he had ever seen. The Bards that came through Gaotha played lap harps that were small and easy to travel with. A few traveled with their Bardic harps, which could still be set upon their laps. But *this* harp was not going to be perched on anyone's lap or slung casually over one's shoulder. For it stood at least as tall as he was, prominently displayed in the largest bedroom he'd ever seen. He tore his gaze away from it to find the tall Bard looking back at him quizzically.

"Is this my uncle's room?" Shay asked.

Cyral came to stand next to him. "Yes, it is."

"And ... is that his harp?" the boy asked in a hushed voice.

"No," the Bard replied. "It's mine." He stood for a moment gazing at the beautiful instrument, and his chromafield, bright with tawny, amber, teal, and indigo, was abruptly shot through with streaks of grey. Shay glanced up into the Bard's face and found it filled with a blend of sadness and longing. Without thinking, he reached out and gently touched Cyral's arm.

"I'm sorry it makes you so sad. I shouldn't have stopped."

Cyral shook his head slightly. "My room is right there," he said, indicating the door opposite the Master's. "He knows I can hardly help but see it," he murmured under his breath.

"I haven't seen very many harps before," Shay said, "but that must be the biggest, most beautiful one in all Eire."

Cyral smiled. "Let's take your things to your room. We've been busy preparing for our journey, and Master Ferghus needs to go to Aille-Mara for a few hours this afternoon. I'll be staying here, however, and can show you my two smaller harps then."

Shay nodded and followed him to the room on the right that abutted Cyral's own. It was a spacious bedroom, with two closets, a large chest of drawers, and a trunk. He stared at the bed in awe. It was nearly as large as his whole bedroom in the Grovekeeper's home had been and was covered with soft quilts and pillows. *Three of me could sleep on that!*

"The closets and the top drawer are full of clothing for you, and there's a pair of new boots in the chest." The Bard smiled at Shay's surprised look. "Master Ferghus gave me a pretty good idea of your height, but I still had to guess at the size. For the clothes, I tried to get some that will fit now, and others you can grow into. Perhaps you can try them on later and let me know if I succeeded."

"Thank you!" Shay felt overwhelmed. "Everything I owned was lost in the fire." He bit his bottom lip and fell silent.

"Master Ferghus told me what you've been through," Cyral said gently. "And I know myself how hard it is to be given to someone you've never met. Your uncle understands that, too, which is why he decided to tell one other person everything he knew about you and his brother. He wanted you to have two people you can talk freely with, who will never betray your confidence when and if you choose to give it. I'm honored to be the one he chose."

Shay's eyes filled with unexpected tears.

"It must feel strange to suddenly have an uncle in your life," Cyral continued, "but having a nephew in his life doesn't feel strange to your uncle. He's absolutely delighted to have you here with him, and he's not just calling you his nephew to keep you safe. As far as he's concerned, you *are* his nephew, every bit as much as if you'd been born to his brother. Now, I'd best get you something to eat before he comes in and chides me for not having fed you yet."

Shay stood still for a moment, then followed the Bard into the kitchen and offered to help. By the time his uncle returned to the house, he and Cyral were munching on apple slices, cheese, and toast spread with blackberry jam, deep in a discussion about the differences between the bay of Aille-Mara and the cove of Gaotha.

"I see Shay isn't the only one in need of a second breakfast," Ferghus observed dryly.

"Well, it would be impolite, Master, not to join him," Cyral said, brushing crumbs off his robe.

"In that case, my boy, I could do with an extra bite myself." Ferghus sat down and looked at Cyral expectantly.

The Bard chuckled and headed for the kitchen. Shay rose to help, but the Master shook his head.

"Let him do it himself, lad. It's good for his soul and gives us a chance to talk a bit."

Shay reluctantly sat back down. In his experience, most adults talked a bit with a long-winded lecture, and sure enough, the Master gave him a stern look.

"I suppose my brother has regaled you with any number of stories about your uncle?"

Shay's eyes widened in surprise. "Why ... yes, he has."

"Well, then, nephew, I strongly advise you to forget them."

Shay suppressed a grin. "All of 'em, Uncle Ferghus?"

"Every last one," Ferghus confirmed. "None of them are likely to be true. Or at least, not the *whole* truth."

A spluttering sound came from the kitchen.

"Are you having difficulties slicing my apple?" Ferghus demanded.

"No, Master," Cyral said as he emerged and deposited a plate of fruit and cheese in front of Ferghus. "Your toast will arrive shortly." He turned, gave Shay a wink, and returned to the kitchen.

Ferghus settled back comfortably. "Now, then. Let's see about setting your skewed version of our family history straight."

The next morning Shay woke up early and lay for a moment wondering where he was. Memory returned and he stared at the window, grey in the pre-dawn light, feeling strangely reluctant to rise and begin this day. He liked Bard Cyral and his uncle, but today they seemed like distractions, intended to keep him from noticing that this was not a day like any other. For Shay knew in his soul that it was not, knew with deep, inner certainty that this was a day he did not wish to experience. He sighed and left his bed, dressed, then washed his face and hands in the basin on the nightstand without bothering to light the candle next to it. He walked silently down the dark hallway and out the front door, closing it quietly behind him. The sky was just beginning to lighten behind the hills, the sun seemingly as unwilling to face this day as he was. In front of him the bluff drew him inexorably toward it, the waves below crashing relentlessly against the rocky cliffs. The boy walked to a grassy spot near the edge of the bluff and stared sightlessly out to where the mouth of the bay met the open sea beyond.

Ferghus watched as his nephew made his way to the edge of the bluff. *He knows, Daithi.*

I know.

Are you certain you're doing the right thing?

For Shay? No. It's a terrible thing to do, and I can only hope that someday he will understand ... and forgive me for it.

The Grove is but a circle of trees! The words flew from the Master without his consent and would not be stopped. *What could that possibly be worth compared to that youngling standing out there, waiting for the world as he knows it to come to an end?*

Silence fell between them.

Forgive me, Ferghus said at last. *What you're about to do is hard enough without me upbraiding you for it. But couldn't you stay longer? Until we leave, perhaps?*

I've stayed until I knew he was safe. Staying longer, with him knowing, would be a cruelty he does not deserve.

Couldn't you visit him, then, by following your bond to him?

I won't light a false hope in him. You will not be within reach for long, and then he'd be devastated all over again. If I must hurt him, I'll do it quickly and but once. Keep him safe, Ferghus, and love him as you have always loved me.

Ferghus couldn't answer.

Goodbye, brother.

The Master's hand touched the windowpane, tracing a crooked path down it, mirroring the tears trickling down his face.

"Goodbye," he whispered.

On the bluff, the boy stood waiting, though he could not have said what he was waiting for.

Shay.

And then he knew. Knew it like he knew the colors of the Grovekeeper's chromafield. Knew without looking that whorls of grey sorrow were moving slowly through it, just as the slate grey of dread was streaking his own.

No, he whispered. *Please don't!*

I must leave you now.

Why? The cry rang through his mind, shattering every hope that tenaciously clung there.

I must return to the Grove.

You knew you would leave me! the boy accused. *You knew it from the beginning! Why didn't you tell me?*

You needed to learn as much as I could teach you in a short amount of time. And I wanted your memories of our last two weeks together to be good ones, not filled with sorrow.

I lost you once, and now I'm losing you again, he cried. *And this is even worse! You're doing it when you don't have to.*

I have no— Even as he spoke, he knew it for the lie it was. So did Shay.

You have a choice! And you're choosing the Grove … instead of me.

The truth left only silence in its wake until Daithi broke it. *That doesn't mean I love it more than you. You'll have a good life where they're going, Shay. I've seen it.*

I don't want a good life! I want you. I'll travel back with you in your chromafield, he said hopefully. *Then no one can hurt me and I can stay with you in the Grove.*

No! Daithi said sternly. *For you would exist as a conscious awareness bereft of its soul.*

Shay stared at the edge of the bluff and the empty air beyond. Just a few steps … a few moments of plunging through the air to the rocks below. Soul and awareness would be released together … and he would refuse the stars like the Grovekeeper had and stay—

No. Not like that, Daithi said gently. *As much as I want to have you with me, I won't let you do that to yourself. You deserve to live your life, Shay. With a real family, not just a ghostly father.*

A father wouldn't send me away!

A father would love you enough to let you go. Go with Ferghus and Cyral. Embrace the Bardic Order that is taking you in, for there you have an important role to play. There is nothing for you here in Eire but sorrow and death.

And you!

For a time. Keep my ring close, and know that part of me will always be with you.

For an endless moment that was far too short, emerald and honey gold, cerulean and silver swirled through Shay's mind … twined with his own colors … tenderly touched the bond they shared. Then, with the utmost gentleness, the colors faded and left.

Against his chest, the Grovekeeper's ring flared with all four colors. Then those, too, faded away.

The sun lifted its face above the hills, brushing the patches of cowslips with vivid yellows, the grasses with emerald green, the sky and sea beyond an aquamarine blue, but the eyes of the boy who could see the colors of everything around him saw none of this. He stood in a dim, colorless world as if turned to stone, his eyes hot with unshed tears, his mind raw with pain. For a long, terrible moment, the bluff seemed to beckon him, the colorless grasses waving toward its edge like inviting fingers. He took a single shaking step toward it. But before he could take a second one, he felt a hand on his shoulder. A familiar voice spoke behind him.

"When my brother was facing a horrible death by fire, he reached out to me and asked me to release his song before the flames reached him. He didn't want your last memories of him to be cries of pain. I did as he asked. Later, he told me that he was pulled toward the stars above, bright beyond belief though there was still daylight below. Their pull was irresistible, but he never found out where the stars would have led him. For he was also pulled toward an ancient Oak far below, where the youngling he loved more than anything else was sitting high in its branches, devastated and alone. So my brother refused the pull of the stars and returned to him until his boy was safe. It takes real love to do that, Shay, to put what's best for another ahead of what's best for oneself. And, as hard as it is for you to understand this right now, he's just done the same thing. He's sending you away and returning to the Grove alone because he's seen that it's best for you. You can argue and rant and be angry. You can be sad and devastated and believe that nothing will ever be the same. But what you cannot do is think that he did this because he didn't love you. Live the life he's given you. Live it, knowing that somehow, perhaps through the ring he left you, he will know, and take joy in it."

Shay turned then, his uncle a blurred vision before him.

"Let your tears come, youngling," the Master said gently. "They are healing tears and will do you good."

The boy let out a sob, and Ferghus held him as he cried, his tears flowing like the endless waves of the ocean below.

Far to the north, in Daithi's Grove, the rowans began to gently sway. Their flowered branches moved in rhythm, as though to aid the faded chromafield slowly making its way through them. As it reached the center of the Grove, the ancient Oak began to glow with faint, colored lights at the crown of the tree, infusing every branch and leaf below with power. The rowans stilled as the nearly translucent chromafield reached the Oak, and the ethereal light of the tree rained down like hundreds of sylvan teardrops of emerald, honey gold, cerulean, and silver into the chromafield below. It flared with renewed brilliance as the one who had claimed the Grove returned to it.

A softly shimmering chromafield of umbar reliability and nurturing sage, bright with russet's rustic charm, approached the Oak.

Welcome home, Grovekeeper.

Alben! What are you doing here? Why didn't you move on and follow the stars?

And let you return to the Grove all alone? Not likely. I knew you'd be coming back, and that Shay wouldn't be, and I promised you I'd always be here for you when you needed me.

I'm going to be here a very long time, my friend.

Aye, perhaps. But not alone. I'll be here, watching out, like ... as I've always done.

For a long moment, silence reigned in the Oak.

I have no idea what I ever did to deserve such a friend as you, Alben. You shouldn't have stayed ... but I'm glad you did.

I'm not the only one who stayed.

What do you mean? Did Cathair—

No, he's murdered no one else I know of. Come, I'll show you.

The two of them moved seamlessly through the rowans to the perimeter of hawthorns beyond. Their branches nearly touched each other, though Daithi knew they had stood well separated before he left. The two of them waited in silence, neither of them wishing to disturb the tangible sense of expectancy that emanated from every branch of the faery trees. Evening fell over the Grove at last, and tiny lights appeared amongst the hawthorns. The sound of voices singing rose clearly, though no living person was there to hear it. The faery trees began to move, their thorny branches reaching even closer to each other, twisting together to form an impenetrable shield around the Grove within.

Do you see them? Alben murmured.

Yes … I see them!

Aren't they the most beautiful creatures? Pure light, they are. Do you think they know we're here?

They know.

They've been busy working with the hawthorns since you left, and it looks like their work is nearly done. They're protecting the Grove for you, sir. No one could enter through such a barrier.

The Grove is indeed safe for now, said Daithi. *But they aren't protecting it for me. They're protecting it for the one who always believed in them, who walked the Grove of an evening to look out for the ones he loved and who stayed here to do the same. They're protecting it for you.*

Truly? came the astonished response.

Truly.

Movement Three

Marcach Gaoithe

mar-kukh gwee-heh: 'Rider of the Wind'

Chapter 26

Two mornings after Daithi returned to his Grove, Cyral and Shay sat in the Master's living room discussing the differences between their respective Gifts. Ferghus had left for yet another Council meeting directly after breakfast.

"So, then," Cyral said, "whereas I can hear the inherent *song* in an object—like one of those shells on the mantle—you can see its inherent energy field, called a chromafield?"

Shay reluctantly nodded. It was hard to discuss chromafields when he was trying not to think of the Grovekeeper.

"What does it look like?"

Shay scrutinized a shell that stood prominently in the front. "That whelk's chromafield has layers of different colors. Aqua at the top, pinks and browns underneath. Pale, but pretty. That rock next to it has a brighter one of mostly blues, greens, and golden browns, and the colors have shapes. People's don't," he added thoughtfully. "Their chromafields are a flow of colors, out and back in again." He frowned, reminded of something, but unable to pin-point what it was.

"What kind of shapes do the rock's chromafield colors have?"

"Well, the browns and greens follow the shape of the rock, but the blues shoot out of it in all directions and have six sides."

"That rock is a rare connellite mineral," Cyral told him. "If you turn it around, you'll see shiny blue crystals with six sides."

Reluctance gave way to interest. "Then the browns and greens must be coming from the rock, and the blues are coming from the crystals. I'd show it to you if I knew how."

"Perhaps we can figure out a way to do that. Am I right in thinking that if your own chromafield overlaps the connelite's, you can send your conscious awareness into it, just as we do by playing its song?"

Shay nodded. "But I don't know if we'd see the same thing or not. I've never seen what you see."

"Well, that's easily fixed. I can play the song of the connellite for you," the Bard offered, "and then you can travel into it with me and see if it's the same."

Interest became intrigue. "I'd like that!"

Cyral fetched his lap harp. "Master Ferghus apprenticed me when I was eight cycles old and taught me how to make this harp."

"Really? That's how old I was when..." All traces of a smile vanished. "When I was taken to the Grove."

"Well, then, since my Master and your father are brothers, I believe that makes us cousins." He smiled into the boy's astonished eyes. "And cousins don't call each other by their Bardic titles." He held out his arm. "Do they, Cousin Shay?"

For a moment, the youngster stared at the Bard's chromafield. Tawny and amber showed him to be dependable and focused; teal and indigo revealed empathy and curiosity. He reached out and firmly clasped the offered arm with his own. "No, they don't ... Cousin Cyral." He gave his new cousin a slight smile. "I feel like I suddenly have a family."

"That's because you do." Cyral set his harp comfortably on his lap and began to play.

Shay had barely a moment to admire the Bard's expert playing before his senses were swept into the connellite. Groups of closely packed crystals appeared, each comprised of thin, brilliant blue hexagons. Shay stared in awe at the forest of crystal needles, each a fragile blue prism giving the connellite its lacy appearance. Then the music of the harp brought him back to himself.

"That was amazing!" he exclaimed.

"Now that you know what it looks like from my point of view, let's see what it looks like from yours. I think, if you focus on the bond you and I have begun to form with each other, then enter the crystal, you'll take me with you in much the same way I just took you with me. As short a time as we've known each other, I can see the beginnings of our bond in my mind. Can you see it in yours?"

"I suppose I could," Shay said reluctantly. "I've never looked since..." He fell silent.

"Since your father left," Cyral said gently. "Go ahead and say it, for you must get used to calling him your father, not the Grovekeeper. And the more often you say it, the less it will hurt and the more you will take pleasure in your memories of him."

Shay averted his eyes. How could he possibly call the Grovekeeper his father without breaking apart like a piece of fragile connelite someone smashed with their fist?

"Let's practice it together first," Cyral suggested. "Just repeat the words after me. My father."

Shay hesitated. "My fa— My father," he said at last.

Cyral smiled encouragement and said the word several more times. When Shay echoed him without hesitating, he added a word.

"My father left."

Shay flinched. "My father ... left," he barely managed to say.

"My father left for the marketplace."

This was easier to repeat, and the Bard said it several times, each time ending with a more preposterous place his father had gone, until Shay couldn't help but chuckle. Then Cyral said the original unfinished sentence.

"I've never looked since my father left."

"I've never looked since my father left." His cousin was right ... it did hurt less. And his father *had* left. *He's just never coming back for me.* The unspoken words cut like a serrated blade.

"Look into your mind now," Cyral told him. "Your bond with your father will still be there, as will all the other bonds you've created in your life. You've just begun to develop one with us, so our bonds will be thinner and fragile looking. As you get to know us better, they'll strengthen. Focus on mine, then keep the image clearly in your mind as you enter the connellite."

Shay shook his head. "I don't want to see my father's bond."

"Why not?" Cyral asked gently.

"Because ... I just don't." How could he tell him that he didn't want to see if the Grovekeeper's bond had disappeared, leaving even his mind deserted and empty?

"I know this isn't easy for you, and I'm sorry to be the one asking it of you, but we'll be leaving soon. You need to be prepared for curious people questioning you about your father, and be able to easily refer to him as such. You and I can practice doing it together, and part of that means facing the bond and the memories you have of him ... pleasant ones and hard, for they are connected."

"Did my uncle tell you to do this?" Shay asked unsteadily.

"No, I'm doing it so he doesn't have to," Cyral told him. "He hasn't the time right now, and better for you to dislike your cousin for asking such a thing of you, than your uncle."

Shay gave him a startled look. "I don't dislike you for it," he said, "and I don't want Uncle Ferghus to have to do it, either. I'll ... try." He concentrated on seeing his own chromafield, unsurprised to find it shrunken and dull in color. Reluctantly, he entered his own mind, hoping he could spot his bond with his cousin before he saw the one he shared with ... his father.

The moment he entered his mind, however, he had eyes only for the Grovekeeper's bond. Their entwined chromafields were still there, the colors pale, as though both of them were asleep. He tore his gaze away and saw two bonds that were new, one of them wisps of his own chromafield just beginning to entwine with his cousin's, the other a surprisingly strong one with his uncle. Shay stared at it, wondering if all the stories the Grovekeeper had shared with him had begun to build a bond with his uncle before he ever met him. For a brief moment, he felt the Master's hand on his shoulder as he stood devastated on the bluff, felt the strong arms holding him as he cried. Then he forcefully yanked his attention away and focused on his bond with his cousin. Taking the mental image of it with him, he entered the chromafield of the crystal.

Again he was immersed in a lacy forest of hexagons, the blue crystalline structures needling out in every direction. Cyral's chromafield shimmered next to him, swirls of lavender compassion drifting through its vibrant colors. Shay returned to himself, blinking back tears, to find his cousin's eyes resting on him.

"That was hard for you, but you did it anyway," Cyral gently said. "You're a brave soul, and I'm proud to call you my cousin. The next time I face a tough decision, I'll think of you, and it will help me make it, however hard it is."

Shay's face brightened, and the Bard continued. "And now we know that we see the same thing, regardless of how we're doing it," he said thoughtfully. "We also know that you can focus on your bond with someone and take them with you. That's enough work for one morning. Let's go have some fun! Can you swim?"

"Swim?" Shay echoed, surprised at both the question and the roguish grin on the Bard's face. "No, I never learned how. Gaotha's bay is too rough and cold for swimming."

"Then it will be even more thrilling!"

"What will?" Shay asked nervously.

"Riding the Easach Falls. It's perfectly safe," he added reassuringly. "Our bodies will stay right on the bank, safe and dry. It's our senses that will go on the ride. You'll see, hear, and feel it just as if you were doing it for real. We'll walk to a place where it's slow and gentle, so you can see what it's like first. Any time you want to stop, just tell me and I'll take you right back."

"But ... how can you play the song of a river?"

"The elements also have songs of their own, which can be played and traveled, although normally only by the Masters. Fortunately, your uncle has allowed me to do so."

Shay hesitated. "Am I going to get in trouble with Uncle Ferghus for going with you?"

"No, for you won't be using the watersong yourself. If anyone's going to get in trouble," the Bard said dryly, "it will be me."

Shay grinned. "In that case, Cousin, let's go!"

Cyral laughed, fetched his full Bardic harp, and they were soon walking north toward the falls.

"Does the size of the harp matter?" Shay asked curiously.

"Besides giving the harpist a greater range of notes, it gives their Gift more strength and power."

"Then the huge harp in Uncle Ferghus' room would be incredible! Why don't you use it?" Shay flushed at the look of pain on his new cousin's face. "I'm sorry," he said, ashamed. "And you've treated me like I'm your family."

"You *are* my family. I don't use it because my Master has forbidden me to for now. I would tell you why if I knew."

Shay looked up in surprise, but made no further comment about Cyral's forbidden harp as they reached the river and headed upstream. Soon they were sitting on the bank in a place where the water swirled gently below their feet, though farther out it was moving rapidly. Shay eyed it nervously. "Have you got any real cousins?" he asked curiously as Cyral removed his harp.

"Quite a few of them, actually, but I don't consider them family. My parents died when I was very young, and my relatives didn't want me because I couldn't talk without stuttering."

Shay's eyes widened. "But ... you don't stutter!"

Cyral smiled. "Your uncle helped me with it."

"So ... your only family is me and Uncle Ferghus?"

"Sometimes the family we choose for ourselves is the best." Cyral indicated the smoothly flowing river. "If I play the watersong now," he said, "you'll experience exactly what I do when we ride the river, but you'll only see what I choose to look at. If I play the watersong while focusing on our bond, you'll be able to see what you wish from your own perspective. Which would you prefer?"

This took no thought at all. "To see what I want to!"

Cyral chuckled, then closed his eyes.

Shay had only a moment to see the burnt orange of adventure blossoming in his cousin's chromafield before a liquid flow of sound came from the Bardic harp. The next moment, he was submerged in water. Panic rose with his mind's insistence that he couldn't breathe here, but Cyral's voice immediately calmed him.

It's normal to feel like you need to breathe and can't, Shay, but your senses have no need of air, and your body is still sitting on the bank, breathing without any problem at all. Focus on me, relax, and the sensation will go away.

Shay focused on Cyral's chromafield bubble shimmering in the water next to him, and the constriction he felt in his throat relaxed. He looked around him in delight. Grasses, clinging to the rocky riverbed below, swayed with the current. Small fish darted here and there among rocks limned in filtered sunlight. From underneath the overhanging bank, a brown trout swam lazily toward them, its golden-brown scales glistening.

I've been holding us here against the current, the Bard told him. *Do you want to go back, stay here, or head downstream?*

Head downstream!

And off they went, swirling down the river.

Faster, Cousin Cyral! Faster!

And faster they went, careening around boulders, zipping around bends, both of them laughing.

Here comes the waterfall! Cyral shouted.

A moment later Shay was airborne, thousands of droplets surrounding him like suspended crystals filled with captured sunlight and rainbows. Then he plunged into a world of bubbles and foam, with no idea which way was up or down, and not caring in the least. He tumbled wildly around, then spun out into calmer water, winded, disoriented, and thoroughly happy.

Can we do it again, Cousin Cyral? Can we? Please?

Cyral laughed and took them back up above the falls. Down they went again, Shay screaming in delight. The youngster came back to himself with an eruption of unrestrained joy.

"Thank ye! I've never had so much fun in my life!" He frowned abruptly, the pleasure on his face turning to guilt as he stared unseeingly at the river. He felt his cousin's eyes resting on him.

"I had a friend once," Cyral told him. "Bryan. He was in a terrible accident and didn't survive it. For over a cycle I mourned him and refused to make other friends because I didn't want to go through that kind of pain again ... you know?"

Shay looked up into amber eyes that had darkened with remembered grief. "Yeah ... I know."

"I regret that now, because I'll never know what wonderful friendships I might have made during that time. Bryan would have wanted me to have them ... would have wanted me to be happy. And your father would want *you* to be happy, too."

You deserve to live your life, Shay. The memory of the Grovekeeper's words spoke clearly in his mind, and Shay relaxed into the smile he gave his cousin. "Yes, he would."

They headed back home to find the Master already there. "Well, now," he said, smiling at them from his chair. "It looks like you two have been having fun together."

"We had a *great* time, Uncle Ferghus!" Shay said excitedly. "Cousin Cyral took me down the river twice ... and we went flying off a waterfall and landed smack in the bay!"

"Did he, now? I'd like to hear all about it soon, lad, but perhaps you could take a short walk along the bluff first. Cyral and I need to have a talk, and then I'll join you there."

Shay was alarmed at the serious look on his uncle's face.

Cousin Cyral must be in a lot of trouble, and all because of me. His uncle's brow quirked in his direction.

"I'll go," Shay said quickly, "but please don't be angry with Cousin Cyral. He only did it for me. He showed me it's okay to have some fun, and that ... my father would want me to be happy."

Ferghus gave his nephew a startled look, but said nothing.

"So," Shay continued, swallowing hard, "if you're going to punish Cousin Cyral, would you let me take his place?"

It was Cyral's turn to look startled.

"Am I to understand," the Master said, looking keenly at his nephew, "that if I should decide to punish Cyral for taking you down the river today without asking my permission, you wish to take his punishment because he did it for your benefit?"

Quailing inwardly at the thought of what awful punishment would be meted out to a full-fledged Bard, Shay silently nodded.

"Cyral committed no offense by taking you with him," Ferghus told him, "nor would I have punished him if he had. I'm happy you had a good time, and that he chose to share his favorite place with you, especially since he did so for your benefit and not merely to show off his expertise with the watersong."

Cyral chuckled.

"I need to talk to him about a different matter, Nephew, and you can rest assured he's in no trouble ... at the moment."

Shay nodded in relief and took his leave. Ferghus turned an enquiring look Cyral's way as the Bard took a seat next to him.

"You actually got the lad to call Daithi his father two days after being abandoned by him? I stand impressed, my boy."

"The credit is Shay's. It wasn't easy for him."

"Oh, I think a bit of credit can also go to ... Cousin Cyral, is it?"

"It is."

"You realize what that means? If anything should happen—"

"—then I," the Bard smoothly inserted, "as Shay's only living relative, will take full responsibility for him. Yes, I know."

"You've taken to him that strongly?"

"I have. And what he just did, offering to take my place for what he thought would be a terrible punishment, is unprecedented in my experience with my birth cousins. They," he said ruefully, "treated me quite differently."

"Our Shay is a good lad. Thank you for giving him his first moments of happiness since Daithi left him. My only grievance is that you didn't wait until I could join you." Ferghus sighed. "With all the stress I've been under lately, a wild ride down the Easach sounds downright soothing."

Cyral chuckled. "I can take you right now, if you haven't the energy to take yourself."

"Another time, perhaps," the Master said. "Right now I have a summons to deliver to you," he said gravely.

The Bard's smile vanished.

"I speak now as your Prime. You are formally summoned to appear before the Council at noon tomorrow. You're to bring your lap harp *and* the harp that currently sits in my bedroom."

Cyral inhaled a sharp breath.

"Remain in the anteroom until Scribe Diarmuid comes to fetch you," the Prime continued. "Then enter the Council Hall with only your lap harp, leaving your other harp in the anteroom." He paused for a moment. "I would prefer Shay not to be left here alone, so bring him with you, but he's to remain outside on the steps and await you there. He is *not* to enter the building or leave the steps, regardless of what he might hear coming from within. Is this clearly understood?"

"Yes, Prime Ferghus, it is."

"See to it that it's clearly understood by him as well. Now, then, I think I'll go spend some time with my nephew." The Master rose and left, leaving Cyral staring after him in astonishment.

Chapter 27

At precisely noon of the following day, Cyral restlessly paced the length of the antechamber of the Council Hall. Shay had eagerly come along with him, bursting with curiosity ... unsatisfied by Cyral, who was bursting with his own. He had left his young cousin on the steps outside with the stern command from his uncle not to move from them until Cyral returned, no matter what he might hear ... perplexing though that was. The walls of the Council Hall were thick stone, and it was difficult to imagine any sound from within reaching the curious boy on its front steps.

Cyral knew all fifteen Masters were seated within the Council Hall, for fifteen cubicles and pegs in the antechamber sported a variety of packs and instruments. As he paced, he wondered why he had been summoned. The only reason he could think of was to reveal his mastery of the elemental songs, but why now, at the height of their preparations to leave? Cyral could see no reason why the Council would agree to allow a Bard the privilege of using skills forbidden to his rank. It was far more likely they'd summarily deny such a request and censure the Master who made it, Prime or not, for flouting tradition and teaching a Bard forbidden skills. Ferghus had refused to answer any questions the night before, deftly changing the subject to the elemental songs.

Not long after becoming a Master of Windsong and Earthsong, the firesong and watersong had touched Cyral's song as well, making him a Master of all four elemental songs. He had practiced diligently with three of them, using Bryan's harp, while his own harp had continued to stand alone and unused in his Master's bedroom. The windsong was still forbidden him, for even though four months had passed, Ferghus still refused to allow that his definition of "soon" had come. Cyral had nearly given up hope that it ever would. Today his hands had trembled as he touched his forbidden harp and forced himself to put it in its case and travel bag. Was he going to be ordered to abandon it? To leave it in the Council's hands for someone more worthy to use it? *No! He would never—*

The Bard abruptly stopped pacing as the door to the Council Hall was opened by a short, balding man dressed in black trousers and a tunic of seafoam green with an insignia of a silver quill on the front left shoulder. The garb of a Scribe. The man bowed.

"Bard Cyral," he said quietly. "I'm Diarmuid, Scribe of the Masters. Please take your place at the end of the Council table, bringing only your lap harp with you." Tearing his disbelieving eyes away from the huge harp standing there, the Scribe stood aside.

Cyral slung his lap harp over his shoulder, then took a deep breath and entered the hall. He paused a moment to glance appreciatively at the mosaics of the elements above the four large windows, each exquisitely crafted from crystals and gems. With a last longing glance at the windsong's mosaic, a vortex of quartz crystals and crushed aquamarine, he approached the table. As with the few other times he had been here for a conclave, a mallet and set of three graduated chimes were positioned in front of Ferghus, seated at the head of the table as Prime of the Council. Seven Masters were seated on either side of him. Cyral had met most of them before, especially Masters Barrach and Liam, Second and Third of the Council, whose territories he had served in, but he felt as nervous as if he were an erring apprentice being brought to task by all the Master Bards of Eire.

Noticing that the Scribe had already seated himself at his desk against the far wall, Cyral quickened his pace to the open end of the table, set his lap harp on the floor, and bowed. "Prime Ferghus," he said. "I've come in response to your summons."

Ferghus nodded, then picked up the mallet and struck the smallest chime three times. "Our meeting will now resume its session." He glanced at the Bard. "I warn you that everything said here is to be held in the strictest confidence. You are not to discuss these proceedings with anyone except a Master once you leave this hall."

"You have my word."

Ferghus turned to the Fourth of the Council. "Fionn, please brief the Council on the construction of the ships."

Fionn cleared his throat. "As you all know, our Prime arranged for ten ships to be built in two different locations. I've visited both," he added, glancing at Ferghus, "and applaud your choices. Inconvenient, perhaps, but choosing uninhabited islands with coves that kept our activities unseen from land and sea was perfect. As was your invention of the bogus 'fishing camps' of Rinn and Cuan to explain the comings and goings." He turned back to the Council.

"To date, the five ships in the cove of Rinn are complete and will arrive here the day before the Summer Solstice, eight days from now. The other five in the inlet of Cuan will not be complete until a fortnight after that and will set sail immediately upon their completion. All of our ships will have a Shipmaster, crew, and at least ten Bards on board, some of them Gifted, which will make communications easier. I've arranged for most of our unperishable stores, including necessary tools and goods, to be loaded onto the ships coming from Rinn, saving us precious time when they arrive. Each ship can take up to seventy passengers, depending on the weight of the perishable stores we must carry, which is frankly impossible to determine at this point." Fionn looked with some asperity at the Prime.

"Not to complain, Ferghus, but what good are these expensive ships of ours if we still have no idea where we're going? Until I know where we're headed and how long it will take to get there, I can't possibly calculate the supplies we'll need."

"We can always flee south to Armorica," suggested Liam.

Fionn shook his head. "Do you suppose there are no Druids along their northwestern coast? Gaul is where ours came from! And even if we sailed farther south to Aquitania, word of our mass migration would soon reach Eire. The Druidic Order might not care where we've gone so long as we stay there, but the Ard Rí will want us back, and take steps to force our return." He shook his head. "What we need is a place where no one knows us ... or better yet, somewhere completely uninhabited."

"So, all we need is the impossible," came a reckless comment from farther down the table.

"Or simply a key to unlock the possibilities dismissed in the box labeled 'impossible'," Ferghus countered. "I summoned Cyral here today because he might be the very key we need, having a Gift like no other this Council has ever seen before. I've relentlessly honed it and submit to you that there is a reason such a powerful Gift has arisen now, when we face extermination at the hands of an Order whose leader desires wealth and power. A leader who sees us as a means to the first, and a threat to the second."

Exclamations of astonishment rippled over the Council table, and appraising glances were turned toward Cyral. The Bard's face grew warm, and he inwardly groaned at his Master's choice of words concerning his Gift. Would they expect miracles from him? What would they think when they discovered he was just a Bard who could use elemental music, the same as they could?

"There's no doubt in my mind, Ferghus," Liam protested, "that your *own* Gift is the strongest among us!"

"No, it is not," the Prime said. "I call for a testing of windsong between the only two Masters of Windsong seated at this table ... myself and Barrach."

The Masters stared at their Prime, none looking more stunned than the Second of the Council. The Bard braced himself, certain he was witnessing the beginning of a war between the Masters. A war waged in a bid to gain the Council's authorization for him to continue using the elemental forces.

"Come now, Ferghus," Fionn remonstrated. "At such a time as this, would you delay the Council just to prove—"

"I'm hardly doing this on a mere whim, nor is it *my* abilities I intend to prove," the Prime stated. He turned to Barrach. "You're Second among us in the Gift, and a Master of Firesong, Watersong, and Windsong. Take your harp, set a block, and call the windsong to rise in this room."

Every eye turned to Barrach, who hesitated only a moment before nodding to the Council Scribe. Diarmuid rose to bring both Master's harps from the antechamber. Barrach's was a beautiful Bardic harp of polished maple. He nestled it against his chest, his brow furrowed slightly as he closed his eyes and began to expertly play. Cyral trembled and his hands clenched to fists as music he was forbidden to play filled the hall.

The Masters watched Barrach with skeptical expressions. Calling the windsong to rise was a simple thing for any Master out in the open where the wind blew freely. It was another matter entirely in a closed hall, even for a Master of the element. Yet the air began to stir around them in response to the Master's deft playing, swirling about the hems of their robes and lifting the edge of the open scroll on the Scribe's desk. Barrach broke off with a gasp.

"Impressive," the Prime said with a nod of respect, and many voices around the table murmured agreement. "Let's see if I can do better." He withdrew the gleaming rosewood instrument and set it on his lap, his weathered face lined deeply in concentration. His fingers began a light dance over the strings. Again the air stirred, the breeze strengthening as the Master's harp echoed the windsong. The Scribe's scroll skittered across the recording table. The chimes began to gently stir, giving voice to their own sweet sounds. Then Ferghus broke off with a grimace and put a hand to his chest.

Barrach frowned. "Are you all—"

"I'm perfectly fine," Ferghus said briskly. He motioned to the Scribe, who hurried to return both harps to the antechamber. When the Scribe had reseated himself, Ferghus glanced at Cyral and indicated the lap harp lying next to him. "If you please."

The stunned silence that fell after this was shattered by the combined objection of every Master at the table.

"By the Maker himself, Ferghus! You can't possibly—"

"*No* Bard is allowed to call an elemental force!"

"Have you lost your senses? Prime or not—"

"Even if he were allowed to, which he is *not*—"

"This is a *Bard,* Ferghus, in case you haven't—"

"Will you flagrantly break our rules before our very eyes?"

The clang of the largest chime effectively stopped the clash of raised voices. Those who had risen to their feet in outrage slowly reseated themselves, their expressions mutinous.

Cyral stood still, wondering if he could fly with the windsong in the enclosed hall when two accomplished Masters of Windsong had barely managed to make it rise. However, though the war had just escalated to fourteen against one, he would still put every spare copper he had on his Master. He stooped down and picked up his lap harp.

"Stop right there!" The commanding voice coming from the Second of the Council froze the Bard in place for a moment. He straightened, held the lap harp to his chest, and waited for the skirmish to begin.

Barrach glared at Ferghus. "Leaving aside, for the moment," he said tersely, "the fact that *Bard* Cyral has no right whatsoever to be calling the windsong—"

"As the Tester," Ferghus interrupted with a voice of iron, "*I* have the right to give any test I wish to anyone I choose. And my *Bard* has the responsibility to obey any command his Master gives him, without interference from you or anyone else!"

This gave Barrach pause, and Cyral stared at Ferghus. This was not the Master whom he had grown to love so dearly. This was a Prime in the full strength of his authority as the undisputed leader of the Bardic Order. Little wonder his Master's primary element was the indomitable earthsong.

Then Barrach slapped the arm of his chair. "Even so, this is hardly a fair testing! A Bard with a lap harp, going up against two Masters of Windsong? Who's next on your list?" he demanded. "Our Scribe, armed with his *quill?*" He gestured toward Diarmuid, who paled and dropped the slender writing tool.

When Ferghus' inflexible expression did not change, Barrach barked a laugh and threw up his hands. "Fine," he said. "Go right ahead and let him try calling the windsong to rise in a closed hall with a mere lap harp! How you can expect him to succeed is beyond me." A murmur of agreement rose from around the table.

The Prime turned to Cyral. "I can and do expect it," he said with quiet emphasis. "And I expect it to be done to the best of his ability, holding back nothing."

"Soon—" the Bard began.

"—is now," the Master finished. "But you're restricted to this room," he warned, "and must not leave it."

Cyral's heart hammered in his chest, torn between his intense desire to do as his Master commanded and the uncertainty of what might happen if he did. Putting aside his misgivings, Cyral sat in the chair the Scribe hastily fetched. He slid the small harp onto his lap, closed his eyes to the riveted scrutiny of the Council, and set a strong block. Then he placed his fingers on the strings and opened his awareness to the song he had longed to play since he first flew with it, a song he had not dared to even listen to since that day.

Come to me!

The windsong came instantly to his bidding, as though it had been impatiently waiting for his command. Then, focusing on the still air within the Council Hall, the Bard began to play the music that filled his soul.

The air around him rose instantly in response, swirling upward as the Bard's awareness rose ecstatically with it. The exultation of a long-denied freedom blew all uncertainties away as he spiraled blissfully toward the ceiling, oblivious to all else.

I can fly with you at last!

Scrolls flew off the scribing table, outpacing Diarmuid's frantic reach. Books and manuscripts from the open pigeonhole cabinet next to it followed, one after the other. The Masters' hair blew wildly and their white robes whipped about their chairs as they hung on to the edge of the Council table in the rising tempest. The chimes swung crazily, their voices clashing in dissonance as they fell, Ferghus barely managing to catch them. Upward soared the whirling windsong, battering against the constraining walls until it reached the windows high above. The sudden crash of splintering glass rent the air as the window beneath the windsong mural burst from the pressure, raining shards down upon the ground outside. Some fell inside, narrowly missing the Scribe, who sat clutching his desk and moaning in fear as it began to move away from the wall.

Cyral had but a moment to gaze longingly at the enticing breach in the enclosed hall before an authoritative voice spoke in his mind.

Return to me! Now!

Only a flicker of rebellion crossed the Harpist's mind as his fingers slowed and he commanded the windsong to be still. It stopped as suddenly as it had risen, and the gale in the hall died with it.

Cyral opened his eyes to a scene of utter chaos. Glass littered the floor, a confusion of books and manuscripts were piled in the corners, scrolls lay scattered all over the hall, and the set of chimes lay on its side, still clutched by the Prime. The mallet was nowhere to be seen. For a long moment, no one moved. Exclamations of hushed disbelief and wonder began to circulate.

"I don't care *what* Ferghus says. *That* ... was impossible!"

"Who could have imagined such—"

"*No* one could!

"Why, if he hadn't stopped—"

"—he could have killed us all!"

Fourteen Masters stared at Cyral with various combinations of awe and fear. Liam gingerly touched his right ear and winced at the blow the mallet had inflicted as it flew from the table.

"I must admit," he said slowly, "that was the most impressive breaking of a stricture I've ever witnessed. Any *more* impressive, and I might be missing an ear ... or an eye."

Cyral began to apologize, but the Master shook his head.

"A Bard who does as his Master commands owes no one an apology for it."

"True enough," agreed Barrach. "But I would demand an accounting from his *Master* for commanding his Bard to break our rules, regardless of how spectacularly he did it!"

Ferghus frowned. "Am I speaking to a gathering of newly robed apprentices, that I must explain the obvious?" His eyes swept the slowly recovering Council. "You've seen what our two Masters of Windsong can do with cycles of experience and their full Bardic harps in hand, and you've seen what Cyral can do with *no* cycles of experience on a mere *lap* harp. If strength in the Gift were the only criterion for becoming a Master, then clearly our new Prime would be sitting at the other end of this table!"

Ferghus set the chimes upright and glanced at the wide-eyed Scribe. "The mallet, if you please," he murmured, and the Scribe moved from his frozen position and went to hunt for it under a pile of books. No one spoke until it was retrieved and the Scribe pushed his table back into position and took his seat.

"Not to take away from his stunning accomplishment," Fionn said, "but how long has Cyral been calling the windsong?"

"This was his second time," Ferghus returned evenly.

Freshly shocked faces turned Cyral's way.

"Done at my request," the Prime added.

Heads swiveled back to Ferghus.

"*You* requested it?" Fionn exclaimed. "The Prime who's a stickler for the strictures he demands that every Bard know and follow? And what on earth happened the *first* time he used it?"

"His affinity with the wind was immediate, and he flew as a Master of Windsong through my open door to the bay and well beyond, nearly out of my reach to retrieve him."

"With a *lap harp?*" Liam asked incredulously.

"The same one he holds now, which he also used to become a Master of Firesong, Watersong, and Earthsong."

Stunned gazes traveled collectively back to Cyral, who sat as immobile as the stone table he was staring at.

"You're all doing an excellent job of missing the point," Ferghus testily continued. "Do begin to think. If Cyral stirred up a wind like this with a lap harp, and blew out a window with it before I stopped him, what could he do with a full-sized Bardic harp?"

"He could undoubtedly blow up this hall, and everyone in it!" Barrach stated, throwing his hands in the air as if illustrating the explosion. "And of what use would *that* be, except to underscore why Bards should not be taught what only Masters should know? You're a superb Prime, Ferghus—the best our Order has had for generations—but this is not something any of us can let pass."

Ferghus turned his eyes upon Cyral. "Go now," he commanded, "and bring your harp here for them to see."

Wordlessly, Cyral rose and fetched it, then removed it from its travel bag and case and stood it before them, his hands possessively holding onto its frame. He looked up to find fourteen sets of disbelieving eyes fixed upon it.

"Cyral has had a dream since he was a youngling," Ferghus told them, "a dream of making the biggest, most incredible harp ever to be seen in all of Eire."

"I'd say he succeeded," Barrach said dryly, giving Cyral a nod. "Congratulations." He turned to Ferghus and began to speak, then abruptly stopped and gave the huge harp an appraising look.

The Prime shoved his chair back and stood, commanding every Master's attention. "The windsong touched Cyral's song before he felt any fear of it," he declared. "He then traveled far beyond the bay with a mere lap harp. How far do you think he could go with a full Bardic harp?" His voice rang through the hall as he gestured meaningfully toward the harp in Cyral's hands. "How far could he go with *that* one? And what might he find with it?"

Utter silence fell over the hall.

Liam was the first to break it. "A place for us to go," he murmured in awe. The quiet utterance of six words released a veritable tidal wave of speech.

"By all the—"

"Why, he's absolutely right! A harp like *that!*

"Wielded by a Bard with a *Gift* like that!"

"Who'd have thought our Prime could have—"

"Are you inferring that us *older* Masters are—"

"No, no! Of course not!"

Soft chuckles came from the head of the table.

"Just imagine what he could find!"

"A place of safety!"

"We could live free of Druids *and* Rí!"

"A Bardic refuge ... all our own!"

Barrach dealt both arms of his chair a ringing slap, bringing the confusion of voices to a stop. "Sionnach glic!" he exclaimed. "You crafty old fox! Once again, you've given us a chance!"

"Can I assume my flagrant breaking of the rules is forgiven?" Ferghus asked with arched brows as he reseated himself.

"I'd forgive you turning *twenty* Bards into Masters before their time if it gives us an opportunity like this!"

Voices from all around the table rose in excited agreement.

Appraising glances turned toward Cyral, whose attention was fixed on his harp.

He wants us to find a safe haven for our people? Then why has he forbidden me to use you? We should have been practicing together night and day, my friend!

"I'd like to hear this harp of his, Ferghus," Liam said, his eyes alight with interest. "Will you allow him to play it for us? Something... less elemental, perhaps?" he added wryly.

Bard and Master locked eyes, the Bard's filled with yearning, the Master's with regret.

"No," Ferghus said gently. "I'm truly sorry, but I can't allow it." He turned his attention back to the Council. "Cyral has played this harp of his but once ... a stunning performance for me several months ago. I have not allowed him to play it since."

"That's harsh, Ferghus ... even for you," Barrach said dryly. "No wonder he's clutching it like he's expecting it to be taken away. Why would you allow him to make such an incredible instrument, only to forbid him to play it?"

Ferghus looked directly into Cyral's eyes. "Because the next time he plays it," he quietly said, "he will be filled with all the pent-up desire his hands are trembling with now, a desire whose flames I've intentionally stoked by forbidding him its use, and except for today, forbidding him to fly the windsong as well. For he will need to fly far and long, and such emotion will give him a great deal more power to do so ... and return to us safely again."

Cyral sat down abruptly, as though his legs could no longer support him.

"I have indeed been harsh," the Master told him. "And though I know you have silently questioned and protested such treatment, you have obeyed, having no idea why I was forbidding you the instrument you love and the windsong you ache to fly. Until now."

Cyral briefly closed his eyes, his hands still clutching the frame of his harp. He rose and returned the instrument to its case, then cinched it tightly in its travel bag. Setting it next to his chair, he turned and faced the Prime.

"My Master," he said clearly, "does nothing without good reason, whether it's forbidding me the use of my harp or commanding me to break a stricture in front of the Council. I will continue to accept your restriction of my harp and the windsong until you give me permission to do otherwise." He didn't see the looks of respect the members of the Council gave him.

The Prime held the eyes of his Bard for a long moment before speaking. "While Diarmuid catches up with his recording," he said with a pointed glance at the Scribe, who hurriedly took up the quill and inkwell he had saved from the maelstrom and began frantically writing, "I ask the Second of the Council to scan Bard Cyral's mind for any impediments that would preclude him from using the windsong to find us a new homeland."

Barrach frowned. "Are you certain, Ferghus? You realize what I will do if—"

"I'm quite aware." Ferghus turned to Cyral. "Open your mind to Master Barrach."

Cyral turned his attention to the Second of the Council and looked steadily into the Master's eyes. A song appeared in his mind, different than his own Master's. It moved slowly through his thoughts and memories, much like the sparkling notes from the granite had when he'd propelled them into the Stone. When at last it finished its methodical circuit, the song paused for a moment.

Thank you for allowing my scrutiny. Our Prime has placed this venture of his in good hands. You will have the full support of myself and this Council.

Before Cyral could reply, the song was gone. He blinked as the Second of the Council rose to his feet.

"I find Bard Cyral free of impediments, though he's perhaps a bit stunned at the moment," he said with a brief smile. "I will also say that I've never encountered a Gift of such incredible strength in anyone before. Little wonder all four elements touched it." He sat back down and Ferghus stood.

The Prime struck the middle chime twice. "Let me state for the record that Cyral has passed all his Bard Tests in the Gift to my complete satisfaction ... and you all know how difficult that is to achieve," he added dryly.

A ripple of amusement went around the table, releasing the emotionally charged atmosphere. Nearly every Master at the table had taken their Bard Tests under Ferghus.

"Cyral has served well and faithfully in three territories," the Prime continued. "He has a thorough knowledge and understanding of Bardic Law. As our Second has just verified, he is free of impediments. He's not only fully eligible to become a Master, he's already proficient in everything a new Master is customarily taught. *And* he's a Master of all four elemental songs." His gaze swept the table. "I therefore propose we advance Bard Cyral to the rank of Master, subject to twelve votes of agreement among the Council. Do both the Second and Third of the Council agree with putting this proposal to a vote?"

"Yes," Barrach and Liam chorused together.

Ferghus tapped the middle chime twice, then turned toward the Second of the Council. "How do you vote?"

Cyral, still grappling with the reason his Master had forbidden him his harp and the windsong, barely heard each vote as it was given and duly recorded. The vote was unanimous. He was a Bard no longer.

Cyral couldn't find his voice to speak as an enthusiastic wave of congratulations came from his new colleagues. Nor could he find it when the Prime accepted the book of Bardic Law the Scribe brought to him, and told the former Bard to approach. But as he walked numbly to the head of the table, the weathered face of his Master broke into a smile, like the sun coming out from behind the clouds on a rainy summer day. And Cyral found his voice at last as

Ferghus held out the book and told him to place his right hand upon it.

"I, Cyral, accept the rank of Master Bard offered me by this Council. I will uphold Bardic Law, as far as it lies within me to do so. I will place the welfare of our people before all consideration of myself, and work to ensure that the music, song, and lore of our land does not die."

He removed his blue robe and silver cord, then reached out and accepted the white robe from Ferghus' hand. He pulled the robe on, and Ferghus himself tied the gold cord securely around it. The Council rose to their feet and acknowledged him with one voice, a shout of approval and hope that set the silver chimes dancing on their pedestal.

"Master Cyral!"

Chapter 28

Cyral left the Council Hall in a daze, too numb to even notice Shay's exclamation of surprise at seeing his cousin emerge in the white robe and gold cord of a Master Bard. The boy fell silent as they walked along the coastal path, as though sensing Cyral's need to process whatever had happened in the Council Hall without being pestered with questions.

The former Bard came to a sudden halt. "I'm sorry, Shay," he said. "I've ... a lot to think about."

"That's okay, Cous—can I still call you my cousin?" Shay wanted to know.

"Of course you can. I'm still the same cousin who took you down the Easach."

"But, you're a Master now," Shay said in a hushed voice.

"*And* your Cousin Cyral."

"Then ... can you tell me what all the noise was?" Shay's eyes lit with excitement. "It sounded like the biggest windstorm ever! And then there was an explosion ... and glass came flying out when one of those huge windows broke! I didn't move from the steps," he hurriedly added when one of Cyral's brows lifted in his direction. "They go all the way to the corner of the building, and I just happened to be looking around it. My feet were on the steps the whole time you were gone, truly!"

Cyral nodded. "I would tell you what happened if I could," he told the youngster. "But I'm sworn not to speak of it to anyone but a Master. Not even a trusted relative," he added with a smile.

They walked on in comfortable silence, but when they arrived at the Master's home, Cyral found himself too restless for the house to contain him. He left to walk along the bluff, pacing back and forth while Shay made dinner for the three of them, pausing occasionally to check on his cousin through the window. Cyral continued trampling the grass near the cliff's edge, never noticing when Ferghus arrived home, studied him for a few moments, then entered the house. At last Cyral headed back, so distracted by his thoughts that he knocked on the door. His Master opened it and unexpectedly swept him a formal bow.

"Master Cyral."

Cyral swept his Master a deeper one.

"Prime Ferghus."

They looked at each other and grinned. Ferghus extended his right arm in offered friendship, and Cyral stared at it in surprise.

"Take it before it falls off," Ferghus advised. "You've become a *full* Master, not a newly robed one with much to learn. We are equals now."

Cyral grasped the proffered arm firmly. "In rank, perhaps. But you are my Prime and will always be my Master."

Back inside, they enjoyed the lamb stew Shay had prepared. The three of them talked about everything except what had happened in the Council Hall. Shay helped Cyral with cleaning up, then, obeying a meaningful nod from his uncle in the direction of his room, the lad excused himself and headed down the hall.

"Any particular reason why my bedroom is still hosting your harp?" Ferghus asked as they took their seats by the fireplace.

"I'm not sure what I'm allowed or not allowed to do, or which harp I'm allowed or not allowed to do it with. Until all of that is made clear, I don't trust myself to keep my harp in my possession."

"Do you truly think I would forbid a Master the use of his own instrument?"

"I certainly do!" came the emphatic reply. "Our robes may match, but as Prime, you can still forbid me whatever you wish."

"I will no longer forbid you your harp."

Cyral gave him a disbelieving look. "So, I could fetch it this moment and play it all I like?"

"Absolutely," Ferghus affirmed. "But you won't."

Silence fell between them. "No," Cyral said at last. "I won't. But, leaving that aside for the moment..." He took a deep breath and looked directly into Ferghus' eyes. "What possible reason could you have had for turning me into a Master today? I expected the conflict you started. I expected you to win it and gain the Council's approval for my wielding of the elemental forces. I did *not* expect to walk out of the hall in a Master's robe!"

Ferghus cocked a brow. "Must I have a reason beyond bestowing a rank I feel you deserve?"

"Yes."

Ferghus frowned. "You can't simply enjoy receiving a robe you've earned with the superb mastery of four elemental songs?"

"No."

"Trusting that I know what I'm do—"

"No."

"So," Ferghus said dryly, "you knock on my door like a stranger, tell me I will always be your Master, and then demand that I account for myself?"

"Yes. Blame the earthsong for my stubbornness and upbraid me all you like for daring to dictate to my Prime ... but I'll have your reason first."

Ferghus gave his former Bard a hard stare, one that just that morning would have produced instant compliance. "Did the explanation I gave the Council not satisfy you?" he demanded.

"No," Cyral said flatly. "You've been telling me that my Gift is the key to our survival, and now I understand why … you want me to use my harp and the windsong to find a safe haven for us. But what made you think that I could even do such a thing? Being Gifted was no guarantee that I'd bond with the elements, so how did you know that I would? And why do I need to be a Master in order to search for a new homeland? All that was needed was the Council's authorization, not a Master's robe to go with it!"

Silence fell between them, broken at last by a deep sigh from Ferghus. "Very well, then. Do you remember the day I took you from Harpist Ultan's home?"

"Of course I do," Cyral said, startled by the unexpected question. "How could I not? It was the best day of my life."

"And did you think I just happened to walk through your village, decided to check in on the local Harpist, and much to my surprise, found a boy I thought might be nice to have around to fetch and carry for me?"

Cyral stared at him, nonplussed. "At the time, I didn't question it," he finally said, "because you promised to teach me how to make my own lap harp. I'd have gladly gone with anyone who promised me that and took me away from a Harpist who only wanted me to do his chores. Later, I assumed Ultan had sent word to you that I was Gifted, and since the Gifted can only be apprenticed by a Master, you came to get me."

"Ultan sent me no word, and only the Maker knows how long he'd have delayed doing so. He took one look at my face and apologized profusely before running off to pack your bag and hand you over. I went to your village to fetch you because I already knew you were there. I knew what you looked like because I'd seen your black hair, amber eyes, and shy smile long before I met you."

Before Cyral could register his surprise, Ferghus threw another question his way. "Do you remember when I summoned you here to inspect the Stone I'd found the day before?"

Cyral nodded wordlessly.

"Did you think I was out for a morning stroll and amongst all the thousands of rocks on the beach, I just happened to come across that one?"

"I'm guessing not."

"I went to the beach that morning because I already knew the Stone was there. I saw it wash ashore clearly enough to know its approximate location. I also knew the importance it would play in honing your Gift."

Cyral stared at him, nonplussed. "Are you telling me you have the Sight?"

Ferghus sat back in his chair and gave the young Master a deeply offended look. "Hardly that," he said testily. "I'm no village soothsayer, my boy! It's more of an … intuitive ability."

"An intuitive—but you can actually see the future!"

"A very *strong* intuitive ability."

"Don't you believe in the Sight?" Cyral wanted to know.

"Of course I do," Ferghus said stiffly. "I also believe that the unfortunate souls who have it are pestered day and night with people wanting to know their futures! I am fortunately *not* one of them, since I merely have strong *intuitions.*"

Cyral suppressed a smile. "I see. Very well, then, what did you *intuit* that made you decide to turn me into a Master?"

Ferghus' golden eyes gleamed. "I saw that you would make a great harp and would use it to find something we desperately needed. I could hardly help but notice that you were wearing a white robe. Don't ask me the details of what you'll find—I don't know—but I do know you'll find it."

Cyral stared at him.

"And then," Ferghus continued, "the need came—the most pressing need we've ever had in all our history—and your harp was nearly finished and you were still robed in blue. So, I did what I could to fix the color."

Cyral blinked. "You … fixed the color."

"And now you know the need, your colossal harp is finished, and you're robed in white," Ferghus said with quiet satisfaction. "The emotional frustration of having been kept from your harp and the windsong will be fully released the next time you play it, for today's curtailed trip with it would have only increased it. Your next flight will be to find a safe haven for us. You already realize this, of course, or your harp would not be standing in my bedroom."

Cyral frowned. "So, I should just snatch it out of your room and ride the winds across the ocean until I bump into somewhere no one knows about?"

"Absolutely."

"Just like that?"

"Do you know a better way?"

Cyral threw his hands in the air. "You've lost your mind! How, exactly, am I supposed to pull off a miracle like that?"

"Not by insulting your Prime, that's certain," Ferghus said reprovingly. "If you can blow out a window in a closed room on a mere lap harp, think what you can do in the open air with that monstrosity of yours!"

"Which brings up another question I want answered," Cyral said, his temper rising. "You knew perfectly well I'd only ridden the windsong once! What if I hadn't been able to stop when you ordered me to? What if you'd all been swept up and dashed against the walls until you were battered to a pulp? What if I'd brought all four of those priceless mosaics down on your heads? Did you stop to consider *that* before you ordered me to whip up the windsong for you?"

Ferghus regarded him levelly, his eyes glinting with a trace of the masterful Prime Cyral had seen at the Council session. "If you're waiting for an apology, you'll be sitting there a long time. I've seen you use the windsong to find what we so desperately need, and you will be a Master when you do it. I have seen it! Time is of the essence, so I did what needed to be done. Cathair will attack at the Summer Solstice whether we're ready or not."

Cyral frowned. "Do we even know where he is?"

"He left Gaotha by sea a fortnight ago. There's little doubt who picked him up, or where they headed. They left two Celtic warriors in his place, who would have succeeded in finding Shay and killing him if Daithi hadn't arranged for his escape. And Tadhg told me Shay warned him about two riders approaching as they rounded the estuary. They were able to hide themselves before two Celts rode past and took the road west. Why, one wonders, would they head that way? Who might be coming by sea to pick them up so close to Aille-Mara? Or, more probably," he said darkly, "drop warriors off to join them so they can attack us by land *and* sea?" Ferghus locked eyes with his horrified colleague.

"Don't waste time fearing what your Gift might do. Use it!" The Master's fist punctuated his words against the arm of his chair. *"Use* it to find a place we can go! We must make our move before the Summer Solstice, nine days from now. We have five ships that are ready to sail and can arrive here within a day's time. We only need a direction. Use your Gift to give us one, or do nothing and watch us perish!"

Cyral sat frozen.

"You're a Master now," Ferghus said more gently. "What you do must be by your own choice or you won't use the strength of will the earthsong has given you to succeed. And you'll need more than the earthsong's willpower. You must *believe* in what you seek with the passion of the firesong, *hunt* for it with the creative flow of the watersong, and *fly* to it with the freedom of the windsong."

"And, if I don't succeed?" The words were rough with anguish.

"Then we're no worse off than we are now, and you'll have at least *tried,* using everything you have to give." Ferghus observed the conflict on Cyral's face and quietly continued. "You have become more than you ever imagined being. You have a tremendous, highly developed affinity for songs, an affinity that attracted all four elemental songs to touch yours in the space of a single season! If I *did* believe in impossibilities, that would certainly be at the top of the list. The rest of us have more experience directing the wind-song, but we can do little more than bring a welcome breeze on a hot summer day or subdue the violence of a winter storm. None of us can travel the wind far enough to find a new homeland, out of sight and knowledge of Eire. You alone can ... and you *will* find it. I haven't seen the place myself, but I've seen your success. I believe implicitly in it. Yet I repeat, the choice is your own."

Silence fell once again between them, broken when Cyral abruptly rose. His gaze lingered on the fire as he walked to the window overlooking the bay, remembering the first time he had entered the flames and traveled their fiery depths. He stood staring out at dark waves limned in moonlight, remembering the thrill of traveling under them in the sunlight for the first time. He remembered being on the beach below, taken swiftly down through a crack in the bottom of a bucket, pulled by the strength of the earthsong. He remembered the incredible moment that vast force had touched his song. He heard the keening of the wind over the bluff and re-membered the first time he had immersed himself in its song, remembered the indescribable feeling of flying with it, the longing to continue moving freely with it forever. He remembered ... and knew in his soul that all of it had been possible only because of the Master who sat behind him, silently awaiting his decision.

"In the face of your belief in me, how can I not try?"

A smile transfigured Ferghus' face. "When will you go?"

Cyral's brow furrowed in thought as he began to pace the Master's living room. He said nothing for a long time as Ferghus silently watched. At long last Cyral addressed the table.

"There are things to consider," he informed it. "First, our direction. There's no sense in heading east," he told a chair, as though it had foolishly suggested it. "For even if we managed to evade the Ard Rí's notice, no other country would welcome us. And south is no better," he admonished another, "for the Druids of Gaul aren't any more likely to roll out a welcome mat." He shook his head at a third chair. "We can't risk going north, the direction the warriors will be coming from. That leaves west," he said emphatically, as though daring any chair to argue the point. Having settled the matter without opposition, he turned and paced the other way.

"Then," he mused, "there's the question of distance. How far can I fly with the windsong before I need to turn around? Not having ridden it enough to know, I'll have to go by how I feel when I ride the other elements and know I need to return." Satisfied with this decision, he turned and strode to the window overlooking the bay, where he stood for a long moment.

"Navigation shouldn't be a problem," he murmured, "for the windsong will keep me headed in any direction I command it to. When I've either succeeded or begin to tire, it will bring me straight back. And," he brightened considerably, "after this place of ours is found, I should be able to direct the windsong to take our ships there. So ... I'll leave at dawn," he announced to the window. Then, with a look of determination, he strode off to fetch his harp and set it in readiness by the front door.

The two Masters promised each other they'd try to get some sleep, both of them knowing the other one wouldn't. Then Cyral left for his room, pausing when he heard the soft snick of a door closing farther down the hall. His eyes narrowed, wondering how much of their conversation Shay had heard.

In the pre-dawn light, Cyral rose and found Ferghus already up and motioning him to a hearty breakfast. Cyral ate quickly as Ferghus sat silently at the end of the table. When the young Master rose to leave, he paused next to Ferghus.

"Halfway from here to Aille-Mara is a place where the cliffs jut out toward the bay and there are a few boulders to sit on," Cyral told him. "It's isolated from the road and far enough from here that I won't need to set a block."

Ferghus nodded. "I know the place."

"Make sure that Shay doesn't follow me, like he did Daithi." Cyral quietly added. When Ferghus glanced up in surprise and nodded, Cyral took the Master's hand in his own and pressed it to his lips. Then he slung the great harp over his shoulder and left.

Ferghus cradled his hand and closed his eyes. "The Maker be with you, my boy," he murmured, "for the sake of us all."

"Aren't you going to help him?" came a young, accusing voice.

Ferghus' eyes flew open to see Shay standing at the hallway's entrance, looking at him in distress. The Master regretfully shook his head.

"There's no further help we can give him now except to wait and not interfere."

The boy's eyes gleamed with stubbornness as he took a step toward the door, but stopped when Ferghus raised a hand.

"No, lad, you must not follow him," the Master said gravely. "For if you do, you'll be taken up into the music of the wind as well, the added burden of having someone with him will take his strength all the sooner, and you will both be lost to the wind."

The youngster stood biting his lip, then looked at his uncle and nodded a silent promise.

"If there was anything in this world I could do for him now," the Master told him, "you can rest assured I would be at his side, doing it. But this..." He sighed heavily. "This is something only Cyral can do. And he must do it alone."

Chapter 29

Cyral sat on a large boulder near the edge of a sheer drop into the sea, overlooking the northern bay of Aille-Mara. His harp stood in front of him, ready to be played. The wind was not strong this fine morning, merely a gentle breeze that caused the tall grass around him to sway gently back and forth, and the hem of his robe to ripple across his legs.

The young Master tried in vain to calm his nerves and stop his hands from trembling as they took their place on the strings. The only time he had given this harp its voice, he had played a medley of his memories of Ferghus, taking them both on a journey to the past. Today he would play the windsong in search of his people's future. He was afraid, not of riding the wind, but of riding it and finding nothing out there ... of returning to face the devastation on his Master's face. He firmly pushed that thought aside. He was no longer an apprentice, determined never to disappoint his Master again. Nor was he a Harpist or Bard under someone else's direction. He was a Master, who must make his own decisions and live with their consequences. His fingers steadied as he reached out with his mind and spoke to the wind.

Bring me your song!

The windsong flooded his mind as though it had been waiting

on the very threshold of his awareness. His heart beat quickly, matching the capricious music that tripped lightly across his mind, stirring his thoughts and emotions as easily as it stirred the grass surrounding him. He dropped all expectations of musical form and rhythmic consistency and opened himself to experience the song of an element that seemed inherently wild and unpredictable. Yet even as he thought it, he amended the description to a single word.

Flexible. Able to go anywhere and find the homeland we need. Without conscious thought, Cyral's fingers began to dance across the strings, playing the music flooding his mind. The song of the wind.

The harpist barely noticed the wind rise around him, was hardly conscious of the vortex that the music from his harp evoked. He only knew that something deep inside him soared with it, and the next moment his awareness was high above the cliff, facing the open sea. For a moment he nearly panicked, realizing how far away from his own body he was about to travel and what it would mean if he lacked the strength to return. Eventually his hands would tire, the strings would fall silent, and his body would perish. What would happen to his mind, to his conscious awareness of himself as an individual? Would he forever ride the wind, unable to direct it with his playing? Or would the song of his mind unravel, note by note, to be scattered far and wide?

Better that than refusing to give our people the chance they need to survive!

The willpower of the earthsong possessed Cyral so strongly in that moment that he nearly switched elemental songs. Firmly, he kept his fingers dancing across the strings in deft mimicry of the windsong. Then, with the indomitable force of the earthsong's will, he commanded the windsong to take him west. West over the ocean at blinding speed. The windsong responded instantly, blowing him over the bay in a mere heartbeat and out to the open sea. Joy and terror filled him, and he frantically slowed the tempo so he could regain his composure and take his bearings.

He gasped in relief as the wind slowed enough for him to see his surroundings. He glanced behind him at the quickly receding coast of Eire. Thinking of himself on the cliff, still playing, was disorienting and unnerving, so he turned his attention to the sea below. He could see the Scaelaga Islands not far to the south and the Blasca Islands to the north, but to the west only the empty ocean met his searching gaze, the waves patterned ripples on its azure surface. Though he had been determined to make this journey, doubt clouded his mind, and Cyral held the music in stasis, keeping him where he was. For this, he realized, was his true moment of decision … here, away from all influence of the Council or the many people who needed him, away from his Master's belief in him. Those things had gotten him this far, but for him to move forward, he must find the strength to do this within himself. He must fully trust the harp he could only feel the strings of, and the windsong that would take him onward … or back. And it seemed to him in that suspended moment of time that his mind stepped aside and his soul rose up and made the choice to trust … and move forward.

Yet it was the windsong that moved first, bringing two words up from the very depths of his harp. They swirled gently into his mind, words he instantly recognized as the harp's true, Celtic name. In pure exultation, Cyral shouted it into the wind.

Marcach Gaoithe! Rider of the Wind.

At its utterance, windsong and Harp formed a bond with each other and with the Master who commanded them both, a bond the like of which Cyral had never felt before. Marveling, the Master took firm hold of the reins of the Windsong and the strings of his Harp and moved forward in the sheer joy of riding the wind as he flew faster and farther from the shores of his homeland.

Long he played, long he rode the wind with no sense of the passage of time. He visualized land, trusting the windsong to understand his need, and his course altered slightly to the north. After endless waves had passed below, and the coast of Eire had long since been lost to view, he began to feel like he did after riding the earthsong as far as he dared, and knew he needed to head back. Cyral continued to scan the western horizon, loath to return without having found what he sought, but nothing met his searching gaze.

He was about to turn back when he spotted something in the distance breaking the monotony of the waves. The windsong swept him toward it, and to his joy, a group of islands came into view. He wondered if, back on the bluff, tears were streaming down his face, mirroring the ones flooding his mind at their welcome sight.

Cyral slowed the tempo of the windsong as he approached the largest isle from high above it, the peak of a tall mountain rising in the northwest. To the east lay a smaller island with vast stretches of forest, and to the north of this was the smallest island with precipitous cliffs that plunged into the ocean. Northwest of this was the second largest island, densely forested with a chain of three mountains. To its southwest was the fifth isle, which seemed to be mostly open grassland with no visible mountains. Nowhere did he see any signs of human habitation; no villages or towns met his eye, not a single ship or boat plied the waters below.

With a cry of triumph, the harpist sent the wind back the way it had come. He made no effort to hold back the tempo until he saw the distant shore of Eire. Then, fearing what kind of maelstrom he might visit on his own homeland, he slowed the tempo of his aching fingers, gradually bringing the speed of the wind down to a strong breeze. When at last he saw himself playing at the top of the cliff, Cyral was dizzy with exhaustion. With a last burst of effort, he commanded his fingers to continue playing ... yet still they slowed, as sluggish as the mind struggling to command them. His hands fell from strings he could no longer feel.

The wind died. On the bluff far below, the harpist slumped against the frame of his instrument as he lost consciousness. The

Harp fell and took him with it to the grass. He did not stir.

An hour later, Ferghus was doing an excellent imitation of his former apprentice, pacing back and forth across his living room in growing agitation. Surely Cyral had finished his initial search by now! He should have come back and reported without delay, either in person or by traveling their bond. Ferghus could travel it to Cyral, but distracting him while he was riding the windsong was dangerous, for if the harpist stopped playing he would be lost to the wind. Nor could Ferghus go to him, for the same reason he had given Shay, who was silently watching him pace from the depths of Cyral's chair. So the Master had waited … and worried … and agonized over the validity of his intuitive visions.

Suddenly a voice spoke in Ferghus' mind, freezing him in place. It was Tryg, the Bard in charge of the five ships in the cove of Rinn, waiting for the command to set sail.

Prime Ferghus! I'm sorry to take such a risk, but you need to know!

What's happened?

One of our hunters saw Celtic warriors in the hills above our camp early this morning. There's nothing of possible interest to them here unless they've gotten wind of our ships and are searching for them. So I ordered all five ships to leave. We set sail just before the warriors reached the deserted camp. They sent a flurry of arrows that caused a few injuries and one death. I know I did this without—

You did exactly as you should have! When do you anticipate arriving in Aille-Mara?

Late this afternoon. The Bard's relief was palpable.

We'll be ready. Never mind the risk … notify the other Masters! Tell them Faolán has decided not to wait for the Solstice. They must implement their evacuation plans immediately, on my authority, after which they're to meet me at the Hall.

Yes, Prime Ferghus! Tryg's presence vanished.

Ferghus uttered an oath that shocked Shay to his core. Then he ordered his stunned nephew to pack his belongings immediately and stormed from the house, slamming the door behind him with enough force to set his wind chimes dancing in protest. He went around to the shed, hitched Sásta to the cart and brought him around to the front of the house. Then back and forth he went, loading the open-backed cart with crates of valuable scrolls from his room, Shay scrambling to help. The Master collected their instruments, a few necessities, and some items he couldn't bear the thought of Cathair or Faolán getting their hands on. Then he stored what Cyral would need in the young Master's packs, thinking furiously. Faolán must have found out about the ships being built at Rinn and sent his fianna to take them. He would have timed his sea warriors coming from the north to reach the bay of Aille-Mara at the same time the commandeered ships arrived from the south. With such a force as that set against them, their own ships unexpectedly filled with warriors, every Bard and Master in Aille-Mara would have been killed. Thanks to Tryg, their five ships were still in their own possession, giving them a chance to escape.

There was no time to lose. Whether or not Cyral's mission was complete, Ferghus had no choice but to interrupt him and get the young Master to the wharf and onto a ship. Nothing took precedence over that, for he knew Cyral was the one irreplaceable key to their survival. If the young Master hadn't found a refuge for them, he would have to hunt for it from the ship after they escaped.

Shay quickly loaded the last of the crates while Ferghus took a final, cursory look around his home. Then he resolutely shut the door for the last time, trying without success to shut out the many memories that clamored for his attention from the other side. Most of those memories were of his boy. He told himself he could pack up his memories and let go of this place, certain that Cyral would be going with him, for his intuition had never been wrong before. *And it had better not be wrong now.* He loaded Cyral's packs into the cart and settled himself onto the seat next to Shay. Then, with a brisk slap of the reins, they headed down the road toward Aille-Mara.

The moment Ferghus neared the promontory Cyral had spoken of, he rode straight onto the verge and down the grassy slope. Shay cried out and pointed to the crumpled figure near the edge of the cliff. The great Harp was lying on the ground, one of the harpist's hands lying protectively across its frame. Ferghus' heart lurched. "No!" He drove the pony as close as he dared, then jumped down from the cart and broke into a run with Shay right behind him. He fell to his knees by Cyral's side, muttering savagely.

"No, you *can't* be ... you aren't allowed to be ... you're absolutely and utterly *forbidden* to be!" He turned Cyral onto his back, looking frantically for any signs of life, immeasurably relieved to see the rhythmic rise and fall of the young Master's chest.

"He's alive!" Ferghus told his stricken nephew. For a few moments he tried without success to revive Cyral, then eyed the enormous Harp that Shay was determinedly trying to set upright. His nephew had it right ... Cyral's Harp was their only chance. Ferghus rose and took the Harp from the youngster's hands, then sat on the boulder with the instrument in place before him. "He's lost," he murmured brokenly to it. "My boy is lost in the wind."

The Master pulled the Harp close, feeling dwarfed by it. He tried to settle his nerves and calm his racing heart. His boy needed him, and Ferghus would be of no use to Cyral if he played in a state of panic, exciting the wind currents to take Cyral even farther away. Cyral's body was safe, but his conscious awareness was gone, apparently unable to return before his fingers had left the strings. Ferghus traveled swiftly through their bond, but encountered nothing but the confusion of a mind taken over by the wind. With the stark realization that he had no way to communicate with Cyral,

Ferghus began to play, forcing his fingers to move slowly up one arpeggio and down another. He felt an instant affinity for this Harp his boy loved so much, and the sweet tones began to calm his fear. Gradually his breathing returned to normal, and he turned his attention to the wind with the determination of a prodigious Master of Earthsong. He was about to set a block when a young mind abruptly appeared inside his own.

Shay! How on earth—you need to leave me! Now!

No!

Ferghus found himself in a rare state of speechlessness. Shay took instant advantage.

If Cousin Cyral is lost in the wind, you need me to find him, and I need you to take me. You can only see his song, and that's small and has no color, but his chromafield is huge and full of colors I can see from a long distance. I'll find him, Uncle!

Continuing to send arpeggios up and down the Harp strings, the Master stopped the furious repeat of his order that was about to erupt. He had never seen a chromafield, nor had he thought to ask Daithi how large they were, but if there was the slightest chance the youngling was right...

Very well, then, Nephew. Let's do it together. The Master focused on the windsong, listening until the music became clear, then began to play what he heard ... softly, gently, not calling it to rise as he had the day before. Called by Cyral's Harp, the windsong instantly responded, taking the Master's mind aloft with such strength that he nearly lost his focus. *As if it's aware ... as if it knows this Harp and has bonded to it like it has to its Master!*

Having no idea which direction to go, Ferghus made no effort to direct the windsong. He lost all sense of time as he gently played, blown here and there with the wind above the cliffs of Aille-Mara. He simply immersed himself in the music, wandering along one variation after another as the wind played about the bluff. He called out often to Cyral in his mind, but there was no answer, and with every moment that passed, his despair grew. His traitorous mind insisted that finding a song in the wind was impossible, that he could pass right next to it and never know.

Nothing is impossible, he growled to himself. *We'll find him! I saw him on the ship with his Harp!*

Before his mind could take issue with this, Ferghus called to Cyral again ... and again ... but no answer came to him on the wind.

There he is! Shay shouted excitedly. *He's moving with the wind to the northeast, behind the hills!*

With equal measures of hope and disbelief, Ferghus commanded the windsong to take them in that direction, Shay calling out adjustments as they went. At last, when the boy insisted they were right next to Cyral's chromafield, the distraught Master heard a phrase that didn't fit. A small fragment of music that was not a part or variation of the windsong, yet was held and kept aloft by it. It played in his mind like the familiar, beloved song that it was.

Cyral!

Master? The voice, weak and confused, reached him like the lost, uncertain notes of an unresolved chord.

Ferghus pulled Cyral's song close and issued a fierce command to the windsong to take them back. As though startled by the strength of the directive, the windsong sped them back to the harp's location on the bluff.

A few moments later the Master stilled the vibrating strings of Cyral's Harp and opened his eyes to the wonderful sight of his boy trying unsuccessfully to sit up.

"You came for me," Cyral hoarsely murmured. He looked at his beaming cousin. "You both came for me."

"Well, of course we did, my boy," Ferghus said gruffly. "After all, someone has to watch out for you, Master of Windsong or not. And," he said with a smile for Shay, who was holding his waterskin for Cyral as his parched cousin thirstily drank it down, "I wouldn't have found you without my nephew to guide me. But the next time you go flying off with the windsong, have the good sense to come all the way back before you release the strings!" He reached for the Harp's case and began packing the large instrument up.

A wry smile flickered crossed Cyral's face. "I tried ... couldn't."

"Did you find it?" Ferghus asked in a hushed voice.

"The Bardic Isles. Beautiful ... completely uninhabited."

"The Bardic—you named them?"

"It just came to me before I lost touch with the strings and ... couldn't think at all."

"A good name. Which direction?"

"West of here, and a bit north. Five islands."

"I asked you to find us a place ... and you found *five* of them?"

"Yes."

"Just like that?"

"Just like that."

Tears welled up in Ferghus' eyes and trickled down his cheeks. "You *did* it, my boy! You've saved us all."

Cyral shook his head, then closed his eyes at the dizziness the movement caused. "No," he said. "You and your strong intuitions did." He managed to push himself up and looked around, dazed. "Strange. I flew high and far and didn't feel disoriented at all. Now I'm resting on solid ground and I'm too dizzy to see straight."

"Do you know how far away it is?"

"Not really. I passed the Scaelaga Islands early on, but after that there were no reference points and no way to know how fast I was going ... but it was incredibly fast. Even with the windsong's aid, best to count on several days, at least. Maybe more."

Ferghus wrestled the Harp into its travel bag and managed with Shay's help to get it loaded into the back of the cart and lashed securely to the side. Then they went to help Cyral.

"Come on, young Master of the elements," Ferghus said. "Let's see if you can master your own two legs." With a great deal of effort, sweat, and an occasional muttered expletive from Ferghus, they helped Cyral get to his feet and stagger to the cart. He managed to boost himself into it, then curled onto his side in the narrow space by the Harp and was asleep before Ferghus snapped the reins.

They were soon rumbling through the streets of Aille-Mara. Panicked people hurried everywhere as Bards urged them to evacuate. As Ferghus drove down to the equally busy wharf, the men stacking crates on the docks stood still at the sight of a ship entering the bay. And *such* a ship as had never been seen before ... a beautiful new ship with snowy white sails and graceful lines. Behind it, four more appeared, causing a great deal of excitement and cheering on the docks. Tears sprang to the old Master's eyes as he watched the five ships sail proudly in, the culmination of three cycles of effort and planning. He recognized a young Bard standing next to two others on the dock and sent him a mental directive. The Bard whirled around immediately, spotted the Master, and all three Bards hurried over. They stopped short at the sight of an unconscious Master in the back of the crowded cart.

"Prime Ferghus!" one of them exclaimed. "What's—"

"Never mind what, Tiernan," Ferghus said brusquely. "I want you to see that my nephew here and Master Cyral—"

"Master *Cy*—"

"—are put on one of those ships, along with all those crates, instruments, and packs. Take special care with that Harp of his." He eyed the flabbergasted Bards sternly. "This takes precedence over *anything* else you might be commanded to do by any other Master. Am I understood?"

"Yes, sir!" they chorused, then eyed Cyral and his Harp appraisingly, as though calculating what it would take to get these overgrown specimens to the wharf.

"Once you have him on a ship, one of you will remain with him and see that he eats and drinks when he regains consciousness."

Tiernan nodded. "I'll see to it myself."

"Do not fail me in this. More depends on it than you know."

He turned to Shay. "You're to stay with Cyral as well," he sternly told him. "Don't leave his side, and keep an eye on his Harp. The two of them *must* be kept together. Do not disobey me this time, Nephew."

"I won't, sir!" the wide-eyed boy promised.

The moment the wagon was unburdened of luggage, Harp, and Master, Ferghus slapped the reins and headed for the Council Hall through the crowded streets. He grimaced slightly at the twinge of pain in his chest. He had felt it more often of late, but the pain was getting worse. There was certainly no time, however, to cater to his own needs. They were on the eve of an influx of warriors they couldn't hope to fight against. This would be no glorious battle for Bards of the future to sing about. This would be a slaughter, with not a single Bard or Master left alive in Aille-Mara to compose a lament for their passing. Their only hope was to save as many as could be crammed onto the ships, and leave with the morning tide for the open sea before Faolán's sea warriors reached them from the north. He fervently hoped the fianna that had failed to confiscate their ships were on foot and would not have time to reach them from the south.

Chapter 30

Ferghus strode into the Council Hall to the clear sounds of arguing, which stopped the moment he entered. He walked briskly to the head of the table, making no move to sound the chimes. Instead, he removed a thick cloth from his pack, wrapped the chimes in it, then stowed them with the mallet in his pack.

"Diarmuid," he said. "Bring me the Book of Bardic Law."

The Scribe hurried to obey the unusual request. Ferghus stowed the tome in his pack, then handed a small bag to the surprised man. "This is the remainder of your wages, and more for the excellent job you have done," the Master told him. "Now, gather together as many of your records as you can carry and board one of our ships in the harbor, along with your family. Leave the rest of the records here for us to carry to the cart outside."

The scribe nodded and hurried to do the Master's bidding.

Hope lit Barrach's eyes. "He found it?"

"He found five uninhabited islands for us ... the Bardic Isles!" Ferghus hushed the flurry of excited questions that greeted this announcement and quickly told them what he knew. "We didn't plan to leave so abruptly, with only five of our ships ready, but there's no help for it. We don't have another week to prepare. We leave in the morning, so drop whatever you were all arguing about. The rest of our evacuation plans must be implemented now!"

The brief silence was broken by Fionn. "Some think the ships should be filled with *all* the members of the Bardic order in Aille-

Mara, not just the Bards and Masters," he said. "especially now that there are but five ships, with no knowing if the other five will be able to follow. I, along with several others, do not agree."

"Nor do I," Ferghus said. "I'm truly sorry to leave so many of our people behind, but they should be safe as long as they leave Aille-Mara before sunrise. Bards and Masters will not be safe anywhere in Eire. And, if we're to survive in this new land of ours, we need families with children. We need tradesmen, craftsmen, and holders. We need scholars and healers." His arm swept the table. "We need our history, firmly stored in the minds of every one of you. We need our music to create and maintain the balance between our people and our new land. And there's every reason to believe the other five ships will soon join us, for Cormac assures me they are undiscovered. I've instructed him to oversee their completion, load them as quickly as possible, and be ready for refugees from Aille-Mara. They're to keep a sharp lookout for any warriors in the vicinity and set sail the moment any are spotted, or as soon as all five ships are ready. They will sail west, and Cyral can keep them on course once they get close enough to communicate." He arched a brow at the relieved expressions that greeted this.

"Now," he said sternly, "are you truly going to waste time sitting here, stubbornly believing in what you *wish* were true, instead of what *is?* Those of you with territories on the eastern coast should know better! Do you think what will happen here will be any different than the raids you have there? This attack is being made, not as Druids against Bards, but as sea warriors raiding a seaport, who will take their payment by looting it and killing anyone who gets in their way! The majority of our Order perishing will be a tragic coincidence. Odhran is sure to weep tears of grief in public over it and beg the Ard Rí to put a stop to Faolán's pillaging ways ... thereby handily ridding himself of someone he must otherwise pay from the proceeds of our mine for cycles to come."

Silence reigned for an instant, then Barrach and Liam surged to their feet. "Those of you with assigned sections, come with me," Barrach ordered. "Harpists and Pipers can help bring all those willing to come with us down to the wharf as quickly as possible. Warn those unwilling to come to evacuate. Spread the word that those in the Bardic Order below the rank of Bard are ordered by the Council to be gone from Aille-Mara with their families before dawn's light. All Bards are ordered to go to the wharf to help with the loading and be ready to board."

"The rest of you follow me," Liam said. "We'll load the cart with the rest of our records for Ferghus to take. Torin and Bran, bring the animals down to the wharf, grabbing as many Bards as you need to help. The rest of us will arrange the cargo already there for loading onto the ships as they come in."

The Hall was soon buzzing with activity as the Masters organized themselves and left, each with an armful of records for the cart. Ferghus drove it down to the wharf, worrying afresh about Cyral. There was no knowing how much rest the young Master would need to regain his strength. Ferghus forcefully shoved his worries aside. His boy would recover in time. If he did not, Ferghus would never trust his intuitions again, for he had seen the ship clearly and Cyral had been on it, sitting on a large crate with his Harp before him and a look of fury on his face.

Never had the seaport of Aille-Mara been as busy as it was that night. Pipers, Harpists, and Masters roused household after household; those willing to leave their homeland were sent to the docks, those unwilling were warned to evacuate Aille-Mara before dawn. Once the tally for the five ships was met, the others who wanted to join them were told to leave at once for Cuan and the five ships nearing completion. Many willing hands came to help with the loading or to hurriedly evacuate their families; those unwilling shut their doors and refused to leave their homes.

At the wharf, Ferghus was relieved to see Cyral awake, sitting on the dock arguing fiercely with Tiernan. The Bard was glowering into the young Master's face and refusing to let him get up, going so far as to push him back down every time Cyral tried to rise. Shay sat next to the Harp, anxiously watching the battle of wills. Relief lit Tiernan's face when he spotted Ferghus coming toward them.

"Prime Ferghus! Thank the Maker you're here! Master Cyral came to himself before we could carry him onto the ship and he refuses to listen to me." The Bard spoke in aggrieved tones, as though Cyral were a piece of uncooperative luggage.

"You did well, Tiernan. Go help with the loading and I'll handle this troublesome young Master."

The Bard wasted no time in doing so. Ferghus raised a brow at Cyral, who looked mutinously back.

"What good is becoming a Master if a Bard will not obey me?" he demanded querulously. "I'm perfectly fine and can help load!"

"A Prime's order outweighs a Master's," Ferghus said pointedly. "If you insist on helping, then help load *that* one when it comes in." He nodded toward the last ship waiting to come in to the docks with the tide. "*After* you drink that flask of water and eat the food Tiernan provided you. You'll be needing your full strength for more important things than loading luggage, my boy."

Cyral made no further protest, finishing off the flask and food while two more ships were loaded, then left to moor themselves farther out in the bay. The last ship approached the docks an hour before dawn. The three of them carried their luggage to the prow of the boat, Cyral taking his Harp, which he would allow no one else to touch. Shay was instructed to stay with their belongings while Cyral and Ferghus helped with the loading. The ship rapidly filled with anxious passengers, and the two Masters rejoined Shay as dawn approached.

The last remaining passengers had just begun to file onto the deck when a shout was heard from one of the ships. They turned to the horrific sight of a currach filled with warriors rounding the entrance to the bay from the north. Eighteen oars flashed as it sliced a path toward the closest ship in the pre-dawn light, aided by a single sail and the drum beats of the warrior in the stern. Behind them, four other currachs appeared. The rhythmic chanting of the rowers echoed eerily through lifting tendrils of mist.

As though appalled at the sight, the wind died, leaving the sails of the Bardic ships flapping uselessly. Those still on the shore fled, some toward the one remaining ship, some toward the town. A confused jumble of yelling and cursing filled the air as passengers tried to push their way off the ship while others were pushing their way on. Ferghus' authoritative voice cut through all of it as he ordered everyone to board the ship and stay there so they could leave. Most of the panicked passengers ignored him. Those people still on the beach were running toward the town, discarded baggage littering the beach behind them.

As if there were not enough disasters to focus on, a band of warriors on horseback descended into Aille-Mara from the hills above. Ferghus groaned; Faolán was indeed a formidable strategist. He apparently had spies of his own that had ferreted out the existence of their ships, and sent a band of warriors to seize them. He had positioned another band on horseback to attack Aille-Mara from the hills, then brought the rest of his men to attack it from the sea. And he had done it a week before he was supposed to, to offset any chance Cathair's plans had been discovered. Thanks to Tryg, the Bardic ships were still their own, giving them a chance to escape, but caught between warriors from both land and sea, Aille-Mara itself stood no chance. Screams from the town mingled with those on the beach as the riders thundered into Aille-Mara. The stampede off the boat became a stampede back onto it. The Master despaired, for there was no way out of the town that did not lead through the warriors, and no way for the ships to leave the harbor with no wind to fill their sails. And the tide had yet to turn.

Slowed by their own slack sails, the warriors in the currachs rowed determinedly toward the ships as their own Shipmaster shouted a command to leave. The crew cast off, tossed the landing platform onto the ship, and leaped onto its deck. Unaided by the tide, the ship continued to rock against the wharf.

Ferghus, realizing for the first time that Cyral was no longer standing next to him, uttered a curse and reached for his harp, intending to call the windsong with it, but Shay snatched it away.

"No, Uncle Ferghus!" the boy cried. "Cousin Cyral says not to! He told me not to let you have it." At his Uncle's glare, Shay suited actions to words and sat against the wall, obstinately clutching Ferghus' harp to himself. "He wants you to use your bond to tell all the Masters on the ships to open their minds to Master Barrach," he recited, "and for all of them except you to link their Gifts to him." He paused for a moment, his brow furrowed. "One of them needs to create a block for Master Barrach," he continued, "and then Cousin Cyral can tell you what he wants them to do. He says you must use your bond to create a block for him, and he doesn't want to use his bond to talk to them."

Though Shay looked completely confused by this, Ferghus instantly understood. Cyral couldn't communicate with the linked Masters without being pulled into the link himself, and he needed to use the power of his Gift independently, without interruption. So he would speak to Ferghus, who would remain unlinked, able to enter and leave it at will through his bond with Barrach. The combined force of the Masters would be enough to move the ship away from the dock against the tide and be ready for whatever else Cyral needed them to do. Having one of the linked Masters create a block for Barrach, and Ferghus create one for Cyral was pure genius, preventing any listener from being taken into their music with them and conserving both Master's strength for using their Gift.

Ferghus sent a command thundering into the minds of every Master and felt the surge of power that began to flow into Barrach as ten Masters swiftly linked their Gift to his. Liam built a strong block and Barrach called the windsong. A strong breeze began to blow from the east, rustling the slack sails above them. Leaving the link, Ferghus quickly traveled his bond into Cyral's mind and created the strongest block he had ever made. He returned to himself to find the ship moving slowly away from the dock as the crew hurriedly adjusted the sails.

"There's a fire in the town!" Shay exclaimed, and Ferghus turned a startled look toward Aille-Mara, where one of the thatched roofs was on fire. The wind intended to aid their ship was also aiding the hungry flames as they spread across the roof.

Cyral had placed a large crate in the center of the deck and was ordering everyone to get down below the rail and stay there. He set his Harp in front of it as people scrambled to obey his fierce commands. Shay stayed rooted where he was, still clutching his uncle's harp, and stared at his cousin as if he had never seen him before.

Ferghus watched in horror as some of the warriors on horseback reached the beach, running down anyone in their path as they headed straight for the wharf. Sand flew under pounding hooves as the riders quickly closed the distance between themselves and the fleeing townspeople, ruthlessly cutting down every adult who had fled the wharf. Swords flashed in the early morning light; screams filled the air and were summarily cut off. Every man and woman on the beach was slaughtered before Ferghus' uncomprehending eyes, their children left wailing as they fled or stood rooted in shock. He watched in helpless fury as two Bards and three Masters who had left the ship to urge them to return to it were slain where they stood. The sheer brutality of what he witnessed in those horrific moments rose like bile in his throat and he found himself retching over the rail as his stomach emptied in protest. Flames rose from more of the town's roofs, rapidly catching hold and spreading. Smoke filled the air, carried on the breeze Barrach continued to send toward the sails of their ship. In the harbor, the currachs came ever closer to the four Bardic ships that lay stalled there. Several warriors on the beach dismounted and raced to the wharf, intending to leap onto the ship slowly moving away from it.

With no warning, harp music filled the air and the ramp to the wharf was torn asunder as the earth underneath it exploded. Pieces of lumber, coils of ropes and crates flew in all directions. Terrified passengers screamed as some of it landed on the crowded deck of their ship. The warrior closest to the ramp was tossed into the air like an ungainly leaf and landed behind the others, who dropped where they stood. Ferghus whirled toward Cyral and stared incredulously at his vision, for the young Master was indeed sitting on a crate, playing the earthsong with utter command and a look of pure fury on his face. More explosions pockmarked the beach, driving the remaining warriors away from the wharf. A fierce order came directly into Ferghus' mind from Cyral.

Tell Barrach to keep using the windsong to move our ship out of arrow range! I'll get it going for them and then take care of the currachs!

Ferghus obeyed the directive immediately and without question. A wild melodic line flew from the strings of Cyral's Harp with the force of the young Master's emotion and the power of the windsong. The notes grew in strength, amplified by the windsong's binding with Harp and Master. A strong wind rose, caught the sails of their ship and hastened it away from the dock.

Cyral turned to face the bay and glared at the currachs that had almost reached the Bardic ships. Again the harpist played, his music fluid and connected. The watersong flowed from the lowest strings, then surged upward in a burst of arpeggiated sound, each note in furious pursuit of the one before it. Ferghus caught his breath as the inversions segued into music that seemed vaguely familiar ... broken phrases from a forgotten nightmare. The harpist hurled them without restraint toward the pursuing warriors. One after the other, four of the lightweight currachs were thrown into the air by a powerful surge of water. Up they flew, then smacked back into the waves and capsized. The air filled with the startled cries of warriors who could swim and the panicked yells of those who couldn't.

The fifth currach, heading toward their own ship, was abruptly taken care of as Barrach, taking his cue from Cyral's actions, produced a surge of water that swamped and overturned it. Cheers erupted from the four Bardic ships that still sat with slack sails in the bay.

Cyral continued to play, the windsong resounding with notes so powerful that Ferghus wondered at the ability of the strings to withstand them. The wind responded instantly to the harpist's will, resounding over the bay like a symphonic thunderclap and rising to gale force as the music accelerated across the strings of the great Harp. The sails of all five Bardic ships snapped taut in the resultant wind. The crews raced to man them and the ships jerked into sudden motion, moving swiftly toward the mouth of the bay.

Then, just when it seemed they would escape, a large warrior ship appeared, heading straight toward the leading Bardic ship. The Master turned toward it with increased fury as the warrior ship, far lighter than the Bardic one, began to close the distance.

The music of the wind plunged downward over the strings, expertly played by the harpist's left hand. His right hand moved upward, sending a capricious melody sparkling over the upper strings in deft counterpoint. Ferghus' mouth dropped open in disbelief as a gale-force stream of wind arose in the opposite direction, seemingly from nowhere, catching only the warrior ship in its path and propelling it toward the shore. The ship careened past them as though the seaport itself were reeling it in. A deafening crack rent the air as the mast snapped in half and the warriors hastened to obey shouted orders. Despite their frantic efforts, the ship foundered and was driven aground.

Shay's jubilant cheers joined those of the crews and passengers on every Bardic ship as he craned his neck to see as much as he could. A burst of sheer admiration filled Ferghus. *He did with the windsong what I taught him to do with the watersong to move objects against the tide! Brilliant, my boy ... brilliant!* As if in response, another terse command came from Cyral.

Tell Barrach to link with me. Now!

Ferghus barked a mental order to Barrach and saw the exhaustion on Cyral's face turn to grim determination as the remaining strength of eleven Masters flowed into him.

The harpist's hands flew faster, playing a passionate storm across the strings, the windsong commanded by his right hand, the watersong by his left. Then he did what no Master had ever done before, blending the songs of two elements together into one. Ferghus watched, numb now with amazement, as a heavy mist rose from the open sea and was taken by the windsong to form thick clouds over Aille-Mara, where before there had been clear skies. Rain began to fall and the fires were soon put out ... but Ferghus knew that no amount of rain would ever wash away the bloodstains the seaport had sustained this day.

This sentiment seemed to be shared by the other refugees as well, for no sound came from them as all five Bardic ships raced toward the open sea. The survivors gazed in grief at the smoking ruins of their home. The harpist's hands fell from the strings as he broke his link with Barrach. He turned away from their last view of Aille-Mara and faced forward, tears streaming freely down his cheeks. One by one, every passenger silently followed his lead, turning away from their old life and facing west toward their hope of a new homeland.

The last person to turn was Shay, who had stood up next to Ferghus to witness the last few moments of their exodus. The youngster's gaze turned north, toward Gaotha and the Grove he knew he would never see again. The ring hanging safely under his tunic flared with sudden heat. He withdrew it and clutched it in his hand as he turned to face west with the others, holding onto it until at last it cooled.

He knows. He knows we made it!

$\mathcal{B}$ehind them, in the port of Aille-Mara, Faolán stormed across the beach, too angry to be grateful he and most of his crew had survived the grounding of his ship. Not far from where he strode, the beach was strewn with the bodies of townsfolk, Bards, and Masters. Inexplicably, the wharf seemed to have been blown to bits, some of his own men caught in the blast. Damaged currachs rolled in and out with the waves, intermingled with the bodies of his warriors.

He had little doubt who was responsible. His enraged mind was filled with images of the Master who had sat on the deck of the last ship to leave and wielded a huge Harp—and who would ever believe that?—to run Faolán's own ship aground. The Chieftain had only heard fragments of the wild music as his ship had been propelled toward shore, but they certainly hadn't been played for pleasure. Indeed, for a brief moment Faolán had locked eyes with the harpist and seen a fury to match his own and a strength of will to match his father's. And the wind! Faolán shuddered. He would not soon forget the howling of the wind as it aided the Bardic ships and somehow, against all reason, grounded his own. And how had a rainstorm formed from a clear sky to empty itself directly above Aille-Mara and put out the fires? Not that Faolán had minded that. Indeed, if he found out that any of his warriors were responsible for starting those, they'd be in serious trouble. Looting came before burning, as any decent raider knew perfectly well. And burning was foolish. Better for a raided town to recover with a sense of false security ... prosperous again and ready for a repeat performance.

Faolán came to a stop at the water's edge and stared at the bay, rehashing the insane things that had happened there. Most stories grew in the telling, but this one required no embellishment to be unbelievable. Cathair, who had opted to distance himself from the attack and remain on Carr, was certainly not going to believe the straight truth of it, and the warrior could well imagine the Druid's fury when he learned that the majority of Bards and Masters had escaped on ships that had appeared out of nowhere.

Of course, Faolán knew exactly where they'd come from. His spy in Aille-Mara had overheard two Bard's quiet discussion about ships being constructed in a fishing camp to the southeast. The Chieftain ground his teeth in frustration. Those ships should have arrived filled with his own warriors, sealing the fate of every Master and Bard in Aille-Mara. Not that Cathair needed to know about that. The Druid had what *he* wanted, after all. The mine was securely in the Druidic Order's possession. The Bards and Masters were gone from Eire, surely never to return. But if ever Faolán met that larger-than-life Master who had singlehandedly destroyed his prospects of commanding a finer fleet of ships than his father had ever dreamed of, he would give that man a nod of profound respect ... then plant his belt knife straight into his chest. Right now, however, there was a seaport to enjoy the spoils of, and no unbelievable Master with an unbelievable Harp to stop him.

As he turned toward the town, he spotted a small object glistening in the sand at the water's edge. A smooth, black stone ... certainly nothing remarkable. Yet his steps took him toward it as if the stone itself were pulling him. He bent down and picked it up. Faolán stared at it for a long moment, wondering at the sensation that something was staring back from its smooth surface. Then he shook himself, fully intending to toss the stone into the waves. Inexplicably, he pushed it into the front of his tunic, then grinned in anticipation as he headed toward the town.

Chapter 31

After leaving the bay of Aille-Mara, no one dared disturb the Master of the Harp that commanded the wind speeding all five Bardic ships onward. Ferghus glanced around at the people on board in an assortment of Bardic robes and the colorful tunics of holders, craftsmen, tradesmen, scholars, healers … apparently the Council had obeyed him to the letter. There were no white robes among the crowd, nor had he seen any in his brief visit to the stern. He had witnessed the murder of three Masters on the beach and knew that ten Masters had linked with Barrach, so they must all be on the other ships. Families huddled against the rail, staring at Cyral as if he were a Gaelic legend come to life. Ferghus told Shay to stay with his cousin, then made his way to the back of the prow and spoke with all the authority of a Prime.

"Use the remaining light to set up oilcloth awnings for shelters and make yourselves as comfortable as possible here," the Master told them, pointing to the pile of materials they would need, "for the hold is full of livestock and cargo, and the Shipmaster will allow only one emergency ship lantern to be used. He will signal the other ships to come about when Master Cyral stops playing, so we can stay moored together during the night." Then Ferghus communicated with one of the Gifted Bards in the stern, instructing him to tell the passengers there to do the same. He notified the Masters on the other ships to do likewise, then returned to help Shay set up their own awning, covering Cyral as he continued to sit on his crate and direct the windsong, oblivious to the activity around him.

An hour later, worried at the increasing exhaustion on Cyral's face, Ferghus gently touched the harpist's hands. Cyral didn't resist, coming back to himself with a gasp of relief and stilling the strings. The Master opened a bedroll and Cyral collapsed onto it and fell instantly asleep. Ferghus and Shay put the Harp back in its travel bag, and then Shay opened his own bedroll and placed it at his cousin's side.

Soon the other ships came about and sails were lowered. Heavy hemp ropes, thick as a man's arm, were thrown from ship to ship, looped around cleats and lashed tight. The ships launched their sea anchors, the large canvas cones rolling into the sea and catching the current to slow their drift. Night fell to the eerie sound of creaking timbers and rolling waves.

At last the refugees rested, some falling asleep, others weeping quietly in the dim moonlight. Shay was sleeping, one hand clasping his cousin's possessively. Ferghus covered them with blankets, then settled himself close to Cyral, wishing to be instantly alerted to the slightest movement the Master of the Harp made. Ferghus himself lay wide awake, trying to focus on the future, but his mind kept pulling him back to the past and the horrific events he had witnessed that day. It was long before he slept, only to be awoken by rain dripping from the awning and the echoing calls of the crew as they hoisted sea anchors, untied the ships, and made ready to sail in the slowly lifting fog.

Cyral sat up and reached for his Harp, ignoring Ferghus' scowl. "This will only take a few moments and cost little energy," the young Master said as he slid his Harp from its weatherproof bag. He placed his fingers on the strings and began to softly play. Instantly a wind moved around the deck, swirling upward and bringing all eyes to the Master who commanded it. For a few moments the wind seemed to hesitate, holding its vortex directly above the ship. Then it swept away, taking the last of the fog with it. The harpist, still playing, opened his eyes and called to the Shipmaster, who hurried over.

"I must rest today," Cyral said. "Keep us headed in the direction the wind is blowing now, for it will change when I stop playing. Wake me every two hours so I can check your heading and keep us moving toward the Bardic Isles."

The Shipmaster nodded and strode off, barking a command to signal the other ships to follow theirs. Cyral released the strings and put away his Harp. Feeling Shay's eyes on him, he glanced up and gave him a brief smile.

The boy's face lit. "The things you did," he said in wonder. "I can't believe what I saw with my own eyes!"

"Neither can I," Ferghus agreed. "Well done, my boy." To his surprise, Cyral frowned and shook his head.

"I should have taken my Harp out sooner," the young Master stated flatly, glaring toward the east as though looking for another target to blast out of the water. Apparently, the anger Cyral had felt during the battle had not yet dissipated, even with sleep.

Ferghus was having none of it. "You were taking your Harp out when I was hurling the contents of my stomach into the sea! With the horror of what we witnessed—" He arched a brow at Cyral. "You alone kept your head, thought of linking the Masters together under Barrach ... kept me free to communicate with them ... devised an excellent way to set blocks for the two of you ... got everyone down so you could see what needed to be done. And then you took your Harp and acted, quickly and decisively! By the Maker himself, my boy, you have no reason to be upset for not having done all that even sooner. And," he added when Cyral's expression didn't clear, "you should not have had to think of linking the Masters and setting blocks that did not require your energy to maintain. The Prime of your Order should have thought of that. Would it do any good to blame myself for not having done so?"

Cyral's face cleared under the Master's lifted brow.

"It will take time for all of us to sort through our emotions," Ferghus said. "In the meantime, get some more sleep." He motioned toward Cyral's packs. "I grabbed what I thought you would need, but I'm afraid I couldn't find the Stone anywhere."

"I keep it with me." Cyral reached into an inner pocket of his robe, then searched every pocket he possessed.

"It's gone!" he exclaimed. "I have no idea how it could have fallen out, but maybe, in all the confusion on the dock—"

"Then let it go, my boy. You've no further need of it."

"No, but I'll miss pitting wits with it. And I have the strangest feeling that the Stone ... well, that it *chose* to abandon me. Foolish though that sounds." He stared east over the waves.

"Such a Stone as that," Ferghus said, "follows its own path."

Cyral glanced at him and frowned. "What have you intuited?"

Ferghus shook his head. "Nothing to worry yourself about," he said dismissively. "The ships will reach the Isles, of that I am certain, and nothing else should occupy our attention until that's an accomplished fact." He waved away Cyral's attempt to argue and would say no more on the subject.

Cyral slept until mid-afternoon. When he rose, he spent time walking around the deck, stopping to talk to each group of passengers, reassuring them that all would be well and that the Bardic Isles were truly there, for indeed, he had seen them himself. The somber mood lifted as he went, everyone trusting that the one who commanded such power over the elements was also able to see a far-away land. Ferghus pressed food and a water skin into Cyral's hands when he returned, insisting that he eat and drink. Afterwards, Cyral reached for his Harp, intending to increase the wind's strength, but Ferghus forbade it, insisting that Cyral and his fingers needed rest more than the ships needed speed.

"You've set the direction for us, which is all we need this day. Lie down and sleep while you can," he said sternly. "I care not that you're a Master now, and very probably the greatest harpist who ever lived. I am still your Prime!"

Cyral, however, made no move to obey. He didn't like the fatigue and pallor on Ferghus' face, or the trembling in his hands. "I will do so only if you take your own advice."

Shay's eyes widened. Ferghus looked up indignantly, but seeing the inflexible expression on Cyral's face, made no objection. The two of them lay down on the deck and were soon fast asleep. Shay woke them for supper, and a crew member came every two hours for Cyral to check their course, but otherwise the exhausted Masters remained undisturbed.

After the first two days of steady, miserable rain, the weather remained fair, the seas calm. Ferghus gave Cyral a knowing look, but the young Master shook his head.

"I've done nothing more with the Windsong than keep all five ships headed toward the Bardic Isles," he said. "I did make a suggestion to Barrach that linking with the other Masters could enable him to improve our conditions, however. Apparently, it worked."

For two more days they sailed while there was light enough to see. They spent the nights moored together under a spectacular display of stars, the light of which limned the waves lulling them to sleep. They had collected as much rainwater as they could and rationed their water and food supplies carefully.

Shay could always be found by the side of one Master or the other and was introduced to all and sundry as nephew or cousin. He soon lost his shyness and struck up a friendship with a boy his own age during the few times he ventured away from the Masters.

"I'm glad you've made a new friend," Cyral told him during one of his few rest periods from his Harp. "And," he added, "I want to thank you for saving my life. Your uncle tells me that, if it weren't for your refusal to obey him, I would have been lost to the wind, and the Bardic Isles would have been lost to us all."

"I knew I could find your chromafield," Shay said. "It's almost as big as Uncle Ferghus'!" He hesitated a moment. "Do you think that's what my father meant when he said it was important for me to stay with you ... that there was an important part I had to play?"

"I do. But my Master thinks he was also speaking of a role you will play in our new land as well. And your Uncle Ferghus has a habit of being right." He laid a hand over Shay's. "I couldn't ask for a better cousin. And," he added dryly, "anyone who disobeys a direct order from Master Ferghus and lives to tell the tale has my sincere admiration. *I* certainly didn't get away with it."

Shay laughed.

As the days passed, Cyral quickly regained his full strength, and could be found helping young and old alike when he wasn't directing the windsong, speeding them to their destination at an unprecedented tempo.

"Wherever these Bardic Isles of his are," the Shipmaster told his crew in wonder, "We're getting there at least twice as fast as we would without him."

Ferghus, however, seemed to grow frailer every day and rarely moved from their shelter. On the afternoon of the fifth day, he collapsed as he attempted to leave it. The young Master rushed to his side, his own heart faltering as he saw his Master's ashen face and felt his weak, thready pulse. Cyral's frantic calls for a healer were halted by Ferghus' own hand, who gripped his with surprising strength. The old Master shook his head and spoke gently. "No need for that, my boy," he said. "I won't be finishing this voyage. I knew it before the ships were ever loaded."

"No," Cyral whispered brokenly. "No!" Next to him, Shay inhaled sharply and sat back on his heels.

"Shay has Daithi's ring. I want you to have mine. Take it from my finger and place it on your own."

Cyral numbly did as the Master asked, slipping the silver ring onto his smallest finger.

"I don't want my song to depart here, between our past and future homelands." His grip tightened. "Take me to this land of ours! I would see it for myself before I go ... and leave from there."

Amber eyes held each other motionless, then Cyral nodded and reached for his Harp. He glanced at the Shipmaster, who had come up beside him. "Continue on your way, keeping to this same heading while I'm gone." The Shipmaster gravely nodded.

Cyral turned to Shay. "Make certain no one disturbs me while I'm playing." Then he poised his fingers on the strings and set a powerful block in his mind.

"Hurry," Ferghus whispered. "There isn't much time." His eyes turned to Shay. "I love you, Nephew. Remember that always. Stay with Cyral ... the two of you will need each other."

Shay choked back a sob and nodded, his cheeks wet with tears.

The harpist swept the strings of his Harp with gentle fingers, and a strong current of wind instantly swirled over the deck. Cyral bent his mind to his Master's, shocked by the stillness within, the song that gave life to his body so faint he could barely hear it. By force of contrast, the song of his Master's essence resonated clearly, every note of it sparkling with eagerness to be off and away. Without hesitation, Cyral pulled the song of his Master close and, instead of releasing his song as he had done with Bryan's, let the windsong take them both.

The music of the harpist swept upward and the wind instantly followed, rising above the ship like a retracting twister before speeding toward the west. The Shipmaster, glancing sorrowfully at Ferghus' motionless form, stooped to take his pulse, then shook his head and closed the amber eyes that would never open again. Then he gave the order for the ships to continue on the course the windsong had set for them.

Oblivious to the activity on the ships, Cyral rode the windsong with his Master, who was laughing and enjoying every moment.

This is marvelous, my boy!

Surely you've ridden the wind many times before.

Not like this, I haven't! No effort on my part, no failing body to return to ... pure freedom! You should try it. Not too soon, mind you. Our people will need you for some time to come.

They need you as well. The windsong faltered as the harpist's hands slowed. *I need you.*

No, my boy. My time is done, and the body I left behind is already gone. You must let me go as well. But before you do, let's have the ride of our lives!

The windsong rallied, speeding them on to where a group of five islands could be seen, the two southernmost ones next to each other, the other three arched over them to the north. In less time than Cyral liked, they approached the one to the southeast. The harpist held the windsong in stasis, and they hovered over vast stretches of forested hills and meadows.

I named our new homeland, Master ... would you like to name the islands for us?

I would indeed! Ferghus said with pleasure. *This island is as pretty as a summer song. I'll name it Lyra, for the Master of Songs who discovered it.*

The harpist directed the windsong to take them north, and they moved leisurely over the newly named island, admiring the rocky beaches that mirrored their abandoned homeland, and the single mountain near the northern coast. Then they crossed the open sea and approached a much smaller island. Here, twisted junipers clung to sheer cliffs that plunged into the ocean. The waves broke stubbornly against them in endless, rhythmic swells. A small, symmetrical peak lifted itself above the woods and meadows of the interior. And everywhere, it seemed, the wind blew.

A true gem of an island! Ferghus exclaimed. *I'll name it Zephyr, for the windsong that loves it so.*

As if delighted with the Master's choice, the windsong rose, taking them northwest to an island larger than either of the others. A chain of three mountains rose in the distance. Two great rivers divided the land, forested hills and a large lake filling the expanse between. Below them came the staccato cries of a wild kestrel as it dove toward one of the rivers. Two fledglings echoed the cries as they folded their wings and dove after it.

This one I'll name Kestrel, for these avians who fly with the wind as freely as we do.

Onward they traveled across the length of Kestrel. Then Cyral directed the windsong to the southwest, where a fourth island, slightly larger than Zephyr, spread before them. No mountain peak broke the landscape here, no cliffs punctuated the coast. The beaches were sandy and strewn with driftwood, the inner part of the island a series of rolling, grassy plains.

From up here, it looks like a nest for a gigantic bird! I'll name it Eyrie, for it's a good nesting place for our livestock and those who prefer an open sky.

They traveled over the island at a leisurely pace, speaking little, enjoying the view and each other's company. Then Cyral took them south. They rounded the western coast of the largest island of the five and hovered over a sandy beach on its southern shore. To the northwest, two peaks of the tallest mountain they had ever seen rose in sovereign splendor, and Cyral was glad he had saved the very best for last.

Bardic Mountain! Ferghus said decisively, as though he had just remembered its long-forgotten name. *Take us to its highest peak, my boy. I'll leave the island for you to name, for this is where you will land. This is truly a wonderful new homeland you've found for us,* he added in a deeply satisfied voice. *Thank you for giving me the joy of seeing it before I go.*

Unable to speak, Cyral bade the windsong to take them, and they were soon skimming over woods and valleys toward the highest mountain in the Bardic Isles. They followed the path of a shining river below until at last they lingered like a fermata over the highest peak. Cliffs of granite gleamed in the sun. A waterfall sent its graceful music into the air.

This is where I want you to release me.

Cyral's song contracted. *No … please, no.*

This is what I wish, my boy. Take good care of Shay for Daithi and me … and let me go.

I can't let go of your song!

My purpose here is done. Yours is just beginning. You will lay the foundation for this new land of ours. You have so much more than the power of your Gift to give. You have the skills you need to make this place a true homeland, a place where our people can live in peace. Use those skills, and know that wherever I am, I will know … and be as proud of you as I have always been.

Silence fell, gently broken by Ferghus. *Look directly below and tell me what you see.*

It was long before Cyral could bring himself to answer. *I see granite cliffs, a small valley with a waterfall … a narrow shelf higher up.*

Do you see that deep niche in the cliffs above the shelf?

Yes.

Remember it, my boy. You will have need of it one day.

Silence fell again.

So those are the wondrous stars Daithi told me of, Ferghus murmured, as if to himself. *It's time for me to follow them. Let me go, my son.*

Son! Cyral's voice filled with heartbreak. *How I always wished I was your son … that you were indeed my father!*

And so we have always been. Did you think I was unaware of it? Our relationship in the Bardic Order changed over the cycles, as it should … Master and apprentice, Master and Harpist, Master and Bard, Masters both … but I have also been the father you can't remember, and you have been the son I never had, and that will never change. You have made me happier in this life than I had any right to be. Do so one more time … and let me go.

Far away, on the deck of a Bardic ship, the harpist moaned in pain, tears streaming down his face. His left hand continued to hold the windsong in place; his right slowed the tempo of his Master's song, each phrase a little slower than the one before, each note a little softer. He released the strings one finger at a time, loath to stop playing the beautiful song. The last note sounded, then died away on the wind.

At the same time, at the very summit of Bardic Mountain, a song rose freely above it. And if songs could smile, this one surely did, its notes sparkling in the last of the afternoon sunlight as they faded from the harpist's sight.

Grief swept Cyral's mind so deeply that both of his hands dropped nerveless from the strings. Yet the repeated notes continued to play, the strings vibrating in the windsong that swept through them, keeping the harpist hovering over the highest peak of Bardic Mountain. Cyral, slowly becoming aware that he was no longer playing, drew a sharp breath and hurriedly placed his hands back on the strings. He brought the windsong out of stasis and moved slowly away from the mountain his eyes remained fixed on. He never remembered the windsong taking him back across the ocean to where the ships were moored again for the night.

Gradually he became aware of the rhythmic flow of the ocean waves beneath him, and opened his eyes to the lifeless body of his Master. The weathered face was pale but peaceful, the mouth curved in a slight smile. Next to him, Shay was silent, his head bowed over his uncle's hand, clasped gently in his own.

The harpist pulled his Harp toward him then and, releasing the block he had set, began playing a spontaneous variation of the song he and his Master had composed together. It was played with such poignant grief that all activity on the ships ceased. The windsong rose, gently swirling from deck to deck, bringing the music clearly to every ear on every ship. Every voice was stilled, every face turned toward the harpist, all of them pulled into memory after memory of the gentle man who commanded such devotion from his protégé. They saw the Master meeting a young boy whose burning desire was to build the biggest harp in all Eire. They saw the Master teaching him, challenging him, encouraging him to think and explore every possibility and become more than he thought he could be. They saw the Master's song lift free and high above a mountain peak, and they caught their breath at the sheer beauty of song and mountain. They saw ... and wept ... and knew that they had just heard the Master's elegy, and the name of the island they would land on.

The poignant music came to an end. The strings stilled beneath the harpist's hands, and the windsong stilled with it. The listeners slowly returned to their preparations for sleep as the sun slipped below the horizon with a final blaze of color. Cyral sat listening to the Shipmaster's quiet comments concerning his Master's remains, for the body couldn't stay onboard for an unknown number of days, nor could fire be used for a floating pyre.

"At morning's light," the Master murmured, and the Shipmaster nodded and left him alone to hold vigil with Shay.

When dawn came, Cyral stared sightlessly at the two crewmembers who silently approached, wrapped the body of his Master onto a plank with weights, and slid it to its final resting place in the sea. Shay let out a cry of grief and Cyral held him fast, his mind still filled with more memories than he could ever count. He wondered if the people of the Bardic Isles, untold cycles from now, would remember the true name of the Master who had saved them. For, though all the ship's passengers were convinced it was Master Cyral who had saved them from certain death, Cyral himself knew better. It was the Master who was no longer with them who had done that, the Master who, following his convictions in the face of steady opposition, had refused to believe in impossibilities.

His Master, who had made all of it possible.

Chapter 32

Three days after Ferghus' death, land was sighted, to cheers of joy and relief. They came, as the Master had told Cyral they would, to the southern coast of Elegy, the twin peaks of Bardic Mountain clearly visible in the northwest. Four of the ships anchored near a likely looking cove as their own ship began cautiously navigating it, the crewmembers using a weighted line to estimate the depth.

"By the mark eighteen!" the line reader cried.

Cyral approached the Shipmaster with Shay by his side. "I'd be happy to find a safe path for you," the Master offered.

The Shipmaster looked at him in relief and issued an order to anchor. "This is a good, sheltered cove for our ships, but the western side, where you see those ripples, looks to have rocks beneath the surface, so we're making our way in on the eastern side. If you'll check the depth and see if it's clear of any hazards below, Master Cyral, I'll be even more in your debt than I already am."

"You owe me nothing."

The Shipmaster shook his head. "I owe you my life, the lives of my crew and passengers, and the fastest, best navigation of this ship I could ever have wished for."

Cyral settled himself on a crate Shay ran to fetch for him and set his Harp in place. "Keep anyone from disturbing me while I'm playing," he told Shay, who solemnly nodded.

"Chart the whale spouts," Cyral told the Shipmaster. "They'll show you where there are dangers, or depths that are too shallow."

Before the astonished Shipmaster could ask any questions, the Master closed his eyes, then opened them a few moments later. "I contacted the Masters on the other ships," he said, "and they'll tell their Shipmasters to do the same and then follow you in." He closed his eyes again, set a block, and began to softly play. The first mate approached the Shipmaster, scanning the water uneasily.

"Did I hear him say we're to chart *whale* spouts? Why, no whale would be so crazy as to—"

Foom! The first mate yelped as a spout of water broke the surface not far from them. Shay laughed in delight, then clapped his hand over his mouth and darted a worried glance at his cousin. The Shipmaster grinned and marked the spout's location while the first mate cast a wondering glance at the harpist.

Foom! A second spout broke the surface farther away and a third soon followed.

"So, *this* is the mischievous sprite that supposedly brought whales into the bay of Aille-Mara," the Shipmaster murmured, chuckling. He soon had a detailed chart of the areas to avoid and was delighted when Cyral stilled the strings and told him everywhere else was free of obstruction and ranged from eighteen fathoms to four fathoms before becoming too shallow. "A good place to build a wharf," the Shipmaster said in satisfaction. It wasn't long before all five ships were anchored near a wide, sandy beach and began lowering their landing boats.

Cyral put away his Harp and went to help with the unloading, his eyes often straying to the highest peak of Bardic Mountain. His Master was at peace, he knew, and had gone from this life where and how he wished to. Cyral determined to honor the man who had been both father and Master to him by doing what Ferghus would have done ... everything he could to ensure that the transition to their new homeland went as smoothly as possible.

To this end, he began thinking about their social structure, for there were no fiefdoms, no lords or Rí to rule over them here, as there had been in Eire. At last he put quill to parchment and spent his early mornings writing, the rest of his time helping with the organization of their camp and mapping out likely places for their crops. His respect for the Masters increased even more as he worked closely with them for the first time, impressed with their skill in dealing with the myriad issues that came along with establishing a new homeland. Late one afternoon, he paid Barrach a visit and was greeted warmly.

"Cyral! Good to see you. I'd ask you in, but it's a bit crowded in my shelter. Perhaps we could sit outside."

"I see your outdoor Council Hall has some new furniture," Cyral said, grinning at twelve stumps arranged as if around an invisible table.

"Yes, it's all the latest," Barrach said with a laugh, "and will serve for our Council sessions once we get better organized."

They each took a stump, and Barrach gave him a sympathetic glance. "I'm truly sorry for the loss of your Master. I don't know if you're aware of this, but the two of us were close friends from the time we were Bards." He smiled when Cyral glanced at him in surprise. "Oh, we tangled at Council sessions now and then, but I meant what I said about Ferghus being the best Prime we've had in generations. He will be sorely missed."

Cyral nodded, his loss still too raw to permit discussion.

"And you have my fervent thanks for what you did for us in the bay of Aille-Mara."

The young Master frowned and looked away.

"Ah," Barrach said quietly. "I see our excellent Prime was right once again."

Cyral gave him a sharp glance. "What do you mean?"

"You and Bryan were serving my territory when his accident occurred, so I was well aware of the impediment you were forming.

When you refused my attempts to discuss the matter, I contacted Ferghus, thinking he would be better able to help you. He agreed and decided to recall you to his side, for, he said, you found it difficult to free yourself of guilt, even when it was unwarranted. After you played your Harp for the Council, I wasn't happy when he chose me to scan you, because I knew that if that impediment was still there, I'd be forced to bind your Gift ... and then face Ferghus. I've never been so relieved in my life to find an impediment gone."

Cyral stared at him, astonished, and the Master continued.

"The third night of our voyage, Ferghus contacted me, telling me he would not survive the trip and refusing my plea to send every healer we had to him. He told me his concern was for you, that you were going to have a difficult time coming to grips with what you'd had to do in order to save us, and with what he was going to ask of you. I tell you now, what you did for us *and* what you did for your Master were the best things you could possibly have done. So it grieves me to see you recreating an impediment to your Gift, a Gift we will need in the difficult cycles to come."

For a long moment, they regarded each other in silence.

"What I did for my Master caused no impediment," Cyral said at last. "For I released him as he asked, and his body was already gone. But what I did on that ship ... that was intentional murder, and nothing will ever change that." He turned his face away from Barrach and stared sightlessly out over the empty Council stumps as if clearly seeing the accusing stares of ghostlike warriors hovering over them.

"I killed with my Gift," he said in a voice tight with pain. "So many ... dead because of me." His hands closed into fists. "I know I had to do it. I know it was better for the warriors to die than to stand back and let them kill us all. I know I'd do it again if I had to. And, if I'd reacted when they first appeared, I could have used the earthsong to kill even more of them, and more of our people would have made it to the ship in time and been here with us now, instead of slaughtered on the beach." He gave Barrach a haunted look. "I regret every death I caused ... yet wish I could have caused more of them! How am I supposed to live with that contradiction?"

"By looking forward, not backward," Barrach told him. "Something I must do every day as well, for I also killed with my Gift and the Gifts of eight other Masters who trusted me to use them well. Would you tell me I did not?"

Cyral looked into the Master's eyes and saw his own pain reflected there, and a depth of understanding he had not expected.

"No," he said. "I wouldn't."

"Then don't blame yourself for using your own Gift well." Barrach paused for a moment. "You wouldn't be the Bard Ferghus trained into an incredible Master if you didn't regret the deaths you caused, the thought of which will haunt you now and then. When it does, look around you, now or many cycles in the future, and know that all the lives you see wouldn't be there if it weren't for you. And every last one of us thanks you for it."

Cyral felt something hard within him relax and melt away at the Master's words. "Are you going to scan me again?" he asked.

"No. After what we went through, none of us would pass one," Barrach said wryly. "We'll all need time to deal with our anger and grief. There'll be time enough later for scanning and helping those who haven't been able to do so."

A smile crossed Cyral's face. "You're more like my Master than I realized, and will be an excellent Prime."

Barrach's brow lifted. "I'm a Master of three elemental forces. You're a Master of all four, and clearly one without peer. If you wish to become our Prime, I won't challenge you for it. Young as you are, you've accomplished more with your Gift than all of us combined. If that's what you came to discuss, you can rest assured the position is yours for the taking, with my full support."

Cyral shook his head. "We both know there's more to being Prime than expertise with elemental forces. I lack the experience such a position requires, and it will be cycles before I obtain it. Far better for the Bardic Isles to have you as their Prime until then."

Barrach regarded the younger Master appraisingly. "Experienced or not, few men would refuse such a position."

"Did I not recently take a vow to put the welfare of our people before all consideration of myself?"

Barrach looked at him with respect. "A vow I see you intend to keep. I had expected you to call our first Council session to ratify your position as Prime, but now that I know your mind, I'll call it myself. It's time the Council met."

Cyral nodded and pulled out a few parchments from his pack. "I've a proposal for the Council's eventual consideration. This is the outline of it, and I'll fill out the details if you approve it."

The older Master's eyes widened as he took the parchments and began reading. "This is quite the proposal."

"A premature one, for we'll be busy ensuring basic needs are met first. But eventually, we'll need to organize ourselves in a different way than in Eire. Brehon Law won't serve us here, where no túatha or Rí exist. Bardic Law will govern our own Order, but I doubt the trades or crafts will agree to abide by it."

Barrach grimaced in agreement. "Barely a week since we arrived and we're already arbitrating their disputes." He finished reading the outline and gave it a nod of approval. "Well, Ferghus may have taken twenty cycles longer than the rest of us, but the single apprentice he found was certainly worth the wait. This is an excellent outline, filled with good suggestions, and I'll be in your debt if you finish the details for us." He tapped the pages thoughtfully. "And it's not too soon to let the trades and crafts see this and begin implementing what they can. Our people need something to look forward to, and a secure structure in place ... if only to know exactly who to complain to," he added with a chuckle. "So I believe I'll put this forward as a proposal for the future ... goals, drafted by the legendary Master Cyral himself." He put up a hand to forestall

Cyral's objection. "I won't take credit for another Master's hard work. And you underestimate your reputation. If I fraudulently present this as my own proposal, it will be subjected to endless arguments and debates from every craft and trade. If I present it as the proposal of the legendary Master Cyral, they'll leap to embrace every line of it."

Amusement flickered across Cyral's face. "Perhaps the 'legendary Master Cyral' would best serve the Bardic Isles as your Scribe, then, so he can draft *all* your proposals."

Barrach gave him a scandalized look and pointed to a set of two stumps a short distance away, one taller than the other. "Poor Diarmuid!" he exclaimed. "Forfeiting his brand new desk and chair to you would devastate the man. Why, have you any idea how many times he's dusted them?"

They looked at each other, laughed, and in that moment, became firm friends.

"I like your suggestion to elect one Master for each island, and have each of the trades and crafts choose similar leaders," Barrach said. "It will be a long time before we're ready to expand to the other Isles, but we can begin with exploratory parties, giving our ships a useful occupation and bringing us back needed supplies that might not be found here. You could help in that endeavor, finding likely bays for them to use."

"Any Master could do the same," Cyral said.

"If they take lessons from a whale," Barrach said dryly. "Or perhaps from the sprite of Aille-Mara's bay, who apparently hitched a ride with us."

Cyral laughed.

"Ah, so *here's* our living legend!" came a cheerful voice from behind them. Fionn approached with a broad smile, then stopped short at the expression on Cyral's face. "Are you ill?"

"No, but if one more person refers to me as a 'living legend', I'm *going* to be."

Fionn laughed and wagged a finger at the sour-faced Master. "Don't discount the power of legends," he admonished. "Our people are frightened by what's happened to them, unsettled at being transplanted so far from Eire, unsure if this place can really become our new home. Some are clamoring to return, if you can believe it. Nerves are frayed, tempers short. You may dislike the term being applied to yourself, but a living, breathing legend is *exactly* what we need to bring us all together. Yet, while I can't thank that legend enough for all he's done for us, I must ask if he would be willing to do yet more."

"What is it you need?"

"I'm worried about the five ships we left behind. They should set sail soon. I've tried to contact Cormac, but it's too far for mental communication. Could you try to reach him?"

"I've tried, and was also unsuccessful. I was about to ask our Prime if he would like—"

"Our Prime?" Fionn looked inquiringly at Barrach.

"Subject, of course, to the ratification of the Council," Barrach said, "and only because Cyral himself refuses the position."

Fionn glanced at Cyral in surprise as Barrach continued. "I'm going to propose that Cyral be given the honor of becoming our first Free Master, so that he can focus on using his Gift and Harp freely throughout the Isles."

"A superb idea!" Fionn exclaimed, then turned back to Cyral. "Now, then ... about our ships?"

Cyral blinked, taken aback at Barrach's proposal and Fionn's ready acceptance of it. "Well," he finally said, "what I *can* do is ride the windsong toward Eire and contact Cormac if I can get within range before tiring. I can find out when they intend to leave, and tell them how long a trip to plan for. Then, once they've cut enough distance between us, I can use the windsong..."

"—to blow them straight here, like you did for us!" Fionn enthusiastically finished. "Wonderful!" He dug into one of the pockets of his robe. "I just so happen to have a list of a few essential tools I'd like them to bring that we didn't have time to pack."

"It seems you came prepared," Cyral commented dryly.

Fionn handed him the list and shrugged. "Well, I didn't know if you'd have a way, but since we all know you subscribe to your Master's firm belief that there are—"

"—no such things as impossibilities," Cyral deftly inserted.

"—I had every confidence that, if you didn't *have* a way, you'd soon *find* one." Fionn grinned and extended his arm. Cyral laughed and clasped it firmly with his own, letting the support and friendship of these two men ease a little of his heartache.

Several days later, Prime Barrach called a general meeting of all Bardians in the newly named settlement of Tuirling, their "place of landing". Liam and Fionn, Second and Third of the Council, stood to the right of him on a makeshift platform, and Cyral was firmly escorted to stand at his left. Barrach began with congratulations.

"We've accomplished a great deal in a fortnight," the Prime told them. "Everyone is settled into temporary accommodations, our able Holders have begun clearing land for our crops, and Healers have been scouring the countryside for useful herbs and plants. Fishermen and hunters have been providing us with food from the sea and the woods. There is much yet to do, but we've made a good start. I know you're all wondering about the five ships we left behind, and hoping some of your friends and loved ones will be on them. I can assure you that our own Master Cyral has things well in hand. Cyral, if you would..."

Cyral, his eyes promising Barrach they would have words later, had no choice but to step forward and explain that the ships had set sail two days ago, which brought a flurry of excited exclamations. He went on to say that he would use his Harp to facilitate their arrival here, which brought a roar of approval. He waited until they quieted down, every face bright with hope as they looked up at him. They might well argue with and doubt each other, but they had complete faith in the one who had brought them here. Cyral inwardly groaned. He was not, it seemed, going to be able to evade his new reputation.

As Barrach passed out copies of "Our goals for the future, drafted by Master Cyral's very own hand", Fionn's eyes danced knowingly at the young Master's discomfiture, and Cyral sighed. If being a legend was what the Bardic Isles needed, then fine. He'd be a legend. There were worse molds a man might be forced into, he supposed, though he couldn't actually think of one. A memory of his Master came unbidden to him, and he glanced in amusement at the distant peak. *We never did get around to discussing my 'charmingly reclusive nature', Master, but I'm sure you'll be happy to know it's about to get fixed ... whether I like it or not.*

Though Cyral had felt much of his outline was too premature to make public, Barrach and Liam had swiftly overridden him, saying that the sooner they had everyone's attention focused on the future and away from the past, the better. Looking now at the faces brightening as they glanced at the plans he had drawn up, Cyral knew the Masters had been right.

Barrach turned to Cyral. "Perhaps," he murmured, "our living legend should bring the meeting to a close now, while their hope is still fresh and their questions few."

Cyral glanced at Shay, looking proudly up at him, and forced himself to step forward once more. "Many of these plans won't be started now, or even during this cycle or the next," he told them. "But these are the goals we will strive to meet in this new homeland of ours. I'm confident that the tradesmen and craftsmen will create Guilds here that will far surpass anything we were allowed to have in Eire." Those dressed in the garb of traders and craftsmen beamed approval.

"Our ships will be put to good use, not only amongst the Isles, but in bringing us needed materials and supplies from afar. I will sail with the crew, keeping them safe and bringing them into and out of their chosen port in southern Armorica, well away from the notice of Eire. Master Ferghus brought the remainder of the Bardic Order's coffers with him, and every last bit of it will be used to bring us what we need." Shouts of approval met this welcome news.

"In Eire," Cyral continued, "learning how to read and cipher was the privilege of those with the coin to purchase it. In the Bardic Isles, schools will be built in every village, the first one right here in this settlement, to ensure that *all* our children will be given that opportunity." Clapping broke out among the parents in the crowd. "We in the Bardic Order are trained to keep the knowledge of our heritage here," Cyral touched his forehead, "and here," he placed a fist over his heart. "Now that knowledge will be scribed for everyone, so it is never lost to us."

He looked up challengingly. "This is the proposal that the Bardic Order has to offer you," he said in the strong voice of a Master of Earthsong. "What say you, Bardians of the Bardic Isles?"

The crowd erupted in cheering that soared upward on the summer breeze. Cyral cast his gaze to the mountain beyond, glad the windsong was blowing toward it ... and hoped the tribute would fly with it to reach the one who deserved it the most.

Movement Four

Bardic Mountain

forty cycles later

Chapter 33

In an isolated home on the northern coast of Elegy, Master Cyral put aside his quill and sighed, for it was late and he was unspeakably weary. He looked about his comfortable home and was struck once again by how empty it seemed compared to his previous home in Tryl, Elegy's seaport on the eastern coast. His son Sean, named for Ferghus, the "Sean-Sionnach" of their Order, had often visited him there with his wife and two children until two cycles ago, when the young family had moved to Kestrel. Sean wanted to begin a life of his own in its new western settlement, where the shadow of his father's legend would not reach him, and where his talent for wood carving would be highly valued.

Cyral understood and had not opposed the move, but he would miss them every bit as much as he missed his wife, Aisling, one of the two Gifted female Bards who had made the trip with them. Women born with the Bardic Gift were not common in Eire, and Ferghus had believed it was because the Sight was far more common in women than men. "A good trade for us," he had said with a sniff, "for what sane man would want the Sight?" Cyral had suppressed a smile and wisely said nothing. Whatever the reason, few women were Gifted in the Bardic sense, and most of them had chosen to remain in Eire with their families and relatives.

Cyral felt a familiar spasm of grief at the thought of his wife's death three cycles ago. The two of them had fallen in love fourteen cycles after the landing and were overjoyed when Len Aisling had quickened with child a cycle later. Twenty-two wonderful cycles had followed, and Cyral had been bereft at her loss. Losing his son to Kestrel a cycle after her death had solidified his desire to move here and spend his last cycles in the peace he had always craved, away from the constant demands the Bardic Order put on the living legend in their midst ... a legend he had never wanted to be.

Shay, too, had left Tryl long ago. He had developed a passion for learning, and had eagerly absorbed every scroll any Bard or Master would loan him. He had also developed a fine hand for scribing, and had copied dozens of scrolls, giving the copies back to their owners and storing the originals in the fledgling storerooms of Caer Wynd on the island of Lyra, where they could be safely kept for future generations. When Caer Wynd officially opened their doors, Shay had eagerly entered them as a student, becoming first a Scribe, then an Adept Herbalist. Thanks to his uncanny skill with growing things, gardens of exquisite beauty soon graced the grounds. Six cycles later he attained an Adept rank in two other fields, healing and storytelling, giving him the rank of Scholar. He chose to stay at Caer Wynd, teaching a variety of subjects, and did so in such an entertaining way that the classes of Scholar Shay were soon filled to capacity.

When the founders decided the flourishing complex needed a leader, Shay was unanimously voted in as the first Loremaster of Caer Wynd at the age of thirty-five. To the surprise of all the Masters except Cyral, Loremaster Shaylor refused the Council's gift of a silver ring proclaiming his new position, preferring to wear Daithi's ring alone. Cyral had visited him as often as possible and was as proud of his cousin as he was of his own son.

The same cycle that Cyral had handfasted Aisling, Shay had done so as well with a beautiful young woman named Fiona. Three cycles later, she gave birth to their only child, a daughter named Dáire, who had the same Gift as Shay and Daithi, the ability to see and travel chromafields. Cyral had been pleased when his son had fallen in love with Dáire. Two young people, both strongly Gifted in different ways ... what, Cyral often wondered, would his grandchildren or great-grandchildren inherit from such a union?

The Master rose and went to sit in his favorite chair by the fire, his Harp standing in its accustomed place next to it. Though it was early summer, his home overlooked Bard's Landing on the northern coast, and the winds buffeting the coast were always cold. There were no other homes nearby, for the small bay provided no shelter to ships, though they could stop long enough to transport Bards and Masters to and from the rocky shore. Cyral had chosen this isolated area for the Meeting Grounds for the Bards, and Council Grounds for the Masters. It was out of the way, certainly, but he considered that to be its chief attraction, giving Bards and Masters a needed and welcome respite from their busy lives. And, though no one knew it but himself, Cyral loved his unobstructed view of Bardic Mountain and the lofty peak where he had released his Master's song so long ago. He was glad he had given in to his son's insistence that he keep a mule here for his forays into the wooded hills, and to more easily take his Harp with him on his trips to Tryl.

Cyral sat back comfortably in his chair and enjoyed the flickering flames. He was content, he told himself. He was sixty-six cycles old now, a good count by any standard, and certainly entitled to the solitude he had always wanted. He'd had a good life here, and done everything he could to ensure that the Bardic Isles would continue on, strong and free, long after he was gone. Were he to see his Master's face again after passing on himself, he knew he would see no disappointment there. The only regret of his own was his failure to find an apprentice, someone who could inherit his Harp when he was gone. His son, strongly Gifted though he was, had declined to join the Bardic Order. Since Sean had no knowledge of or interest in musical instruments, Cyral had successfully petitioned the Council not to bind his son's Gift, in case the binding precluded the Gift from being passed on to his children.

Cyral sighed and reached for his Harp, wondering what would become of it when he was gone. Perhaps he should bequeath it to the Council, to be kept until someone arose with the ability to wield it. All of the other eleven Masters from Eire had long since passed away. Not counting himself, there were only five Masters now, one for each of the islands. All five had tried to play Cyral's Harp, but had broken off with a gasp of pain after only a phrase or two. Cyral was as perplexed by it as any. How, he didn't know, but his Harp had grown in power over the cycles, and his own hands were the only ones the Harp would allow. Even more strange, lately it had begun to play itself, the strings humming softly, as though the windsong that was wont to swirl gently through them had grown invisible fingers.

Cyral sighed once more and began to idly strum the strings. He spoke to his Harp, as he had done since the days he had spent making it. For it seemed to him that the great instrument could somehow hear and understand him, and if that was a foolish notion, it had nevertheless always brought him comfort.

"We must find you a new owner soon, Marcach Gaoithe," he murmured. "Someone who can ride the windsong with you when I'm gone. I would not leave you alone."

As though in response, the Harp came to life with music. The Master didn't resist, his fingers following the Harp's lead as he willingly played the song he heard coming from it. The song swept him far above his home, then sped him north, to the island of Kestrel. At first he thought the Harp was taking him to see his son. To his surprise, the song bypassed the woodworking settlement and took him to a more remote area high in the northwest mountains, a place he knew was still uninhabited.

He found himself in an unfamiliar, crowded village square, his attention taken, as everyone's was, by the music of a Master Bard Cyral did not recognize. To his amazement, the Master was expertly playing an outlandish flute, the likes of which Cyral had never seen, nor would he have ever imagined. The flute wasn't considered a Bardic instrument in Cyral's own day, but this instrument must surely be, for it was much longer and had keys and levers that gave the Master the impressive command of a three-octave range. If what Cyral was seeing was a vision, it must be many generations in the future. He watched the Master scan the crowd as he played, and was astonished by his vivid blue eyes.

An ungifted Master? How could that be?

Suddenly the Master's gaze fixed upon a young boy who sat listening, enthralled by the music. Cyral inhaled sharply as he recognized the distinctive posture and stubborn chin, the pronounced dimple in the right cheek of a boy who could have been his own son. Shocked, he realized he was seeing the fruit, generations later, of the union between his son and Shay's daughter, both Gifted, Sean in songs, Dáire in chromafields.

Cyral watched the boy, seeing his amber eyes fixed upon the Bardic flute in longing ... recognizing the inhibited Gift within him that would grow greater the longer it was suppressed. He marveled at the music the boy had composed and sequestered behind walls of grief and fear, for unlike any of the songs he had ever seen, these shimmered with color, a veritable kaleidoscope of music. He saw the boy rise and follow the Master, and perceived the love that would grow between the two, Master and apprentice, as surely as it had between himself and Ferghus. He saw all this and so much more in the colorful song of the boy that the Harp sang for him. Yet, as the vision continued, Cyral's face paled and his fingers fell nerveless from the strings as he became painfully aware of what this young descendant of his would have to endure. Yet Cyral was not lost in the wind, for the Harp continued to play without him, the windsong sweeping the music from the strings and carrying the Master safely home.

Cyral came to himself sitting in his chair before a hearth whose fire had long since cooled to ashes. He closed his eyes and sighed. "Ah, Marcach Gaoithe, you've waited all this time to show me my incredible apprentice, and he's a son of my own blood who won't be born for untold cycles?" A faint smile crossed his face. "I don't think either of us can wait that long, my friend."

To his amazement, the Harp came to life once again under his fingers, its song this time wild and insistent, and his fingers flew to play the notes that sparked across his mind. Once again, the windsong swept him up, taking him this time to the south, the notes sending another crystal-clear vision into his mind. Again, he knew that this was the song of a future event, something that would happen as surely as the boy he had seen would one day be born and follow an ungifted Master out of his village. Unlike that vision, however, this one was filled with unspeakable horror, sending a shout of pure defiance ringing through his mind with the strength of the earthsong itself.

No! This I will not allow!

The Master flew home in a rage he had not felt since Faolán's warriors had attacked Aille-Mara. The windsong instantly obeyed his command, transporting him back at vivace tempo. He came to himself at the edge of his chair and released the strings, his heart pounding with emotion, his mind screaming in protest.

The Master of Songs did not sleep that night. He sat silently before a cold hearth and twisted his ring in growing agitation, unaware of anything except an overwhelming desire to do something—anything!—to avert the disaster he knew would be visited on his cherished homeland. At last, as the first light of day brought a misty rain to patter rhythmically against his windows, he looked sadly at his Harp.

"There's only one thing we can do, you and I," he softly told it. "And we must do it now, before I lack the strength to make such a journey." His mind made up, he rose with determination and went to his desk. Taking up parchment and quill, he began to write. He opted not to use plain words in describing his visions, which might well be discounted by future generations as the ramblings of an old man ... who then wandered off alone, never to be seen again. Cryptic verses, he thought, might stand the test of time, as generations of those coming after him puzzled over their meaning ... meaning that would become clear only to the boy they were intended to reach. The words came to him with the creativity of the watersong, so rapidly that he could barely keep up with their flow. Wave after wave of verses and music he wrote, hoping that some of them would survive the cycles and help guide the boy he knew was the only hope his homeland had of surviving what was to come. At last, the daylight nearly gone, his energy nearly spent, one last song came to him. He wrote the verses and music swiftly.

Over sea and over stone,
Over cycles yet to be,
Lies a Bardic treasure caught
In time, for need alone to free.

Come, you Pipers, blow with might!
Come, you Harpists, play!
Masters, keep the land of song
From silence in that day.

Where, oh where, the young sprig growing
On an old tree, so alone?
Awake the Harp, the Master's Harp,
That lies forsaken, trapped in stone!

Mute, my Harp is left in anguish,
Waiting for the one to hear
Music from the crying mountain,
Drawing him, despite his fear.

Put aside your doubts and wonder,
All depends upon your choice.
Listen to the mountain's song!
Then wake my Harp with hands and voice.

Exhausted, Cyral released his quill and barely managed to cap the inkwell. He staggered to his bed and fell into a deep, dreamless slumber. Upon rising the next morning, he wrote letters to his family and the Council. He told them he was leaving and would not be returning. He told his family that he loved them and was proud of each and every one of them. Leaving the letters with the stack of verses on his desk, he packed the mule with his Harp and supplies and left. He set his face west, toward Bardic Mountain and the niche near the top of the peak his Master had said he would have need of one day.

The day had come, he told himself. The day had come, and he would not look back.

Chapter 34

On a fine, clear summer morning, Cyral stood in what was surely the highest, most beautiful gem of a valley in all the Bardic Isles. Hidden from the view of anyone on the lower slopes, the only thing that would draw an appreciative eye upward was the waterfall that spilled gracefully down the southern slopes of the mountain. It had taken Cyral over a month to arrive here, where a deep pool provided the waterfall a brief respite before continuing its downward course. He looked up above it to the highest peak of Bardic Mountain. Though not visible from where he stood, he knew the niche his Master had shown him was up there, within his reach at last.

The journey had not been an easy one, even with the mule to carry the burden of his supplies and Harp, for Cyral was no longer the young man he had once been. But, though his steps were slower, his Gift burned as brightly as ever. He had used the watersong to sweep fish directly into his net, and skillfully regulated the tempo of the firesong to keep his fire from going out during the night. He had called upon the windsong to blow clouds and fog away, and since leaving the banks of the Chyrn river, had used the earthsong to forge a way around the obstacles in his upward path and provide him access to the niche above.

Cyral unloaded the mule, then led him back through the tunnel they had come through to reach this valley, the first of two the earthsong had forged for him. He gave the animal a fond farewell pat when they emerged, for the remainder of his path was not one the mule could travel, nor was it one that anyone coming after him would easily find.

Upon returning to the waterfall, Cyral sat on a flat rock facing the pool and liberally rubbed ointment into his sore muscles and joints, sighing in relief as the herbal remedy worked its magic. Then he took out a few carving tools, positioned his Harp in front of him, and carved his name into the column. When he was finished, a whisper came to him from the windsong swirling through the strings of Marcach Gaoithe. He listened, then nodded and carved another name beneath his own.

Kaelin

As though the carving of his name had brought him, a clear vision of the boy he had seen before appeared in front of the pool, the boy he knew to be the apprentice of his blood and heart, and the rightful inheritor of his Harp. Cyral looked searchingly into the boy's face, so like his son's, and into the deep amber eyes, so like his own, and spoke gently in his own mind. He inscribed every word there, creating a memory with notes from his song that already twined with the boy's. A duet that would last until the day the boy came here to this place and heard it echoed in his mind.

You will come here someday to find me, wondering if I am real or just a dream. Believe in your dream, for it will lead you to what is real.

Taking a small rosewood box from his pack, Cyral went to the cliff face near the waterfall. He picked up a piece of granite lying there and slipped it into his pocket. Then, for the first time since Ferghus had given it to him, Cyral twisted the silver ring off his finger. For a long moment he looked at it, emotion blurring his vision as he followed the twisting staff with tiny notes carved into the band. He placed the ring inside the box and gently laid it against a crack in the cliff face. Returning to his Harp, the clear vision of the boy still before him, he focused on the earthsong and began to play. The earthsong responded instantly to the Master's desire, creating a cavity the box slid into, then covering it smoothly over.

As he put his Harp into its travel bag, Cyral unexpectedly thought of Daithi. Though the Master had never met or spoken to Ferghus' brother, he felt a sudden kinship with the Grovekeeper, who had seen Shay safely to them and returned to his Grove alone. He wondered if Daithi still existed among his trees. There were indeed, he thought, difficult paths one could choose to follow, though it tore one's heart to do so. The choice Daithi made had saved Cyral's life when he was lost to the wind after discovering the Bardic Isles. And someday it would also give rise to the only one who could save their new homeland. With renewed resolve, Cyral spoke once more to the vision of the boy.

There is only one way to save our people. I will leave my Harp for you up near the highest peak of Bardic Mountain. When the need for the Harp arises, it will draw you with the power of the mountain itself to find it. Do not fail it ... or me, for I shall be there too, waiting.

Leaving his pack and Harp case behind, the Master slung the great instrument over his shoulder and approached the waterfall. He turned briefly and locked eyes with the silently watching boy, knowing the music of this memory would one day reach the youngster and help him make the decision he would need to make if the Bardic Isles were to survive. Then he turned to the waterfall and, following the path he had seen the earthsong make for him, stepped through the bracing spray.

The cleft hidden behind the waterfall opened into a dark, narrow passageway that twisted away from the falls. Lightly touching the wall, Cyral followed it to its end, where sunlight streaming through an opening overhead illuminated the rough steps the earthsong had fashioned for his use. He touched them gently, sending a thread of gratitude into the stone. Then he climbed to the top, emerging at the foot of a wooded slope. He hiked steadily upward until he reached the opening of the second tunnel the earthsong had forged. He entered this and soon emerged onto the stone shelf he had seen with his Master from high above. Looking up the cliff face, Cyral spotted the deep niche he needed to reach. A jagged line of granite led upward toward it, forming rough steps the Master could navigate.

He made the final climb with only his Harp and his memories of Ferghus, which burned more brightly with every difficult step he took. The kindness in the Master's eyes when they first met, and his wondrous promise to teach him to make his own lap harp. The Master's never-ending questions that taught him to think for himself, and his look of bright expectation as he watched his apprentice pace back and forth, formulating questions and searching for answers. The pride in the Master's eyes as he handed him the blue robe and silver cord of a Bard, and the smile that lit his face when he handed him the white robe and gold cord of a Master. The gentleness in the Master's voice as he called him his son and asked him to let him go ... high above where Cyral now sat, straddling a narrow ledge the earthsong had made for him that spanned the opening of the niche from one side to the other.

With the unnerving awareness of open air on either side of him, he pushed himself and his Harp forward along the ledge until the Harp's pillar rested firmly against the opposite wall. He removed the chunk of granite from his pocket and set it next to his Harp. Then Cyral placed his hands on the strings for the last time. One last song, played by the Master of Songs.

I'll still be with you, he told the magnificent instrument that had been his confidant during the cycles of its construction and his constant companion for so many cycles afterwards. It had suffered with him under his Master's imposed separation, had taken him to the Bardic Isles on the wings of the windsong it had bonded to, had fought a battle with him ... had since refused any other hand but his own to touch it.

The Master turned his attention to the piece of granite resting next to his Harp. It's song came readily to his mind, and his fingers began to flawlessly duplicate it on the strings of his Harp. Effortlessly, he sent his awareness into the granite. Memories assailed him as he surveyed the ensemble of songs before him. He chose the same one he had taken from the piece of granite sitting on his Master's table so long ago. The song of mica. The harpist played the sparkling descant with his right hand, skillfully untangling it from the complexity of the layered music. Continuing to play it, he turned his attention to the gleaming, translucent song of quartz. With his left hand, he played and untangled it as well, then combined the two freed songs into a duet played with his right hand. His freed left hand began playing the dominant song of the granite, the rich, rhythmic song that seemed to come from the very heart of the earth itself, expressed in the granite's smooth grey feldspar. He drew all three songs into his Harp in the same way he had once drawn fragments of songs into a Stone with no music of its own.

I'm sorry, he whispered as the piece of granite, the songs of its three primary components gone, crumbled with his departure and was blown from the ledge. Cyral turned his attention to the three melodies he was playing. None of them complete in their own right, all of them but fragments of the whole, yet the hands of the Master Harpist wove the three together into a song complete in itself. Again and again he played it, increasing its dynamic range from the softest pianissimo to the loudest fortissimo, until the song echoed among the cliffs and rolled down into the valley below.

The sun crossed the sky westward toward the horizon, for once not assisted in its descent by the singing of the mountain birds. For all was silent on Bardic Mountain as the harpist played, on and on, until the sun flared red as it touched the edge of the sea. Then, his strength nearly spent, the Master called the windsong and earthsong to his aid. The wind blew from behind him in sudden tempest as the Master of Songs struck the final, augmented chord and released his own song into the wind, which carried it directly into the Harp. The mountain shook with a violent force that was felt all across Elegy.

The wind died as the mountain's travail ended. The ledge was empty except for the Harp, which stood alone. For the earthsong had fused its column to the cliff as seamlessly as if the great instrument had grown from the mountain itself. Within the Harp, the song of granite had increased in strength and power with each repetition and gained ascendency as the dominant theme. The Harp began to gleam with the earthen tones and properties of granite, its strings silenced in fine, immovable strands. The frame of feldspar glistened in the fading light with flecks of mica and streaks of quartz. Cyral's Harp was solid stone ... stone that would withstand the many cycles that must pass before the rightful heir to the Harp would be born.

The song that was Cyral was freed in a moment of exquisite wonder that would have taken his breath away, had he a body to draw it. Held within the stone Harp, his song felt as free as the windsong swirling through the stone strings. He exulted in it, understanding now the laughter his Master had shouted into the wind as they had flown with the windsong toward the Bardic Isles. Time no longer existed unless he chose to pay attention to it. One moment, he realized, could be a cycle, or a cycle a mere moment. His song was intensely, vibrantly alive, and he heard every song within the Harp clearly, each of them alone or all of them in a veritable symphony of intertwined melodies. For it was not only the song of granite he heard, or the songs of the various woods the Harp had originally been made of, but all the many songs he had ever played on the great instrument, imprinted into it forever. Perhaps, he thought, several lifetimes of being confined here with only his Harp to communicate with might not be so terrible a fate for one who had once believed that his Harp was the only companion he needed. The tremor that rippled through his song was the pang of one who had long since learned differently.

Then he heard laughter, and saw the one song he loved above all others. A song not imprinted in the Harp, but shining free and clear before him. And in that single, blinding moment, Cyral saw and understood that he was not alone ... that indeed, he never had been.

You didn't really think your Harp had a mind of its own, did you, my boy?

Master!

All the joy of the universe was in his voice.

End of Book Three of The Bardic Isles Series

Songs in the Wind

All things are created with music,
All things have a song of their own.
At times our songs twine with each other
And sometimes they travel alone, it seems,
Sometimes they travel alone.

One day we will journey together
On a voyage far over the sea.
And though I am sure you will find what we seek,
You will arrive without me, I know.
You will arrive without me.

And when it seems certain I've left you,
Fall not into grief or despair.
For songs, once created, are songs evermore,
Never to scatter or fade in the air.
Our songs will not fade in the air.

The stars far above will call to my song,
To follow their path, bright and true.
But I will refuse them and call on the wind,
And the wind will carry my song to you,
Carry my song back to you.

And though you won't know that I'm with you
Or realize how close I will be,
One day you'll release your own song in the wind,
And the wind will carry your song to me,
Carry your song back to me.

All things are created with music,
All things have a song of their own.
At times our songs twine with each other
And sometimes they travel alone, it seems...
Yet never alone ... never alone will they be.

I hope you enjoyed your trip to the past in the Bardic Isles Series!
If you would like to hear the music described in this book, all of
which was composed by the author, you can experience it in a
one-of-a-kind audiobook, available on all major audiobook plat-
forms, including Audible (Amazon), Spotify, Apple Books, Google
Play, Barnes & Noble, Audiobooks.com, Chirp, and Kobo.
Samples of the music (including the vocal song above) can also
be found on the author's website, mhimedabooks.com
or simply scan the QR code below.
See the books ... hear the music ... experience the wonder!

Glossary of Basic Music Terms

Accent: (>) to play the note(s) with emphasis or stress

Adagio: a slow tempo, between largo and andante

Andante: a moderate, walking tempo

Allegetto: a moderately fast tempo

Allegro: a fast tempo

Arpeggio: the notes of a chord, played consecutively

Articulation: markings on notes that define their smoothness and duration, such as a staccato or accent

Augmented: a major chord with raised top note; has an uneasy or strange sound

Cadence: a series of chords that brings closure

Chord: usually three or four notes played together

Coda: a passage that brings the piece or movement to an end

Counterpoint: the combination of different melodic lines

Crescendo: a gradual increase in volume

Da Capo al Coda: a direction to go back to the beginning, then take the "coda" ending

Descant: the highest melodic line

Diminished: a minor chord with top note lowered; has a suspenseful sound

Diminuendo: a gradual decrease in volume

Dominant 7th, or V7: a chord comprised of a major triad and a minor 7th, such as C-E-G-Bb; has an unresolved sound

Dynamics: the range in volume of a piece

Embellishment: the ornamentation on a note, such as a trill

Fermata: a dot with a curved line over it that prolongs the length of a note or rest, at the discretion of the player

Forte: (f) loud or full in volume

Fortissimo: (ff) very loud or full in volume

Half Step: the closest possible distance between two notes

Interval: the distance between two notes

Inversion: a chord whose main (root) note is not the lowest; thus C-E-G (root) is inverted first as E-G-C, then G-C-E

Key Signature: a series of notes (most often a major or minor scale) that defines the tonality, the sharps and flats of which are usually notated at the beginning of the staff

Legato: to play smoothly connected, usually marked with a slur

Major Chord: the 1st, 3rd, and 5th notes of a major scale, played together; has a feeling of well-being

Marcato: (^) to play the note(s) with strong accentuation

Measure: fixed number of beats between two vertical staff lines

Minor Chord: the 1st, 3rd, and 5th notes of a minor scale, played together; has a feeling of sadness

Piano: (p) soft

Pianissimo: (pp) very soft

Presto: an extremely fast tempo

Scale: a series of notes from which melodies and harmonies can be built, the most common being major and minor

Slur: a curved line connecting two or more notes to be played smoothly connected, or legato

Staccato: a dot above or below a note, played short and light

Tempo: the speed of a piece

Time Signature: convention defining how many beats are in one measure, and what kind of note receives one beat

Tonic: first note of a major or minor scale, or a chord built on it

Tremolo: two notes played rapidly back and forth

Trill: a note played in rapid alternation with one a whole or half step higher

Vivace: a very fast and lively tempo

Whole Step: an interval comprised of two half steps; notes a whole step apart have only one possible note between them

Acknowledgements

Writing a novel is not a solo event, it's the work of an ensemble, and I'm incredibly fortunate to have such a wonderful team surrounding me. My most fervent thanks to my two editors, Charis Himeda and Dawn Hollison, for their meticulous scrutiny of all things great and small in this newly created world of mine. I could not get along without you!

Jeff Brown, of Jeff Brown Graphics, has done it yet again, creating a wonderful cover that brings to life the western coast of long-ago Eire, and the Master Bard who became a legend in his own time. I can hear the windsong being masterfully duplicated across the strings of his Harp.

A special thanks to Matt Wilson for recommending "The Hidden Life of Trees" by Peter Wohlleben. A wonderful book, filled with delightful information about trees that helped me bring the Druidic Gift to life.

And, as all you audiobook lovers know by now, I have a marvelous narrator for my series, Will Hahn, who once again has done a sterling job of bringing an entire orchestra of new characters to life with his voice. Narrator and friend both, though the only place we've ever met is in the Bardic Isles. Thank you again for your wonderful portrayal of my fantasy world, and your continued support of my compositions for it!

About the Author

Marla Himeda is a lifelong musician who taught piano and clarinet for eighteen years at Punahou Schools and for over half a century in her own studio. She teaches her own theory and composition courses, coaches ensemble groups, composes music, and is a prolific arranger of chamber music for winds. She has performed in the Seattle Opera House, the Seattle Art Museum, and many concert venues in Hawaii, where she lives near Mount Olomana, whose twin peaks sparked the birth of Bardic Mountain. She is a member of the National Music Teachers Association, Opus 5 Winds, and is an active member of the Honolulu Wind Ensemble.

Titles in the Bardic Isles Series have won eleven international awards, including the IAN Awards Fantasy Book of the Year and Young Adult Finalist, the IP Awards overall Oustanding Audiobook and Gold medalist, the Readers' Favorite Audiobook Gold & Silver Medalist, the B.R.A.G. Medallion Honoree, the BookFest Awards Audiobook Silver Medalist, and The Wishing Shelf Awards Fiction and Audiobook Finalist. The Bardic Isles Series is a merging of two passions—music and writing—and portrays a unique world that the author unabashedly admits loving to escape to. She believes that we should all have a Master Bergid in our lives, and her own life was blessed with three of them: Michiko Miyamoto and Professor Randolph Hokanson, both amazing piano teachers, and Frances Walton, an inspiring Youth Symphony director.

Visit her at mhimedabooks.com